PORTENTS AND ODDITIES

SOPHIE FEEGLE BOOK 2

GWEN DEMARCO

CHAPTER 1

"*I*s she okay?"

"What happened?"

"I think it was a panic attack."

Ignoring the whispers, Sophie tried to take slow even breaths, turning her focus towards the small and inconsequential details around her. It helped lessen the tightness in her burning lungs. She started to look over to the autopsy table but forced her attention away quickly.

Don't think about it, she commanded herself.

Sophie noted the coldness of the floor under her butt. She tried to find patterns in the flecks of gray in the waxed white linoleum tiles between her feet. She took deep breaths of air, savoring the sharp smell of antiseptic flavored with a hint of cloying sweetness. Hugging her arms around her middle, Sophie dropped her head on her knees. She felt like she was going to shake apart at any minute.

In a detached part of her brain, Sophie watched what was happening around her like a movie reel playing out.

"Wow. I've never seen her freak out like this before. That guy's death vision must have been awful."

"That's what's so weird. Sophie never even touched the guy. She took one look at his face and had a panic attack."

Slumped against the wall, Sophie listened as her co-workers talked – not as quietly as they believed. Letting her eyes wander around the autopsy room, she noticed that the wheels from the gurneys had run a wagon wheel rut across the floor, leaving permanent indents from the thousands of times dead bodies had been rolled along the same path. Only from her position on the floor with the bright lights gleaming overhead would she have ever noticed the grooves.

"Does she know this guy? Is he a friend or something?"

"I'm not sure. I think she said he was a lumberjack."

Sophie absently noticed that one heel on her favorite black boots had started to separate from the rest of the shoe. Then she shifted her focus to the crumpled brown bag that Ace had shoved into her hands and commanded her to breathe into, trying to help stave off her earlier panic attack. It was from that new restaurant that specialized in sandwiches made with waffles instead of regular bread. She'd been meaning to check that place out.

"Well, he certainly looks like a lumberjack," Amira noted.

Reggie, her boss and friend, knelt in front of her, dropping his face into Sophie's line of vision. His sweet round face was filled with worry as he gently chafed one of Sophie's cold, clammy hands between his.

"I'm fine," a disembodied voice said. It took Sophie a moment to realize that the flat voice was hers.

"Are you up for telling us what happened?" he asked in a soft, soothing voice.

Sophie opened her mouth to respond when a bellowed "Sophie!" reverberated down the hall outside the autopsy doors. Ace opened the door and waved a frantic-looking Mac inside. Mac came hurtling into the room, scooping Sophie onto his lap and sitting back on the floor with his back pressed to the wall.

She clung to him like a limpet, feeling only slightly embarrassed by her display of weakness. Out the corner of her eye, Sophie noticed Reggie and Amira exchange surprised looks.

"What happened?" he demanded to the room, running a gentle hand over Sophie's back. With a slightly clinical touch, he started checking her over for injury.

"We were about to start a priority one autopsy, but as soon as Sophie saw the victim, she had a panic attack," Reggie explained, wringing his hands, his cheeks creased with worry.

"It's the lumberjack," Sophie whispered, nodding her head towards the body on the gurney on the other side of the room.

"Lumberjack? What do you mean? Wait... from the nightmare you had last night?" Mac asked, eyebrows raised in surprise.

"Yes, it's the same guy from the nightmare. The one I dreamed that I stabbed in the throat," Sophie explained, picking at a loose thread dangling on the knee of her scrubs. Mac rubbed Sophie's back as she shuddered at the memory. If she turned her head, she could just see the edge of the black body bag containing the corpse across the room. Sophie carefully kept her vision averted.

"Are you saying that the guy you dreamed you murdered is real? Are you certain it's him and not just someone who maybe looks similar?"

"It's him," Sophie said, her voice thick.

"What dream?" Ace asked, looking around at everyone else in the room like they would have a clue.

"Last night, I was sleeping on Sophie's couch when I woke up because she was yelling out in her sleep. When I woke her, she said that in a dream, she stabbed a lumberjack in the neck," Mac explained to Reggie, Ace, and Amira.

Reggie knelt on one knee next to Sophie, his voice low and his eyes pained. "Can you tell us more about what happened in the dream?"

"Yeah, I can try," Sophie said, trying to wiggle out of Mac's arms, but he pulled her firmly back against his chest. Sophie

3

settled back in his lap with an exaggerated sigh of defeat but was secretly pleased. "In the dream, I was in some sort of bar – typical old-school pub – not super nice but not quite a dive. I was wearing a blonde wig and a black dress. I was drinking tonic waters but making it look like they had alcohol in them and pretending that I was getting drunk. I was there for Lumberjack – like I had followed him there and was trying to lure him to me. After being there for a couple of hours, I left the bar, and he followed me into the alley next door. I attempted to inject him with something – I don't know what it was – but I accidentally dropped the syringe. Lumberjack started to freak out when he saw the needle, so I pulled a spike-like knife out of my pocket and stabbed him. I stabbed him in the neck... it was so gross. Once he was down, I left him in the alley bleeding to death."

"Can you remember any other details? Did you get the name of the bar?" Mac asked.

"You think this might be real?" she whispered. "I mean... maybe I'm mistaken, and it's not the same guy."

"With you, anything might be possible. The one thing I know is that you didn't murder anyone last night. I was in your apartment the whole night. I would have noticed if you left," Mac said with a wink. Sophie was just glad that Mac left off the fact that he was in her bed in front of the team. No need to air that dirty laundry. "Take a minute and see if you can remember any other details."

"What time did you have the dream?" Reggie asked.

"I woke up sometime between midnight and one, but I didn't look at my watch, so I can't be completely sure," Mac answered when Sophie shrugged her uncertainty.

Sophie sighed, feeling fragile and worn thin like old cotton. She needed to get her shit together; she was freaking her friends out. Fatigue settled on her shoulders, her mental energy sapped of its usual strength – exhaustion caused by the panic attack. Seeing the face of the man that she murdered in a nightmare the night before created an immediate visceral reaction, like being dipped in a well of horror and panic. As she looked down at her unsullied hands, she could almost feel the man's warm blood on them, feeling the echoes of that sticky sensation in the webbing of her fingers.

"I never saw the name of the bar. One bartender was dark-haired, maybe in his late twenties, medium build. The other bartender was a little older, probably in her late thirties. She had short, spiky blonde hair, stockier build," Sophie said, screwing her face up in concentration. "Wait! I do remember something else. In the dream, as Lumberjack was dying, he asked me why I stabbed him. I said, 'You know why, Troy.' Do you think that guy's name is really Troy?"

"I will find out," Mac promised.

"Perhaps if you touched him and got his death vision, you could see the real killer, and that would help you feel better," Amira suggested.

Nodding, Sophie started to get up. She whipped her head around and stared at Mac incredulously when he helped heft her to her feet with a hand on her butt. Mac's face was a study in innocence, making Sophie give him a narrow-eyed look and shake her head.

"I'm fine," Sophie assured the gathering of mother hens surrounding her. Her only relief was that Fitz wasn't here to add to the hovering crowd. Reggie circled Sophie like a nervous hummingbird. She patted his shoulder reassuringly.

With gargantuan effort, Sophie shut up the manic chattering in her brain and turned toward the body. She watched her feet tread a reluctant path towards the autopsy table. She could feel everyone's eyes on her. It was so quiet that Sophie could hear the squeak of her boots against the shiny linoleum. The fluorescent lights overhead cast the dead man's blood-splattered features in garish relief. Sophie noted by the man's waxy washed-out complexion that pallor mortis had set in, making the splashes of rust-colored blood stand out even more against his pale face. There were deep lacerations on the left side of Lumberjack's throat, in the same spot as the dream. Sophie flexed her right hand, feeling the phantom of the weapon in it.

Sophie whispered her thanks when Ace handed her fresh nitrile gloves but struggled to pull the thin blue gloves onto her dread-dampened hands.

Once she finally got the gloves on, Sophie reached out to place her hand on the lumberjack's arm, where his red and black flannel was rolled up. She froze, her hand hovering an inch away from his skin. Sophie watched as Reggie grabbed his phone to record her vision. Sophie flexed her fingers but couldn't seem to close the gap between her palm and the victim's forearm.

"Come on, hellraiser. I thought you were tougher than this," Mac taunted. Sophie's spine snapped straight in indignation.

"God, you are *such* a dickhead," Sophie griped, but his taunt had its intended effect.

Gritting her teeth, Sophie pulled on her bitch face and placed a hand on the dead man's arm, mumbling faint curses under her breath. Sucking in a sharp breath through her nose, Sophie closed her eyes as Lumberjack's final night on earth unraveled before her.

"Okay. I got it. I see Lumberjack walking down a street. It's dusk, and the streetlights are just coming on. He heads into a bar. The sign over the entrance says 8th Avenue Pub – not a very original name," Sophie scoffed. "Yeah, this is the same place from my dream. It's kinda dark and gloomy inside. There's a fireplace off to the side, but it's not lit. He orders a Guinness from the male bartender, who he calls Rob. He avoids the other bartender. He seems uncomfortable around her. She's outspoken and brusque. He sits at the bar for a while as the place fills up for the night. He watches the front door in the mirror over the bar, observing each person who comes into the pub. When he sees the flash of long blond hair, he straightens in his seat, trying to get a better look at the woman in the entrance."

Sophie lifted her hand off Lumberjack's cold, clammy arm and shook it out. Clenching her teeth, Sophie forced herself to put her hand back on his arm.

"Damn, that looks like me. I have blonde hair, but that's my face," Sophie stated, swallowing thickly. "Why do I see myself? I thought I'd see the murderer."

"Are you sure it's you?" Reggie asked, but looked sheepish when Sophie squinted open one eye and gave him a look.

"I know my own face, Reg."

"Right, sorry." Reggie shrugged, his puppy-dog eyes making Sophie regret her sharp tone.

"Lumberjack watches me – well, the woman who looks like me – drink for several hours. He moves away from the bar and watches the woman from a darkened corner. I think he's trying to avoid her notice. He doesn't approach her – he just watches. He would normally never hunt at his local bar, he thinks, but she's impossible to resist. Just his type. Blonde, thin, small, with big, sweet, innocent eyes. When he overhears her mention to the bartender that she's on a road trip exploring the country by herself for the next month, he knows he won't be able to resist. She's meant to be his.

"He usually picks women who are beneath society's notice – prostitutes, runaways, the homeless. He calls them his Forgotten Ones. But *he* hasn't forgotten them. He carries them always, each special girl, in his heart and his memory. He decides to break his cardinal rule of never hunting at home. She's worth the risk. Besides, no one will be looking for her for a whole month.

"As the bar continues to fill up, it gives him enough cover to watch her covertly without being discovered. By the time midnight is starting to approach, the girl is visibly drunk. She's tilting slightly in her seat. She's making this so easy. Leaving a few bills on her table, the woman stands up and heads out of the bar, drunkenly bumping into the doorjamb on her way out. Lumberjack rushes after her, wanting to make sure he keeps her in his sights. As he exits the bar, he sees the woman run around the corner into the alley with a hand pressed over her mouth like she's about to be sick. When he rounds the corner, she straightens up from leaning against the wall. He asks her if she is okay. He wants to see if her hair is as silky as it looks, so he starts to reach for it, but he accidentally bumps her hand when she reaches for him at the same time. She drops a syringe that cracks open and spills its contents on the alley floor. She starts crying about insulin, but Lumberjack saw the look on her face. He recognizes the eyes of a predator. He sees them in the mirror every day. Whatever was in that syringe was meant for him. Lumberjack realizes that this bitch was trying to attack him. Him! He's going to make her suffer for this insult. He starts to reach for the girl, expecting her to make a run for it. Instead, she darts towards him and stomps on his instep. Then she hits him in the throat. For a moment, he thinks that she punched him until a sharp ripping pain registers. She stabs him several more times before he has a chance to react. He grabs his throat and feels blood beneath his fingers. He tries to apply pressure to stem the blood flow but there's too much. The bitch shoves him hard in the chest, making him fall on his ass, sprawled on the ground. She's talking, but he can't focus on her words. When he asks her why, she leans over him, bringing her face close, giving him a sweet smile... the kind of smile that's impossible to resist – the kind of smile he likes to ruin. 'You know why, Troy,' she says, then twirls out of the alley humming a happy tune. The last thing he sees is her animal-print high heels walking away."

Removing her hand from Lumberjack's arm, Sophie stepped back from his body, flexing her cold fingers.

"Well, we know it wasn't you," Amira announced, giving Sophie a gamine grin. "Animal-print high heels? Do you even own any shoes that aren't combat boots?"

"Ha ha." Sophie scowled at Amira but ruined her frown when a chuckle bubbled up her throat.

"It sounds like your dream and Lumberjack's death vision match up. Was there anything different from your dream?" Reggie asked.

"It all matched. The dream was from the murderer's perspective is the only difference from Lumberjack's vision."

"My question is: why did you see your own face? Is there some kind of spell or a psychic power that makes this possible? It has to be a Mythical of some kind," Reggie said. "Perhaps a witch or a powerful Fae."

"If I had to guess, I'd say that the murderer has a way of blocking anyone from seeing her. Anyone looking for this person only sees a reflection of themselves; that's why Sophie only saw her face in both the dream and the vision. However, I've never heard of any kinds of Mythical beings with the ability to block visions. I need to call the Chief of Police. He's going to need to be informed about this situation. And I'll ask if he's ever heard of a power or spell that hides a person's identity from psychics," Mac said.

"I read once that every person alive has six doppelgangers in the world. I wouldn't rule out the possibility that she just looks very similar to Sophie," Ace suggested.

"She didn't look similar. It was like looking in a mirror. What are the odds that the person I'm seeing a vision of looks exactly like me?"

"I'm just saying, it might be unlikely, but you shouldn't rule out the possibility that it's just a strange coincidence. Weirder things have happened," Ace argued.

Reggie picked up the victim's chart and gave Sophie a strange look. "You were right, by the way, the victim's name was Troy Weatherby. And he was found in the alley next to the 8th Avenue Pub."

"Well, we figured that I probably had all that stuff right,"

Sophie said, trying for a nonchalant shrug. She peeled off her gloves and tossed them into the bin.

"Have you ever had any other dreams where you've witnessed a murder? Especially from the murderer's perspective?" Reggie asked.

Sophie's heart felt like it was going to pound out of her chest. "Shit. Yeah, I think I've had a couple of them."

When Sophie's ears started to ring, Mac pulled her into a hug, gently rubbing her back. "We'll figure this all out. Don't stress. I'm going to make a few calls. I'll be just down the hall if you need me, okay?" Mac whispered.

"It sounds like Lumberjack, aka Troy, is some kind of serial killer or a rapist. The dude seemed seriously creepy," Amira said.

"I agree. I'm going to try to see if he has a record," Mac said, brushing a soft kiss across Sophie's lips. As he turned to leave, he caught one of Sophie's hands, giving it a reassuring squeeze. His hand felt warm against Sophie's cold and clammy one. The rough rasp of his calluses sent a pleasant shiver up her spine.

After watching the door swing shut behind Mac, Sophie turned back to look at Troy. He had seemed menacing in the visions, but death had reduced him to nothing more than a cold, empty husk.

Sophie's mind swirled with too many questions and possibilities. Hopefully, Mac would find some answers.

"You gonna be okay?" Ace asked, his normally curt voice soft and concerned. Without lifting her gaze from Troy's ashen face, Sophie tried to reassure her friend, stating that she was fine. She could hear Ace's and Amira's softly murmuring voices fade as they headed out of the autopsy room.

"Why don't you sit this one out? I can have Amira assist with the autopsy," Reggie suggested once they were alone again.

"Like hell am I going to let Amira do my job. I can do this. Don't treat me like I'm weak, Reggie. It was just the shock of finding out the guy from my dream was real. It just caught me by surprise, that's all. I'm fine. Seriously," Sophie argued. Straightening up to her full – albeit not terribly tall – height, Sophie dared Reggie to try and keep her from doing her job.

"I don't think you're weak. But you've been put through a lot lately. Everyone has a breaking point, so don't let your need to be strong push you past your limit. No one will think less of you if it all gets to be too much."

"Reg, I'm fine. Really. If everything gets to be too much, I will let you know, I promise," Sophie replied, bumping her shoulder against Reggie's.

After a final reassurance, they got to work.

CHAPTER 2

By the time they finished with Troy's autopsy, Mac still hadn't returned. Sophie had to stop herself from continually glancing back at the door, hoping to see him come through. She zipped up the body bag, hiding Troy from her view, and deposited him back in the walk-in fridge with a sigh of relief.

"What type of Mythical was Troy, anyway? Usually, I can figure it out from their death vision, but I didn't pick up on anything," Sophie asked Reggie as she rolled in a gurney with their next scheduled autopsy on it.

Reggie picked up the chart, skimming over the limited information he had on Troy. "He was a redcap."

"A what?"

"Redcap. They're similar to goblins; most of their stories are out of Scotland and England, I believe. Legend says that they got their name because they dyed their hats red with their victims' blood. They usually lived around castle ruins and killed travelers that wandered too close to their lair. I've heard that in real life, they're usually loners and keep to themselves," Reggie explained. "They don't even necessarily wear hats."

"Does a redcap look human, or are they like Burg and have a different form?"

Burg, the owner of the pub next door to her apartment, was a Mythical who usually looked like an old-timey circus strongman. His true form was a ten-foot-tall ogre with olive-green skin and tusks. Burg had an enchanted tattoo that let him transform between his natural ogre form and his human one with just a few magically spoken words.

"In the legends, redcaps look like short old men with long sharp teeth, skinny fingers tipped with talons, and large red eyes. Think of a hideously gruesome garden gnome. I'm not sure if Troy had a separate redcap form or what we saw was what he really looked like," Reggie explained, making Sophie's eyebrows rise in interest. Sophie had noted a tattoo on Troy's arm during the autopsy. "However, he did have a sigil tattoo, so we can assume he probably had a second form. But that's not a guarantee, since almost all Mythicals have at least one charmed tattoo."

"So that tattoo on his arm with the red hat and the spear was probably a transformation sigil, right? What other kinds of magic tattoos are there?" Sophie asked while rolling a new gurney with a fresh body onto the weighing station. "And how can you tell a magic tattoo from a regular one?" Every day Sophie found out something new about this strange new world where beings from myth and legend were real. Sometimes, it felt like she was treading water in a sea of information that kept sweeping over her head. There was so much to learn.

"There are all kinds, from simple to complex. There isn't a single way to tell a sigil tattoo from a nonmagical one. Most of the tattoos are imbued with a spell to make Mythicals appear human, and typically they have the same basic designs for each species. So, if you see a redcap tattoo on what appears to be a human, you're most likely talking to a redcap. Most of them have an incantation tattooed around them. Those words need to be chanted to activate or deactivate the glamor."

"So, if I knew the words to the spell on someone's tattoo, could I activate their spell?" Sophie asked intrigued.

"No," Reggie said, shaking his head at Sophie. "The only person who can activate their tattoo is the person the tattoo is on. Plus, the spells don't have a standard language they need to be written in, so it could be in hundreds of different languages. Even dead ones. My tattoo is in Greek, and the only Greek words I know are for my tattoo."

"Wait, you have a tattoo? I would not have pictured you as the tattoo type," Sophie asked, eyes bright with suppressed curiosity.

"Just the one. It's to correct my eyesight," Reggie said, rolling his sleeve up and showing Sophie a small tattoo of an anatomical eye with an indecipherable script under it.

"The detail is amazing. So accurate," Sophie said the only positive thing she could think of, biting her lip to keep from grimacing.

Reggie snorted his amusement. "It's easier, and cheaper, for the tattoo artist to bespell an accurate representation of what needs to be fixed or changed rather than create an abstract, artistic image. It's not pretty, but it works."

"Do you think you'll get any more? I've found that once you get one, you get addicted to adding more."

"No. They're quite expensive, so most Mythicals usually only have tattoos for important problems or required concealment, like Burg's. He can't live in the human realm in his true ogre form, so he needed a tattoo to help him look human. He might have other sigil tattoos – you'd have to ask him – but I would be surprised," Reggie explained.

"Really? I would think people would get glamored to look more beautiful or thinner or something."

"It would be way cheaper to get plastic surgery than to get a sigil tattoo. It took me years to save for mine. The only reason I even decided to get it was because my nearsightedness was causing issues with my work."

"If a sigil tattoo is so expensive, why not just get Lasik or something?"

"Well, I had corrective lenses until I could save for the tattoo. It's worth the price and wait because not only does it give me guaranteed perfect vision, it also gives me night vision. I had a couple of other features added like magnifying and infrared vision."

"Infrared! That sounds so cool. How do you get one? Is there a special place you have to go to?"

"There are a few Fae-owned tattoo parlors around the city that specialize in sigil tattoos," Reggie explained, rolling his sleeve back down.

"Silly me. Of course there are."

"You ready?" Reggie asked, setting up his phone to record the new autopsy.

JUST UNDER AN HOUR LATER, AS SOPHIE WAS ROLLING THE WOLF shifter they had just finished up into the fridge, Amira popped out of her office with a gleeful expression on her face.

"What?" Sophie asked cautiously, her shenanigans alarm sounding a warning in her head.

"So... You and Mac. You two looked very cozy," Amira said, dramatically fluttering her ridiculously long eyelashes.

"I was in the middle of a panic attack. He was just comforting me."

"Comforting, huh? Is that what they are calling it nowadays? He looked at you the way Fitz looks at focaccia," Amira said with a conspiratorial smirk. "I saw him kiss you. What exactly happened after we left your place last night?"

"Ugh. You suck," Sophie said. "Yes, something happened last night. Well, more like this morning, but whatever. After he woke me from my nightmare, I asked him to sleep with me. Just sleep!"

Sophie reiterated when she saw the glee start to form on Amira's face. "Something about the dream freaked me out, and I didn't want to be alone. In the morning, we made out a little. Nothing more than that!"

"That's it? Boooring!" Amira singsonged. "I want juicy details. Not some PG-13 romance bullshit."

"*So* sorry to disappoint you."

"No need for sarcasm," Amira said, but Sophie disagreed; there was every need for sarcasm. "So, what happens next with you guys?"

"I don't know yet. It's so new. I was hoping to keep it under wraps for a bit."

"You're a dumb ass. Everyone knows. You're both super obvious. Seriously, there's sparks flying. So... do you think it's serious?"

"I think it could be serious one day. There's potential there. He was going to take me to breakfast after work tonight, but now I don't know what's going to happen," Sophie replied.

"Well, when you get some juicy details, I want 'em," Amira announced gleefully, making 'gimme gimme' grabby hands.

"Sure thing," Sophie placated, pushing the gurney away from her possibly crazy friend, with absolutely no intention of sharing personal 'juicy' details with anyone.

Rolling the gurney into the main autopsy room, Sophie spotted Mac talking to Reggie. At the noise of her entry, Mac turned his head and captured Sophie's dark eyes with his bright blue ones.

"Everything okay?" Sophie asked, unable to decipher the look on Mac's face.

"Reggie was just telling me that the estimated time of death aligns with when I woke you up from your nightmare. This is good news because it means you have an alibi. However, I talked with the chief, and he wants me to take your picture to the pub and see if anyone recognizes you, just to cover all our bases. He also insists that based on your visions of Weatherby's murder, and your previous assistance in discovering Edwyn's plan, he needs to meet you in person. He said that he needs to make sure you are on the 'up and up' – which I politely told him is bullshit. However, he has the power to ban you from helping. If the chief thinks you're dangerous or going to cause problems, he can get you fired. He's coming here at 5. He wants to talk to the whole crew but especially you, Sophie."

"Oh, come on! If I were the murderer, do you think I would have confessed to the dream? I could have lied or pretended I'd never seen Lumberjack before, and no one would have been the wiser. If I were the murderer, none of my behavior tonight makes any sense," Sophie said, rolling her eyes.

"I don't think Chief Dunham believes you are the murderer. He just wants to observe the situation here since he's putting a lot of faith in your visions," Mac assured Sophie. "He insists on witnessing one of your autopsies, just to warn you."

Sophie huffed in annoyance, feeling like a sideshow freak performing for others' entertainment. She could understand intellectually that the Chief of Police needed to see her ability for himself, but it made Sophie feel awkward and untrusted.

Shaking off her less than helpful emotions, Sophie finished rolling the gurney over to the x-ray station. When Mac cleared his throat, Sophie looked over to see him holding up his phone with a chagrined look on his face.

"What?"

"I need to take your picture to show the bartenders."

"No," Sophie whined, looking down at her worn scrubs and scuffed-up boots.

"Chill out. I just need a picture."

When Mac lifted his phone to take the picture, Sophie stuck out her tongue and gave him the finger. Mac snapped a quick photo of Sophie before she dropped the face she was making.

"I'm setting that one to my wallpaper. Now stop making faces and let me take the damn photo."

After Mac took the picture, he promised to return before Chief Dunham arrived in a few hours.

"And once we are done dealing with Dunham, I *am* taking you to breakfast," Mac vowed.

CHAPTER 3

"I have a question," Sophie said, cleaning and sanitizing the surgical implements and power tools before they started on their next autopsy. "That last autopsy – that was a human killed by a vampire, right? So what happens to the vampire now?"

"What do you mean?" Reggie asked, looking up from the chart where he was making his final notations.

"Well, I mean, will they arrest him? A vampire can't exactly go through the normal court system, right? I can't imagine that they could put vampires in a regular jail. Is there like a vampire jail?"

"Any crimes committed by Mythicals fall under the Conclave's jurisdiction. They will hear the details of the crime and decide what happens to the perpetrator. Depending on the nature of the crime, they will typically leave the punishment up to the vampire's Domus. Sometimes, the Conclave will order an execution for something particularly heinous. Justice tends to be swift and 'conclusive' in the Mythical world compared to the human one," Reggie explained. "The Conclave has a place where they house those awaiting judgment, but they do not operate a prison for Mythicals. They also have a few cells at the police station to temporarily house Mythicals. The bars on the cells had to be reinforced so no shifters could bust out."

"Huh," Sophie said. "That sounds like a better system."

"I suppose, but only if you trust your leaders' judgment and intentions implicitly. Having power over someone's life is serious. If they get bad information, if they're biased, or are compromised or corrupt – all these things can lead to a system where innocent people get abused. Swift justice only sounds good in a perfect world. The real world is messy and complicated. That's why what we do is so important here. We can't have crimes committed by Mythicals go unpunished and we can't have them discovered by unsuspecting humans. But we also have to make sure that the Conclave gets the most accurate information possible so they can rule fairly."

"Ugh. No pressure then." Sophie winced. "I didn't think about the possibility that if I get my visions wrong, I could be hurting people."

"Don't think like that. Your visions still have to be backed up by facts and proof provided by the police. Your visions might help point the police in the right direction, but they can't be used to convict anyone. The burden is on the police to obtain irrefutable proof."

Before Sophie could respond, voices from outside the room caught her attention. She immediately recognized Mac's gruff tone, but the other deep voice was unfamiliar. Just as she finished sanitizing the last tool and set it on the tray, the door to the autopsy room swung open, and Mac stepped through accompanied by a strange man. The man, possibly in his late fifties with a drooping, bushy mustache, was just behind Mac. Thick glasses framed baggy eyes that quickly glanced around the room with a skeptic's air. A few wispy hairs crowned the top of a head encircled with a ring of hair that was more gray than brown. The man was large in every sense of the word: large body, large eyebrows, large gut, large presence.

Sophie stared into piercing ochre-colored eyes with such deep bags under them it looked like ruffles of fabric. She got the immediate sense that he wasn't impressed with what he saw in front of him. He didn't seem like the type of guy to put up with bullshit, and Sophie was just brimming with bullshit.

"This her?" he asked, turning toward Mac.

"Yes, sir, this is Sophie Feegle," Mac replied. "Sophie, this is Chief of Police Wilford Dunham."

"Nice to meet you," Sophie said, suppressing the weird, sudden urge to salute.

"I'd offer to shake your hand, but..." Dunham said, nodding his head towards Sophie's gloved hands, making Sophie snort.

Maybe this won't be so bad, Sophie thought, starting to believe that her initial impression of Dunham was wrong. Perhaps he had a sense of humor after all.

"I'd like to observe one of your death visions and then ask you some questions. Any objections?"

Sophie shook her head and let Dunham know that she would return in a moment with the next autopsy. When she wheeled in the new gurney, she and Reggie quickly got through the preparation steps of weighing and x-raying the body. Reggie locked the gurney wheels and moved the swivel arm on the bright overhead light into position, highlighting the woman on the gurney.

"You ready, Soph?" Reggie asked, his finger hovering over the record button on his phone.

Sophie cleared her throat a couple of times and wished for a moment she had stopped at the water fountain before nodding and stepping up to the side of the cold metal gurney. Bruises were visible on the woman's pale arms. Sophie placed her hand on an unblemished section on the back of the woman's hand.

With a slow exhale, Sophie started relaying the vision unraveling in her mind.

"She's sleeping, and a noise wakes her up. Looking over at her husband, he's snoring, but she notices that his phone is lit up with a message. She thinks it's weird that he's getting a text so late at night. Maybe there's an emergency. She picks up his phone. When she looks at the screen, she sees a message from someone named Giselle. She knows there is a woman in Victor's office named Giselle. He told her that Giselle was overbearing and gossipy. He said that he was annoyed that he had to attend that conference with her a few weeks ago, and he couldn't wait to get home and away from her constant chattering. The text says, 'Missing you tonight. I don't like sleeping without you anymore.' She wakes Victor up, demanding to know why Giselle is texting him in the middle of the night. Victor tries to tell her that the text is a practical joke his co-workers are all playing on each other. Then he says, 'Renee, I am not cheating on you. Giselle is obsessed with me. I've told her to leave me alone, but she keeps texting me. I didn't tell you because I didn't want you to worry. I think Giselle might be unhinged.'

"Fed up with his obvious and weak lies, she starts typing a response to Giselle. When Victor sees what she is doing, he leaps out of bed and tries to grab the phone from Renee's hand. Realizing what he's trying to do, she quickly backs up and locks herself in the master bathroom. As Victor beats on the door, she scrolls through old messages on his phone. Renee yells out in a wordless rage when she sees all the texts and nude photos the two have exchanged. Opening the bathroom door, she calls Victor a bastard and throws the phone at him. She screams that she wants a divorce. The phone hits Victor right in the eye. Oh man, she nailed him. This enrages Victor; he calls Renee a fucking bitch and pushes her. She trips and hits her head on the way down on the toilet or maybe the tub; I can't tell which. She's dazed from hitting her head, and everything is going in and out of focus. Kneeling on her, he starts hitting Renee, and then he starts choking her when she tries to fight back. She tries to speak a defensive spell to knock him back, but she can't get the words out because he's squeezing her neck so tightly. The last thing she sees is him swearing that she'll never leave him – that he'll kill her first."

Sophie opened her eyes and stepped back from the gurney. She stared for a moment at Renee's face. She had to take several deep breaths to push down the rage she felt for Victor. Sophie wanted to go track him down and beat the shit out of him on Renee's behalf. See how he liked it. Plus, she needed some eye bleach after seeing those photos of Victor's junk.

"Is that how it normally goes?" Dunham asked, rousing Sophie from her murderous thoughts.

"Generally," Sophie replied. "Sometimes, the vision is like watching through someone else's eyes, and sometimes it's more vivid, like I'm there in person. When I first started getting the readings, it was all more indistinct and dreamlike. Once I realized it was all real, I started attempting to focus on the details. Now, I can sometimes even pick up on the victim's thoughts. Usually, I am aware of where I am and that I'm watching a vision play out. Very rarely, I get sucked into the vision entirely, losing awareness."

"We've theorized that the closer to the time of death that Sophie touches the victim, the more vivid the vision. My other theory is that the person who died has magic that Sophie's magic reacts more strongly to," Reggie explained.

"I see," Dunham said. "What usually happens next?"

"We conduct an autopsy on the victim. Then I send the audio file of Sophie's vision, along with the autopsy report, to Mac to make sure the detective on the case gets all of the relevant information," Reggie explained. "Would you like to stay for the autopsy as well?"

CHAPTER 4

$\mathcal{T}$o Sophie's utter disappointment, Chief Dunham did decide to stay for another autopsy. Thankfully, it was the last autopsy scheduled for the night, so she just had to get through one more, swallowing down any complaints about being treated like a sideshow freak.

By the time they finished, Sophie was annoyed and out of sorts. It was not that the police chief was obtrusive or rude in any way; she just didn't like having him there.

"Please forward me both the audio recordings and your autopsy reports from tonight. I would like to compare them to the official police reports when I get back to my office," Dunham said to Reggie.

"Do you not believe the authenticity of Sophie's visions? How can you possibly question her after seeing how the autopsies matched the details of her visions? That first woman had a contusion on the back of her head and had died from strangulation, just like Sophie stated," Reggie argued.

Dunham raised a placating hand to halt Reggie's rant. "I'm not questioning the authenticity of Sophie's visions. I am only doing my due diligence here. I can't authorize her visions to be used in cases unless I have concrete proof of their accuracy. I have to report this to the Conclave, and I need to be able to justify this decision with my superiors."

"No worries. That makes perfect sense to us," Sophie interjected, sliding between Reggie and Dunham, wanting to make sure Reggie didn't say anything else that might piss off the Chief of Police.

"Sophie, I need you to come down to my office at 9 this morning. I will have a few more questions after I finish reviewing the police reports from both autopsies," Dunham informed Sophie.

"I request permission to attend that meeting," Mac, who had been silently observing until this point, interjected.

"I will allow it. I'll see you both at 9. Actually, you know what? I'm going to need breakfast. It's been a long night. Let's meet at 8 instead at The Mission Bean."

Dunham turned to thank Reggie for opening his autopsy room for observation before either Mac or Sophie could respond, exiting the room with a preoccupied air.

"Not exactly a warm and fuzzy kind of guy, huh?" Sophie murmured, making Mac chuckle.

"Not really," he agreed. "Damn it. I was going to take you to breakfast."

Sophie shrugged in a 'whaddya gonna do' gesture.

"I'll make it up to you," Mac vowed.

"Hey." Sophie nudged Mac, whispering just in case Dunham was still nearby. "What kind of Mythical is Dunham? Is he a bulldog shifter?"

"What? No. Why would you think that?"

"You don't think he kinda looks like a bulldog in human form? He's got the jowls for it," Sophie said, making Reggie and Mac chortle.

"You know that's not how being a shifter works, right? Do

you think I look like an opossum? Don't answer that. I don't want to know," Reggie teased.

"So, what is Dunham?"

"He's a bear shifter. Grizzly, I believe," Mac said, chuckling at Sophie's shocked expression. "I recognize that look in your eye – that's my boss. Actually, my bosses' boss, so don't ask any inappropriate questions in our meeting later today," Mac said, ignoring Sophie's pout.

"What did the bartenders say when you showed them Sophie's photo?" Reggie asked, changing the subject.

"They weren't sure. Both the bartenders remembered a blond woman, but it was a busy night, and they didn't pay her much attention. One of them thought that you might have looked familiar but couldn't say for certain. Have you ever been to that pub?" Mac asked.

Sophie shook her head. "So, what does that mean for me?"

"Nothing. You already have an alibi. I have a contact at the Conclave that is a magic expert, so I've sent him an email to see if he's ever heard of someone being able to block their identity from psychics," Mac said.

"I'm not a psychic," Sophie exclaimed, thinking of the stereotype of a Gypsy woman in a long skirt gazing into a crystal ball.

"You have visions of people's final moments… What do you think that's called?" Mac growled, softening the words with a grin.

"Nobody likes a smartass," Sophie mock-growled, pursing her lips at Mac.

A buzz from the phone in Mac's hand interrupted his retort. As he read whatever was on the screen, Sophie watched Mac's eyebrows rise.

"What?" she asked.

"The lead detective on the case has found a bunch of evidence in his apartment that Troy Weatherby was a serial killer. There were dozens of photos and trophies from his victims all over his place. They are now theorizing that Troy's murder was possibly either self-defense or an act of vengeance."

"That aligns with my visions. The murderer was specifically targeting Troy. That makes me feel better. Is that weird? I mean, I know I didn't kill him. It's just that the dream was so realistic that it *felt* like I murdered Troy. Finding out he was a serial killer makes me feel less guilty."

"I don't think that's weird. You shouldn't feel guilty either way. I was there when you woke up, remember? You were horrified," Mac said. "You have nothing to do with this except being an unwilling witness."

"According to my dream, Troy's murder wasn't self-defense. That leaves vengeance as a possible motive. However, it didn't feel personal. If Troy had hurt her or someone she cared about, wouldn't she have been filled with rage? She was... I don't know exactly. But it was like she was having fun. It felt more like vigilante justice than personal revenge," Sophie explained, trying to put into words the feelings she picked up from the murderer's vision.

"The detectives investigating will be focusing on Troy and any possible connections the murderer could have to him. They will be concentrating on family, friends, and victims. I think we need to focus on your visions," Mac stated. "Let's go over what you can remember from any previous dreams, so we can have that information if the chief asks."

"You guys can use my office or the main office, but the morning shift will probably start arriving soon. And they're almost all human," Reggie said.

"Why don't we take this to the police headquarters? The top floor is reserved for the exclusive use of the Mythical division of the SFPD, so we'd be safe to discuss matters there. Plus, it's only a few blocks away from The Mission Bean, so we could walk there afterwards."

"Hell yeah! I want to see where you work. Where you solve

crimes in a blaze of intellectual glory," Sophie said, making Mac roll his eyes heavenwards like he was seeking divine patience.

Reggie declined an invitation to join them, stating that he wouldn't be much help but to let him know if they had any need for his medical expertise.

"I'll drive. It's only ten minutes away," Mac offered.

"Sounds good. Let me change out of my scrubs. I'll meet you in the lobby in just a couple of minutes," Sophie said.

Back in her street clothes, Sophie headed out into the lobby.

"Bye, Miss Zhao. Have a nice day," Sophie called out to the immaculately dressed receptionist as they exited the Medical Examiner's office a few minutes later.

"Goodbye, Sophie. Have a nice day, dear," Miss Zhao called out from her domain behind the receptionist desk.

"How old do you think Miss Zhao is?" Sophie said quietly, unreasonably concerned that Miss Zhao would overhear her, despite being outside the building in the parking lot. Something about Miss Zhao made Sophie use caution when so little else did. "She looks like she might be in her mid-thirties, but I'm not sure. She's got this ageless wisdom about her – like she's seen it all and won't suffer fools."

Mac glanced back in the direction of the ME's office's lobby, where Miss Zhao was safely ensconced behind the reflective glass doors.

"It's hard to say. There's not a lot of information known about dilongs. Chinese dragons are a secretive bunch. She might be a century old for all I know. Or she might be exactly what she appears: a thirty-something woman in a blue pantsuit," Mac said, shrugging.

Mac steered Sophie over to his immaculately clean and immensely boring four-door sedan. Mac started to unlock the door but stopped, turning and leaning against the side of his shiny gray car.

"I'm sorry about all this," he replied.

"Sorry about what?"

"This is *not* the breakfast date I had envisioned for us," he groused, sweeping a lock of Sophie's hair behind her ear. Sophie's breath caught as he leaned closer, but instead of kissing her, he unlocked the door and ushered Sophie inside.

The drive took less than ten minutes. San Francisco's police headquarters was just north of the ME's office, on the other side of Dogpatch, one block away from the bay's edge.

Much like the ME's office, the building that housed the police headquarters was a large, shiny square box – all sharp-edged modern design. Next door, in contrast, was a red-brick fire station, its old-timey charm making the police station's stark aesthetic stand out even more. The fire station almost looked like it was nestled back into the police headquarters building. Like the SFPD was hugging the fire department in its cold, indifferent arms.

Sophie admired the dichotomy of San Francisco's landscape: old, grand architecture tucked in between soaring, modern developments and run-down warehouses. New shiny progress crushed the old beneath its technological foot in other cities, but the old hung on with a tenacious, fierce grip here.

If the police headquarters hadn't gleamed quite so brightly, it would look exactly like a prison. Sophie grinned at the irony that the police were working diligently to put criminals in a place that looks so much like where they willingly spent their days.

Sophie followed Mac through a large, echoing lobby filled with concrete, natural wood, and glass walls. It was stark and unwelcoming, with only one rounded cloud-gray couch to break up the repeating pattern of rectangles. Mac walked by a large reception window heading to a bank of elevators. Using a keycard, they entered the elevator and headed to the fifth floor.

"Nice place," Sophie said, trying to muffle the sarcasm that wanted to bubble forth.

"Sure is. It has all the warmth and welcome of a cistern," Mac deadpanned. Sophie laughed, the tension that had been slowly ratcheting up her spine, loosening its grip on her muscles.

Mac kept tugging at the collar of his button-up shirt and shrugged under the suit jacket.

"Do you have fleas?" she asked.

Mac looked at Sophie, startled. "What? No, why would you ask me that?"

Sophie smirked, imitating the way Mac kept tugging at his shirt.

"This suit is irritating me," he explained. "Not everyone gets to wear whatever they want to work. I have to be professional."

"Hmm, I do like the suits," Sophie teased, letting her eyes linger on Mac's suit-covered form.

"Soph," he growled. Mac had a way of saying her name like it was a warning. Mac started to reach for Sophie, but the ding of the arriving elevator had Sophie dancing away with a mischievous laugh.

Exiting the elevator, Sophie followed Mac through a wide-open floor filled with a sea of beige cubicles.

"This is the bullpen," Mac said, waving his hand toward the ordered rows of desks. "This entire floor is dedicated to the Mythical division of SFPD. We cover any shifter or Mythical crimes from Sonoma down to San Mateo. My desk is over here."

Mac stepped into one of the fabric-lined cubicles in the second row of the cubicle farm. Snagging an office chair from the cubicle across from his, Mac rolled the chair next to his. Accepting the seat, Sophie sat and looked around at Mac's pristine workspace. Grinning like a gremlin, she slid a slow finger across the leather desk protector, pushing the five perfectly placed pens next to a notepad out of alignment. Mac snatched the pens away with a huff and opened his desk drawer to hide them away from her.

"Wait," Sophie yelped, stopping Mac from closing the drawer. Sophie took in the little storage boxes filled with an assortment of office supplies, running her fingers over the landscape of containers filled with paperclips and pens and staples, all perfectly lined up and ordered. "Do you have OCD?"

"No! I'm organized. Something you wouldn't know anything about," Mac snarked.

"Puh-lease. I'm organized," Sophie argued, earning an eye roll from Mac.

"Cut the shit. I've been in your apartment, so I know that's a lie. Everything should have a place. It means I don't have to waste time looking for something. I always know exactly where everything is. Do you know how many times I've seen you misplace your phone just this week alone?"

"Clutter is normal. This is not normal," Sophie teased. "It's practically robotic."

As they bickered, the mostly empty floor started to see a slow trickle of arriving detectives. Mac pulled a small leather notepad from his inner jacket pocket.

"Before we meet with Chief Dunham this morning, I want to go over any previous dreams you've had that might be related to Troy's murderer," Mac explained.

"I'm not sure if I'm going to be able to remember much. I didn't think they might be real, so I didn't pay that much attention to them. I just thought they were vivid nightmares."

"That's okay. Let's just see what you do remember."

A brown-haired man wearing an old-fashioned tweed fedora with a slightly askew striped tie stopped and leaned his elbows on the half-wall of Mac's cubicle. Sophie glanced between this intruder and Mac, waiting for Mac to acknowledge the man's presence.

"Hey Volpes, who's your friend?" the man finally asked.

"Fuck off, Turner," Mac responded without looking up from his notepad.

"Charming, as usual," the man said. Sophie watched as he

shrugged nonchalantly, then winked at her before wandering off, seemingly unfazed by Mac's attitude.

"Did he piss in your Cheerios?" Sophie asked, using one of Ace's favorite phrases.

"What? Who?" Mac asked distractedly.

"That guy, Turner. Is he a jerk? Or a weirdo or something?"

"Turner? No, he's fine," Mac responded, quickly plucking a pen out of a tray filled with its brothers. "If we let him, he'd stay here all morning chatting our ears off. Better to cut him off before he gets started."

Sophie smirked, reflecting on the first time she met Mac several weeks ago and what a jerk he had been to her. She probably shouldn't enjoy that he was such a dickhead, but she did. Mac was a gruff asshole, but he was her gruff asshole.

"I'd like to work backward from your most recent dreams to the oldest. Sound good?" Mac asked. When Sophie nodded her agreement, he waited silently with an expectant air.

Sighing, Sophie closed her eyes, turning her focus inwards, trying to pull the last dream from her hazy memories.

"I dreamed that I lured a man to a hotel. It was a nice enough hotel room, I suppose, but not high-end. It was generic enough that it could have been anywhere. I mixed myself and the man a drink, but I spiked his cocktail. The man was bald and pudgy, maybe in his early fifties. He was wearing a brown suit and an ugly blue tie. I'm not sure of his height; he was sitting on a couch during the dream. I gave him the drug-laced drink and watched him toss back the whole thing in practically one swallow. I remember I mentioned that I was nervous because I had never done something like this before. The man – his name started with a D, like Doug or Dan, maybe – asked me if this was my first time answering an escort ad. When he asked me my name, I told him to call me Snow White," Sophie said. "I woke up at that point, so I don't know what happened after that, but I'm pretty sure I gave him a lethal dose of fentanyl."

"You mentioned Snow White to me before. You said that you occasionally dreamed that you worked as Snow White at Disney, right? That doesn't feel like a coincidence," Mac asked, scribbling his notes in a tight, compact style that fit him perfectly.

"I haven't had any dreams about being a Disney princess for a while now. But yes, that used to be a recurring dream of mine. Meeting kids dressed up as Snow White, taking pictures with them, and signing autographs. And performing in some kind of stage show, I think. It's all a bit fuzzy now."

"Was it at Disneyland or Disney World?"

"I have no idea. I've never been to either. How would I know the difference?"

"One's in Anaheim, and the other is in Florida," Mac replied.

"I still don't know. I don't remember too many details. I remember seeing the castle, though."

"They both have castles. It would help to know which location, but this still helps. Alright, let's keep going on the dreams," Mac suggested.

Sophie recounted as many dreams as she could remember. She told Mac about the man she murdered behind a dance club in a dream, the one where she made a man look like he committed suicide at a playground. In another, she killed a man after pretending to be a prostitute at a sleazy hotel, a fourth killed just off a jogging path, and a final one in his truck in the empty parking lot behind an industrial park.

"Do you think these dreams were visions from the same murderer?" Mac asked.

"Maybe? I mean, in each dream, I suppose I felt the same: resolute, but with this weird sense of accomplishment. That was what made the dreams feel so awful. I was always so chipper in them. I remember when I made the guy on the jogging path look like he OD'ed, I was whistling the whole time, like I was just happily completing a chore, not murdering a man."

"If we assume that all the dreams were visions of the same

killer, that person has killed at least seven men. Historically, women are rarely serial killers, so the whole thing is highly unusual. The motives of female serial killers are typically different than men. Statistically, they kill for profit or revenge, although there are certainly outliers. And female serial killers tend to kill people they are close to, most often family members. Mode of murder is the only thing that lines up with a stereotypical female killer. Using poison *is* common. At least it wasn't arsenic in their elderberry wine," Mac said with a chuckle.

"Elderberry wine? What the hell are you babbling about?"

"It's from the movie *Arsenic and Old Lace*. It's a Cary Grant film. I think you'd like it; it's a dark comedy. These two sisters murder their gentlemen callers by poisoning their elderberry wine."

"Yeah, that sounds hysterical," Sophie snarked. "You and those old movies. Were you born in the wrong era?"

"Nah, I like it now, hellraiser. I just enjoy good movies. I'm adding *Arsenic and Old Lace* to our list of movies to watch together," Mac said, opening his notepad to a back page and writing down the movie title. Sophie snorted when she saw just how many films Mac had written down.

"Alright, let's go over similarities and differences our killer has with a typical female serial killer," Mac suggested. "That might help point us in the right direction."

"Okay, that makes sense. None of those guys seemed to know me, and I didn't know them. At least not personally. I definitely sought them out specifically, but they didn't recognize me. In the dreams, it also didn't feel like I killed for profit. I would guess revenge, but I wasn't angry. It also didn't feel like killing them was sexual. I remember that Lumberjack repulsed me," Sophie explained.

"We need to separate your identity from the killer's. We know you aren't committing these murders, so you need to stop saying things like 'I didn't kill for profit.' We need to make sure no one associates you to the murderer," Mac lectured. "Let's call her Snow White from now on."

Sophie nodded and watched Mac as he reread his notes. She had the urge to smooth the worried crease between his eyebrows with her thumb. When had she become such a romantic fool?

Not wanting to interrupt Mac's thought process, Sophie looked around the bullpen at the other early-bird detectives peppered throughout the space. She played a mental game where she tried to guess what type of Mythical each person might be. There was an exceptionally tall man pouring himself a coffee from an ancient-looking coffee machine who Sophie desperately hoped was a giraffe shifter. Mac's voice pulled her from her musings.

"In almost every instance, Snow White used herself as a lure to get these men alone. She also seems to prefer drugging, typically using fentanyl, to incapacitate her victims. If I had to guess, she makes the deaths look like overdoses," Mac murmurs, reading over his notes. "That's good. We have a basic MO. Aside from all her victims being male, did any of these men have anything else in common? Like age, ethnicity, looks, behavior?"

"Not physically. They all looked very different, and the ages were all over the place. None of them seemed like particularly nice guys, that's for sure. At least two of them hired Snow White as a prostitute or escort. That one guy followed her into a dark and closed park, which sounds like something someone who is up to no good would do. And I felt like the one at the jogging path might have been lying in wait, but I can't say that for certain. I mean, maybe he was off the path taking a piss in the woods, but when he stepped into the path in front of Snow White, she had been expecting him to do so."

"Troy was certainly a predator," Mac said. "The circumstances in your dreams make me think that the other victims might have been as well. It might be unusual, but I'm leaning towards vigilante justice as the possible motive. But I need concrete proof. I wonder how Snow White targeted these guys. Did you get any sense of how she picked them from your dreams?" When Sophie shook her head, Mac turned towards his computer. "I'm going to see if I can find any of these other six victims," Mac said, logging into the bulky computer sitting on the corner of his desk.

"What?" Sophie asked when Mac suddenly growled in irritation.

"Damn it. We're out of time. It's almost 8. We need to go meet the chief. I'll see if I can find any of the victims later. Come on, we need to go if we want to make it on time," Mac said, tucking his notepad back in his pocket and standing up.

As Mac strode away toward the elevators, Sophie was left behind to scramble after him.

"Wait up, Detective Dickhead," she yelled after his retreating back. Sophie heard several snickers from some of the cubicles around her. Mac stopped and looked back at her with a raised eyebrow.

"Move your ass, hellraiser. I want to get there before Dunham does."

"You're so rude," Sophie griped at Mac as they waited for the elevator. Mac gave Sophie an unrepentant smirk but tempered it by gently grasping one of her hands in his.

Outside the police headquarters, the sidewalk sparkled in the morning sun from a brief early-season rainstorm. It must have drizzled while they were inside working. The city still held a glimmer of moisture. The smells of the urban landscape – a metallic coating of fumes, a hint of garlic and onions from a nearby restaurant, old tar, and grimy asphalt trapped in the stagnant, humid air – clung to her nostrils. Still, beneath the smells of the city, there remained the suggestion of damp, fertile earth, and green growing things.

Hand in hand, Sophie and Mac walked the few blocks to The Mission Bean. Before they even turned the final corner to their destination, Sophie could smell the roasted, sumptuous goodness of strong coffee.

The Mission Bean was sandwiched between a salon and a co-op pizza place. The scent of freshly roasted coffee pulled Sophie inside the dim, cozy interior of the shop. To the left was a long wooden bench interspersed with small rickety tables. Tucked into the shop's back, almost lost in the low-lit atmosphere, was a small counter and glass case displaying various baked goods. But what had Sophie's full attention was the enormous coffee roasting machine to the right. Matte black with shiny copper knobs and levers, the well-used machine gave the impression of a bygone era. The cone hopper at the top of the roaster made the entire contraption look like a steam locomotive from the turn of the century. A young man with a long wooden paddle resting against his shoulder supervised the slow churning of the beans roasting. Walking over, Sophie watched, mesmerized as rotating blades stirred the still piping-hot coffee beans in a wide shallow basin. The beans' burnt chocolate color and their rich, heady scent refreshed Sophie's mind, invigorating her senses.

Mac and Sophie admired the hypnotizing motion of the paddles stirring the beans for a moment longer before they made their way through the narrow shop to the bored-looking woman in an orange beanie cap at the register.

"Good morning, Detective Volpes," the employee said, visibly perking up when she spotted Mac. "The usual?"

"Thanks, that would be great, Becky. What do you want?" Mac turned to Sophie as she looked over the chalkboard menu.

After Sophie had picked out a bagel sandwich and Mac chose a healthy, grain-filled muffin, they took one of the empty tables near the entrance to the shop, steaming hot cups of coffee in hand. Sophie slid into the booth with Mac taking the seat across from her. When a customer came in and asked to take the extra empty chair from their table, Mac growled that they were expecting company, startling the person.

Ignoring Mac's rudeness, Sophie cupped her hands around the heat of her coffee mug, looking around the café with an admiring glance. "I like this place."

"Yeah, me too. I come here several times a week."

Sophie watched as Mac broke off a piece of his muffin and popped it into his mouth with relish.

"What?" he asked at Sophie's look of disgust.

"A bran muffin? Really? It's just such a sad meal. Live a little," Sophie teased, pulling a piece of bacon out of her sandwich and waving it under Mac's nose before taking a crunching bite. Sophie hummed happily at the taste of salty, fatty, greasy goodness.

"They make a delicious muffin here. They're good for you, and they're very… *moist*," Mac said with an evil grin.

"Don't you start." Sophie pointed an accusatory finger at Mac.

"You don't like *moist* muffins, Soph?"

"I swear, I will leave you here alone to explain to the Chief of Police how you ran me off with your ridiculousness," Sophie threatened, making Mac guffaw into his coffee.

Sophie looked around the café in admiration. She loved the feeling of an old-school neighborhood coffee shop, from the chalkboard on the back wall with the daily specials down to the dark-stained scuffed concrete floor. Corporate sanitization, where uniformity was valued over uniqueness and originality, hadn't yet robbed The Mission Bean of its original character.

"I wish there were a cafe like this near my place. Oh, look," Sophie said, pointing at a display next to the register. "They sell bags of their freshly roasted beans. Remind me to pick up a couple of bags for work before we leave. The coffee at the morgue tastes like sweaty feet. It's disgusting."

"How do you know what sweaty feet taste like?" Mac teased while Sophie scoffed and rolled her eyes. "Come on, spill all your secrets. I want to know all about your fetishes."

"All my fetishes?" Sophie clarified. "Like sweaty feet?"

"I just wanna make sure all your needs are being met," Mac said, waggling his eyebrows.

"Good. I'll make up a checklist of all my fetishes. Just to make sure you're up for the job at hand," Sophie retorted, making Mac chuckle.

Mac started to respond but snapped his mouth closed and nodded his head toward the entrance.

Sophie watched as Chief Dunham muscled his way through the door, scowling at it like he thought he needed to intimidate the entrance into compliance.

Spotting Mac and Sophie, Dunham indicated that he'd join them after he placed an order. Sophie watched in amusement as Dunham ordered tea and then squeezed so much honey into his cup that he smooshed the honeybear's belly concave.

Sophie turned to Mac bursting with glee. As she opened her mouth to make a bear with honey joke, Mac put a hand over her mouth and shook his head no.

"Shifters have excellent hearing," he reminded her. Sophie huffed a disappointed breath into Mac's hand still over her mouth, then tugged his hand away from her face.

Chief Dunham took the seat next to Mac, diagonally across the table from Sophie.

Taking a long sip of his tea, Dunham stared at Sophie with the implacable gaze of a guard dog. He had a broad face with a large square jaw and probing brown eyes under heavy eyebrows. With his ruddy cheeks and the beginning of rounded jowls, all he would need was a white beard to make an excellent Santa Claus in a few years – if he somehow became jolly in the ensuing timespan. Sophie doubted that being the Chief of Police lent itself to much of a jolly state of mind.

The woman with the beanie brought over the chief's breakfast before Sophie could start asking probing questions about Dunham's plans after retirement.

"So, what have you discovered so far?" Dunham asked around a mouthful of sandwich.

Mac explained his theory that Sophie was having visions of the same murderer. He told Dunham how he planned to see if he could find any of Snow White's previous victims. The hope was that locating other victims would reveal additional evidence and possibly help trace her movements.

"Aside from Troy Weatherby, were any of Snow White's other victims Mythicals? Do you think she could be targeting Mythicals specifically or was it just a coincidence?" Dunham asked.

"I'm leaning towards coincidence. I think she is targeting predatory men. The dreams did not reveal any details whether the victims were human or Mythical," Mac answered.

"Based on preliminary evidence found at his apartment, it looks like Troy traveled all over the country for his job as a millwright. He used the cover of his work travel to hunt for victims far from home. Since he liked to keep trophies, we are hoping to be able to track down all his victims, but it could take weeks, if not months," Dunham said, pinching the bridge of his nose. "It appears he was targeting women that wouldn't be missed, like prostitutes and runaways, but every single one was blond, and most were petite."

"I got fifty bucks that say his mom was blond and petite," Sophie replied with a snort.

Dunham sucked air through his nose with an annoyed whoosh. Mac looked over at Sophie with raised eyebrows that said, 'See, it's not just me you annoy.' When the chief glanced down at his watch, Sophie narrowed her eyes and stuck out her tongue at Mac.

"What's a millwright?" Sophie asked, changing the subject.

"A millwright is someone who repairs and maintains large-scale machinery. Weatherby specialized in repairing certain types of factory equipment," Dunham explained. "He traveled extensively."

"That might explain all the dirt and grime we found under his fingernails during the autopsy," Sophie murmured.

"Based on your visions, you don't think that Troy Weatherby's murder was personal? That it was vigilante justice? The lead detectives on this case believe that Weatherby's murder was either a matter of self-defense from a potential victim or more likely a revenge killing by a relative of a victim."

"I don't care what those detectives think. Not my problem. I'm not going to concern myself with their case. I am only interested in following up on the other murders from Sophie's visions of Snow White. I won't be interfering in their investigation in any way," Mac assured Dunham.

"If you do find anything relevant to their cases, you will forward that to me. I will deal with parsing information to the lead detectives on their cases. Do not step on any more toes within the department, Mac. You can work on this angle as long as it doesn't interfere with Chan and Novack's investigation."

Mac raised his hands in aggravation, muttering, "Fine."

"From here on out, I need all copies of Sophie's autopsy visions forwarded to me instead of you, Volpes. You are not to act as any kind of intermediary between Sophie and the detectives assigned to the cases she has visions for. Also, Miss Feegle, I need you to start keeping a journal of *all* your dreams. I don't care if it's a recording or a written account, but I would like that sent to me weekly. Unless you have a relevant dream, which I want immediately," Dunham stated.

"What! You can't cut me out of this," Mac argued. Watching him, Sophie couldn't shake the mental image of a dog with its ruff raised in aggression, showing its teeth, a low growl rolling from its throat.

"You have to understand my problem here," Dunham said, spreading his hands out. "Comparing the recordings of your visions to the police reports and autopsies, I don't see any errors in your visions. That would typically be enough to greenlight your work, but now we have someone who seems to be able to circumvent your magic. How can I trust your visions now?"

Dunham calmly took a large bite of his sandwich while Mac visibly tried to swallow his anger. Sophie watched as a small blob of egg salad caught in Dunham's thick mustache.

"I found Sophie. I'm the one who figured out her gift. She is an important asset to the department. But even more important, I'm her friend and will do whatever it takes to protect her. The more people who know what she can do, the more danger that poses to her. Don't cut me out," Mac said, his fist thumped on the table, rattling the half-empty dishes. "Someone needs to be watching out for her."

"That's another problem. I believe you are emotionally compromised," Dunham said, pointing a thick finger at Mac. "It is clear, based on your body language alone, that you are overly invested in Sophie. I am concerned that you are biased."

Sophie pushed her plate away despite having only eaten half of her bagel, no longer hungry.

"Biased?" Mac said through gritted teeth. "I'm *not* compromised. I care about Sophie, yeah. But all I do is forward her visions to each relevant detective exactly as she dictates them. I don't alter what she says, and I don't tell the detectives what to do with that information. Sophie's visions aren't proof. They're a guide. Any detective that doesn't understand that isn't worth their weight in salt," Mac argued. "This is bullshit. I am not biased. I'm a damn good detective. And my record reflects my ability, judgement, and commitment."

Sophie liked that Mac was so confident and sure in his abilities.

Anger rolled through Mac's blue eyes, revealing the predatory side of his fox shifter nature. Occasionally, Sophie would forget that Mac wasn't entirely human, and then his well-concealed aggression reared its head. Was it only a few days prior that Mac, in a partially shifted fox form, dispatched several wolf shifters with only his claws and fangs right before Sophie's eyes? Events in Sophie's life had been moving at warp speed. The battle at the top of Coit Tower felt like it happened weeks ago rather than just a few days.

"I reviewed your file. Can you explain your spotty employment history?" Dunham asked Sophie, shifting gears.

Sophie felt her bitch-face drop into place at what Dunham's tone implied.

"Is this a job interview?" Sophie snapped.

"Yes, actually. Answer the question," Dunham deadpanned.

"I only got my Associate's degree. Without a Bachelor's, most jobs I could find were in retail. It turns out that customer service is not my forte. It's not in my nature to put up with bullshit. I like working at the morgue because the customers don't complain about my attitude," Sophie said. The joke landed between them with the grace of a dead duck falling from the sky.

"And how did you not know about your gift until recently?"

"I wasn't exactly going around feeling up corpses, now was I? I'd never touched a dead body before I started working at the ME's office," Sophie retorted.

"I find it peculiar how you got the job. You have zero previous experience in the medical field. You just *happened* to rescue the opossum shifter who runs the Mythical division of the Medical Examiner's office, and he offered you the job. You don't find that unusual?"

"To be honest, I find the whole thing unusual. The fact that Mythicals exist is unusual. But you know, you're right. You got me. I planned the whole damn thing so I could perform autopsies in the middle of the night. It was my master plan.

"You know what? I don't need to put up with this bullshit. Do you think I enjoy reliving people's last horrific moments? You think I'm having fun?" Sophie asked, angrily starting to push out of her seat to leave. Mac reached across the table and rested a quelling hand on Sophie's arm. The reassurance embedded in his touch calmed Sophie as nothing else could.

Taking a deep, cleansing breath, Sophie sat back down and turned to look at Dunham. "Why would I lie? What could I possibly be getting out of this? What do I have to gain? Frankly, it kind of sucks. Don't get me wrong, I love my job, but the visions are often horrific, and they take a toll on me."

"You're right," Dunham said, making Sophie's anger deflate almost as quickly as it started. "I needed to meet you. See your reactions myself before I can approve the use of your visions in the Mythical division. I needed to see for myself that you were the real thing and not just some clever scam artist or a glory hound."

"Glory hound? This was a test?" Sophie said through clenched teeth.

Dunham gave her an unapologetic shrug.

"You sure you're not Fae?" Chief Dunham asked, giving Sophie mental whiplash with how quickly he kept changing gears.

"I'm human. Some of the others at the morgue think that I might have a Fae ancestor or something to explain my ability," Sophie said. "But as far as I know, my entire family was human."

The chief took an obvious sniff of Sophie. She firmed every muscle in her body to keep from cringing away from Dunham. Being so obviously sniffed made her paranoid that her deodorant wasn't working. However, she refused to have a single sign of her discomfort to register on her face. She focused all her attention on the piece of egg still clinging to Dunham's mustache as it quivered with each deep huff.

"You don't smell Fae. You smell like a regular old human to me. Strange, but you wouldn't be the first human with magical abilities," Dunham said with a one-shoulder shrug. "I reviewed all the cases where you had visions. It was good work. I was impressed by the details you managed to uncover. A couple of times, you even helped solve stalled cases."

"Uh... you're welcome?"

"Chief, I am requesting to continue to receive copies of Sophie's visions. Just to reiterate, I will not interfere with any investigations. I just want to be kept in the loop," Mac cut in, turning in his chair to fully face Dunham. Sophie watched how Mac clenched his jaw, realizing that he was about to dig in his heels.

"Your request has been noted. And rejected. Sorry Mac, Miss Feegle's autopsy visions will be routed through me from now on. You will no longer be her main point of contact. Do not argue, Volpes. It's a done deal," Dunham held a stern finger up when Mac opened his mouth, his face red with anger.

Out of the corner of her eye, Sophie noticed that beanie-lady had started to come around the counter, a worried look on her face.

"I want Mac to be my point of contact with my dream visions," Sophie said quickly, cutting Mac off from escalating the argument with Dunham. "He's the only person I will entrust with my dreams."

"Acceptable," Dunham stated. "I expect a weekly report of all her dreams, Mac, even the mundane ones. Summaries will suffice, I don't need the details unless they're relevant. High-priority dreams need to be forwarded to me immediately. Unless you have anything else to discuss, you can go. I'd like to finish my breakfast in peace. You're both bad for my digestion."

Without another word, Mac jerkily stood up and motioned Sophie to do the same. He swept out the exit on a wave of anger. Sophie decided to buy the coffee beans some other time. She just wanted to escape.

As she started to follow Mac to the exit, Sophie stopped and turned back to Dunham, "By the way, you have egg in your mustache."

Sophie watched through the big front window as Mac turned and realized that he'd left Sophie behind, so he returned and held the door for Sophie to join him outside. Without another word, Sophie walked away from Dunham, following Mac into the growing flow of morning foot traffic.

Mac stalked down the sidewalk, muttering angry expletives under his breath. Once they turned the corner away from the café, he stopped in the middle of the walkway. He just stood there, shoulders tensed up and heaving aggravated breaths like a winded horse.

"What. An. Asshole," Sophie stated since she believed they were far enough away from The Mission Bean not to be overheard by sensitive shifter hearing. Mac took a long inhale and then rotated his neck before responding.

"He's the Chief of Police and in charge of all Mythical crimes for NorCal," Mac said as if that explained everything. "Plus, he has to answer to the Conclave. A nice guy would get chewed up and spit out within the first two days on the job. He's tough and shrewd, but he's fair. More importantly, I trust him. I'm just pissed that he's cutting me out."

"You trust him?"

"Yes, I trust him to do his job. He will utilize your gift, and he will protect you because he knows the value of your abilities. However, I don't trust anyone but myself and the rest of the Odd Ones to put your safety over the job. You can trust Dunham to always put the job first," Mac promised. "We're your friends. He's just your boss."

"I could still forward the autopsy visions to you. He doesn't need to know," Sophie offered.

"No, you don't need to do that. I only compared your visions to the case reports and forwarded them to the assigned detectives, so I don't need to be involved. He's right that I've been pissing off a few of the guys in the department. Now that I'm calming down, I realize he's probably right. The detectives have to take your visions seriously if they come from the Chief of Police."

"Doesn't mean I like him. He has no sense of humor," Sophie complained. "I don't trust anyone who doesn't laugh at my jokes."

"Uh, Soph… I hate to be the bearer of bad news, but no one laughs at your jokes," Mac teased, making Sophie shove him with her shoulder.

"You are so full of it," Sophie grumbled, sniggering when Mac nodded in agreement.

"Come on, hellraiser. Let me drive you home," Mac offered. Taking his hand in hers, Sophie felt the worry and stress from the talk with Dunham melt away.

CHAPTER 5

$\mathcal{A}$s Mac pulled into the curb in front of Sophie's apartment building, she admired how the glistening morning sun made the building – she had affectionately named it Brown Betty – look almost regal. The rain still clung to the curlicue woodwork along the steep gables reflecting the bright crystalline morning sun, temporarily camouflaging the dirt and slow-creeping decay.

With a final glance back at Brown Betty sparkling in the morning sun, Sophie turned to Mac while the car idled beneath them both. The space suddenly felt much smaller. The naked heat in Mac's eyes made Sophie feel caught somewhere between being a prey animal and a temptress. It wasn't a feeling Sophie was used to, but she was enjoying it.

The snick of Mac unclipping his seat belt sounded overly loud in the quiet of the vehicle. As he leaned across the console, all Sophie could see was the frosty blue of his eyes. The look in his eyes was intense and thrilling – like a predator's. He was entirely focused, as if ready to pounce. Sophie felt a sudden kinship to a gazelle on the savanna. Sliding his hand along her shoulder, cupping the back of her neck, Mac held Sophie in place as he brushed a thumb along her pulse point. His grip somehow added to the feeling of being willing prey. A thrill of pleasure skated up Sophie's spine. Mac held still, a breath of space between them, waiting for Sophie to cross that last millimeter. He left it all up to her. Sophie waited almost a beat too long, savoring the moment of anticipation, that space where heat and desire grew.

Tilting her head up, Sophie slowly pressed her lips to his. Placing one of her hands on Mac's chest, Sophie could feel the low rumble beneath her fingers of an inaudible growl. Mac turned the soft kiss fierce, filled with possession and heat, robbing Sophie of higher thought. Sliding her arms around his neck, Sophie pulled him closer, wanting to touch every inch of him. Mac dragged his mouth away from Sophie's lips, kissing his way to her neck. A searing path of heat followed in the wake of his lips. When Mac's teeth nipped Sophie's shoulder, his name escaped her lips in a hiss.

With a snarl, Mac pulled away and practically threw himself back across the car, pressed back against the far door. For a moment, Sophie was confused and ready to snatch him back, but the noise of traffic and passing pedestrians broke into her awareness.

Raking his hands through his hair, making the caramel blonde strands stand up in wild tangles, Mac said, "You should go before I lose control and we give Birdie an eyeful."

"Birdie?" Sophie repeated in confusion, still trying to gather her scattered thoughts. Mac's kiss had knocked the sense right out of her. Mac nodded his chin towards Brown Betty's façade.

Sophie turned in her seat to gaze at her apartment building. Looking toward her neighbor's window, Sophie snorted when she spotted Birdie plastered in her front window with an ear-to-ear grin splashed across her face.

Sophie looked back at Mac, trying to hide that she was out of breath and squirming in her seat. The look in Mac's eyes told Sophie she was not fooling him.

"Since our breakfast date this morning was ruined, would you join me for dinner and a movie at my place tonight before you go to work? I could order Indian from this place down the street that makes the best chicken vindaloo," Mac offered.

"I'd like that," Sophie replied, annoyed at the breathless quality of her voice.

"I'll pick you up here at 6. I can drive you to work after, so you won't have to take the bus," Mac suggested. "Anything you want to make sure I order?"

"Nah, I like it all."

"I'll see you tonight then," Mac said, leaning back across the car.

Meeting him halfway, Mac gave Sophie a brief, almost chaste, kiss.

"See you tonight," Sophie said, reluctantly getting out of the car. "Looks like Birdie wants to say hi."

Sophie pointed to the enthusiastically waving octogenarian pressed up against her window.

"Hi, Miss Birdie!" Mac bellowed, waving back.

Birdie blew an exaggerated kiss at him. Mac pretended to catch the kiss and tuck it into his jacket's inner pocket.

"Did you just put that in your pocket?"

"Yes, I'm saving it for later," Mac replied. The sharp quip startled a laugh out of Sophie.

Ugh, I'm turning into a giggler. Gross. Get your shit together. You're supposed to be a badass bitch, Sophie mentally lectured herself, rolling her shoulders.

With a final wave, Sophie turned and walked up Brown Betty's slightly sagging steps leading up to the tiny foyer.

After finishing the last few steps to the third floor, Sophie was not surprised to see Birdie waiting for her in the open door to her apartment. Without a word, Birdie nodded for Sophie to get inside. Sophie was feeling like a crummy friend because it had been several days since they'd been able to share a cup of tea and watch some trashy TV. Sophie made a silent vow not to let the craziness of her life interfere with spending time with her small collection of friends.

Sophie headed to her usual spot on the loveseat while Birdie shuffled into her tiny kitchen.

"You want tea?" Birdie called out.

"Yes, please." Sophie gave the only appropriate response.

Ginsberg, Birdie's tortoiseshell cat, sauntered out of the bedroom and gave Sophie a long, penetrating stare full of feline disdain. Ginsberg pointed his delicate nose in the air and started to stroll across the living room. It was clear that Sophie had been judged and found lacking. Sophie dangled her hand in offering and made kissy noises to try and entice Ginsberg over, but he gave her a haughty sniff and scampered into the kitchen to see what his mistress was up to instead.

A few minutes later, Birdie came out carrying two delicate saucers bearing matching teacups. Thin tendrils of steam curled from the liquid's surface. Ginsberg trailed behind Birdie as she handed Sophie her drink. Sophie blew across the top of the cup before taking a small sip. Humming happily at the hint of tart orange in the dark, smoky tea, Sophie took another sip.

Sophie chuckled as Ginsberg stopped in front of her and gave a demanding *mrow*. He turned in three precise circles, then flopped across Sophie's feet, purring like the engine of a motorboat.

"Oh, I see. *Now* you want attention. Fickle feline. What changed from three minutes ago?" Sophie questioned as she leaned down and obligingly scratched Ginsberg under his silky chin. Ginsberg allowed the chin scratches for a minute before turning and rubbing his cheek against Sophie's fingers. Turning his body, forcing Sophie's hand to rub along his neck to his shoulder, he leaned his weight on her busy fingers. Sophie followed the motion of Ginsberg's movement, running her hand along his back. He did this several more times before suddenly turning with an indignant yowl and batting Sophie's hand with his paw. He turned and raced out of the room and back to the sanctuary of Birdie's bedroom after giving her a brief glare.

"Crazy cat. At least he had his claws retracted," Sophie commented, watching as Ginsberg peeked his head back around the corner. He glared at Sophie and then disappeared again with a final swish of his tail.

Birdie headed back into her kitchen and returned with a beat-up box of vanilla wafer cookies. Birdie joined Sophie on the loveseat, lowering herself onto the flowered cushion with a groan. Placing the cookies between them, she picked up the TV remote and put on a morning talk show. They ate cookies dunked in tea while watching a bird-thin blonde woman and a dark-haired man with a threateningly bright smile talk to various celebrities.

Sophie hid her smile behind her hand as she listened to Birdie gripe about missing some man who used to host the show before the overly polished young fellow joined the cast.

"How is it going with you and Mac?" Birdie asked, setting her tea down on a side table and turning to Sophie in the middle of a commercial break.

"It's going good. We have a date tonight," Sophie answered. Sophie couldn't tell if the warm glow in her belly was the hot tea or the realization that she had a date.

"Good, I'm glad. I'm happy for you both. Although, I admit I was surprised you went for a shifter," Birdie replied. "Not that I don't understand. He's a fine-looking man. I would've given him a tumble back in my day."

Sophie sputtered into her drink, spilling hot liquid over her hand.

"Ugh, girl, watch my sofa," Birdie lectured, getting up and bringing Sophie some paper towels to mop up her clothes and chin. Birdie carefully cleaned the spilled tea off her orange floral upholstery.

"Wha—How did you know?"

"What? It's obvious that boy is a shifter. If you know what to look for, most of them aren't very good at hiding their true nature."

"What do you mean? How could you tell?" Sophie asked, wondering, *If it's so obvious, why don't more humans know about Mythicals?*

"Well, for one, he growls at you every time you annoy him – which is constantly. If the light hits his eyes just right, sometimes you can see the golden sheen in his iris. I've only ever seen that with shifters. He also has the banked aggression found in most of the apex shifters," Birdie explained, ticking off points on her age-gnarled fingers. "With Mythicals, a lot of their nature shows in the way they behave or sometimes even dress. For example, if you ever meet a man or woman who always wears a gold coin, they might be a leprechaun. But a sure way to know you're dealing with a leprechaun is that they will constantly touch the coin – it's a compulsive need for most of them."

"Huh, weird. How do you know about Mythicals in the first place? I only recently found out on accident," Sophie asked.

"Girlie, please. I've lived my whole life in this city. San Francisco is teeming with nonhumans. Plus, I dated a tiger shifter in my early twenties. Oh, that man was terrific in the sack. So good with his hands," Birdie said, a dreamy expression on her face. She cackled when she saw that Sophie had plugged her ears and was chanting "la la la" under her breath. "Prude," Birdie declared, then shushed the retort on Sophie's lips because the commercial break had ended.

They watched the rest of the show in companionable silence,

and then Sophie headed home to get some sleep after a very long night.

Before Sophie slipped into bed, she grabbed the notepad she used for her grocery list and a pen. She set them on the wobbly table next to her bed, keeping them easily within reach in case she had another vision in her sleep.

CHAPTER 6

Sitting on the top porch step, waiting for Mac, Sophie turned her face up to the gray sky looming above her. The temperature had dropped in the past few days as autumn started its march towards winter. The first tentative foray of the rainy season looked like it was sneaking over the city. Closing her eyes, the soft drizzle, barely more than a mist, felt like tiny ice needles on her cheeks. Fishing her thick knit cap out of her coat pocket, she tugged it tightly over her hair, making sure to cover her ears.

Everything was silent except the soft sound of drizzle hitting the buildings around her.

"Hey, Soph!" a deep voice called out, breaking into Sophie's wandering thoughts. Looking to the right, Sophie spotted Burg standing in a warm splash of light spilling out from his pub. "What're you doing out in the rain?"

"Got a hot date, Burg! I'm waiting for my ride."

"Tell Mac I said hi." Burg gave Sophie a small smile and a wave before opening the door to head back inside his bar. He was wearing an olive-green cable knit turtleneck stretched tight over his drum-shaped chest. He paused in the doorway, the lights inside the pub highlighting the ribs of the thick knit momentarily golden. "How are you doing? I haven't had a chance to check on you since our little adventure."

"*Little* adventure?" Sophie repeated with one raised eyebrow.

The little adventure Burg referred to was from just a few days ago: him turning into his ogre form, killing two corrupt cops who were about to put a bullet in Sophie's head, then climbing up the outside of the Coit Tower with Sophie clinging to his back like a tick. At the top of the Coit Tower, Sophie watched the Burg-ogre mow through a crowd of Mythicals who were trying to close the portal to the Fae realm permanently. Sure, "little adventure" indeed.

"Okay then, how are you doing since our big adventure?"

"I'm good, Burg. No need to worry." The last thing Sophie wanted was another worrywart hovering over her. She had a gaggle of them at this point.

With a parting offer to share some whiskey and company soon, Burg headed back into the warm glow of his pub, The Little Thumb.

A few minutes later, just as Sophie's butt had started to turn into a block of ice, Mac smoothly pulled up to the curb directly in front of Brown Betty. Checking her watch, Sophie chuckled when she realized that it was precisely 6. *Figures.*

Mac rolled down the passenger window and gave Sophie a devilish grin.

"Am I at the right place for the bi-weekly meeting of Cults and Witchcraft Anonymous?"

"You are, but it's by invitation only. Sorry, we don't just take in any ole weirdo off the street," Sophie quipped, standing up from where she was lounging on Brown Betty's porch steps. Skipping down the few steps, Sophie got into Mac's sedan.

Sliding into the passenger seat, Sophie held her fingers to the vents, sighing in bliss as the heat sent warm tingles into the tips of her fingers.

"You ready to watch *The Maltese Falcon?*" Mac asked, an eager smile on his face.

"Can't wait," Sophie replied, knowing how excited Mac was to share one of his favorite movies with her. Sophie leaned over, giving Mac a small kiss hello.

"Argh! Your nose is like ice!" Mac yelped, which only made Sophie shove her face against his neck. When he tried to pull away, Sophie clung to him like a spider monkey, giggling maniacally. Finally, Mac tickled his fingers into one of Sophie's armpits, making her jolt away from his questing digits.

"Hey, cut that out!" Sophie laughingly complained.

"Me? *You're* evil," Mac protested, shaking his head.

"How's your shoulder?" Sophie asked, thinking about the gunshot wound Mac suffered a few days earlier.

"Good as new."

"That's crazy. It's great, but crazy," Sophie said, shaking her head.

"The perks of being a shifter."

"Any news on the Lumberjack or Snow White?" Sophie asked as Mac pulled into the scant traffic in front of Brown Betty.

"Yeah, I think I might have tracked down one of Snow White's victims. A guy named Daniel Charles Blummer III. He was found dead in a hotel in Burbank just over a month ago. He'd overdosed on fentanyl and alcohol and fits the physical description you gave me. Here's where it gets interesting: when his niece was clearing out his house, she found polaroid photos of what appeared to be dead women. It looks like Blummer might be a serial killer ~ just like Weatherby. I reached out to the Mythical division in LA and told them about Snow White and her possible link to Blummer. They forwarded me his files. They're in my bag," Mac said, hooking his thumb over his shoulder, indicating a messenger bag on the seat behind him.

"That makes her a serial killer that murders other serial killers. That's super weird."

57

"It's all very Dexter-like," Mac agreed.

Sophie snagged the bag from the backseat and pulled it onto her lap.

"It's all in the green folder."

Sophie pulled the folder out and sat it on the bag on her lap, hesitating. "What about Lumberjack?"

"I haven't heard any news on Weatherby. They're still processing all the evidence they pulled from the crime scene, not that there was much. Snow White did a good job of not leaving anything behind."

Taking a deep breath, Sophie forced herself to open the folder. The first thing Sophie saw was the police report, which she just skimmed before flipping to the next page. Staring up at her was a mug shot of a middle-aged man with thinning brown hair. The breath Sophie was holding whooshed out of suddenly tight lungs.

"Soph?"

"That's the guy. He's the one I dreamed about."

"You sure?"

"I'm positive. He looks younger and thinner in this photo, but it's him. I wouldn't forget his face," Sophie responded woodenly.

"That makes sense. That mugshot is from six years ago. He got arrested for soliciting a prostitute," Mac said, glancing at the photo Sophie held in her hands.

Flipping the photo over, Sophie quickly rifled through the rest of the documents in the folder. She paused at an image of the crime scene. Daniel Blummer was slumped over on a plush tan couch.

"I think this is the hotel that was in my dream too. The couch and the painting of the mountain look familiar. Although they're both generic enough, I could be wrong," Sophie said after examining the photo, turning it sideways, trying to get a better look at Blummer's tie. She remembered that in the dream, he was wearing a blue tie with a ghastly paisley design. It was the right color, but Sophie wasn't sure if it was the same one from her dream.

The rest of the documents were scans of the polaroids found in Blummer's house. After the first two pictures, Sophie closed her eyes and took a couple of calming breaths. The photos weren't gory or graphic; if it weren't for the marks around the necks, they would look like photos of sleeping women. But knowing they were all probably dead made Sophie queasy. Opening her eyes, Sophie quickly skimmed over the last couple of pictures, but none of the images triggered any memories.

Flipping back to the first document, Sophie took another look at the full police report.

"They ruled it an accidental overdose. Or possible suicide," Sophie murmured.

"Yeah, until I called this morning, they didn't have any reason to believe otherwise. There was no evidence left at the scene to indicate otherwise. You should have heard my contact at the homicide division in LA flip out when he found out that a serial killer was operating in his territory, and he didn't know it."

"Was Daniel a Mythical?"

"No, he was completely human."

"Well, that blows up the theory that Snow White is only targeting Mythicals. Did you find any of the other guys from my dreams?"

"Not yet. I think if I narrow the parameters of my search to only California, I might have more luck. You wouldn't believe the sheer number of men who have OD'd in parks and bar parking lots this year. Snow White appears to be very good at hiding her tracks. The only reason I found Daniel was because you knew his first name started with a D and because his case was flagged after they found the polaroids at his house. We would never have figured out what was happening if you hadn't dreamed about Snow White's murders," Mac explained.

A short drive later, Mac pulled his sedan into the tiny

driveway in front of his Mission-style house in Potrero Hill. As Mac unlocked the dark-wood front door, Sophie admired the little house's cream-colored stucco and red-tiled roof. It made her think of how until the mid-1800s, Spain used missions to occupy much of California. The imprint of that time's architecture, art, and culture could still be found throughout San Francisco and the surrounding areas well over a century later. Layers of history were settled throughout San Francisco like sedimentation – you never knew when around the next corner if you'd see some ode to a past age in the architecture or even etched into the landscape itself.

Kicking off her tattered boots and leaving them next to Mac's tan suede oxfords by the front door, Sophie followed Mac into his living room in stocking-clad feet.

"You want a beer?" Mac called out from the passthrough between his kitchen and living room.

"Sure. I can only have one or two, though, since I have to work in a few hours."

A moment later, Mac wandered back into the living room with the neck of two amber bottles dangling from his fingers. Handing one to Sophie, he tugged her up from where she was sprawled in the corner of his ridiculously comfy couch, sliding in behind her. Resting her head on Mac's chest, Sophie sank so deep into the cushions it felt like it would require a rescue team to retrieve her. With a soft snick, Mac uncapped her beer and handed her the bottle. Clinking bottles, they both took deep pulls from the ice-cold bottles, humming in contentment.

"God, that's so good," Sophie said on a gust of breath.

"The brewery is just a few streets over from here. You can take a tour of the facility."

"And I assume you've taken the tour," Sophie teased.

"Of course I did. Anchor Steam managed to survive two earthquakes and the Prohibition. I had to check it out."

Sophie happily snuggled into Mac's chest, enjoying her beer and Mac's enthusiasm for history.

"You hungry? I placed an order earlier. It should be here soon. I got a little of everything," Mac explained.

"That sounds perfect. I'm starving."

"Hey, did you have any dreams today?" Mac asked suddenly, setting his now-empty beer bottle on the side table.

"Yeah, but they were nothing special. The only one I remember is that I dreamed I bought a bunch of candy from a Safeway, including like six boxes of Good & Plenties. The absolute worst candy in the world. Black licorice is disgusting," Sophie replied with an exaggerated shudder. "I assume that was a dream of Snow White. She's evil enough to like black licorice." Shifting on the couch, she worked her fingers into her front pocket and pulled out a crumpled sheet of paper, handing it to Mac.

"So, you *did* have a nightmare," Mac murmured, taking the paper from Sophie's hand and straightening it out. "What is this?"

"I wrote down the dream as you and Dunham requested."

"You expect me to give my boss a weekly report of your dreams written on crumpled, barely legible notes? Look! Your grocery list is written on the other side," Mac growled, shaking the offending piece of paper in front of Sophie.

"Hey! I didn't have anything better in my apartment," Sophie protested. "You're lucky it wasn't on a napkin. I will pick up a journal or something tomorrow."

"No need. I have something for you. Wait here," Mac responded, helping Sophie sit up so he could slip out from behind her.

Sophie watched as Mac trotted around the corner to the hallway that she knew led to his bedroom. He reappeared only a moment later, holding two items. Mac handed Sophie one of the packages, a plain brown paper bag. The somewhat heavy, shifting weight inside the bag surprised Sophie. Glancing into the bag's opening, she gasped in surprise. Several bags of coffee from The Mission Bean sat inside the bag. Pulling one bag out, Sophie took a long smell of the rich coffee scent emanating from the sealed bag in her hand.

"Hmmm, hazelnut," Sophie sighed in bliss. "You remembered. Thank you."

"No biggie. I picked it up on my lunch break. Here, I got you something else," Mac said, handing the second package to Sophie.

"A present?"

Immediately, Sophie knew she was holding a journal for her dreams. Tearing off the paper in excitement, a moment later, Sophie was left gaping in horror. A hot pink, glitter-covered book was sitting in Sophie's hands, featuring a cartoon image of a white unicorn with rainbow wings rearing up dramatically, a fluffy cloud under its hooves. Sophie glanced up from the unicorn to Mac's face, his eyes glittering with merriment.

"What in the world?" Sophie asked, looking back at the pink eyesore clutched in her hands.

"You needed a dream journal. I saw this, and I *knew* you'd love it. Look, it comes with its very own pen."

When she followed Mac's pointing finger, Sophie laughed at the rainbow-striped pen with a small fluffy ball on top strapped to the journal's spine.

"Do you like it?" Mac asked with a barely repressed glee.

"Well, I certainly won't lose it in my apartment," Sophie replied, thinking of her penchant for dark furnishings and upholstery. The diary would practically glow in those surroundings. Mac started cackling like a deranged maniac. "You think you're funny, don't you?" Sophie complained.

Mac exaggeratedly nodded his head, clearly pleased with himself.

"Well, joke's on you. I do love it. I am totally going to use this as my dream journal."

Whatever Mac's response was going to be was interrupted by

the ringing of his doorbell. Mac lifted his nose in the air and took a deep sniff. Turning to Sophie, he announced, "Food's here!"

Before Sophie could claw her way out of the prison he called a couch, Mac strolled back past with a bulky plastic bag hanging from each hand.

Scrambling after Mac as he entered his tiny kitchen, Sophie started opening drawers and cupboards to locate plates and silverware.

"Are you sure you got enough? That's a ton of food," Sophie teased, looking over the multitude of takeout boxes spread across his kitchen counters.

"Shifter metabolism," Mac said with a shrug.

"Do you eat your meat raw?" Sophie asked suddenly.

"What! No. Why would you think that?"

"You're part fox—"

"No," Mac said flatly.

"When you're a fox, do you eat small fluffy animals?"

"No. Just no. Even in my fox form, I'm still me. Why would I eat raw meat when I can have a burrito? Plus, as a fox, I would be eating fur and bones and stuff. Gross."

"I didn't realize I was dating a werefox with such delicate sensibilities."

"Werefox! I'm a fox shifter!" Mac mock-growled, starting towards Sophie.

"Kidding! I'm just kidding!" Sophie shrieked, scurrying out of the kitchen, clutching her overflowing plate protectively.

Once Mac finished filling his plate, they opted to eat on the couch rather than at the dining room table. Picking up the remote, he started the movie while they dug into their food.

"Hey! That's the Bay Bridge! Is the *Maltese Falcon* set in San Francisco?" Sophie exclaimed as the opening credits scrolled across the television.

"The guy who wrote the book was an actual private investigator at the Pinkerton Detective Agency here in the city back in the '30s."

As they watched the movie, Sophie couldn't believe the quantity of food that Mac could plow through. Shifter metabolism, indeed.

"Wait a minute. Someone just murdered his partner. You'd think Sam would be a little more broken up about it," Sophie commented, watching as Sam Spade examined the crime scene where his partner's body was still splayed out on the side of a hill.

Sophie quickly became absorbed into the mystery and intrigue of the old black-and-white film.

"He slept with his partner's wife! How could Sam do that to Archer? That scoundrel! And I thought *you* were the dickhead detective."

"Sam Spade is a private investigator, *not* a police detective," Mac growled, making Sophie roll her eyes with a grin. "Also, if you keep talking over this movie, I'm going to muzzle you." Sophie mimed zipping her mouth closed, locking her lips, and then tossing away the key.

Once they finished their meals, Mac opened his arms for Sophie to cuddle up with him. Sophie settled into his side with a contented sigh, ready to finish watching as Sam Spade figured out who murdered Miles Archer and Floyd Thursby.

Cradled in Mac's arms, Sophie kept sneaking glances up at him as he watched the film. She loved how engrossed in the movie he was. When he silently mouthed the words of the world-wearied Spade – "When you're slapped, you'll take it and like it." – Sophie had to smother the urge to giggle.

Sophie might not have much 'serious' relationship experience – sneaking out after a random hook-up being her norm – but she knew things just felt right with Mac. He had her back, always. She could talk to him about anything. He might get snarky – frankly, so could she; they were well matched in that way – but he always took her concerns seriously. And he listened. She just liked him, everything about him.

She'd never believed in any kind of destined, star-crossed lovers bullshit before, but maybe she needed to have a little more faith.

All she knew was that she wanted to see where things went with Mac.

Wanting – and planning – for a future farther away than next week felt strange. It created a jittery feeling in her gut. Assuming that she was going to get a happy ending felt like courting disaster. Things had rarely worked out for Sophie in the past. She worried that everything was going so well now, the universe was bound to notice her happiness and take the necessary steps to rectify the situation. Sometimes, Sophie felt like maybe she didn't deserve happiness. She'd lost her parents in a car accident when she was nineteen; she'd made it through community college by the skin of her teeth. She'd been skating by for several years, not taking charge of her destiny. Ever since getting her Associate's degree, she had been floating from job to job, just trying to make ends meet. She never looked further than her next paycheck. Every opportunity she either squandered or ruined, usually because of her mouth. And a month ago, she had been facing the real possibility of becoming homeless. Knowing it was mostly her own fault was the annoying cherry on the shit sundae.

The direction of her life had turned around so quickly Sophie almost felt like she should have whiplash. She landed a job she loved, found more friends besides the little old lady next door and her favorite bartender, discovered a hidden magical talent, and found someone she wanted to date. It all felt too good to last. And she was a generally decent person despite sometimes acting like a snarky bitch. She never kicked someone when they were down. She was kind to animals, kids, and the elderly, she paid her taxes – mostly. Maybe she was a terrible person in her previous life, and that's where this feeling of not deserving happiness originated. It wasn't logical, but she couldn't shake the feeling of impending doom, nonetheless. But she wanted a happily-ever-after desperately, and she wanted it with Mac. She wasn't going to let herself ruin it this time.

If she closed her eyes, she could envision a future filled with days like this, snuggled on Mac's ridiculous couch together, sharing meals and old black-and-white movies. Maybe she just needed to get out of her own way and not overthink things.

CHAPTER 7

"Maybe Snow White has stopped killing. Or maybe she's moved away from the city and is out of your psychic range," Fitz suggested around a mouthful of spinach. "Do you think there's a limit on your reach?"

Sophie shrugged noncommittally while picking the crust off her sandwich and ripping it into tiny shreds.

It had been several days since Mac had given Sophie her dream journal, and it was mostly empty. What was inside the journal was mostly small snippets from what little she could remember of her dreams. Despite keeping the journal close at hand, each morning, as Sophie tried to scribble her remembrances down quickly, they floated away like gossamer threads in the wind, impossible to hold on to. The only dream that had stuck with Sophie was one featuring Troy, who had been back on the autopsy table. In the nightmare, he opened his eyes and accused Sophie of not trying hard enough to save him. His eyes were milky white and bottomless, and his mouth bubbled over with blood so dark it had been almost black. Sophie pushed away what was left of her sandwich, appetite gone with just the remembrance.

"It's only been four days. I have gone weeks, even months, without having a dream about a murder. There's no point in getting pessimistic yet," Sophie reminded her co-workers who were gathered around the lunchroom table for a shared meal before getting back to their respective jobs.

"I hope that's not the case. You need more dreams so we can apprehend the killer soon," Reggie said. He slapped his hand over his mouth, eyes round and shocked, when Sophie gave him a droll look. "I mean, I don't want anyone to die! And I wouldn't wish those dreams on anyone, but the killer needs to be stopped, and you have the ability to do it," he added softly.

"It's okay. I know what you meant. And you're right – Snow White needs to be stopped. I feel bad that I didn't realize the dreams were real sooner. Maybe I could have prevented some deaths."

"How could you have possibly known any different? No one wakes up from having a weird nightmare and thinks, 'Hey, maybe I'm having a vision!' You have nothing to feel bad about," Amira retorted, shaking a motherly finger at Sophie.

"Besides, it sounds like Snow White was just getting rid of the riff-raff. If those guys were all serial killers like we suspect, then she was possibly saving lives by disposing of them," Ace argued.

"What! No one should be allowed to kill indiscriminately. We don't know what Snow White's motivations are. Plus, you know how I feel about the death penalty! What if she gets one wrong and kills an innocent man? What about the burden of proof?" Amira retorted, leaning towards Ace, feline disgust painted across her features.

As Ace and Amira started to quarrel, Sophie gave Reggie a pointed look and nodded towards the exit. Hiding a smirk behind his hand, Reggie quietly stood up from the chair and left behind their arguing co-workers with Sophie hot on his heels.

"My god, those two! I swear they're worse than siblings,"

Sophie whispered once they reached the peace and sanctity of the hallway, shaking her head in bewilderment.

"It's been a lot better since you joined the team," Reggie responded, laughing when Sophie gasped in mock horror. "Go get the next patient, funny lady, and I'll meet you in the autopsy room. Oh hey, the next autopsy is one of Mac's. He messaged that he wanted to be here for it, so let me text him. He said he'd be at the station, so he should be able to get here in a few minutes."

Sophie ignored the eager flutter of her heart and headed to the walk-in fridge to find the next body.

By the time they finished scrubbing up, Sophie and Reggie only had to wait a few minutes for Mac to arrive. The squeak of the door to the autopsy room opening had Sophie turning away from organizing the tray of medical tools with an anticipatory smile plastered on her face. Peeking his head into the door, Mac answered her smile with one of his own.

"Mac! Good evening," Reggie exclaimed enthusiastically, apparently almost as pleased to see Mac as she was.

"Hey, Reg," Mac said, raising a hand in greeting to Sophie's boss.

Skipping over to Mac, Sophie pushed him back out the door and into the privacy of the hallway.

"Hey, hellraiser," Mac purred in Sophie's ear as he wrapped her in a hug.

"Hey, dickhead," Sophie replied, burrowing into his chest. Sophie's hand slid up his neck and found its way into Mac's hair, scratching her nails over his scalp. Mac pushed his head into her hand, moving into her fingers like a cat. "Since we've officially had our first date, are you ready to break up with me yet?"

"Hmmm, I'm still undecided. Perhaps we should have another date – you know, just to make sure. Maybe you can do something to change my mind?" Mac asked, waggling his eyebrows suggestively.

"You wish," Sophie snorted, giving him a retaliatory poke in his side. "Are you here for a reading?"

"Yeah, it's a gruesome one, just to warn you." Muscles ticked along Mac's jaw, showing a sudden tension.

"Lovely. It must be truly horrible to put that look on your face," Sophie said with a sigh. "By the way, what are you doing two Saturdays from next? The night of the 19th. I got tickets to the night tour at Alcatraz."

After checking his phone, Mac let her know that he was available that night.

"It's a date then."

"Hell yeah. Let's get spooky, baby."

"You're such a weirdo." Sophie shook her head and smiled to herself at Mac's antics. He was such a grumpy bastard with everyone else; Sophie felt like she was the only one who got to see the goofball hidden beneath the scowl.

"Let's not leave Reggie waiting any longer. The sooner I take a reading, the sooner it's over," Sophie suggested, tugging Mac back into the autopsy room.

Mac peeled off from her side and took his usual spot against the wall. Stepping up to the gurney, Sophie took a small breath and held it for a moment before reaching for the zipper on the body bag and revealing its contents.

"You weren't kidding," Sophie said on a soft exhale. A middle-aged man with a neat, short beard and graying hair was lying in the black bag. He looked like he'd been the rope in a horrific game of tug-of-war. Sophie suppressed a shudder when she noticed that one of the man's arms had been ripped almost entirely off and was only hanging on by a few bits of flesh and sinew. Seeing the arm placed next to his body, rather than attached to it, made Sophie swallow several times convulsively before calming herself.

"You ready?" Reggie asked, finger hovering over the record button on his phone.

With a nod, Sophie placed a hand on the man's severed arm.

"He was on his way home from work when a group of people grabbed him. I can't see much, but it looks like he had just finished parking his car in a residential area. He didn't get a good look at his attackers. They put something over his face too quickly, but he can feel several hands holding him. At least three people, maybe more. He struggles, but they easily throw him into a vehicle. They drive for a while. Not sure how long – maybe an hour? Each time he tries to speak or fight back, they hit him. He's sitting between two of them, so I'd guess he's in the backseat of a car. I think they're both men, but I can't guarantee that. No one says a word.

"The car finally stops, and they pull him out of the car. He can hear another car pulling up. It might be more than one. He starts to yell for help, but someone punches him in the gut. He almost falls to his knees from the pain, but they haul him back to his feet. They frog-march him for several minutes. He can hear laughing and whispered conversations behind him. He can feel the crunch of leaves and branches beneath his feet. He thinks he must be in a forest of some kind because there aren't any sounds of the city. Poor guy – he's scared out of his mind. He starts pleading for his life. Suddenly, he gets pushed and falls on the ground hard, landing on his hands and knees. He scrambles back, ripping the bag off his head. It's almost pitch-black out, and he can barely make out the trees around him, but he can see the shadows and silhouettes of a group of people standing about ten feet away. There must be at least a half dozen people. But it might be more than that, possibly up to a dozen. There is a little bit of moonlight filtering through the trees for him to see their shapes. It's hard to tell; they keep shifting around and moving.

"He asks them what they want from him. Asks why they took him. He offers them money to let him go. A few laughs echo through the crowd again, but then a deep voice barks at him to run. He asks 'What?' in confusion, and then the same voice roars

71

at him to run. That bellow tapers into a long howl. The whole crowd starts growling and snarling. They don't sound human; they sound like wild animals. In total terror, he scrambles away.

"He's just running blindly through the dark. He can hear them chasing him, practically at his heels. His dress shoes are slippery on the wet ground, and he keeps losing his footing. Tree branches and roots are tripping him up; branches are slapping him in the face. Howls are echoing all around him. Something heavy knocks him off his feet. He screams as sharp teeth clamp onto his upper arm and flip him onto his back, tearing into his shoulder. Standing over him is a huge black wolf, snarling. It has bright glowing, amber eyes. Another wolf darts in from the side and bites his leg, trying to pull him from under the black wolf. This starts an awful tug of war between several of the wolves, who are ripping and tearing into him. The black wolf snarls and snaps at the others, which backs them all away. The wolf turns back to the man, growling menacingly, stepping back over him. His arm's not working right, but he tries to crawl away. He thinks he's dying; there are too many wounds and cuts all over his body, and something feels broken inside him. The wolf lunges and grabs him again, throwing him around. The wolf tears into him for several minutes, slashing his abdomen with his claws and biting him all over, tearing his flesh. The black wolf finally backs away, and the rest of the wolves gather close, howling and snarling. He can hardly see anything anymore – his vision is failing – but he can hear their growls. Just before he fades away, he thinks he hears sirens in the distance, and they sound like they are growing closer."

Sophie removed her hand from the man's arm, opening her eyes and looking down at his face. It was surprising to see that his face looked so peaceful and serene after witnessing his horrifying final moments. Somehow his face remained unscathed after all that. Other than smudges of dirt, he almost appeared to be merely sleeping. Over the scent of blood, Sophie could smell the sharp scent of pine resin still clinging to his clothes.

"I don't even know his name," Sophie whispered, staring at the man's countenance. "They just hunted him down. It was sick. And pointless. The guy couldn't have possibly gotten away or fought back. He was no match for them. Those assholes just toyed with him, scared him to the point he pissed himself, and then tore him apart."

"His name was Derek Gibson," Mac said from a few feet behind Sophie. "I'm going to do my best to find the bastards who killed Derek, and when the Conclave finishes with them, it will be as if they never existed."

"Did my vision help?"

"It confirmed what we suspected. I just wish he had seen even just one of those assholes' faces."

"Soph, why don't you take an early lunch break? I'll have Amira help me finish this autopsy," Reggie suggested. "Mac, if I find anything that can help you figure out who they are, I will send you a text."

"You sure?" Sophie asked. Reggie nodded before turning back to the body on the gurney.

"Sounds good. If you find any body fluids that aren't his, have Ace put a rush on the DNA testing," Mac called back as Reggie waved them both out the door.

Fifteen minutes later, Mac and Sophie were seated on a bench outside the Medical Examiner's office eating gyros and talking about Derek Gibson.

"If the first cops on the scene had only arrived a little bit sooner, they might have been able to save him. The initial report believes that he'd only been dead for a few minutes when they got to him. And your vision corroborates that," Mac said, picking out the onions from his gyro.

"Did they catch any of the killers? They were right there when he died," Sophie asked, snatching the onions from Mac's fingers and stuffing them into her gyro.

"No, they must have heard the sirens and scattered. We have a couple of shifters trying to track the perpetrators' scent trails through the woods, but I don't have much hope for that. Shifters are good at hiding their tracks. Plus, there were just too many of them."

"How did the cops get there so quickly? I've been to Muir Woods. There's not much nearby."

Mac explained that a good Samaritan had put a call into the police when they saw a group of men dragging a man with a bag over his head into a car. The person followed them to Muir Woods and called the police from the visitor's center.

"The person had to break into the closed visitor's center to make the call. They said they didn't have a phone."

"Can you imagine what kind of weirdo doesn't have a cell phone on them in this day and age?" Sophie teased, making Mac roll his eyes at her.

"We found two cars abandoned at the visitor center, but both were stolen, so no leads there," Mac said. His face looked strained, so Sophie bumped his shoulder with hers. "They're being processed, so maybe something will be found in one of them."

"You'll figure it out. I mean, a bunch of wolf shifters grabbed a guy right off the street. That's bound to draw some notice, right?"

"That's just it. We're almost certain that this isn't the first time this has happened. We've heard rumors of other humans going missing. This is the first time it was anyone important. Derek Gibson was a member of the Planning Commission for the city. All the other murders were of homeless and displaced people. They're almost impossible to track because of their transitory nature. Over the last year, we've found two other victims – both in shallow graves in heavily wooded areas. One was found near Mount Diablo and the other in Muir Woods. I suspect that there is a group of shifters hunting humans for sport. Probably wolf shifters, but I'm not ruling out coyotes or wild dogs yet. I find it strange that they went after someone prominent. That's going to raise flags and get them noticed."

"You think they're hunting humans for sport?" Sophie clarified; horror etched over her features. Sophie could still hear Derek's screams in her head, inhuman wails filled with pain and terror. Swallowing thickly, Sophie set aside her gyro as her stomach roiled and bile creeped up her throat. Her stomach was threatening to expel its contents. If she closed her eyes, Sophie could still see the black wolf shaking his head, flinging dark blood off his muzzle, and howling a triumphant song over his victim. Sophie forced the memories out of her mind and turned her focus back on Mac.

"We thought it was a lone wolf or two, but based on your vision, we have to take a harder look at the local packs."

"How many wolf packs are there?"

"Four main packs in the city. Three more in Marin County and the surrounding areas. Heading south, there are five packs between here and LA. Plus, there's possibly a few loner, straggler packs that might have enough members to fit our criteria."

"That sounds like a lot of work."

"It is. But it doesn't matter; I'm going to find these assholes and make them pay." A sheen of yellow rolled over Mac's eyes so quickly that if Sophie hadn't been staring directly into them, she would have missed it. A shiver tried to work its way up her spine, but Sophie squelched it. She'd have felt sorry for those shifters if she didn't wholeheartedly agree that they needed to pay.

CHAPTER 8

As she trailed half a block behind her quarry, she wondered at the sudden change to his routine. It was pure luck that she decided to head to the café across from his house to wait for him a few hours earlier than usual. Typically, after the man got home from work, he didn't re-emerge until hours after the sun had disappeared beyond the horizon. Until today, she could usually set her watch to him.

Every night, he walked – stalked, really – around the neighborhood, stopping and talking to shop owners and residents. Most nights, she would follow him, trying to catch him alone. It seemed like he almost always had a sycophant or two with him. She had nicknamed him Slippery Dick because he was so wily to follow. He could weave and flow through swarms of people like a river around rocks. Crowds magically parted in front of him like a ship through ice floes, sealing behind him just as seamlessly, making it challenging to keep pace behind him. She'd lost his trail more than once, unwilling to run after him and give away her presence. She felt much like a pinball in an arcade machine, bouncing from person to person on the crowded sidewalks.

She was sitting at the long wooden table in the café window facing the man's house, enjoying the light rain pattering against the large storefront window, when she noticed a vaguely familiar man approach the house and ring the bell. She'd seen this man with Slippery Dick several times. Slippery Dick exited his home a few minutes later, and the two men had an intense-looking conversation on his front porch. Squinting her eyes, she was sure she recognized the new fellow from a few of Slippery Dick's late-night wanderings. She'd had to abandon her drink to make sure she didn't lose track of them as they settled their dispute and strode purposefully down the street, seemingly uncaring of the drab weather.

Slipping into a doorway of a shop, she watched Slippery Dick as the rain plastered his shirt to his body, the fabric lovingly clinging to each of his bulging muscles. Slippery Dick always walked with an aggressive swagger. He had the kind of raw physical strength that came from prolonged manual labor – or an intense love of the gym with a possible dose of steroids on the side. He barely looked human. The permanent sneer on his face didn't help. He was the type of man that looked at the world through a filter of arrogance and contempt. His every move and action plainly stated, 'I'm better than you.'

He's going to learn differently, *she thought with a grin.* Well, if I can get him alone, that is.

The other man was leaner, but his shoulders still strained against his rain-soaked t-shirt. Like everyone else she had ever seen interact with Slippery Dick, the man seemed cowed by him. Almost deferential.

When the men went down to the BART station, she almost turned back since it would be too risky to get caught. Being in the open allowed more anonymity and the ability to slip away quickly if things got too dangerous, but she couldn't pass up the opportunity to see what Slippery Dick was up to. He rarely roamed so far from his usual haunts any of the other times she had tailed him.

Thankful that the platform was crowded, she managed to slip onto the subway unnoticed by either man. At the opposite end of the carriage, she watched as they carried on a quiet conversation. They were so immersed that they never noticed her. She watched them out the corner of her eye, pretending to be engrossed in her phone, hoodie pulled low over her face. At each stop, as each person entered the car, the men gave everyone a quick assessing look before dismissing them all. Just where she liked to be with people like them – ignored until it's too late.

When the men exited the subway car, she waited until the last moment as the subway car doors started to close before slipping out onto the crowded station platform, wanting to put more distance between herself and her target.

Rushing up the steps to exit the BART station onto the main street, she was grateful that the plethora of restaurants and shops on this avenue created a buzzing hive of activity that hid her presence from her mark, even in this dreary weather.

After a few blocks, the two men split up after a brief discussion on the sidewalk. One turned into a storefront, and the other kept walking, continuing on the same path as their original direction. Once she came even with the shop, she peeked into the front window and sighed in defeat because the bakery was small and practically empty. Nowhere to hide. Slippery Dick was at the long glass display counter, arguing with the employee behind the case. There was no way her presence wouldn't be noticed if she entered the shop. She didn't want Slippery Dick to see her until she was sure that she would be the last thing he ever saw. Slowing her steps, she watched him for a minute but scurried on as he started to turn in her direction.

Looking away from Slippery Dick, she saw the other man just as he disappeared around the corner of the bakery. Stopping for a moment, she double-checked her bag and tool kit, then peeked her head around the corner, grinning to herself when she saw that it was a darkened alley.

What is it with all these alleys lately? *she thought with a smirk.*

~

SOPHIE'S EYES SNAPPED OPEN, AND SHE LURCHED UP FROM HER pillow with a choked gasp. Lunging out of bed, she tried to grab her phone off her dresser. Her duvet tangled around her legs, spilling Sophie onto the floor with a thump. Sophie clawed her way out of her bedding, cursing under her breath.

"Shit! *Shit shit shit.*"

Snatching up her phone, she dialed Mac while running to her front door. As she stuffed her feet into unlaced boots, Sophie remembered the taser Mac had given her the night of the Coit Tower incident.

"Hey, Soph. You're up earl—"

"I just dreamed about Snow White," Sophie said, cutting Mac off. "She's following a guy, like right now – actually, two guys. I recognized the bakery where she was. It's only a few blocks away. She was heading into the alley behind the Three Pigs Bakery on Market Street. I have to stop her."

Skidding into the kitchen, Sophie ripped open her junk drawer and grabbed the taser.

"Don't you dare go after her! It's way too dangerous," Mac bellowed. "I'm grabbing my keys and heading there now. Do *not* try to intercept her. Stay home. I've got this."

"I have to. I'm not going to confront her. I'm just going to follow her. I've got to make sure she doesn't hurt anyone else. I'm the only one who knows what the guys she's after look like. I'll be careful, I swear."

Running out her apartment door and down the narrow stair-well, Sophie had to pull the phone away from her ear as Mac loudly ranted in her ear.

Flinging herself out of Brown Betty's front door, Sophie hid the hand clutching the taser under her pajama top. Her feet slid on the rain-slicked sidewalk as Sophie turned and raced in the direction of the Three Pigs Bakery, running as fast as she could in her loose boots. Over her panting breath, she could hear Mac on his end of the call barking out commands to his co-workers.

Finally, with a stitch spreading its claws along her right side, Sophie spotted the intersection for Market Street up ahead.

"I'm almost to Market Street," Sophie told Mac, slowing her

steps as she got to the corner. Looking both ways as she crossed the street, Sophie spotted the sign for the bakery in the distance.

"Sophie, I have several cars converging on that location. And I'm on my way. Pull back and wait for me," Mac tried to demand, desperation and frustration lacing his tone. Sophie could hear traffic over the phone, so she knew he was in a car, heading her way.

"I'll be careful. I'm just going to look around. I'm just going to see if I can locate Slippery Dick or his friend. They'll never even see me."

"Slippery Dick? What in the hell are you talking about?"

"That's what she calls the guy she's following. She was following Slippery Dick and a friend of his. They split up. Slippery Dick went into the bakery, so she followed the other guy around the shop's corner into an alleyway. Tell the other cops to turn off their sirens and come in quiet. I don't want you guys to alert them to our presence. I need to find them to figure out who Snow White is, but I don't want her to know that we're on to her."

"This isn't my first day on the fucking job, Soph. Everyone's in unmarked cars and plain clothes. Give me a description of both men so my team knows what to look for."

Sophie walked along Market, peering carefully into each shop as she passed them, describing Slippery Dick and his sidekick. She slowed her steps as she reached the Three Pigs Bakery. Using the phone and her hand to conceal most of her face, Sophie glanced into the storefront, trying to locate Slippery Dick. Although there were several patrons inside the shop, none of them were oversized black-haired muscleheads.

"Slippery Dick's not in the bakery," Sophie whispered into her phone. "I'm going to walk past the alley and see if anyone's there."

"Damn it, Soph. I'm almost there."

Strolling past the corner of the bakery, Sophie stepped off the sidewalk and pretended to casually glance into the darkened alley. Pale watery light highlighted a grimy dumpster, a few crates, and a pile of black trash bags stretched to capacity with garbage. Vehicles passed by the far end of the alley, muted by the distance, where the narrow passage spilled out onto Mission Street.

"Shit. It's empty. No one's here," Sophie whispered furiously to Mac.

A soft, rattling sound, like the moan of an old house settling, caught her attention. "Wait. I heard something."

Something about that quiet noise raised all the hairs on Sophie's body. The sound of Mac's voice faded as she focused all her attention on the gloomy space looming in front of her. Step by slow step, Sophie worked her way further into the alley. Gripping her taser like a lifeline, she crept past the pile of trash and approached the dumpster.

Another low sound followed by a rustling noise. Sophie dipped down and peeked one eye around the dumpster. She came face to face with the thick rubber sole of a boot. Her eyes roved up the shoe up to a pair of legs clad in dark jeans, then a chest covered in blood. Sophie was moving before her mind even registered that she was looking at Slippery Dick's friend. Slumped against a grimy concrete wall, the man was clutching his ravaged neck as blood poured over his fingers, staring at Sophie with dread. His hazel eyes rolled in terror like a spooked horse, the white of his eyes shining at Sophie out of the gloom.

Scrambling over old food wrappers and smeared trash, Sophie covered the man's hands with her own in a futile attempt to stop the blood seeping over his fingers. Sophie could hear herself screaming to Mac to send an ambulance in a detached part of her brain. Mac's voice came from where she dropped her phone but she couldn't understand what he was saying.

"You're okay," Sophie said, lying to the dying man in front of her. "You're going to be okay. We'll get you to the hospital, and they'll fix you right up. Just stay here with me, okay?"

As Sophie continued to mutter soothing words to the man, she watched as his eyelids started to droop and the blood flowing over her fingers began to slow.

"No, no, no!" Sophie yelled as the man listed sideways in her arms. "Mac! He's dying!"

As the man slumped to the side, Sophie desperately tried to hold him, but he was a solid weight in her arms, dragging them both to the ground.

A rolling, deafening roar from the far end of the alley made Sophie's head snap up. The noise swept down the passage towards her as Slippery Dick came charging around from the back of the bakery and straight at Sophie.

"This isn't what it looks like," Sophie tried to yell, raising her bloodied hands, but the tide of his roar washed out her voice. Sophie scrambled to her feet, managing to snatch up the taser from next to the now-dead man's feet.

"You bitch! I'll kill you," Slippery Dick screeched, his roaring voice ending in a howl.

Bellowing, teeth bared in a rictus of rage, Slippery Dick galloped towards her. Time slowed for Sophie as she watched, frozen in shock, as his teeth grew and sharpened in his mouth – too many teeth in an ever-widening mouth. A sour taste filled Sophie's mouth, and her breath hitched in her lungs.

Sophie's death was plowing toward her, and the measly taser in her extended hand wasn't going to stop it. Scrambling further back, Sophie toppled over the dead man's legs, catching herself on the side of the slimy, rusted dumpster.

A flash of movement out of the corner of her eye was all the warning Sophie got before a body leaped between her and imminent death. Sophie wanted to sag in relief when she recognized Mac's tousled brown hair, but she firmed her spine, got back to her feet, and readied her hand on the taser.

A long, vicious snarl erupted from Mac's lips as he pointed his gun at Slippery Dick. For a moment, Sophie thought that Slippery Dick was going to keep on charging them despite the weapon, but she saw the moment that his higher thought processes clicked back on in his eyes.

Slippery Dick skidded to a halt, inches from Mac, almost plowing into him. With only a breadth of space between them, Slippery Dick growled right in Mac's face, then jerked his head to the side to stare at Sophie over Mac's shoulder. He had the stare of a hungry predator sighting its prey. She could see the promise of death in his maddened eyes.

"Move aside, fox. This bitch murdered Roger. As alpha, I demand justice."

"No, Alphonse, Sophie didn't murder your pack member. She works with me. She called me, trying to stop this from happening. She was trying to help."

"She was following us. I know when some human is following me." Sophie's eyebrows snapped together over the way he sneered the word *human*. "Roger and I split up so we could trap her, and I come around the corner to witness her murdering Roger," Alphonse bellowed, pointing at Roger's body slumped next to the dumpster.

Both men faced off, sneering in each other's faces, aggression in every line of their tense bodies. Sophie watched, in fascinated horror, as their faces slowly shifted, their mouths starting to elongate, sharpening teeth bared in snarls.

Were they getting taller? And bulkier?

"Uh, guys—" Sophie started to say, worried that both men were about to go furry in the middle of the day. At least they were partially hidden from the street traffic by their location in the alleyway.

"Did you see her actually murder Roger? Or did you find her kneeling over him, trying to stop the bleeding? Where's the murder weapon, huh? Also, did you see the face of the woman who was following you? There is no way you could have because you'd know it wasn't Sophie. A woman might have followed you, and that woman killed Roger, but that woman wasn't Sophie," Mac growled, stepping closer to the other man, getting right in his face. "Smell the air. There are two distinct scents."

"I can barely smell anything over all this garbage."

But Alphonse turned his nose up in the air, taking several slow breaths. Stepping back from Mac and closer to Roger's body, Alphonse leaned over his dead friend, his head weaving back and forth, nostrils fluttering. His motions were creepy as hell. Sophie futilely tried to smell the air too, but all she could detect were the smells of yeasty baked goods and steamed dumplings from the place across the street mixed with the rotten stench rising from the dumpster.

"Police! Freeze! Put your hands in the air!" a chorus of voices barked from behind Sophie.

Jolting her hands over her head, Sophie looked over her shoulder to see half a dozen uniformed police officers, with guns drawn, pointing their weapons at them.

"On your knees," a particularly burly cop bellowed as the group surged toward them. Sophie dropped to her knees like someone had cut her puppet strings.

Kneeling in what she prayed was an oil slick and not something disgusting, Sophie grimaced as the cold, wet liquid soaked into the knees of her favorite pajama pants. Not sure if she should stay put or not, Sophie watched from her kneeling position as Mac showed his fellow officers his badge and started explaining the situation to them.

"Ma'am, you can get off your knees now. Let's get you checked over," the beefy cop said in a much friendlier tone, approaching Sophie and holding out a helping hand.

"No, leave her there," Mac suddenly barked out from where he was talking to some other police officers. "Who knows what kind of trouble she'll get into otherwise."

"Haha, you're so funny, Detective Dickhead. Don't listen to him. He's always just trying to get me on my knees," Sophie advised, smirking at the suddenly blushing officer. Wiggling her bent elbow at the man, Sophie got the officer to grab her arm and haul her to her feet since blood covered both hands.

Chaos reigned around Sophie. The flashing lights of an ambulance filled the dark alley, strobing bright and garish. Several EMTs were working on Roger in a futile attempt to revive him. Alphonse was talking to two officers off to the side, waves of aggression radiating from him. The two officers were holding their own, but the hunch in their shoulders showed what it was costing them. Alphonse's eyes snapped to Sophie's and caught her in their angry beam. When his lip raised in a partial snarl, Sophie turned her back on him, not wanting to give him the satisfaction of seeing her cower.

"Miss, are you injured?"

A gentle hand on her arm made Sophie jump. Jerking her elbow out of the soft grip, Sophie turned to give the person who startled her a piece of her mind. But one look at the kind-faced paramedic, and the words died on her tongue.

"I'm fine. Thank you," Sophie told her. Holding up her blood-covered arms, she explained, "None of this is mine."

Another officer came over and used a swab to take a sample of the blood from her hands. Once he was satisfied with his evidence samples, the paramedic gave Sophie some wet wipes to get the drying blood off her hands. Sophie grimaced at the blood caked under her fingernails that only a good scrubbing would remove.

"Detective Volpes, Miss Feegle."

Turning again, feeling a bit like a spinning top, Sophie spotted Chief Dunham striding into the area. His mouth was down-turned in irritation under his bushy mustache.

"Santa looks pissed. Damn, now I'm gonna get coal for certain this year," Sophie whispered to herself and then broke out into inappropriate laughter.

"What are you laughing about, bitch? You think this is funny?" Alphonse growled at her from across the alleyway.

"Listen here, fuckwit, I'm stressed. This has been a pretty shitty day. Where were *you* when—" Sophie's words were cut off when Mac placed his hand over her mouth, muffling the rest of what she was trying to say.

"You better watch your back," Alphonse threatened Sophie.

"Don't threaten me with a good time, asshole," Sophie said, pushing Mac's hand off her mouth, rolling her eyes at the ridiculousness of the entire situation.

"Back off, Alphonse. Don't threaten her. She was trying to save him. You owe her."

"She's a human. I owe her nothing." Alphonse pointed a finger at her, the muscles in his clenched jaw rippling. Sophie's eyes widened when she noticed that his finger was tipped with a long claw instead of a normal fingernail. Alphonse turned on his heel without another word, striding after a police officer into a waiting cruiser.

"What a jerk!" Sophie griped loudly.

"Oh my god! Could you just not?" an exasperated Mac said, throwing his hands in the air. "Did you not see he was barely holding on to his human form? I swear you would poke a lion with a stick just to see what would happen."

"Me?! He started it."

"Are you a six-year-old? You do not antagonize the alpha of the city's biggest, most dangerous wolf pack. You're going to give me gray hair."

"You'd make a hot silver fox," Sophie said, startling herself with the joke. She tried to silence a choked giggle but lost that battle. "Get it? You're a fox."

Mac gave a defeated sigh and pinched the bridge of his nose. Letting go of his nose, Mac gave Sophie a flat look.

"Now is not the time for your jokes. I'm so pissed at you right now that I can't think straight. What were you thinking? I *told* you not to interfere."

"What would you've had me do, huh? Stay at home and let that guy die?"

"Yes! That's exactly what you should've done. You needed to stay out of it."

"Stay out of it!" Sophie yelled. "Well, I can't do that! I can't sit on my ass while people keep dying. That's not who I am. Because of what's happening, I get a front-row seat to watch people die. I'm the one who can stop these things from happening."

"You can't just keep rushing into danger. You're going to get hurt. Or worse. You're just a—"

"If you say I'm just a human, I'm going to kick you in the balls so hard, they'll come out your nostrils."

"I was going to say civilian," Mac retorted. "But yes, you're also a human. If Alphonse had gotten his hands on you, he would have torn you to literal pieces. You can't keep risking yourself."

"Are you two finished yet?" a dry voice asked. With mouths still open, mid-argument, both Sophie and Mac turned to see Dunham standing next to them, arms crossed, impatiently tapping a finger on his bicep.

Despite her most fervent wish, the asphalt did not open and swallow Sophie whole when she realized that she and Mac had been bickering in front of the Police Chief. She had forgotten about his existence, her focus solely on Mac.

"Alphonse was threatening Sophie," Mac said to Dunham, not acknowledging the fight or Dunham's color commentary.

"Yeah, I overheard him. Don't worry about the alpha. I'll take care of him. I'll ensure that he understands that Sophie is under the department's protection."

Mac didn't look convinced but didn't say anything else.

As the adrenaline finally started to drain out of Sophie, she realized just how cold she was. Her clothes were wet and she was shivering, so she hugged her arms around her torso in an attempt to keep warm. Her tank top was plastered papyrus-thin against her skin from the rain. The fine drizzle had soaked through her clothes, leaving her cold and bedraggled. She tried to push her hair back from her face, but it was stuck in stringy clumps, clinging to her face and neck.

"I'd like both of you to head back to the station. I want a meeting so we can discuss and document what happened here. I'd also like to move out and leave the scene for the forensic team to process," Dunham commanded them.

"We can meet you there. I need to get Sophie into dry clothes, and then we'll see you at headquarters," Mac replied.

Dunham acknowledged the request with a dip of his head. He turned on his heel and issued commands to each police officer on the way out of the alley.

The rough rasp of a zipper, overly loud in the alley, ran fingertips of dread up Sophie's spine. Turning her head, Sophie watched as the paramedics finished zipping a body into a familiar black bag. Frustration bubbled up her throat. She was overcome with the desire to punch something. She gave the dumpster a narrow-eyed look. Beating the dumpster would not change the last half hour no matter how satisfying it might feel, and it would probably land her a psych evaluation.

Something heavy dropping on her shoulders made Sophie jolt and skitter away. Twisting around with fists raised, Sophie found Mac standing behind her, hands raised in capitulation. Glancing down at herself, Sophie realized that he had put his jacket over her shoulders.

"You looked cold."

"It's okay. You just caught me by surprise."

Mac caught the lapels of the jacket and pulled Sophie into his warm, dry arms.

"Llamas?" Mac asked.

"Huh?"

Mac quirked an eyebrow down at Sophie's pajamas, his eyes crinkling in humor, their argument forgotten for the moment.

"I was sleeping. I didn't exactly have time to get dolled up," Sophie huffed, defending her plain tank top and teal-colored flannel pants covered in cartoon llamas doing yoga poses. "Besides, they're comfy and super soft."

"I bet," Mac purred, making Sophie duck her head. With a mischievous grin, he tucked Sophie's arms into his jacket and flipped the collar of the coat up to keep the rain off her neck. "For real, though, are you okay?"

"I guess. I'm freaked out. And I'm pissed that I was too late."

"You couldn't have gotten here any faster. There was nothing you could have done," Mac assured her, pulling Sophie into a hug.

The alley wasn't cozy by any means. It was cold, damp, and gritty. It smelled of soggy trash, rancid cooking oil, and blood. But as Sophie pressed her nose into Mac's collar, into the warm, intimate space at the base of his neck, she felt cocooned in warmth.

"Come on, hellraiser. I can get one of the guys to give us a ride back to your place in their cruiser."

"Do you mind if we walk instead? As much as Birdie would enjoy seeing me in the back of a cop car, I'd rather walk."

With a nod, Mac caught one of Sophie's hands. He laced their fingers together, leading Sophie out of the gloom of the alley.

CHAPTER 9

*S*ophie had never been so glad not to run into Birdie. Usually, she looked forward to seeing her naughty neighbor, but she had no idea how she would've explained why she had been running around in the rain clad only in her pajamas. Breathing a sigh of relief, Sophie closed the door to her apartment, cutting off the rest of the world from her and Mac.

"I'm taking a shower," Sophie announced, heading towards her bedroom to get some clean clothes. Mac cleared his throat, making Sophie stop and look back at him with a raised eyebrow.

"The forensic team is going to want your clothes," Mac said, handing Sophie a bag with an apologetic shrug.

"Even the shoes?"

When Mac nodded, Sophie whined, "Aw, man. These are my favorites. Will I get them back?"

"Eventually," was all the answer Mac would give her.

The pipes rattled and groaned as Sophie turned the knob on the shower as far as it would go. Tossing her shoes and crumpled, damp clothes into the bag, Sophie stepped into the limp spray from the shower nozzle. It was barely lukewarm. She had a brief but vivid fantasy of throttling her landlord Moe. The cheap bastard refused to upgrade anything in Brown Betty, even though the water heater was on its last legs.

"My kingdom for hot water," Sophie muttered, grabbing her shampoo and aggressively scrubbing the day out of her hair.

LESS THAN AN HOUR LATER, SOPHIE FOUND HERSELF SITTING IN Mac's cubicle, sipping a Styrofoam cup of what Mac referred to as "coffee". Sophie suspected whatever was in her cup was more closely related to toxic sludge.

"Is this how you get criminals to confess to their crimes? By torturing them with burnt tar pretending to be coffee?"

"This is nothing. Wait until it's been sitting in the pot a couple more hours. Once it pours out like thick, tainted molasses, then we use it to torture criminals." Mac flashed a wolfish grin at Sophie before taking a large slurp of his cup of coffee.

"What are we waiting on?"

"We're waiting for the chief. He wants to be there when you give your statement. And once Dunham is finished with Alphonse, he'll want to talk to you," Mac said, nodding towards the chief's office, from where Alphonse's angry voice could be heard drifting over the office buzz.

"What's Alphonse saying? I can't make out anything."

"He's just being his usual asshole self. Complaining and strutting around like he thinks everyone should bow down and be thankful that he graced us with his presence. He's overly fond of the sound of his own voice."

Looking away from Dunham's office, Sophie stared out of the bank of large glass windows facing the bay. She admired the view of sparkling water of the bay with Oakland in the distance that Mac and his cronies got to enjoy every day.

The blinds to Dunham's office were open, so everyone in the bullpen watched as Alphonse paced around the office, yelling and waving his arms in his agitation. The look of rage and disdain on the man's face gave Sophie a glimpse of the actual person under the handsome veneer.

"Do you know Alphonse well?"

"Not well, but as a detective in the Mythical division, I have to deal with him often enough. His pack still clings to the old ways of predator hierarchy, so I have had to deal with a ton of dominance fights gone too far. I think he fancies himself some sort of warlord. Frankly, he's just a blustering asshole with a God complex. And because I'm a fox shifter – 'not a *true* apex shifter' – he acts like I'm something he scraped off his boot. I can't stand him, but I have to keep my composure as a police officer. Plus, he has a lot of sway with the Conclave. His pack is the biggest in the area, meaning that he has a lot of power. So, try not to piss him off too much, hellraiser."

"Who, *moi?*" Sophie pressed her hand to her chest in mock innocence.

When Mac didn't say anything back, Sophie looked up to see a strange look on his face. He was staring at something behind Sophie.

"What is it?" Sophie asked, starting to look over her shoulder to see what had captured his attention.

"Don't," Mac whispered, leaning forward to put a quelling hand on Sophie's arm. "It's Marcella, from the Conclave. I don't want her to see you here and figure out that you're our psychic. She's already seen you at Coit Tower and might start to put things together."

"I doubt she'd even remember me from the Coit Tower. No one at the time was paying much attention to the measly human in their midst."

Still, Sophie sank down in her seat, watching Mac's face as he followed Marcella's progress across the office. Mac's eyes narrowed as he watched her head directly towards Dunham's office. Holding her cup of coffee in front of her face as a partial shield, Sophie glanced over her shoulder through a curtain of hair to watch. Marcella's sharp, angled features and demeanor made Sophie think of a bird of prey. She and a man in a long, flowing gray robe strode into Dunham's office without even pausing to knock. As the man accompanying Marcella opened the door for her, Sophie got a look at his face. He looked like every wizard ever described in a fantasy novel, complete with gaunt features, a beaky nose perched over a scraggly gray beard. He even had deep bags under his icy pale eyes. He scanned the room as if gazing into the distance, his eyes taking in everything but not settling on any one thing. Then, without a word, he turned on his heel and followed Marcella into the office. This man was reminiscent of a knotted stick, thin and gnarled, but there was a core of strength there.

"Who's the off-brand Gandalf? I've never seen anyone wear a cloak like that in real life."

"I don't know. Based on that outfit, I'm guessing Fae. Some of them like to dress as if they're extras from *Lord of the Rings*. Whoever he is, I've never seen him before." Mac watched, his brow wrinkled, as the wizard lookalike leaned over and whispered something in Marcella's ear. Marcella looked back at the man, her eyes as dark and sharp as a raven's.

Sophie and Mac spied on Marcella and her companion as they talked to Dunham and Alphonse. Whatever they were saying seemed to finally calm Alphonse down. The mystery wizard-man tried to pat Alphonse's shoulder, but he shrugged off the touch with a sneer.

"Do you think he left his wooden staff at home? Who's gonna stop the Balrog?"

"You are *such* a nerd," Mac replied with an eye roll.

The group inside Dunham's office talked for a few more minutes before Alphonse strode out with Marcella and Old Gray

Beard on his heels. Dunham called out to Alphonse, reminding him to give his formal statement to Detective Turner. Turner popped up from his cubicle like an over-enthusiastic prairie dog, waving Alphonse over to his desk.

"I really don't like him," Mac muttered as Alphonse looked around Turner's cubicle with obvious disdain before taking a seat across the desk from him.

"I'd be pissed, too, if one of my friends just got murdered."

"You'd think that's why he's being an asshole, but no. He's always like that."

"Yeah, not exactly Miss Congeniality, is he?" Sophie whispered as Alphonse imperiously waved his hand at Turner to get started with the interview. "If Snow White was after him, does that mean Alphonse is a serial killer? I mean, it seems like a strange coincidence that we got that guy in the morgue the other day that a bunch of wolves had murdered. Do you think that Alphonse and his people killed that guy, and that's why Snow White was after him?"

"It's certainly possible. I don't want to put too much conjecture into this situation because when you start to do that, your bias might make you start fitting the facts to confirm your hypothesis. And I already have a lot of bias against Alphonse. As of now, I'm leaning towards Roger as being her intended target since he was the one that got axed. I'm going to see what I can dig up on him. See if there are any skeletons in Roger's closet. Or we could be entirely wrong about Snow White's motives. It's all just speculation at this point. Dunham wants to see us," Mac said, turning Sophie's attention towards Dunham, who was standing at his office door, waving them over.

Sophie took one of the two seats across the imposing wooden desk centered in the room. The desk was a massive slab of mahogany designed to intimidate anyone unfortunate enough to find themselves in front of it. Sophie noted that the chair Dunham sat in was bigger and taller than theirs so that Dunham would be looking down on them once he sat. The whole office seemed to be designed to put others at a disadvantage.

As Dunham finally closed the blinds facing the bullpen, Sophie looked out the window at the view of the bay. The weather-darkened skies had washed the usual deep blue of the water into a churning pewter gray.

Dunham took his seat behind his desk with a sigh. Sophie didn't know him well, but he looked a little worn around the edges. She imagined that days like today were why some people kept bottles of Jack hidden in their desk drawer.

Dunham slid half-moon bifocals onto his nose and started clicking around his computer with a look of utter concentration.

"Who was the old guy?" The words were out of Sophie's mouth before she could think to censor them.

"Huh?" Dunham replied, looking up at Sophie from his computer.

"The guy with Marcella – who was he? He looked important."

"That was Bramwell. He's the Seneschal," Dunham replied, his attention already back on his computer screen.

"Bramwell? I've never heard of him. What's his last name?" Mac jumped in, leaning forward and resting his forearms on Dunham's desk.

"And what's a seneschal?" Sophie interjected.

"If Bramwell has a last name, I don't know what it is. He's just Bramwell. His job is to watch over the interests of the Fae Queen here in this realm. I don't know what that entails. Frankly, I just try to stay off the Conclave's radar. No news is good news when it comes to the Conclave."

"That's not fucking ominous or anything," Sophie muttered to Mac, who snickered in response. Dunham gave Sophie a droll stare in response.

"Why was the Seneschal here? Should we be concerned?" Mac asked.

"I wouldn't worry if I were you. I believe that Magistrate

Venturi and Bramwell were out together when Alphonse called Marcella in a meltdown over Roger Lammar's murder. The last thing any of us need is the alpha of the largest pack in the area on a rampage, so she headed over to calm him down," Dunham said with a careless shrug. "The Seneschal's presence here was just a coincidence. I wouldn't worry about Bramwell."

Easy for you to be all nonchalant, Sophie thought sourly. *It's not your ass everyone is gunning for.*

Breezing past Sophie's lingering concerns, Dunham had Sophie record the events of the day. He had her go step-by-step through her dream, then her mad dash through the rain, ending with her discovery of Roger's body behind the bakery.

Sophie's respect for Dunham steadily grew as he stopped her periodically to ask probing questions, helping her remember details she'd initially dismissed or forgotten. Once Dunham finished recording Sophie's recollections, he and Mac worked together to create a second sanitized police statement that would be used for public record. There was no mention of dreams, Snow White, or any other magical, non-human elements in that document. According to the heavily edited version of events, Sophie happened to be walking past a backstreet when suspicious movements in the darkened alley caught her eye. She realized someone was being attacked and ran into the alley while calling her friend Malcolm Volpes, a police officer for SFPD. Her yelling chased off the assailant. It all happened so fast that Sophie never got a good look at the murderer. The report suggested that Sophie interrupted a robbery gone wrong.

"Did Alphonse tell you what he saw? Did he get a look at Snow White?" Mac asked Dunham once they finished and submitted the report.

"Alphonse said that he and Roger started to suspect they had a tail as they exited the BART at the Civic Center station. They didn't specifically see anyone; Alphonse just said he had a feeling. He had Roger head into the alley, and he was going to cut through the bakery and head out the backdoor exit. The plan was to trap the person between them behind the shop where they wouldn't be observed. It might have worked if the owner of the bakery hadn't stopped Alphonse and hassled him as he tried to sneak through the kitchen."

Mac hummed in thought, staring unseeingly at the tiled ceiling.

"Did Alphonse see Snow White?"

"Maybe. When he was inside the bakery, he saw a small figure in dark clothing linger for a moment out front. He said that it looked like they were looking for someone inside. He assumed that the person was searching for him. He didn't get a good look at his stalker, but he thought it was a woman. She was decked out in dark clothes, a bulky jacket, hair hidden under a hat. When I pressed him on what he saw, Alphonse conceded that he thought it was a woman, but it could have been a teenager or a petite man."

"Should we tell Alphonse about Snow White? Give him a warning that he might be in danger?" Mac asked.

"No. If you're right about Snow White's motive, then either he or Roger have been killing people. We're going to be putting Alphonse and Roger's lives under a microscope, and I'd rather not tip Alphonse off to our scrutiny. We don't want him to start trying to cover his tracks. Plus, I'm going to put some of my best scouts on him. They can protect him from Snow White while also tracking his activities. Besides, after what happened to Roger, Alphonse is going to be hypervigilant anyhow. It was quite a blow to his ego that one of his people was murdered practically under his nose. You know how alphas are," Dunham said with a roll of his eyes.

Actually, I don't, Sophie thought, *but I can hazard a guess.*

"What if Snow White attacks Alphonse or another of his pack mates and we didn't warn him of the possibility? What's our liability?" Mac asked.

"If things go south, I will deal with it. Besides, I did warn him that another Mythical in the city was recently murdered in a similar fashion." Dunham shrugged as if having to deal with a dangerous, enraged alpha werewolf was no big deal.

"Is there any connection between Troy Weatherby and Alphonse, Roger, or anyone in the Sunset District pack?"

"I asked Alphonse if he knew Weatherby. He said he didn't. Weatherby lived in a territory that overlaps a corner of the territory Alphonse's pack claims, but so do a lot of other Mythicals. I believed him, but we'll be checking all the same."

"Does Alphonse have any enemies? You know, in case this isn't really what we think it is?" Sophie suddenly asked.

"He's the alpha of the largest wolf pack in the city. Plus, he's a massive asshole. It'd be easier to find people who don't have a problem with him than to list all of his enemies."

Dunham's muffled snort signaled his agreement with Mac's blunt statement.

"What did you tell him about why Sophie was there?" Mac asked.

"I told him that Sophie was walking past the alley and noticed two people in a fight. When she realized that Roger had been stabbed, she called 911 and then called you."

"Did he question why Sophie knew to call me?"

"Yes, I told him that you two are a couple," Dunham said with a raised eyebrow, daring Mac to dispute that statement.

"Did he believe you?" Mac asked instead of responding to Dunham's unspoken prompt.

"Yes, he has no reason to doubt me. Now, I have a boatload of paperwork to get through, so you're both dismissed," Dunham stated, turning his attention to his computer screen.

"You're not going to lecture Sophie about running around the city chasing phantom serial killers? You're okay with that?"

"If some ignorant human gets herself torn to pieces by thinking she's tougher than she is, that's on her. I'll be annoyed about having to deal with more paperwork, but Sophie's an adult, and if she wants to do something stupid, who am I to get in the way?" Dunham deadpanned, leaving Mac sputtering in outrage.

"Seriously?" Mac finally managed to retort.

"Yes. Now go. You're dismissed."

Mac stood up from his seat, ramrod straight, and turned on his heel, striding out of Dunham's office like an agitated robot. Sophie scurried after Mac, giving one last look to Dunham as she exited his office, but he was already hunched over his desk with a deep scowl aimed at his computer screen, Sophie and Mac dismissed from his mind.

Sophie followed Mac back to his cubicle while he muttered darkly under his breath. She caught only a few words like "idiotic death wish" and "I'm the only sane one here". Sophie swallowed the urge to laugh, not wanting to get Mac more worked up than he already was.

He quickly stuffed a few items off his desk into a messenger bag.

"I want to head back to the crime scene and look around. Can I drop you off home on my way?"

When Sophie nodded, Mac tucked her under his arm and started heading toward the elevator.

"You do realize that I'm an adult, right?" Sophie asked, wrapping an arm around Mac's waist and giving him a squeeze.

Mac blew out a huff of aggravated breath. "Yeah, I know, Soph. I'm sorry for acting like an overprotective asshole. I'll—"

"A human, Volpes? Really?" a voice called out. Snapping her head around, Sophie realized that their path had brought them within a few feet of where Alphonse was giving his statement at Turner's desk. "You couldn't do any better than that? She's going to dilute an already weak bloodline," Alphonse sneered. Mac puffed up like an enraged bull, aggression in every line of his tensed body. Sophie squeezed his arm before he said whatever was already forming on his lips.

"Don't rise to the bait," she whispered, but she couldn't resist giving the xenophobic dickwad a hard stare while scratching her eyebrow with a middle finger. Not waiting for a reaction from Alphonse, Sophie turned and tugged Mac towards the waiting elevator.

CHAPTER 10

"You sure you're okay?"

"Yes. And if you ask me again, I'm going to punch you in your ear," Sophie threatened, balling up her fist and shaking it at Mac, only partially joking.

"Sorry. I'm not trying to be a pain in the ass; this whole situation just has me freaked out."

"I know. Neither of us handles stress particularly well," Sophie replied, reaching across the console and giving the hand Mac had resting on his thigh a squeeze. Before she could pull her hand back, Mac turned his hand and laced their fingers together.

"I want you to start taking some self-defense classes," Mac announced. "I know a couple of people who would be willing to teach you to fight. The next time you're faced with an enraged alpha, I need to know that you can handle yourself."

"Okay."

"What? Not gonna argue with me about this?"

"I don't argue about everything," Sophie huffed. "I've had a few lessons in the past but today definitely showed me that they weren't enough."

Sophie could see the tension leach out of Mac's shoulders at her easy acceptance. Sophie gave Mac's hand a reassuring squeeze.

The rest of the ride was made in silence, both of them lost in their thoughts.

As they neared Brown Betty, Sophie rubbed her temples, trying to stave off a looming headache.

"Hey, can you drop me off here? I need to pick up a couple of things," Sophie asked, pointing to the tiny market two blocks from her apartment. She planned to pick up a super-sized bottle of aspirin, a cheap bottle of wine, and maybe some junk food to make up for the colossally shitty day.

After a few minutes of slow, drugging kisses and one extracted promise to call Mac before work that night, Sophie stepped into the convenience store with a bit of renewed vigor. A makeout session was just what she needed to reset her crappy mood. The chime of the door opening had the store clerk jerking her head up from the phone she had her nose planted in, turning to see who had entered her domain. When she spotted Sophie, the plump older woman set her phone down on the counter and followed Sophie's progress around the small shop with narrowed eyes and a sneer distorting her mouth.

Sophie could tell exactly what the woman was doing; watching to see if Sophie was going to steal anything. Even at her poorest, Sophie never resorted to stealing.

"Can I help you with anything?" the woman asked stonily, giving Sophie a head-to-toe look that conveyed her thoughts. Sophie curled her toes in her worn sneakers, wishing she was in her favorite boots. She was about ready to leave and take her business elsewhere. There was another store only a ten-minute walk further away.

Sophie ignored the question and continued with her shopping. If the woman thought she looked disreputable now, Sophie should come back in her scuffed combat boots and her threadbare anarchy t-shirt. That'd probably scare a few years off this judgmental woman's life.

She quickly stalked through the aisles, picking up her items with the woman's stare burning a hole in her back. Quickly finishing her shopping, Sophie dropped her items on the counter with a clatter, biting back the comments forming in her mouth. She just wanted to get home and unwind before work, not start a standoff in the Quickie Mart. The woman gave a final *harrumph* before begrudgingly ringing up Sophie's items. Snatching up her change and bag of goodies, Sophie turned her back on the clerk and strode out of the store with her head held high. She felt the woman's eyes on her all the way out the door. Just before the door closed behind her, Sophie raised a middle finger at the cashier. The indignant gasp that followed her out the door brought a smirk to her lips.

Sophie stomped her way home, going on an I-can-wear-whatever-I-want diatribe and muttering darkly under her breath about rude, judgy store clerks. She should be able to wear ripped jeans and old graphic tees without being singled out as a possible thief. By the time she reached Brown Betty, she had come up with several witty comebacks she wished she'd used on the cashier.

"I should be able to dress in rags and still not be treated like a damn criminal," Sophie informed her apartment door as she inserted her key into the scuffed, scratched doorknob. The door was silent on the topic, but Sophie could tell it agreed.

She poured herself a healthy slug of dime-store wine in the first cup she found in her cupboard – a chipped coffee mug nicked from a greasy spoon in her old neighborhood. Sophie downed two Advil with a sigh of relief, happy to be back in the sanctity of Brown Betty. Plopping down on her futon, she kicked her heels up on her beat-up coffee table and ripped open a bag of chips. *Mmmm, crunchy salty goodness*, Sophie hummed, reaching over to grab the romance novel she picked up earlier in the week from the used book store on Valencia Street. It had a gratifying number of ripped bodices and heaving bosoms – enough to satisfy Sophie's need for escape.

When she realized that the book wasn't on the side table where she thought she'd set it, Sophie groaned in annoyance. She must have left it in her locker at work by accident again. In a huff, Sophie grabbed a well-worn, dog-eared favorite from the pile on the floor. The familiar story was as soothing as a warm blanket. Sophie nestled into her couch, ready to join Ender Wiggin in saving the world from buggers.

After a satisfying hour of reading, Sophie received a text from Mac letting her know that he hadn't uncovered anything new at the crime scene. Cobbling together a quick pasta dinner, Sophie tried to eat while reading but couldn't get back into the story. After reading the same paragraph for the third time and still not registering the words, she tossed aside the paperback in resignation. Tracing the hairline cracks in her plaster ceiling with her eyes, Sophie reviewed the afternoon in her mind, step by step, trying to figure out if there was something she could have done differently to save Roger Lammar.

"Stop wallowing in self-pity. You're going to make yourself crazy with 'what if's," Sophie announced out loud. Popping up from the couch, Sophie looked around her apartment for some kind of distraction. "That's it. I gotta get out of here."

Snatching up her messenger bag, Sophie marched out of her apartment and directly to The Little Thumb next door. As she stepped into the pub, the sounds of traffic and construction were muted and replaced with the welcoming din of conversation and soft music coming from hidden speakers.

Glancing up at the sound of the bell, Burg took one look at Sophie's face and pointed a finger at a stool at the far end of the bar where the lighting was dimmer, giving the illusion of privacy.

"You want a beer?" Burg called out.

"I have to work in a bit," Sophie replied, shaking her head.

"You want a Lullaby Lady?" Burg asked with a smirk. Sophie was particularly fond of the drink that was the Mythical equivalent of a Shirley Temple – a kid's drink.

"Nah, I need some caffeine. I'll take a Coke."

Burg tossed a coaster on the counter in front of Sophie and deposited a tall glass filled to the brim with fizzing cola.

"You alright, Soph?"

"I'm good. It's been a long, strange day, but I'm doing okay," Sophie lied, pulling the coaster closer and taking a long sip from the tall glass.

"So… we're good, yeah?" Burg asked tentatively.

"Why wouldn't we be good?"

"Well, I haven't seen you very much lately. Not since you saw my true form. I was worried that I might have scared you or something," Burg replied, pointedly wiping the counter and not looking Sophie in the face.

"Burg," Sophie chastised. "I feel privileged to have seen your true form. And you didn't scare me or anything like that. I've just been crazy busy with work, I swear. I haven't been avoiding you. You're still one of my closest friends."

"Yeah?" Burg stopped, staring unseeingly at the counter and glanced up at Sophie with hopeful eyes.

"I promise. Work has been crazy. Well, and I have been seeing quite a bit of Mac," Sophie said. She was gratified to see the scared look melt off Burg's face.

"What's been going on with work that has you so busy? Are the dead bodies just starting to pile up?" Burg teased, but before Sophie could answer, someone at the end of the bar called out for a refill.

"Ever since that blog write-up, it's been so busy here I'm thinking of hiring a second full-time bartender. My sister fills in occasionally, but she can't work as often as I need. She's got her hands full with my nieces and nephew," Burg complained before heading over to the thirsty customer.

I wanna see baby ogres, Sophie thought. She could just imagine little green ogres with adorable tiny tusks and big attitudes.

Tossing his white bar towel over his shoulder, Burg headed back over to Sophie after getting the customer served.

"I have a weird question," Sophie said when Burg stopped in front of her. "Do you know any of the wolf packs in the city? I met the alpha of the Sunset District pack today. Alphonse. You know him?"

"Alphonse? I don't know him personally, but I know about him. Since I'm considered neutral territory, I get plenty of wolf shifters here, especially the packless ones. I haven't met him, but I've heard plenty."

"What have you heard?"

"That he's an asshole," Burg said with a shrug.

"From what I experienced today, I can confirm that he is unquestionably an asshole. A ginormous asshole. But is he dangerous?"

"Absolutely. He's a Mythical and the alpha of the biggest wolf shifter pack in the whole city. Mythicals are all dangerous, at least compared to humans, and alphas are more dangerous than most. Why do you ask? What happened with him today?"

Sophie shrugged, not sure how much she should share with Burg about her newfound abilities. Dunham told her not to tell anyone, not that she felt particularly compelled to follow his edicts.

"I met Alphonse this afternoon. It was work-related, so I can't tell you much. I just wanted your opinion on him. Is his pack dangerous? Have you heard any weird rumors about them?"

"His pack's dangerous because they will do pretty much whatever Alphonse tells them to. They follow 'traditional' pack hierarchy."

"Like a wolf pack? What do you mean by hierarchy? Like alphas and betas?"

"Pretty much. Alpha at the top of the pack – the top dog.

Then next there are his or her betas. They are the inner circle, the alpha's right-hand men and women. They enforce the alpha's rules – make sure everyone's toeing the line. Then there's the rest of the pack beneath them. There's usually a strict pecking order that is generally established through dominance fights. That's what most shifter packs look like, especially in the wolf and other apex predator packs. They try to model their hierarchy on natural wolf packs. Which is hilarious because that's not how wolf packs in nature work."

"They're not? That's how *I* thought they worked."

"Back in the '40s some scientists were studying wolves and their behaviors. The problem was, they were studying wolves held in captivity. They took a bunch of wolves that were unrelated to one another and threw them together, rather than watching wolves in the wild. These scientists deduced that a pack always had a lead, or an alpha male and an alpha female from watching these wolves. Their faulty research has led the whole world to believe that wolves live in packs with a strict hierarchy and fight for dominance. In reality, wolves in the wild are typically a family group with the mom and dad in charge and their pups following them."

"Seriously?"

"Yeah, it'd be like aliens showing up on Earth, locking up a group of random strangers in a mall and being all 'see, this is how human families work.' It was just bad research, but now all these shifters emulate the hierarchy. Frankly, I find it rather amusing. They take it all so seriously."

"Can you imagine if the aliens chose a Walmart? We'd scare them out of the solar system. I've seen the strangest things there. Maybe that's why aliens have never made contact. They observed a Walmart and decided we weren't worth their time."

"Hey, no knocking Walmart. Not everyone wants to spend their life savings on artisanal, organic yogurt made from cows that only graze on daisies and drink water harvested from glaciers. At least Walmart has parking," Burg griped, wagging a finger at Sophie. Decent parking was as hard to come by in San Francisco as four-leaf clovers and unicorns.

"Parking's not an issue if you don't own a car." Sophie shrugged. She was perfectly content to use public transport rather than having to deal with a car. Having a vehicle in the city was more work and money than Sophie was willing to do and spend. Not that she could afford a car right now, anyway.

The bell over the entrance door jangled, drawing Sophie's attention to the man entering the bar. It was one of the regulars – an older man named Sal. As Sal took his usual stool further down the bar, his gnarly gray beard reminded Sophie of the wizard-lookalike from earlier – Seneschal Bramwell of No Last Name. Watching Burg pour Sal his pint, Sophie tried to figure out what it was about Bramwell that had rubbed her the wrong way. Why did she care? She had enough problems without adding an odd wizard man to her bullshit bucket. That bucket was starting to feel like it was overflowing.

Burg ambled his way back to Sophie, refilling her soda without needing to be asked.

"Marcella seemed like she was very interested in getting to know you better at Coit Tower. She said ogres don't tend to get involved in Mythical politics," Sophie said, noting the look of distaste on Burg's face. "You don't want to work with the Conclave?"

"I've been avoiding the calls from Marcella and the Conclave for the last week. I have no interest in getting pulled into court intrigue and crappy Fae politics. They're only interested in using me as a bodyguard or enforcer. To them, I'm just cannon fodder, a meat shield. It wouldn't even occur to them that I have a brain in this old noggin," Burg complained, knocking his knuckles against the side of his giant bald head.

"Do you know them very well? The Conclave, I mean. Because I met this weird old guy today. He looked like a mysterious wizard. If I didn't know better, I'd swear that he was ready to lead a fellowship to destroy a ring – you know what I mean? Someone said his name was Bramwell. They said he was a seneschal – not that I know what that means. But I got strange vibes from him."

"You've been meeting a lot of the heavy hitters lately, huh? Welcome to the big leagues, Soph. Bramwell is like the Fae queen's right-hand man, her fixer. Bramwell is only interested in himself and the Fae Queen. Everything and everyone else comes second. He's her loyal little toady, from what I hear. Probably in love with her. I can't imagine how anyone could love someone rumored to be so cold and callous. But whatever floats your boat, I guess."

"What's a fixer?"

"A fixer... You know, like, in the mob?" At Sophie's blank look, Burg explained, "They solve 'problems'. Whether that's getting rid of someone or just making sure to get things done. Usually, in the mob, fixers are often the guys who clean up crime scenes and get rid of the bodies."

Sophie was suddenly glad she decided not to introduce herself to Bramwell.

"He kills people?" Sophie asked, thinking back on the whip-thin older man in the floor-length robe incredulously.

"Eh, probably not. The queen has an army of assassins. But he'd be the guy who orders the hits, not necessarily carry them out himself."

"How can he work for the Fae queen? I was told that coming to this realm was a one-way ticket. So why would he still work for the queen? Plus, how do you communicate with someone in a different realm? I feel like my cell service doesn't cover other realms."

"Maybe he's a telepath. Or it could be that the queen is. She's got a ton of power, from what I hear. You'd have to pack a powerful punch to be able to stay on the throne for as long as she has. The Fae court is a nest of vipers."

"Telepathy. Why, of course; it makes total sense."

Burg grinned at the sarcasm, flicking his fingers from his brow in a salute of agreement.

"The queen has several names, but most people call her Queen Maeve." Burg dropped his voice to a whisper when he said the queen's name as if worried that saying her name out loud would summon her.

"What's she like?"

"Who? The queen? I've never met her. But I've heard that she's beautiful, cold, calculating, and deadly. She's supposed to have strong enough magic to pull the air from your lungs with just a thought." Burg shuddered, shimmying in disgust at the thought.

The pub started to fill up as the after-dinner crowd came in, so Burg was too busy to do more than occasionally stop by Sophie and refill her glass. Sophie got up to leave and to head to work early. She needed to tell the team about what happened this afternoon with Roger and Alphonse. It was hard to believe it was only a few hours ago. Sophie dropped a few dollars on the burnished bar top and waved goodbye to Burg.

DRAGGING HER SORRY, TIRED ASS INTO THE MEDICAL EXAMINER'S office lobby, Sophie took a deep breath of cool, dry office air. It'd already been a long day, and the night ahead loomed before her with no end in sight. The dreary weather made Sophie's mood sour. Outside, the air had been so thick and damp it was almost wet with moisture. Breathing the sanitized, air-conditioned office air felt refreshing in comparison.

"Good evening, Miss Zhao," Sophie greeted the receptionist sitting in her usual spot behind the long front desk counter. "Is Reggie here yet?"

"Dr. Didel arrived about 10 minutes ago. He's in his office," Miss Zhao responded, popping her head up from her computer screen to give Sophie a small, prim smile.

Sophie called out her thanks as the doors to the restricted part of the building unlocked with a buzz. Pushing through the doors, she headed straight to Reggie's office. After a quick knock on his door, Reg's voice called out to enter.

"Sophie, you're early," Reggie said, a happy smile plumping up his round face even more. "Is everything okay?"

"Yeah, but some stuff happened today that I wanted to tell you about. Have you talked to Mac today?"

Reggie picked up and glanced at his phone, shaking his head. "No messages from Mac."

A small part of Sophie was amused watching as Reggie's eyes got comically wider and wider as she described to him how she chased after Snow White only to discover Roger's dying body.

"I don't think you should have gone after Snow White," Reggie lectured. "She's deranged. I don't want you to get hurt."

"Not you too," Sophie complained. "Mac gave me a ton of shit for it earlier. I can't just ignore someone in danger like that. I had to try and stop her."

"You can't risk your life like that. You're too important."

"My gift is too important," Sophie corrected, forcefully keeping away the pout which was trying to make it to her face. She was proud of how level her voice sounded. She understood that what she could do was important, but she was more than just her ability.

Reggie gave her a reproachful look. "If you think your gift means more to me than your friendship and your life, you don't know me very well. No one can replace you. I want you to promise me that you'll be more careful."

Sophie sighed. "Alright, I promise. From now on, I'll always wait for backup. No more rushing headfirst into danger. Plus, Mac is insisting that I start taking self-defense classes."

"Oh, that's a good idea," Reggie said, nodding his head in approval. "It's too bad you didn't get a chance to see Snow White's face. It's going to be difficult to stop her until we know what we're looking for. Hopefully—"

The buzz of the phone intercom interrupted his words.

"Dr. Didel, you have a visitor. He is requesting to observe an autopsy scheduled for tonight," Miss Zhao's voice asked, sounding tinny and thin through the speaker.

"I'll be out in just a moment," Reggie responded, rising from his chair, patting Sophie on the shoulder as he headed out of his office.

Sophie trotted after Reggie, curious to see the person who would be watching them conduct an autopsy later that night. The only audience they'd ever had was a handful of police detectives. And the detectives had never put in a request for a viewing – they just appeared.

"Do you often get random people asking to watch you perform an autopsy?" Sophie asked.

"Our spectators are usually detectives, as you've probably noticed. But I'll get the occasional high-ranking official. The last time a Conclave member died, we had to get folding chairs brought in because almost the whole council and their toadies showed up to observe," Reggie replied as he pushed through the exit doors.

Reggie stopped so suddenly once he entered the lobby that Sophie ran into his back with a grunt.

"Uh, alpha. I wasn't expecting you," Reggie stammered. Sophie popped her head over Reggie's shoulder at the word alpha to see Alphonse glowering around the lobby as if it personally annoyed him. The two hulking men with him emulated Alphonse's glower with perfect mimicry. One was a shaggy, dark-haired man in a Giant's jersey and jeans. The other had military-short blond hair and a sharp suit.

"Oh shit," Sophie whispered, swallowing the sudden lump in her throat.

Alphonse was dressed all in black, wearing slacks and a turtleneck. Sophie thought he looked like a self-important douchebag, though, admittedly, she was highly biased.

"You!" Alphonse bellowed before Sophie could execute a strategic retreat. Turning his glower at Reggie, Alphonse growled. "What is she doing here? She's a suspect in my beta's murder. What are you up to? This is improper. You think you can fool me?" His roaring voice echoed around the lobby. Sophie spared the two unfamiliar men with Alphonse a glance before turning her attention on the real threat in the room, Alphonse.

No one paid attention as Sophie tried to explain that she wasn't a murder suspect. She'd been cleared of any wrongdoing. Alphonse and his two henchmen were too busy glowering at Reggie.

"She works here. That's how she knows Detective Volpes. This is all just a coincidence. There is nothing improper happening in my morgue," Reggie replied over Sophie's attempted explanations, holding up his hands as if to fend off the enraged alpha in front of him.

Alphonse growled loudly, his shoulders hunching, looking like he was readying for a fight.

"What do you expect me to believe? I refuse to allow her to be present during Roger's autopsy. What if she tampers with evidence?"

Stepping from behind Reggie, trying to pull Alphonse's attention away from her friend, Sophie opened her mouth to try to refute his words. She couldn't risk Alphonse turning his growing anger on Reggie. He was one of her few friends, and he had done nothing to deserve the alpha's wrath.

"What kind of fucking place are you running here, rodent? I will throw this bitch out myself." Alphonse took a menacing step toward Sophie.

"Rodent!" Sophie squawked. "You fu—"

Before she could finish her insult, Sophie realized that she was suddenly looking at the back of a head. Sophie practically had her nose pressed into a sweep of sleek black hair pulled into an elegant French twist. Jolting a step back, Sophie shook her head in astonishment. She would recognize the woman clad in a crisp dove-gray pantsuit in front of her anywhere. She had never even saw Miss Zhao move, but now the diminutive woman was standing directly in front of her.

A subsonic rumble rolled out through the lobby like a train pulling into a station. The sound raised every hair on Sophie's body. Feeling like frightened prey, Sophie realized that what she was hearing was a dragon growl. Filling the room with pressure more than sound, the growl landed in Sophie's gut and tossed her back into a primordial place of instinct and fear – a time when Sophie's ancestors were still running around with spears and hiding from sabertooth tigers. Locking her jaw, it took all of Sophie's efforts not to whimper out loud.

"Take care with your next words, alpha," Miss Zhao warned quietly, raising a warning finger to ward off Alphonse. Her words were polite, serene even, but still somehow as sharp as a dagger. A blizzard brewed beneath her civil tone. Alphonse growled back, but it sounded petulant and weak compared to the subsonic rumble of a dilong shifter. The shadow of umber brown scales ghosted across Miss Zhao's raised hand, appearing and disappearing in the blink of an eye. The feminine pale pink of the receptionist's painted fingernails and delicate jade jewelry juxtaposed against the scales made the implicit threat feel even more deadly.

"Everyone in this building is in my domain. They're under my care. You would do well to remember that fact, wolf."

"I meant no disrespect, Zhao. However, I cannot allow a suspect in my beta's death to be present for his autopsy, much less participate in it. It is an insult to my pack and my intelligence. My wolves are under my care even after death. You cannot believe that this should be allowed. It is my right as alpha to demand impartiality and justice for my pack mates. If I must, I will take this directly to the Conclave."

"I'm not a suspect. I've been cleared," Sophie tried, but no one in the tense group made any indication they heard Sophie's words.

"There's no need to involve the Conclave," Reggie said. "If you'd given me a chance to explain, you would know that Sophie wouldn't have been assisting at your beta's autopsy. We hadn't even had a chance to check the schedule for tonight, so we didn't see your beta's name on the roster. It's standard operating procedure to keep individuals with any conflict of interest or tie to the victim out of the autopsy room. If I'd had a chance to check the roster, I would've been aware that your pack member was scheduled to be autopsied tonight and could have prevented this misunderstanding. Sophie will not be in attendance for the autopsy. However, you can also rest assured that she would never interfere with an investigation. Her reputation is above reproach here."

"I don't give a shit about some human's reputation. I don't want her anywhere near my pack or me." Sophie returned Alphonse's sneer with a flat look. He made the word 'human' sound like something you would scrape off your shoe.

Reggie gently tugged Sophie away from the group. Turning them both away from Alphonse, keeping Miss Zhao between them and the enraged alpha, Reggie wrapped an arm across her shoulder. Reggie whispered, "I think it would be best if you got out of here. I don't think it's a good idea for you two to be in the same building right now. Why don't you take the night off?"

"You want me to go? I didn't do anything wrong. I tried to save that asshole's friend, for fuck's sake. I understand why I shouldn't be in there for the autopsy, but why do I have to go home?"

"This is not a punishment. I just think you would be safer far away from here. He is too volatile right now – like a powder keg. I don't trust him to keep his temper under control. Maybe Mac could come get you, so you don't have to take the bus," Reggie suggested.

"Won't you need my help?" Sophie whispered.

Sophie desperately wanted to do a reading on Roger in the hopes of seeing Snow White's face.

"Amira can assist me tonight. We can't risk incurring the wrath of the Sunset District pack. It's best if you just head home."

Sophie wanted to protest and throw a hissy fit at being kicked out, but watching Reggie's worried face and the way he was wringing his hands deflated the outrage right out of her.

"Fine," Sophie huffed. "I left my bag in your office. Let me call Mac and see if he can come get me."

"Of course. I'll deal with Alphonse," Reggie murmured. Firming his lips, Reggie wiped the nerves from his face and turned back toward Alphonse.

Heading towards the doors, Sophie called out, "Miss Zhao, can you buzz me back in?"

"Of course, my dear," she responded. Looking back over her shoulder, Sophie gave the tiny, scary receptionist a grateful look. Miss Zhao gave Sophie a warm smile before a flash of gold sparked then faded from her eyes, there and gone before Sophie could blink. Sophie watched as Miss Zhao, in her low-slung, classy heels, walked over to her desk, as regal as any queen, and primly sat in her office chair.

Turning back to the door, she waited for the telltale buzz of the security system unlocking the swinging doors. Sophie almost lost her composure and laughed aloud when she noticed Fitz, Ace, and Amira's enthralled faces pressed against the small glass window in the door. Instead, she just shook her head and gave them a broad smile.

"Holy shit! What is happening out there?" Ace whispered after

Sophie swept through the doors and past her gawking co-workers.

"Come with me, and I'll tell you everything. First, I need to get my phone and call Mac, though," Sophie whispered back, waving her friends to follow her.

"I thought Miss Zhao was gonna eat him," Ace said with an alarming amount of glee.

"I wish," Sophie replied. "I don't think I'm that lucky."

Grabbing her bag from Reggie's office, Sophie headed to the ladies' changing room, assuming Alphonse wouldn't look for her there. Heading into the women's room didn't stop Fitz or Ace from following her, however.

"What was that all about?" Amira demanded as soon as the door closed behind the group.

Sophie quickly caught her friends up on the day's events.

"Um, are you sure it was a good idea to chase after Snow White? You could have been hurt," Fitz said once she finished her story.

"Oh my god. Enough lectures for one day, guys. Mac and Reggie both already got on my case."

"Dude," Ace said, gripping Sophie's forearm in a tight, worried grip. "You're lucky to be alive. Alphonse could have killed you."

"Aww. I didn't know you cared," Sophie teased. "Don't worry, I'm fine. Mac got there in time to defuse the situation. But as you can imagine, I can't be at the autopsy for his beta. So, I'm being sent home. Plus, Alphonse hates me just because I'm human, even though I tried to help save Roger."

"Does he know about Snow White? Does he know about the dream visions?" Fitz asked, worry clouding his eyes.

"Hell no to both, and we need to keep it that way."

All her friends nodded their agreement. Amira pantomimed zipping her lip, locking it, and tossing away the key. *What a goof*, Sophie thought fondly.

"I need to call Mac and see if he can get me out of here," Sophie announced, pulling her phone out of her messenger bag.

Scrolling quickly through her contacts, Sophie was about to call Mac when Ace's snickering stopped her.

"What?" Sophie asked, looking at him. With a bemused expression, he silently pointed to the name she had saved for Mac's number. 'Detective Dickhead' still made her grin every time she called or texted Mac. He'd earned that moniker, in her opinion. Sophie pressed on the name and brought her phone to her ear.

"Hey, hellraiser. I didn't think I'd hear from you so soon. Is everything okay? Missing me already?" Mac's voice asked in her ear, his words low and warm, settling Sophie's nerves.

"You wish, dickhead," Sophie replied, soft and flirty. Seeing Amira bite her lip to keep from giggling reminded Sophie that she wasn't alone. Sophie cleared her throat and pulled the sappy look off her face. "I've got a situation here. I need you to pick me up."

"What? What's happening? Are you okay?" Mac demanded, all serious now.

Sophie explained the situation while Mac swore. He had an impressive arsenal of vulgarity.

"Damn it. There's nowhere else to perform a Mythical autopsy within 100 miles. I should have thought of this. I should have warned Reggie. He would have realized that you would need to be pulled from the schedule tonight."

"You're too hard on yourself. We've had a lot on our minds," Sophie reminded him.

"I'm grabbing my keys right now. Give me fifteen minutes. I'll text you when I arrive. Just lay low and stay out of sight. We don't need Alphonse kicking up more of a fuss than he already has."

"I deserve some ice cream. Today has officially sucked. I want double fudge," Sophie demanded.

After extracting a promise from Mac for ice cream, Sophie

hung up and started haphazardly pulling everything out of her locker and stuffing it into her bag.

"I wonder what Alphonse and his beta were doing in that part of town. Their territory is on the west side of the city. What were they doing east of Twin Peaks? If they were on Market Street like you said, they would have been encroaching in either the Invicta Domus or the Dragon's Gate pride territory," Fitz said, a thoughtful look on his thin face.

"What is up with all these territories that you guys keep talking about?" Sophie asked, wondering how anyone could tell where one territory starts and another ends. Maybe all Mythicals got issued a map. Or mystical runes etched into the sidewalks denoting each territory.

"The city is carved into a ton of tiny territories and mini-kingdoms. San Francisco is crisscrossed with dozens of little Mythical fiefdoms, many of them overlapping depending on the breed of Mythical. Except for work, most Mythicals generally stick with their own kind. Especially the tighter-knit communities like vampires and wolf shifters," Amira explained.

"What about you guys? Do you have to stick to your own territory? Or get issued a hall pass or something? Does that mean this office is in dragon territory since Miss Zhao said this building and everyone in it belongs to her?"

"It's complicated. It's almost in layers," Ace said. "Miss Zhao is part of the Dogpatch clutch. There are five dragon domains in the city. The biggest one encompasses Chinatown, of course. But there are other Mythical territories within each domain. They are split; they overlap. The lines are always shuffling and shifting as different clans jostle for real estate. Frankly, it's often hard to even know which pack or pride or clan's land you are even walking through. It's not a problem for us peons. If we were leaders or alphas or members of the Conclave, it would be more complicated, but even they can move about the city without much trouble. I mean, I wouldn't generally be able to purchase real estate in another Mythical territory without permission. Still, no one's going to have a problem with me shopping at the Safeway in the Financial District even though it is located smack dab in the middle of the goblins' domain or eating in a restaurant in vampire territory."

Something about real estate bobbed to the surface of Sophie's mind. A thought flickered through her like a school of minnows, too slick for her tired brain to retain. Closing her eyes, Sophie tried to concentrate on the thread of thought that was bothering her, but she lost her hold on the idea when Reggie's voice called out for Amira. It felt like an important detail just disappeared into the void.

Come on, gray matter. Don't fail me now. But Sophie's silent pleas were to no avail. Whatever it was, it was gone. Maybe she could bring it up with Mac later and see if anything triggered with him.

Reggie's voice calling for Amira a second time pulled everyone out of their discussion of territories.

"Looks like I'm going to be assisting in the autopsy room tonight," Amira said with a resigned sigh before heading out of the women's changing room to track down Reggie.

"I guess I should wait out front for Mac," Sophie said, checking her locker to make sure she didn't forget anything.

"Let me scout ahead and make sure the coast is clear," Ace suggested.

Once Sophie got outside, she realized that she forgot to mention that Marcella and Bramwell had come to check on Alphonse earlier at the police station. She wanted to know what Reggie thought about them and the situation.

Sophie had barely settled herself on the bench outside the ME's office when Mac came screeching into the parking lot. Getting into the gray sedan, Sophie let Mac fuss over her for a few minutes. She deserved a little babying after that shitshow inside.

"That jerk called Reggie a rodent. It was so disrespectful. I should have had Miss Zhao set Alphonse straight."

"Yeah, I've heard it before. Regular shapeshifters get called stuff like that by certain types of apex predators. Things like rodent, misfit, vermin. Frankly, I'd take being a rodent or a misfit over being anything like Alphonse and his ilk any day."

"Definitely," Sophie agreed. "You should have seen Miss Zhao. I thought she was going to wipe Alphonse off the face of the planet for a minute there. She's terrifying – like shit-your-pants scary."

"If Zhao inserted herself into the situation, then it must have been more dangerous than you indicated on the phone. How bad was it?"

"I'm fine. Everything's fine. Wipe that perma-scowl off your face. It's gonna get stuck like that. Oh no! It's too late!" Poking the deep line between his eyebrows, she tutted in mock-sorrow. Mac nipped his bright teeth at her fingers, making Sophie squeal and yank her hand back, hiding it in her armpit protectively.

"I could lodge a formal complaint with the Conclave, but it would be a wasted effort. I don't want them looking too closely at either of us, anyhow. We just need to be cautious. And you need to stay far away from Alphonse," Mac warned.

"No worries. I don't want to be anywhere near that asshole."

"Let's get out of here," Mac suggested, putting his car into drive, and pulling out of the parking lot and into the sparse traffic. Sophie reminded Mac that she had been promised ice cream.

CHAPTER 11

*A*fter sharing a giant bowl of double fudge chocolate ice cream – complete with nuts and whipped cream – with Mac, Sophie decided that maybe the day hadn't been a total loss after all. She would typically be right in the middle of an autopsy at this time of night, but instead, she got to share ice cream with Mac, sunk into his ridiculous sofa.

When Mac went to take the empty bowl into the kitchen, Sophie grabbed her messenger bag and started pawing through it.

"There's my book!" Sophie announced triumphantly, pulling it out of the bottom of the bag, surrounded by candy wrappers and crumpled receipts. "I was worried that I'd lost it."

"If you're only interested in reading a book tonight, I must be doing something wrong," Mac teased.

"I guess I could be tempted away from my novel. You know… if I had something worth my time."

Mac reached over, clasping her wrist in a gentle hold, rubbing his thumb in a soft circle on her wrist. Desire rolled up Sophie's spine, centering on his touch on her arm, fanning out in ever-widening circles until they encompassed her entire body. Mac pulled Sophie so she was straddled across his lap.

"Sophie," he murmured into her hair, his voice gruff and smoky. Sophie lifted her head from his shoulder and met his eyes. She stared for a long, breath-held moment, watching as his gaze dropped to her lips. Sinking her hands to the back of the couch on either side of his head, Sophie leaned in and kissed him. She wanted to drown in his kiss. Mac cupped a hand around the back of her head, tilting her chin to pull her further in. His other hand splayed across the small of her back. Coiling her arms around his neck, Sophie hung onto Mac as their tongues tangled. Sophie threw herself into the kiss, leaving the worries of the day behind her. All her troubles fell away as her world became solely focused on Mac's lips against hers and where his hands touched her body.

Mac's hand slid down from the back of her head, sweeping down her back, pulling her more firmly into his chest. Sophie writhed on his lap, trying to get as close as possible. Mac grabbed Sophie's ass with both hands to still her movements. He lifted her slightly, scooting forward on the seat, then stood up with Sophie firmly grasped in both hands. Sophie wrapped her legs around his waist, clinging to Mac, not wanting to lose contact with his lips. With Sophie held tight in his arms, Mac turned towards his bedroom.

Sophie didn't stop kissing Mac, didn't bother looking around. Hunger for him roared through her veins. She needed Mac's touch. He opened his bedroom door and stumbled in with Sophie wrapped up in his kiss. She was suddenly enveloped in the lingering scent of cedar and Mac's cologne. The smell of him hung in the room, like he'd spent so much time there that his essence was embedded into every crevice of the space. Sophie wanted to roll in it.

She heard the door slam behind her, and realized that Mac must have kicked it shut. She pulled back and took a quick gulp of air before diving back in to kiss Mac some more. Mac tipped her back onto the bed, following her down onto the mattress. Between kisses, he started to tug her shirt up her torso. Raising her arms above her head, Sophie held her breath as Mac began to pull the shirt over her head. The sleeves of the shirt caught on her elbows, with the shirt covering part of her face. With a low chuckle, Mac whispered in a villainous voice, "Trapped. I've got you now."

Sophie growled and tried to wiggle out of the shirt, but Mac had her firmly caught. She stopped fighting when he placed several long kisses along her exposed neck. Humming low in his throat, Mac kissed along the swell of Sophie's breast. The heated imprint of his lips paired with the rumble in Mac's voice made Sophie arch up off the bed, trying to press closer. With Mac busy being enthralled with her chest, Sophie ripped the shirt off her head with a triumphant grin that quickly morphed into a gasp as Mac nosed his way into the cup of her bra.

Mac sat up, scrambling off the bed to remove his clothing. Not to be outdone, Sophie wriggled out of her jeans, bra, and panties, tossing them over the side of the mattress. Crawling back onto the bed, Mac reached for her ankle, giving it a lingering kiss. He took his time kissing each ankle, working his way up her calves, then the inside of each knee. Sophie whined her impatience, but he ignored her unspoken pleading. Hooking her hands under Mac's arms, Sophie tugged him right where she needed him.

"So demanding," Mac purred with a slow lazy grin, trailing his gaze up her body from his place between her legs.

The first touch of Mac's tongue had Sophie bowing up and grasping the bedding in a desperate grip. The second had Sophie calling out to the ceiling. Mac quickly had Sophie climbing the pinnacle, muscles strung tight, hands clawing the sheets.

Kneeling up, Mac reached across Sophie, opening a drawer in his nightstand. A quick ripping noise had Mac sheathed and ready. Sophie grabbed his shoulders and yanked him until he covered her body.

"Ready?" he asked, his eyes bright and wanting. Biting her lip, Sophie nodded. His eyes burned ice blue, filled only with raw need.

As Sophie welcomed Mac into her body, the relief and pleasure tore a moan from her throat. Pressing her face into his throat, she tried to muffle the sounds of pleasure pouring out of her mouth to no avail. Mac leaned up on his elbows to take her mouth in a long, drugging kiss.

Pulling away to pant and groan, Sophie then gripped his shoulder in her teeth, tasting salt and sweat, feeling animalistic. With the taste of Mac's skin on her tongue, his body thrusting over hers, she wondered if this was how shifters felt – primal and sensual, made of only instinct and desire. Pleasure swamped her, rolling a climax up her spine. A toe-curling, banshee-shrieking, mind-melting orgasm. Sophie's mind whited out as she rode a swell of ecstasy before crashing, limp and panting, back into her wrung-out body.

With a final heave over her body, Mac froze. Sophie watched as his eyes snapped open wide, staring at Sophie's face before sliding closed in pleasure. A low growl slipped from his gritted teeth. A moment later, Mac sagged into Sophie's arms with a contented sigh. She wrapped her arms over his shoulders, rubbing his back in slow, soft circles.

"You're crushing me," Sophie complained playfully after a minute, pushing against his upper shoulder.

"But I'm so comfortable," Mac play-whined, his voice still soft and breathy, panting against her ear.

"You're very lucky you're so cute."

"Give me a minute. My muscles aren't working right yet."

He rubbed his face in Sophie's hair, placing a soft kiss under her ear. Sophie tunneled her fingers through Mac's perpetually disheveled hair, enjoying the silky texture of soft curls sliding through her fingers. He had somehow burrowed his way under her skin, where the blood rushed through her veins – down deep in muscle and bone where her essence lived – and made a place for himself there. She'd feel hollow without him at this point.

Sophie ran her finger over the healed-over bullet wound in his shoulder. The scar had already shrunk and faded, making it look years old rather than weeks. For Sophie, it would always be a reminder that she could have lost Mac before she ever really had him.

Mac peeled himself off Sophie with a long-suffering sigh to deal with the condom. Sophie rolled onto her front, following Mac's progress as he headed into the bathroom. She considered giving his ass a well-deserved wolf whistle, but he had already escaped into the bathroom before she could fully purse her lips. He wasn't the only one who was having trouble controlling their muscles.

A few minutes later, Mac returned. Just as he was about to slide into the bed, Sophie stopped him with an upheld hand. Mac froze, raising his eyebrow in question.

"Can I see your fox form?" Sophie requested. "Or is it taboo?"

"You saw my half-form at the Coit Tower. That's the one that scares most people. My full fox form is just that – a fox, but about twice the normal size. It's just a fox."

Sophie remembered Mac's half-form vividly. She would have assumed that his half-form would be lithe and almost delicate like she'd seen in cartoons. But Mac's half-form leaned more toward movie-monster proportions, with an oversized muzzle and fang-like canines.

"As long as it wouldn't bother you, I'd love to see your fox form."

As Mac backed up toward the space between the dresser and the bed, Sophie propped herself up with a few pillows on the bed. Mac rolled his shoulder and seemed to plant his feet. For a moment, nothing happened, and then Mac's human formed whooshed down, shrinking into a fox the size of a medium-sized dog.

Sophie was expecting to witness the cracking of bones reshaping, fur slowly and dramatically growing from each pore, a snout gradually distorting his human face – something vaguely horrific and grotesque – not a blurred disappearing act. She entertained the idea that she perhaps shouldn't rely so much on movies for this sort of thing. Mostly, Mac just shrank down from a human into a fox. It happened so fast that she was unable to describe later what exactly she had witnessed. However, the *schlep* sound was distinct and would stay with her forever.

She crawled further across the mattress, peeking over the edge. Sophie gasped in delight when a red-furred fox yipped at her.

When Sophie reached out a tentative hand, Mac the fox hopped onto the mattress and rubbed his head into her palm.

"Oh my god, you're so cute. Stay like this forever and be my pet," Sophie cooed, trying to squish Mac's fox face between her hands.

With a zipping-whoosh noise, Sophie found herself cupping Mac's human face again.

"Hmm. I don't know… I think you might miss some of my human aspects," Mac leered at Sophie, comically waggling his eyebrows at her.

Leaning up to give him a small kiss, she conceded, "I suppose you might be right. Thank you for sharing your other form with me."

After giving Sophie a last lingering kiss, he finally slid under the covers, tugging up the blanket from the foot of the mattress to toss over them both. Mac stared at Sophie with a soft smile, cocooned together, the warmth in his eyes making Sophie feel like she was the most beautiful thing he had ever seen.

Mac stroked his hand over her hair, down the sloping line of Sophie's back, flowing over her waist and the gentle curve of her hips. His hand stopped, resting the thumb in the shallow dimple on her lower back.

"Spend the night?" he requested quietly.

Sophie briefly considered leaving, but Mac snuggled close, nuzzling his face into the hollow of her throat, inhaling her scent with a contented sigh.

Who could say no to this?

Sophie nodded her assent, wrapped an arm around his shoulder, and watched as his eyes slowly blinked a few times before sliding closed. The worry line between Mac's brows smoothed away with sleep, but the laugh lines crinkling in the corners of his eyes remained behind, making Mac look sweet and inviting.

Lying in Mac's arms, while he snored lightly in her ear, Sophie realized that she was happy. Mac made her crazy happy, like it was something stolen and would be taken away. As if any minute someone would realize that she didn't deserve something this wonderful. But she took the feeling and held it close to her heart, to savor and protect. Mac was hers, and no one was going to take him away from her.

She was used to the night shift now, so she expected to be awake late into the night, but moments later, she too succumbed to sleep.

CHAPTER 12

*S*training her head, she listened carefully. She held her breath and tried to stop shaking, tried to discern any sound that would tell her where she was. Other than the regular soft ping of dripping water, everything was silent. The damp cold made her think she was below ground. She hadn't seen or heard anyone yet, but the sense of being watched wouldn't leave her. Despite what must have been hours, no one had made themselves known to her.

The air was frigid, and the cold metal table she was lying on had leeched the last of her warmth.

She carefully tugged on the rope that tied her hands to each edge of the table to no avail – then, gritting her teeth, pulled with all her strength. After yanking at the ropes until her arms screamed in protest, she collapsed back on the table with a broken sob. The skin around her wrists and ankles was rubbed raw from her attempts to pull and twist free. If she was bleeding, she couldn't even feel it anymore. She once again rubbed her face along her shoulder, trying to push off the cloth covering her eyes, but it was tied too tight; the knot was digging into the back of her head.

The sound of footsteps made her freeze for a moment before animal-like fear had her thrashing in her bindings. The footfalls stopped just as *quickly as they had begun. She could hear a whisper of movement, a tiny creak of sound as if something was being opened – the familiar quiet rasp of paper against paper. She strained, trying to figure out what was happening around her.*

"Who are you? What do you want with me?" she yelled. Silence answered her.

After a few more minutes, the footsteps resumed, bringing whoever was in the room with her close to her side. She strained to her right, trying to get as far away as possible from her tormentor.

Sibilant whispers started. The words were low and incomprehensible, like ghosts of sound echoing around the empty chamber. They didn't sound like English. Hell, they didn't even sound human. Even though the voice didn't get any louder, it filled her ears. A bright glow tinged with green started to seep around the edges of the cloth covering her eyes. The words came faster and faster without break or breath, flowing and blending.

Something heavy was pressed harshly to her chest, the edges of a heavy object bruising and sharp pushing into her sternum. She thrashed and tried to buck off the thing but whoever was holding it pushed it harder into her chest. A word was spoken, and then a sharp stabbing pain sliced through her chest straight into her heart.

"Ligare."

A scream left her lips as she felt herself falling, slipping away. Her last thought was that it felt like her soul was being sucked out of her body, floating above. She tried to look back at her body, but a bright light was pulling her away.

Sophie came awake with a jolt.

For a moment, she stared at the unfamiliar ceiling above her, still trying to wake up, confused why she wasn't seeing the usual crack that ran its spidery fingers across her bedroom ceiling. The memory of the previous night came back to her in a rush, making her want to squirm in delight. However, duty called first. She needed to record the dream while it was still fresh in her mind.

Reaching for the nightstand, Sophie snagged her dream

journal and quickly wrote down as much of the weird nightmare as she could recall. She was starting to feel like she could distinguish between a regular nightmare and when it was a vision of a real-life event. She was relatively sure this was just a normal old-fashioned nightmare. She never thought the day would come when she would welcome one.

"But here we are," she said, tossing the journal back on the nightstand.

Realizing that she was alone in the bed, Sophie stretched starfish style, soaking in the luxury of a high-quality mattress. So much better than her lumpy old one at home. She would have happily stayed wrapped in Mac's thick duvet forever, but the sound of the shower running finally lured her from her down-filled nest. Scrubbing her fingers over her face, Sophie could feel a sleep-crease marring her cheek.

Shuffling into the bathroom, Sophie paused in the doorway, taking a moment to admire Mac's form on the other side of the steamed-up glass. Sophie let out a piercing wolf whistle.

Jerking his head around, Mac opened the shower door and poked his face out.

"Good morning," he said, waggling his eyebrows at her sleep-rumpled nakedness.

"Good morning. You could have woken me up, and I would have joined you in there."

"You were so tired last night. I figured you could use as much sleep as possible," Mac explained. "Besides… you could join me now."

Mac pulled Sophie into the shower stall with greedy hands.

THIRTY MINUTES LATER, THEY WERE STANDING AT THE BREAKFAST bar, eating bowls of some sugar-free, whole-grain cereal-like food. *It figures I decided to date a health nut*, Sophie grumbled internally. She took great pleasure in the horrified look on Mac's face when she poured several spoonsful of sugar into her bowl.

"Sorry, I have to be at work soon. We probably shouldn't have taken so long in the shower," Mac apologized again.

"Worth it," Sophie replied, bumping her hip into Mac's.

"Yeah. Definitely worth it," Mac replied, relish in his voice.

If Mac wanted to drive Sophie home and still have time to make it to work on time, they needed to eat quickly. Sophie scarfed the cereal down as fast as possible.

"Reggie texted this morning," Mac said, dropping his empty bowl into the sink. "He said the autopsy went fine last night, and he didn't find anything unusual with the victim's death. It's exactly as you described it. Nothing surprising there."

"Did Alphonse cause any trouble after I left?"

"Reggie said it was tense but fine. Having Miss Zhao nearby kept the alpha in line. He didn't try to start any fights or go furry."

Finishing her bowl of cereal, Sophie turned to Mac with a grin. "I heard that Corn Flakes were originally invented by Kellogg's with the intent to suppress people's desire to masturbate."

"You're making that up."

"It's true, I swear!"

"I'm Googling that to see if you're pulling my leg," Mac warned, pulling his phone out of his pocket. "Huh. This website says that Corn Flakes were created to be an 'easy-to-digest, healthy ready-to-eat breakfast'. Not to stop masturbating. However, the creator John Kellogg was all about creating a pure, simple, and *un-stimulating* diet because he believed it would dampen one's sexual urges. Oh wow. Listen to this, he called masturbation 'self-pollution' and 'the most dangerous of all sexual abuses'. He didn't even think married couples should have sex except to procreate. That man's poor wife."

"'Corn Flakes: dampening libidos all across America' should be the new slogan."

"Hey, I like Corn Flakes. Don't ruin them for me," Mac begged.

"Oh no," Sophie announced suddenly, bending over and moaning piteously. "The cereal didn't work."

"What?" Mac asked distractedly, glancing up from his phone.

"It didn't work," Sophie repeated. "Mac. I have these... urges. I don't think I can control myself."

Pretending to convulse, Sophie cupped her boobs crying out. "I can't stop. Kellogg's... you've let me down. I need to self-pollute."

"I would normally love to see that, but I need to get to work," Mac said with a slow, sad shake of his head.

"It's too late for me. Leave me behind," Sophie cried out.

Scooping Sophie up and slinging her over his shoulder, making Sophie yelp, Mac dipped briefly to snag Sophie's overnight bag and headed out his front door.

"Mac, put me down. I need to touch myself," Sophie yelled as Mac walked towards his car in the minuscule driveway out front.

"Oh my god! I live here. My neighbors are probably watching you make a spectacle of yourself," Mac huffed, opening the door to his car and tossing Sophie inside. He shook his head at Sophie while she tried to buckle her seat belt, but she was unsuccessful because she was laughing too hard to get the metal tongue into the buckle.

Getting into the car, Mac turned to Sophie with a sigh. "Are you done yet?"

"I'm not sure. I'll let you know."

Sophie could tell that Mac was trying to hide a grin as he pulled out of his driveway and turned towards the Tenderloin.

Staring out the window at the cityscape passing by, Sophie was glad to see the rain of the last few days looked like it was finally waning, leaving the city washed a little of its usual grime.

At first glance, San Francisco looked like a gleaming metropolis crisscrossed with quaint neighborhoods filled with weaving rows of elegant, stately houses. But if you looked beneath the immediate surface to the real city beneath the candy coating, San Francisco was filled with pockets of darkness. It was where vagrants and homeless slept under bridges and in the clusters of dilapidated buildings or the run-down, seedy corners of the city. Big Money kept washing up on San Francisco's shores, pushing the underbelly of poverty, drugs, and despair into hidden coves. But it was still there if you paid attention. Sophie looked at the sleeping bags filled with homeless under an overpass, trash littered around them, clustered together against the cold.

"I've been reading that history book you got me," Mac said, dragging Sophie out of her melancholy thoughts.

"Yeah? You like it?"

"I do. Did you know that the Golden Gate Bridge wasn't originally meant to be the color it is now?"

"Really? I've always wondered why it's called the *Golden* Gate Bridge when it's orange."

"That color is called International Orange. It was inspired by the primer they used to protect the steel. The architect loved it more than the original list of color options. The book says that the Navy wanted it to be painted in black and yellow stripes so that it would be easier to see through the fog."

"Can you imagine?" Sophie asked in horror, picturing a bumblebee striped bridge spanning the bay instead of the iconic structure. "You ever walk the bridge?"

"Once. And once was enough. Truly amazing view, but between the freezing wind, the traffic, and the signs every four feet begging people not to jump, I've never had the desire to do it again. What about you?" Mac asked.

"Yeah, I walked it once too. Cold as hell. But the views were stunning. Luckily, I went on a day when there wasn't any fog. It was so clear that I swear I could see the Farallon Islands on the horizon."

As Mac drove, he slipped one hand off the wheel, sliding it over Sophie's, pressing their palms together. Weaving their fingers together, Sophie savored the relaxed, unhurried touching. She watched Mac drive, trying to see the fox that dwelled inside of him. The only hint of Mac's other form sometimes showed in his eyes.

"Hey, I have a question," Sophie said. "How is it possible for a 180-pound man to morph into a fox? Where does the missing mass go? Is it just magic? I read that the average fox weighs about 20 pounds. Although I think your fox form was much bigger than that, you're still nowhere near your human size in fox form."

"You've been reading up on foxes?" Mac asked, laughter in his tone. "Find out anything interesting?"

"Yes. A group of foxes is called a skulk. A female fox is called a vixen. Fox urine is supposed to smell heinous," Sophie replied, ticking the facts off on her fingers. "Oh, and foxes are supposed to be pretty noisy when they mate – lots of yips and howls. I didn't notice any yips last night, though I do think I made you howl at one point. Now answer my question."

"The real answer is I don't know. My people consider it magic. But I figure there's a science to it. I believe that once you figure out how something magical works, you find that there's a science to it. I think that most Mythical magic is just undiscovered science."

Figures that he'd be pragmatic about magic.

"Burg told me that wolf shifters gather in packs because they are emulating how they think wolves in the wild live with alphas and such. Do fox shifters live in packs too? Are you a member of a fox pack?"

"Nah, fox shifters tend more towards family groups, unlike the strict hierarchy practiced by wolf shifters and a few others. This means that fox shifters don't have as much political power as other shifters, but they also don't have as much internal strife. My dad is the head of our family group. He's the oldest of his brothers, so that role got handed to him by my grandfather."

"So, will you someday be the alpha of your family group?"

"No, that honor will fall on my older sister's head."

"You wouldn't want to be alpha?" Sophie asked, intrigued.

"And be in charge of all my siblings, nieces, nephews, and cousins? No thanks. Nothing but a headache."

Pulling into the small lot next to Brown Betty, Mac found the last empty parking spot available. Turning off the car, Mac turned to Sophie. Biting her lip, she silently watched him, waiting to see what he would do next.

"C'mere," Mac said huskily, leaning across the console.

Meeting her halfway, Mac kissed Sophie, then brushed his lips under her jaw. Sophie pressed closer, a soft sound crawling up her throat. They jerked away from each other when they heard a thin, reedy voice call Mac's name.

Mac laughed, pointing out Birdie, who was sitting on the rickety lawn chair that had recently appeared on Brown Betty's sloping front porch. She had a large, old-fashioned purse perched on her lap. The stiff green bag looked like it was straight from the '60s – like it should be carried by a woman in a miniskirt and go-go boots. Sophie wondered if it was made from alligator skin.

Do they still make things from alligator skin, or are they endangered?

Bird-thin, delicate, and slightly hunched, Birdie waved enthusiastically from her seat, keeping the large bag from toppling off her lap with one bony hand.

"I swear, she somehow just knows when you're going to show up," Sophie said, shaking her head and waving back at Birdie too.

When Mac cleared his throat, Sophie turned to look at him. Mac got an almost nervous look on his face, running his fingers through his hair. "There's this restaurant that opened up near my house recently. Would you join me for dinner there on Saturday? It's supposed to specialize in California cuisine."

"I'd love to go to dinner with you. But you're gonna take me to In-N-Out Burger? Isn't that what California cuisine means?" Sophie said, only partially joking.

"True. In-N-Out Burger should be listed as the official state restaurant of California. But I'm not taking you there. This place is called Fog Bay Tavern. California cuisine means that it probably just has a lot of avocados in the dishes, and everything is artisanal and organic. I bet they sprinkle micro-greens on every plate."

"Well, I don't know what micro-greens are, but I *do* like avocados," Sophie said with a laugh. "It's a date."

Mac looked so pleased that Sophie couldn't stop from giving him another kiss.

Mac groaned sadly, reminding them both that he needed to go to work. Getting out of the sedan, Mac came around and opened the door to assist Sophie out.

"Ooh, Mac, you're *such* a gentleman," Birdie cooed loudly from the porch.

"If she'd seen what you did to me in the shower this morning, she probably wouldn't say that," Sophie whispered out of the side of her mouth, for Mac's ears alone. Mac waggled his eyebrows at her, an evil grin on his face, likely vividly remembering their time together in the shower.

"Good morning, Miss Birdie," Mac greeted, schooling his face into a less lascivious smile.

"Morning, Mac. Aren't you sweet to drive Sophie home from work?"

Neither Mac nor Sophie corrected Birdie's assumption that Sophie was coming home from work instead of sleeping over at Mac's place.

"You hear that, Sophie? I'm sweet." Tugging on their joined hands, Mac turned Sophie to face him while she scoffed at Mac's supposed sweet nature. "Hey, have a great day. Text me when you get up."

"I will. Call me if there's any news about that case you're working on," Sophie replied, hoping the cryptic words wouldn't arouse Birdie's curious nature. She wasn't ready to explain her powers to Birdie yet, although she knew that day was on the horizon. She couldn't keep this kind of secret from her best friend for long.

At the bottom of the steps, Mac gave Sophie a soft kiss to say goodbye. As he pulled back, Birdie hooted and catcalled them.

"You are such a perverted voyeur, Birdie. I thought that Milton would keep you busy enough to keep you out of my business. Like, once you got your own sex life, you'd butt out of mine," Sophie scolded.

"Mac, I can't figure out why a sweet boy like you is with Sophie. Is she paying you?" Birdie scoffed, ignoring Sophie's presence.

"I wasn't aware that was an option," Mac replied with an intrigued look on his face.

"He can't afford me! This is pro bono work," Sophie huffed, making both Mac and Birdie chortle.

Glancing at his watch, Mac grimaced as he saw the time. "Damn, I've got to go. I'll see you both later."

Both Sophie and Birdie said goodbye, telling Mac they hoped he had a good day at work. When Birdie nudged Sophie's side with her bony elbow, Sophie realized she was standing there, staring after Mac with an idiotic smile on her face.

"Oh yes, that's some man candy, right there," Birdie purred as they both watched Mac walk back to his car.

"You better wipe that look off your face when you're talking about my boyfriend," Sophie threatened with a laugh in her voice. "What are you doing out here anyway?"

"The senior center is going to take a bunch of us on a tour of the Academy of Sciences and then set up a luncheon in the park afterward."

"That sounds nice. Is Milton going to be there?" Sophie asked.

"Maybe..."

"Why are you being evasive?" Sophie asked in consternation.

"I don't know. I just don't want to screw this up. I like him," Birdie said quietly.

Sophie was taken aback to hear Birdie say almost the same fears she'd been having.

"You're not going to screw this up, Birdie. You're awesome. If Milton doesn't get that, then he's a fool. And he doesn't deserve you. It's as plain as that."

"You know what? You're right," Birdie exclaimed. "I am awesome. I don't know why I got myself all worked up over this."

The senior center van pulled up in front of Brown Betty before Sophie could think of anything else to say to reassure Birdie. Watching as Milton excitedly waved from inside the vehicle, Sophie decided to heed her own advice. The young man driving the van hopped out and, with a gentle hand on Birdie's elbow, ushered her into the van to join her gentleman caller.

Waving as the van pulled into traffic, Sophie turned to head into Brown Betty. Usually, she'd be getting home from work about now and going to bed. But she'd slept all night and was wide awake. She didn't think she could stick to her usual schedule.

So what now? The rumble of her stomach decided for Sophie. A measly bowl of bland cereal wasn't going to cut it. She'd burned off a bunch of calories the night before and deserved a yummy, butter-drenched breakfast.

Checking the time, Sophie figured she could beat the crowd to Brenda's French Soul Food if she hustled. After nine, the wait would take forever because the place was so popular, even on a weekday. With good reason too. The menu was a mix of Southern, French, and Creole cuisines served in a relaxed, charming atmosphere. It was one of the hottest brunch spots in the city for a reason. And now that Sophie was getting a steady paycheck, she could afford to treat herself occasionally.

Stepping inside the red and black storefront, Sophie was able to snag one of the few remaining open seats at the bar top running through the middle of the restaurant. Despite her early arrival, the restaurant had already started to fill up.

Sophie ordered a grandma's molasses-black walnut iced coffee when the server dropped off a menu. Her mouth salivated as she looked over the breakfast options. Every item sounded more delicious than the last. Sophie almost ordered the shrimp and grits with tomato-bacon gravy, but at the last moment decided to get the flight of beignets instead. Why choose just one flavor when you can try them all? Sophie planned to eat herself into a carb-coma.

The four different beignets would be too much food to eat alone, so she decided to save the plain and chocolate one to enjoy later. The apple and crawfish ones were going in her belly immediately.

When the server slid the long rectangle plate of pillowy, fried goodness in front of her, Sophie was unable to silence her moan. She knew she sounded like a dying wildebeest. The server seemed unfazed. She imagined he was used to that sort of reaction by now.

Sophie chowed down on a crawfish beignet filled with spicy crawfish and melty cheddar. After sucking the dusting of Cajun spices off her fingertips, instead of the usual powdered sugar coating, Sophie took a big gulp of water to cool the heat on her tongue. After she finished her first beignet, Sophie made herself slow down to savor the apple one. Its caramel sweetness was a perfect counterpoint to the peppery-hot crawfish. It was like having dessert. She could have cared less that she was making a bit of a spectacle of herself. Glancing covertly around, she realized that she wasn't the only patron in the throes of culinary ecstasy. Over the quiet piped-in music was the ambient noise of utensils scraping porcelain and groans muffled by overly full mouths.

The food was delicious, but as Sophie took her final bite of the pastry, she realized it would've tasted even better if she was sharing it with Mac. Man, she had it bad.

After paying for the meal and having her leftovers packed up, Sophie headed out, determined to get some errands done.

On the way home, Sophie stopped at the liquor store around the corner and picked up a bottle of Asbach Uralt brandy for Birdie. After a brief knock at Birdie's door to confirm that she was still on her date with Milton, Sophie considered leaving the bottle on her welcome mat as a surprise, but ultimately decided against it. Leaving alcohol unattended in the Tenderloin just meant you'd never see it again.

Once inside her apartment, Sophie caught up on her bills. Not having to do the mental gymnastics of trying to figure out which bills she could postpone paying and which she had to take care of immediately, figuring out which companies had the worst late fees, and testing out how far she could push the utility company until they turned off the power made Sophie feel glorious. The feeling of just being able to pay them all... Well, it just made her stomach feel lighter. Like she had been carrying a ball of lead inside her everywhere she went – a small constant cannonball of burden and worry that was now gone. It had been getting heavier and denser as the financial hole she'd been in had been getting deeper and more inescapable. But now she had a real job with a steady paycheck, and she could cover her rent and all the necessities. If she was careful, she might even be able to start socking some away for a rainy day or retirement or something. Sophie had even gotten herself a filing box with those olive green hanging folders to organize her bills and receipts and stuff, like a real adult.

Too well rested after all the sleep she got the night before,

Sophie tried to read her book but couldn't get into the story. Maybe it was the sugar from breakfast, but Sophie had energy to burn. Pacing around her tiny apartment, looking for something to occupy her time, Sophie scrunched her toes in her grubby sneakers. Looking at the shoes, Sophie was happy to see they hadn't picked up any stains from the morgue yet. In the short time that Sophie had been working with Reggie, she had learned that if it couldn't be bleached or wiped clean, it would eventually get ruined by some horrendous fluid. Since the detectives took her boots from her yesterday, maybe she should get some replacement ones. Those boots had started to fall apart anyhow.

Double-checking her wallet for her Clipper card, Sophie headed out of Brown Betty and to the nearest BART station.

SEVERAL HOURS AND SHOPS LATER, SOPHIE FINALLY HIT PAY DIRT AT Cal Surplus on Haight. Her usual thrift shop, the bubblegum-pink Out of the Closet, hadn't had any decent boots in her size for once.

Sophie decided to break in her new boots by walking to Alamo Square to enjoy the weather and admire the Painted Ladies with the tourists. Buying a couple of pork tamales from the tamale cart lady, Sophie found a grassy area that wasn't too crowded facing the postcard row of pristine, candy-colored Victorian mansions, back-dropped by downtown skyscrapers. Wishing she'd gotten some extra napkins, Sophie ate her tamales and watched as group after group took the same picture of the houses. Not that she could blame them – the gorgeous mansions with all their architectural details and craftsmanship, the lush, rolling grass, the soaring glass and metal towers in the distance – it was worthy of a picture. The sky was clear enough Sophie could even see the sharp spire of the Transamerica Pyramid stabbing high into the stratosphere above the surrounding down-town buildings.

Which explained why this view was one of the most photographed places in the city. Laying back in the grass, Sophie realized that she hadn't taken the time to just enjoy the park since the annual Hunky Jesus contest in Dolores Park for Easter, which had been almost eight months ago.

With a full belly, the white noise of hundreds of tourists exclaiming over the view, the lush grass cradling her, and the sun warming her, Sophie almost fell asleep there on the hill. Shaking herself from her stupor, she got up and finally headed home to get the sleep she needed before work.

CHAPTER 13

$\mathcal{T}$he soles of Sophie's new lace-up captain boots were still stiff and squeaked on the linoleum floor as she entered the lobby of the Medical Examiner building that evening. The boots, the color of chewing tobacco, made Sophie feel more like herself than her sneakers had. There was just something about a pair of sturdy boots that made her feel like she was ready to take on the world.

"Good evening, Miss Zhao," Sophie called out. "Thanks for coming to my rescue last night. I hope that alpha didn't give you any more trouble after I left."

"I would've liked to have seen him try," Miss Zhao said primly, glancing up from her computer screen with a small, secretive smile. Miss Zhao's fingers flew over the keyboard without skipping a beat. Sophie had always been impressed by people who could type without having to look at the keyboard. She was more the hunt-and-peck type.

"I would pay good money to witness that," Sophie laughed, imagining an enormous copper-brown dragon ripping apart a wolf-form Alphonse and munching on his bones with relish.

Heading through the access doors, Sophie knocked on

Reggie's office door, but there wasn't an answer. Moving further into the facility, she found him in the autopsy room, reviewing the notes on cases scheduled for the night.

"Any trouble after I left last night?" Sophie asked.

"It went fine. Alphonse wasn't happy, but since I've never actually seen him happy, I wasn't worried," Reggie replied. "Here are the notes from the autopsy of his beta. It all was pretty straightforward."

Glancing over the notes written in Amira's flowing handwriting, Sophie snorted at the cause of death. 'Long incised injury found on the front of the neck' felt like a bit of an understatement. Even the 'severance of left carotid artery' didn't quite cover the true horror of Roger's death.

"Is the body still here? I could do a reading and see if I can see Snow White's face or if I still see myself," Sophie offered.

"That's a good idea. We should do that first," Reggie suggested. "Alphonse demanded that we release the body right after we completed the autopsy, but I was able to hold him off by saying the body was part of an ongoing investigation. He was furious that we wouldn't release it to him last night."

"Is that unusual? We've never had anyone claim the body right after the autopsy was done since I've been here. I thought it went to a funeral home or something."

"It's not completely out of the ordinary. For the human side of the ME's department, when a body is ready to be released, it is typically released directly to the crematorium or funeral home. But many Mythicals have specific rituals for their dead, so we will release a body directly to the next of kin, or sometimes their alpha or clan leader. The times I've done an autopsy in front of a family member or a pack alpha or such, they've always requested the body to be released as soon as I'm done. Since they're already here for the autopsy, it makes sense to take the body home right then."

Sophie shrugged since that made sense. She followed Reggie

into the walk-in fridge. Reggie stopped by one of the metal shelves where a body bag sat. Unzipping the bag and parting the flaps, Sophie looked down at Roger's face. Reggie held up his phone, ready for Sophie to get started.

Placing her hand on his chest, well below the gash on his neck, Sophie closed her eyes.

"Okay, he's walking down Market Street with Alphonse. Alphonse tells him that he thinks they've picked up a tail. He points to a bakery up ahead and tells Roger to lead the person into the alley behind the building. He'll cut through the bakery, and they'll trap their shadow and get some answers. Roger slips around the corner and hides behind a dumpster so he can jump out and grab the person. Crouched, he waits for the tail to walk past his hiding spot, but no one walks by. He starts to get worried because if he loses the person, Alphonse is going to be pissed. He tries to sniff and see if he can smell anyone approaching, but the stench of the trash is too strong. He thinks he hears a small sound. It's probably a rat or something, but he tries to peek around the dumpster to see if anyone is approaching. Almost before he can react, something slashes across his throat. A searing pain, and then something shoves him back, so he falls on his ass against the wall. A person in black skips back away from him with a bloody knife clutched in their gloved fist. He is shocked that it's a woman. He can't believe a woman got the drop on him. The woman has the hood of her jacket pulled up so he can't see her face. The alley is too dark. He just gets a hint of feminine lips and chin. She tilts her head, staring at him for a moment, before looking both ways. Turning on her heel, she strides quickly away while Roger tries to stem the blood flow from the wound on his neck. Another noise has him hoping that Alphonse has arrived, but it's me. I'm trying to help put pressure on the wound, but we know how it ended. I was too late."

Sophie opened her eyes and pulled her hand away from Roger's chest. She almost felt bad for him, but she saw how he was looking forward to hurting whoever was trailing after him and his alpha.

"Did you get a look at her? Was Snow White wearing your face again?" Reggie asked.

"I'm not sure. Maybe. Roger didn't get a good look at her, but what he did see kind of looked like me. He just didn't get a good enough look for me to be sure." Sophie shrugged, wishing she had something more concrete to give.

"Could you tell what Roger and Alphonse were doing? Why were they in that part of town?" Reggie asked, pulling Sophie from her contemplation of Roger's final moments.

"No, I didn't catch any hint of what they were up to," Sophie said apologetically.

Reggie shrugged like it was no big deal and turned off the recording. He led the way out of the refrigerator while Sophie rubbed her hands up and down her arms, trying to warm up.

"You ready to get started with our night?" Reggie said once they were back in the hallway.

"Sure, just let me get into my scrubs, and let's get to work," Sophie replied and headed to the changing rooms.

Four hours later, Sophie was munching on her sandwich, listening to the chatter of her co-workers. She enjoyed the normalcy of watching Amira and Ace argue while he attempted to scrub the skin off an apple. Ace had been grumpier than usual lately. Fitz had brought in a batch of orange cranberry scones, the recipe of which he had been trying to perfect. He was dissatisfied with the results, but they tasted delicious to Sophie.

"Did you know that the Swedish call raccoons *tvättbjörn?*" Sophie announced. "It literally translates into 'wash bear'."

Sophie had been reading up on the animals that make up the other half of her friends' souls – hoping to understand them better – when she ran across that little tidbit.

"Well, that's better than trash panda," Amira replied, making Ace snort.

"You about finished? The next one up looks like another OD," Reggie asked Sophie.

"Another one? Jeez. What's up with all these overdoses?"

"The opioid crisis isn't just a human problem. It's an everyone problem."

Reggie got up with a sigh that said he'd seen too many of these deaths. Crumpling up her now-empty brown bag, Sophie tossed it in the trash, following Reggie out of the breakroom.

Splitting off from Reggie as he veered into the main autopsy room, Sophie entered the morgue's walk-in fridge to grab the gurney with the correctly numbered body bag. When Sophie had first started at the morgue, the refrigerator with its shelves of wrapped bodies and rolling tables used to unsettle her. After the last few months, they were no more frightening than office furniture – just a part of the daily landscape after the first few weeks of trepidation.

After parking the gurney in its usual spot, Sophie thoroughly scrubbed up in the sinks just inside the autopsy room. Between having to scrub her hands a dozen times a day and then wearing nitrile gloves, Sophie's hands were perpetually dry and slightly irritated. Amira had steered her towards a hand cream that reduced the irritation after Sophie's hands had become chapped and started cracking during the second week of her employment.

Double-checking the chart against the number on the body bag, Sophie turned to Reggie. "You ready?"

With a nod from Reggie, Sophie unzipped the bag, mentally preparing to see a thin, sickly man. Surprise slapped her when the face of the man that was revealed was unlined and boyishly rounded. Only the bruised and sunken nature of his closed eyes showed the wear and tear of drug use. He had that all-American surfer-boy look with tousled, blond-streaked hair. He looked like the type of guy who called his friends 'bro' and hiked for fun. Glancing back at the chart, Sophie saw that the man, whose name was Zach, was twenty-eight. Most of the other ODs that Sophie had seen on the autopsy table had been aged beyond their years, but Zach still looked youthful. His face and body had not yet been ravaged by drug use.

Reggie grabbed his phone and looked expectantly at Sophie. "Let me know when to start recording," he said.

"You can start now," Sophie replied. Once Reggie hit the record button on his phone, Sophie placed her hand on the dead man's upper arm.

"Into the void," she joked. Taking a deep breath, Sophie cleared her thoughts and turned her attention on the well in her mind where the visions emerged. "He's sitting on a sofa in a what looks like a living room. It's dark – the only light is coming from a small TV – and it's hard to see much. It's all a little blurry and distorted. I think he must be drunk or high because it's hard to focus. There are heaps of empty bottles, empty bags of chips and such cluttered on the coffee table. Two other men with him. They're all kind of slumped around. One is older – maybe early-forties. Brown hair, has a bit of a gut. The other is younger, maybe in his late twenties. He's wearing a red baseball cap, but his hair looks dark blond. Hard to tell. He's thin, almost emaciated-looking. Both are in jeans and t-shirts.

"There's a knock on the door. The thin one gets up and answers. He says that there's someone there to talk to Zach. Zach gets intimidated and nervous when he sees who it is. This dude looks different than these other guys. Cleaner, you know what I mean? He's wearing a black hoodie, but he appears to have dark hair. I can't tell if it's brown or black. He's big. Really big. Now that Zach is standing in front of him, I can see that he must be a few inches over six feet. And bulky. The man tells Zach that he needs to talk to him alone, nodding at the two men on the couch. Zach tells the men that they need to leave. After a bit of grumbling and complaining, they stumble out of the apartment. He tells Zach to take a seat, pointing to the ratty couch he was sitting on before. Glancing at the now-closed door, the scary guy says,

'Humans, really?' Zach says that they serve a purpose with a shrug. He asks Zach if he's been spending a lot of time with humans. Zach shrugs again and says not really. Zach asks him what's going on. He asks if there is a problem or if he's in trouble. He's really rattled. Zach keeps calling the man 'sir'. He hasn't said his name yet.

"The man grips Zach's right shoulder, right by his neck, pinching the nerve there. Staring intently at Zach, he says, 'When we invited you to join the inner circle, you knew what our goal was. What our mission is. You told us you agreed with our stance on humans. And yet... We've noticed you've been spending time with humans, especially the woman. What's her name?' Zach mumbles that there is no woman, but the man digs his fingers harder into Zach's shoulder muscle, making him yelp. 'That's right. Neesa. Her name's Neesa, right?' he says. 'You know what's interesting? Someone called the police the night we dealt with Gibson. No one but us knew what was going down that night. It's an interesting coincidence that the caller was female. Did you tell Neesa about us?' Zach is swearing and promising that he told Neesa nothing. That she doesn't know anything about them. That she doesn't even know that he's a shifter. She thinks he's human.

"'Well, we'll find out if you're telling the truth or not. Jeremiah's paying her a visit as we speak. He'll find out what she knows,' the man says. Zach starts begging him not to hurt Neesa, saying that she's innocent and swearing that he never told her anything. But the man squeezes even harder on Zach's shoulder, shutting him up. 'Doesn't matter, because either way, we can't trust you. You thought you could hide a human girlfriend from us, and we wouldn't find out? Do you think we're fucking stupid? You knew when you joined us what it all meant. Having a relationship with a human just lets us know that you're not up for what comes next.'

"Zach tries to beg the man for a second chance, but he tells

Zach that it's too late. He says that they can do this the easy way or the hard way. That he doesn't care either way, it's up to Zach. Crying, Zach chooses the easy way. The man ties off his left arm while Zach continues to cry. When the man gets distracted for a moment, Zach tries to make a run for it. He barely gets off the couch before the man slams him back down. The man wraps his fingers around Zach's throat and tells him that if he moves a single muscle that he'll have Zach begging for death before he finishes with him. Zach keeps pleading, but the man ignores him as he pulls a syringe out of his hoodie pocket, uncaps it with his teeth, and quickly injects Zach with something. I can't see what it looks like because Zach is determinedly looking away. Recapping the needle, the man sits back on the coffee table and just watches Zach in a detached kind of way. Like he's a science experiment or something. As euphoria washes over Zach, he mumbles that at least it feels good."

Pulling her hand away from Zach's body, Sophie shimmied her shoulder in an all-over shudder. "Ugh. That sucked." Shaking her hand out, Sophie refrained from wiping her hand off on her scrubs. If she did, she'd have to change her gloves. She learned that lesson the hard way her first week at the morgue. Reggie was a stickler for the rules and regulations.

"Wait." Sophie was hit with a sudden realization. "What about the woman? Neesa? Do you think there's still time to help her?"

"Oh gosh, you're right," Reggie exclaimed. "Let's call Mac and see what he can do."

"We're supposed to send my visions to the police chief now, not Mac," Sophie reminded Reggie.

"Oh yeah, I forgot," Reggie replied. "Let me head to my office and call Chief Dunham now."

"Do you think he'll get pissed if we wake him?" Sophie asked, biting her lip with worry. The Chief of Police had the power to make her job and her life quite difficult.

"Don't care. This is too important," Reggie said, heading out of the autopsy room with a determined stride, leaving Sophie alone in the autopsy room.

Turning back towards the gurney, Sophie said to the body, "Looks like it's just you and me now, Zach." Sophie waited to see if Zach wanted to talk – at this point, she didn't think a talking corpse would be all that shocking – but it appeared that Zach had nothing to say.

Sitting sideways in one of the viewing chairs, Sophie settled her feet on the only other chair seat in the room. Sophie briefly considered following Reggie so she could try to listen in to what he said to Dunham but decided it was too much effort to get back up. Besides, Reggie would happily tell her everything that Dunham had to say.

A few minutes later, Reggie bustled into the room.

"Well? What did Dunham say?" Sophie asked, prying herself up from the chair.

"He said he'd take care of it. He also said he wants the full autopsy report as soon as we are done here. I'll need to put a rush on the toxicology screening. He'll want to know exactly what drugs were in the victim's system. It takes a lot to take out a shifter, so I'll also be interested to know what cocktail of drugs was used."

Getting up from her reclined position, Sophie grabbed a new pair of gloves and wandered over to the autopsy table while Reggie bustled about the room. Sophie looked down at Zach's face, wondering why he would hang out with humans and maybe even have a human girlfriend if he was part of some sort of anti-human group. It just didn't make sense. Reggie startled Sophie from her thoughts when he nudged her side with his arm, nodding toward the equipment tray. He prodded Sophie away from the gurney, spreading the flaps of the body bag wide and starting his examination of the body.

"Look at this hematoma on the victim's right shoulder. That matches up with what you witnessed. I wonder if this would have been ruled as simply an overdose without your vision," Reggie said, staring down at Zach with a faraway look on his face.

Shaking himself out of his momentary reverie, Reggie called Sophie back over to help him get started on the official autopsy. "After we finish up here, I will forward this to Chief Dunham right away."

CHAPTER 14

*H*ours later, Sophie zipped up the final body bag of the night with a sigh of relief. Rolling her shoulders to try and release tension from being bent over an autopsy table for hours on end, Sophie glanced at the clock to check the time. If she hustled, she could still catch the bus home.

Reggie wished her a good night, saying that he was headed out. They'd had a bit of a backlog, so they'd needed to stay later than usual. Sophie just needed to drop off the body in the fridge, give the samples to the toxicology department, file the autopsy report, and then she could head home. Her bed was calling out to her. She planned to drop straight onto her mattress and leave the long night far behind her.

"Do you think we can get an update on the investigation into Zach's death from Dunham?" Sophie called out, causing Reggie to pause in the doorway.

"We can ask Dunham or see if Mac would look into it. But there's no guarantee that we will be told. I'm rarely kept in the loop with open cases. Even though the Mythical division does things differently, they don't want any information about ongoing cases getting leaked."

"I'm also worried about the woman. I hope the police found her before the shifters got to her."

"Me too. However, we've done everything we could to help her. We couldn't have done more, so don't worry over something out of your control," Reggie advised.

"I know," Sophie said, turning to unlock the wheels on the gurney.

Reggie left without another word, but Sophie saw the worried look he gave her. She needed to stop dumping her worries on him. He was the sensitive type that wanted to fix everyone's problems.

After finishing the paperwork for the night, Sophie changed out of her scrubs and headed for the exit. Pushing through the double swing doors, a loud snarling voice shocked her into freezing. The door bumped into her side, but she barely paid attention as she looked at the group gathered at the front desk.

"What do you mean you can't release the body?" a familiar voice boomed across the lobby.

Sophie couldn't hear Miss Zhao's response, but she watched as Miss Zhao pointed at some paperwork on her desk and gave Alphonse her patented 'I-suffer-no-fools' face.

"Zach's death is still under investigation? That's outrageous. It was an overdose. You need to release his body this instant," Alphonse bellowed, leaning over Miss Zhao's seated form. "I demand to speak to Dr. Didel this instant!"

When Sophie huffed in annoyance on Reggie's behalf, Alphonse whipped around to glare at Sophie. His eyes narrowed in recognition and anger.

"Shit," Sophie muttered, scooting back into the hallway and letting the door swing closed between them, hiding her from Alphonse's intense glare.

She pressed her ear to the door, listening silently, while Alphonse yelled and blustered at poor Miss Zhao. It took several minutes before he finally seemed to lose steam. Once the arguing died off into silence, Sophie waited a few more minutes before slowly cracking the door open and peeking into the lobby.

Once it looked like the coast was clear, Sophie poked her head further into the room, breathing a sigh of relief when she saw that the lobby was clear of everyone except Miss Zhao.

"It's safe to come out. They've all left," Miss Zhao called out.

Sophie stepped into the lobby, letting the doors swing closed behind her. Approaching the welcome desk, Sophie looked over Miss Zhao, but as usual, not a hair was out of place. She looked serene.

"Are you okay? I'm sorry I left you alone to put up with his behavior," Sophie asked. "I felt like my presence only would have made things worse. He was already looking for a fight."

"You were right to get away from that alpha. He would have gladly dumped his anger on you," Miss Zhao said, dismissing the idea of the misbehaving alpha with a flick of her hand. "Besides, he's all bark, no bite."

"I have a feeling he's both. Maybe not with you, though," Sophie conceded.

"He's not a fool," Miss Zhao replied with a smirk, making Sophie laugh. "He does seem to have a problem with you specifically. He's dangerous, so be careful."

"He has a problem with all humans, not just me. And he's not the only one. It seems like a lot of shifters do."

"Only the short-sighted, narrow-minded ones. It's easy to blame others for your woes. He's not the type to look deeper. He only cares about himself."

Sophie thanked Miss Zhao again and wished her a good day before heading out into the weak morning sun. Walking across the slowly filling parking lot, Sophie shaded her eyes to check the time on her phone. She picked up her pace when she realized that she needed to hustle to make the next bus.

A shadow fell over her as she shoved her phone in her back

pocket. Sophie skipped back a step when she realized that she had almost walked right into a stranger.

Muttering a quick apology, she stepped to the right to go around the man, but he copied her move and blocked her. Looking up from the sidewalk – she usually walked looking down because you never knew what you might accidentally step in on city sidewalks – Sophie realized she recognized that man from Alphonse's entourage the other night. It was the shaggy-haired baseball fan, although this morning he was wearing a faded Brian Wilson 'Fear the Beard' t-shirt.

Sophie cursed herself for dropping her guard. When had she started getting so soft?

Rolling her shoulders, Sophie took a deep breath. She fell back to her usual ploy in a situation where she felt out of depth: bluster and attitude. It was a little strange that her usual mask felt like it didn't fit quite like it used to.

Sophie adopted her best wide-eyed, innocent look. "Can I help you? The Unemployment Office is on Mission. You just need to head down to Acacia Avenue and take the 19 to—"

The man's growl interrupted Sophie's directions to a building she was *very* familiar with.

"They said you were a mouthy bitch," the man said, to which Sophie responded with a gasp of outrage and a hand-on-chest 'who me?' stance. "The alpha has a message for you." The man paused, possibly waiting for Sophie to faint or fall to his feet and beg for mercy.

Despite her racing heart, Sophie rolled her eyes and again tried to sidestep the man she had mentally named Number 1 Sports Fan. "Don't care," she informed him.

The shifter loomed closer, stepping into Sophie's personal bubble, further blocking her from a quick retreat. An intelligent woman would take a step back, but Sophie never considered herself particularly smart. She held her ground, placing her hands on her hips, tapping her toe in a show of irritation.

"The alpha says you need to stay out of Mythical business. You're a human and don't belong with us. You keep sticking your nose where it doesn't belong, and you're gonna get hurt. Humans break so easily, and you look so very—"

Whatever threat Sports Fan was about to make was interrupted by the approach of voices. It sounded like several people were approaching by the chatter of conversation. The voices died off when a small group of people rounded the corner of the building. Sophie recognized a few of the people from the day shift.

"Hey, um," a young man said stepping forward and away from the pack. Sophie had seen him a few times. "Is everything okay here?"

"Actually, no. Could you notify Miss Zhao that I am being harassed out here? She'll take care of it."

"The receptionist? Are you sure?"

"Oh yes. She knows exactly how to deal with trespassers."

Sports Fan threw his hands in the air. "No need. I'm going. But you better take care and listen to what I said," he said, pointing a threatening finger at Sophie.

"Please let Alphonse know that I received the message and will take his words under advisement," Sophie sneered. This time when she stepped around him, Sports Fan let her – stepping back and sweeping his hand as if showing her the way. Sophie strolled towards the newcomers as if she didn't have a care in the world. Her jangling nerves demanded that she look behind her, but her ego wouldn't allow her to do so.

"What the hell was that about?" the young man asked quietly.

"Nothing. Just an unhappy customer. Didn't like the results of an autopsy," Sophie replied absently, watching the reflection of Sports Fan in the building's windows as he got into his shiny white sportscar and peeled out of the parking lot with tires squealing.

After watching the car drive a few blocks and turn south, Sophie waved off the concerned day staffers and hustled to the nearest bus stop. Thankfully, she was able to blend into the large crowd at the stop.

As soon as Sophie got settled into an empty seat on the bus, she dialed up Mac. She quickly gave him a recap of the morning's events.

"That motherfu—" Sophie swallowed a chuckle as Mac bit off his words. It made her feel better to listen to him struggle to rein in his anger. The warmth of having someone care for her gave her an inappropriate smile. She should be copying Mac's serious demeanor, not mooning over having someone angry on her behalf.

"Okay, here's what we're gonna do. I'm in the station right now. I can see the chief in his office. He's in a meeting with the Assistant and Deputy Chiefs – once they're done, I'm going to talk to him. The wolves respect him, and he has the power to make their lives difficult. The chief knows how important your work is, so he'll want you protected. Dunham should be able to make sure they leave you alone. But we're not stopping there. As soon as I hang up with you, I will call Reggie and have him request an Order of Protection for you. Since he's your boss at the morgue and he holds a lot of sway with the Conclave, that should get Alphonse to back off."

"What's an Order of Protection?"

"It states that someone, usually a human but not always, is under the protection of a pack or clan or such. If Reggie puts one in place for you, as the Chief Medical Examiner, it puts you under the protection of the Conclave. The Medical Examiner's office is considered independent of the police department and all government departments. The only entity the ME reports to is the Conclave. And even they can't interfere with any cases or investigations. It gives Reggie a lot of power in the Mythical community. But an Order of Protection issued by Reggie would put you under the direct protection of the Conclave and its considerable assets. No one, not even Alphonse, would try to take on the Conclave. It's our best bet."

"Do you think it's a good idea to bring me to the attention of the Conclave?" Sophie asked.

"We're just going to play it that you're a vulnerable human being harassed by shifters. It might take notice *away* from you. If we're requesting protection for you, it won't occur to them that you're powerful. We'll use their preconceptions about humans against them. We can suggest that your participation in the Coit Tower incident might be why the Sunset District pack is targeting you. The Conclave is trying very hard to keep that whole ordeal under wraps, so they'll want to lock down anything that might bring that incident to light. Orders of Protection are typically only issued for humans, and I don't think Mythicals pay any attention to them because they don't want to bring down the wrath of the Conclave on their heads. I'm also making getting you into fighting lessons my top priority."

"Why do Alphonse and his pack have such a hard-on about me working at the morgue anyway? You don't think they suspect what I can do, do you?"

"No, I think you're just a convenient target for their anger. Your presence at Roger's death and then at the morgue the same day is the only reason they even noticed you. Over the years, that pack has been vocal about not wanting Mythicals to mix with humans. They want all Mythicals to separate themselves from human lives as much as possible. It's not remotely logical or even possible, but there you have it. I have no proof yet, but I suspect that is what is going on here. I'm putting out a few discreet inquiries about that pack and specifically Alphonse. I've got a few contacts within his pack that might be willing to talk to me. Not everyone is pleased to have Alphonse as their alpha. I'm also going to be looking into every death that has occurred to a member of his pack in the last few years to see if any kind of pattern emerges."

"Then you should start with the guy that was brought in last night. It was his body they were trying to pick up this morning." Glancing around the bus to make sure no one was paying her any attention, Sophie proceeded to recap the death vision from the shifter.

Before she could finish the description from the vision, Mac interrupted her. "Damn it. It looks like the meeting in Dunham's office is wrapping up. I need to catch him now before someone else jumps in. I'll have Reggie send me the audio file on that autopsy. I'll call you as soon as I'm done here, okay?"

After saying goodbye and hanging up, Sophie closed her eyes and leaned her head against the bus window, trying to relax until her stop. Giving up after several unsuccessful minutes, she plucked her phone back out of her pocket and sent a quick message to Reggie to let him know what was happening. She warned him that Mac wanted him to issue an Order of Protection for her. Based on the number of exclamations Reggie used when he replied that he would get on it right away, Sophie assumed he was enthusiastic about the idea. Chuckling, she stuffed the phone back in her pocket and tried to relax for the remainder of the ride home.

Thirty minutes later, Sophie finished the climb to her floor in Brown Betty. Passing Birdie's door, she could hear the murmur of the TV. Brown Betty didn't exactly have soundproofed walls. Thinking of the bottle of whiskey waiting for Birdie on Sophie's counter, she decided to grab the bottle and see if Birdie wanted to hang out.

Unlocking the door and stepping inside her apartment, Sophie paused. Everything looked normal, but she couldn't shake the feeling that something was off. Giving her apartment another lingering look, Sophie shook her head when it all appeared to be the way she'd left it the night before.

I can't let those assholes get in my head, she lectured herself.

Heading into her tiny kitchen, Sophie's new boots scuffed over the green and mustard yellow linoleum, the floral design faded from the passage of many shoes. Sophie started to grab Birdie's whiskey when something caught her attention. With her hand hovering over the bottleneck, Sophie leaned closer. The seal on the screw cap had been opened, and a large gap of space was now above the top of the amber liquid.

Sophie froze, a feeling of being trapped crawling up her shoulder blades. Her breath punched from her in shock.

Swirling on the balls of her feet, she took another look at her apartment. Her breath sawed rapidly in and out of her lungs, and sweat gathered along her hairline. Trying to quiet her breathing, Sophie listened but couldn't hear any unusual sounds. Nothing looked out of place.

Tiptoeing back into her living room, she realized that a few small items looked like they had been moved, but only just a little. Her filing box was now sitting in the center of her little desk instead of sitting to the side. As if someone had been rifling through it. Stopping in the door to her bedroom, she noticed that her bedroom window was cracked open. The curtains gently fluttered from the breeze.

Dashing out the front door and slamming it closed behind her, Sophie was dialing Mac before she realized she had even pulled the phone out of her pocket.

He answered after one ring. "Hey, I'm talking to the chief right now. I'll call you back as soon as—"

"Someone's been in my apartment," Sophie huffed out.

"What?"

"Someone's been in my apartment! A few things have been moved around, they opened the whiskey I bought for Birdie, and a window was left open."

"Is anyone in there now?" Mac demanded.

"I don't think so. But I'm not sure. I ran out of there as soon as I realized."

"Okay. Where are you now? I'm heading there right now."

"I'm in the hallway. What should I do?"

"Get out of there. Go to Burg's," Mac suggested.

"Okay. I'm grabbing Birdie first. Just to be safe."

"Good idea. Stay on the phone with me until you get to Burg's place. I'm on my way. I'm bringing backup."

Sophie rapped on Birdie's door urgently, glancing back over her shoulder at her apartment door.

"Girlie," Birdie started to greet, but Sophie held a silencing finger up to her lips. Birdie snapped her mouth shut, eyes drawn in confusion.

"Someone broke into my apartment. Mac is on his way. We need to get out of here," Sophie whispered.

"Okay. Where are we going?"

"Burg's."

Without another word, Birdie scooped up her cat Ginsberg and followed Sophie down the stairs.

Knocking loudly on the glass door to the pub, Sophie glanced over at Birdie shivering in her housecoat and slippers. After a minute without answer, Sophie pounded harder on the door until it rattled in its door frame.

"I'm coming! Jesus!"

Sophie could hear Burg bellow from the depths of the backroom of the pub. Stomping around the corner, she watched the angry scowl slide off Burg's face to be replaced with concern when he spotted Sophie and Birdie huddled in the alcove of his front entry.

Unlocking his door, Burg waved them inside with exclamations of concern. "What are you doing out there in your pajamas, Birdie?" he asked.

After letting Mac know they were safe and ending the call, Sophie quickly explained the situation to Burg and Birdie.

Directing them to a table, Burg handed them each a cup of coffee before grabbing some sugar and creamer.

"Was anything stolen?" Burg asked. When Sophie replied that she hadn't noticed if anything was missing, she saw Burg and Birdie share a troubled look. "Are you sure the bottle hadn't been tampered with before you bought it? I mean, if nothing else was out of place, it doesn't seem like a lot to go on."

"I'm sure someone had been in there. Well... almost completely sure. I *know* I didn't leave the window open. It's been raining so much lately. I specifically remember closing it." Seeing Burg's skeptical face, Sophie sighed and stared into her coffee mug, trying to figure out if this morning was just an overreaction. Sophie shrugged, slowly stirring a dollop of creamer into the steaming coffee. "Someone had been in there, I swear. But maybe I'm just being paranoid. Alphonse sent a pack member to threaten me this morning after I left work."

"He did what?!" Burg exclaimed, starting to rise from his seat. What was he planning to do, go track down Alphonse now?

"Who's Alphonse?" Birdie asked.

"He's an alpha of one of the wolf packs in the city. He has a problem with me working at the morgue in the Mythical division," Sophie explained.

"Why would he care? You're not the only human working with Mythicals. Why is he so concerned about you?" Burg asked.

"Well, it's complicated. And it has to do with an ongoing case, so I'm not sure how much I can divulge," Sophie explained. Burg huffed out a sharp breath but appeared to have accepted Sophie's explanation. At least for the moment.

While Burg went on a short rant about making Alphonse sorry for messing with people under his protection, Sophie determinedly continued to stir her coffee, not looking at either of her friends. She hated lying.

It's not a lie. I don't know how much I can tell them. She promised herself to ask Mac to let them in on her secret power as soon as possible.

"Mac has already talked to the Chief of Police about getting Alphonse to leave me alone. Besides, now I'm thinking I might have overreacted this morning, and no one had been in my apartment," Sophie pointed out, feeling a little sheepish for freaking everyone out over what might be nothing.

"That bear? Puhlease. He thinks because he works for the Conclave that he has any power in this city," Burg scoffed.

"He does have the whole of San Francisco's police department working for him as well," Sophie pointed out. "Miss Zhao also told Alphonse to leave me alone."

"Really?" Burg said, sitting up in interest from his slouch at the table. "The dragon gave an offer of protection. She must think highly of you," he said approvingly, looking impressed.

Sophie hated to burst his bubble, but... "Uh, I don't think she thinks highly of me so much as that she finds me mildly amusing. Like a lion enjoying the mindless scampering of a particularly dumb mouse. Besides, I think it's more that she thinks anything in the morgue belongs to her, including the measly human employees. I'm as important to her as her office chair," Sophie retorted. "Also, Reggie is going to issue an Order of Protection for me, so I'm hoping that will get the Sunset pack to back off."

"Maybe I should put in an official Order of Protection too. Or perhaps I'll just pay Alphonse and his pack a visit."

"It's not that I don't appreciate the offer, but that might start to draw too much attention to me. I'm trying to keep a bit of a low profile," Sophie started to explain.

"Why? You being under the protection of so many Mythicals is a good thing."

Sophie opened her mouth to try and explain, but nothing came out. She just couldn't lie to her friends about why she needed to keep a low profile. A rap on the large glass window saved her from having to come up with an excuse. Sophie leaped up and pushed her chair back with a screech when she saw it was Mac out front. Rushing to the door, Sophie's steps slowed only for a moment when she saw that someone was with him. The man behind turned from surveying the street, and Sophie recognized him from Mac's department. His name escaped her memory.

"Hey," Sophie greeted Mac, trying unsuccessfully for nonchalance. "Did you go up to the apartment yet?"

"No, I wanted to check on you first. Are you okay?" Mac said.

"I'm fine. I'm sorry you came out all this way. I'm starting to think I might have overreacted. I think that Alphonse's threat just got into my head," Sophie apologized.

"You aren't the overreacting type, hellraiser. If you think someone's been in your place, then I'm sure they have. We're going to go check it out. Do you have a key?"

Sophie handed Mac her keys.

"Sophie, you remember—"

"Larry Turner, warlock extraordinaire, at your service. Lovely to see you again," the man said, tipping his gray tweed fedora with panache. Pushing in front of Mac, the man held his hand out for a handshake, a broad smile splitting his narrow face. The wattage of his grin didn't dim even when Sophie hesitated to take his hand.

Sophie shook his hand, perplexed by Larry's aggressively chipper demeanor. "Larry the Warlock?"

A warlock should have a name like Draxir the Wicked or something. Not Larry. Larry is the name of your local mechanic.

"Has a nice ring to it, doesn't it?"

"Um, yeah, sure does. This is Burg and Birdie," Sophie introduced her friends who stepped forward to greet the man. After everyone made their introductions, Sophie turned back to Larry. "Warlock? Is that like a witch or something?"

"Like a *witch*," Larry mimicked, shaking his head like he thought Sophie was being adorable. "Being a warlock isn't like anything else. If I had to classify myself, I suppose a warlock is most similar to human descriptions of a sorcerer or wizard."

"And how exactly are those different than a witch?"

Larry pressed one hand to his heart as if in pain, still holding onto Sophie's hand with his other. "It's completely—"

"Not relevant," Mac growled, cutting off Larry's reply. "We need to check Sophie's apartment. Can you get a read on her now?"

"Yes, yes," Larry mumbled. Sophie tried to extract her hand from Larry's grip, but he tugged her back. "I need your hand for just a moment."

"Why?" Sophie asked.

"I need to get a feel for your aura. Then I'll be able to see if there are any energy footprints left in your apartment besides yours," Larry explained.

Sophie shrugged; that explanation meant nothing to her. Larry droned a few nonsensical words under his breath, his eyes closed in concentration.

"Got it," he announced. Larry turned over Sophie's hand in his, opening his eyes, giving her ringless left hand a pointed look. Sophie yanked her hand out of Larry's and stuffed them into her jean pockets.

"You have a lovely aura," Larry said with a flirtatious wink. Sophie considered knocking his stupid hat off his head and 'accidentally' stepping on it. He was lucky she needed his help.

Larry asked if anyone else present had been inside Sophie's apartment recently. Birdie had visited earlier in the week, so Larry did his mumbling act over Birdie's hand. Sophie felt a little better when Larry shamelessly flirted with Birdie as well. He seemed to be an equal-opportunity Casanova. Mac watched him with an expression of prolonged suffering. Catching Sophie's eyes, Mac rolled his own.

Sophie swallowed the inappropriate grin trying to form on

her face as she watched Mac get annoyed with someone other than her for once.

Pulling Sophie into the pub and away from the others, Mac put an arm around Sophie's shoulder as if comforting her and asked in a hushed tone, "Did you check to see if the clavis had been taken?"

"I didn't hide it in my apartment. It should be safe where I put it," Sophie whispered back.

Sophie cut her eyes toward a golden trophy sitting on a high shelf to their right. Hidden in the bowl of the trophy was a green stone that somehow had the power to close the portal from the Fae realm to Earth permanently.

"You hid the clavis in plain sight in The Little Thumb? In a pub?" Mac asked incredulously. "Does Burg know?"

"Of course not. I didn't tell him anything. It's perfectly safe."

"Are you kidding me? What happens when Burg dusts?" Mac whisper-yelled. "People have killed to get their hands on that thing, and you just left it sitting on a shelf in a bar?"

"That's the cool part. He has a spell on the bar so that he never has to dust anything. You'd need a step ladder to even see inside the trophy. No one even looks at the décor here. They're too busy getting drunk."

"They're too – You—" Sophie watched Mac sputter for a minute. "Argh! I can't right now! You need to get the clavis, and together we'll find a better hiding place. An actual *secure* hiding place."

Rejoining the group, Mac tried to herd Larry out the door, but he side-stepped Mac and continued to chatter inanely at Birdie.

"Enough," Mac barked, apparently having hit his limit with listening to his co-worker exchange coy innuendo with Birdie, who was lapping it up. "We need to go check out the apartment. Stop wasting everyone's time."

Turning on his heel, Mac walked away, stiff-legged and tense, without glancing back to make sure Larry followed. Larry flashed Sophie a wide unrepentant grin, quickly tipped his hat again, and skipped after Mac.

Sophie and Birdie returned to their table while Burg topped up their mugs with fresh coffee. Sophie tried to pay attention to the conversation between Burg and Birdie – Birdie was arguing that Burg needed to start offering food at the pub – but Sophie's concentration kept getting pulled to the clock on the wall. She watched as the minute hand slowly moved around the clock face. The conversation slowly died as her nervousness began to affect everyone else.

Sophie tried to figure out how to distract Burg and Birdie for a minute so she could retrieve the clavis but was unable to come up with a plausible distraction.

"Can I borrow a step stool for a minute?" Sophie asked Burg.

He gave her a confused look but headed to the back of the bar to get the stool. Sophie dragged the folding ladder over to the display wall while Burg and Birdie watched her with perplexed expressions.

"I hope you don't mind, Burg, but I hid something here for Mac. It's for one of his cases. I can't tell you guys any more than that. I'm sorry," Sophie explained.

Climbing the ladder, Sophie carefully reached into the trophy and palmed the clavis. With her back turned to her audience, she slid it into the front pocket of her jeans, making sure that it remained concealed. The jewel left a prominent bulge in her jeans, but there was nothing she could do to disguise its shape.

Burg gave her a suspicious look but didn't comment. Birdie shrugged then turned back to Burg to continue her argument about adding food to the pub's offerings instead of just bowls of pretzels and alcohol.

Eventually, a loud knock on the door made Sophie jolt. She jumped up from her seat when she saw Larry waving her over.

For the first time, Larry's perma-smile was missing. It made

Sophie's feet stutter in her rush to get to the entrance. Yanking the door open, Sophie was already breathless and gasping. "Well? Am I crazy? Had anyone been in there?"

"You were right. Someone has been in your apartment. However, whether you're crazy remains to be seen. You are dating the grumpiest asshole in the force, so it does put your mental faculties into question," Larry teased, some of his natural flirtatious charm seeping back.

Sophie looked over toward Brown Betty, where Mac was still inside her apartment, probably muttering about his annoying, talkative co-worker right at that very moment.

"Ugh, you should see your face right now. Disgusting. I can't believe Volpes has someone of your caliber mooning over him. Such a waste," Larry said, shaking his head with fatherly disappointment.

"The person who broke in… Was it Alphonse or one of his minions?" Sophie asked, waving away Larry's comments.

"That's why I need you to come with me. The aura signature left behind is all muddled. All I'm sure of right now is that it wasn't from a shifter. It's weird. I was hoping that having you there would help separate the footprints. Plus, Mac wants you to pack a bag. He seems a little flipped out. Which worries me because I've never seen him flustered before."

After advising Burg and Birdie to stay in the pub and wait for their return, Larry led Sophie back into Brown Betty.

Opening the door to her apartment, the first thing Sophie saw was Mac's worried face. Pulling her into the kitchen and away from Larry, Mac pulled her close.

"It was her. She was here," Mac whispered urgently. At Sophie's blank look, "Snow White. She was in here."

Sophie reared back in surprise, staring into Mac's eyes, half expecting him to be making a joke. "Snow White? It wasn't Alphonse?"

"No, it's definitely her. I recognize the combination of her perfume, laundry detergent, and her fruity-smelling shampoo."

"You can smell that? When did you get her scent?"

"At Roger's crime scene, I picked up her scent on his clothes and in the air in the alley," Mac explained.

Turning back to Mac, Sophie clung to his arm, feeling like the world was tilting on her. Sophie glanced around her apartment, feeling as if a psycho murderer could pop out at any moment. Of all the scenarios that had been running through her head, it never occurred to Sophie that Snow White would even know who she was.

"How in the world did she find me? How does she even know I exist? How did this happen?"

"She must have been watching the crime scene when you tried to save Roger. I assume that she followed us back here when we walked back to get you clean clothes."

"Are you guys alright? We need to get started. I don't have all day," Larry called out from the living room.

"Are you okay?" Mac whispered to Sophie.

"Yeah. Let's get this over with."

When Sophie turned the corner, Larry grabbed both her hands and tugged her until she was standing in the middle of her tiny living room facing him. Closing his eyes, Larry tilted his face up to the ceiling. After a long moment, he turned his head sideways, as if listening to something only he could hear.

Lifting both of Sophie's hands in front of their chests, he placed each of their palms together like they were going to push one another away. Larry solemnly nodded his head at Sophie as if asking for permission to proceed, so Sophie nodded back. Closing his eyes, Larry spoke more woo-woo magic nonsense words over Sophie's hands. She was beginning to suspect it was all just for show. Larry seemed like the kind of guy to put on a performance. Sophie glanced over at Mac to see if he was buying into this charade, but he watched the proceedings with a serious expression.

Larry's eyes popped open, and he gave Sophie a bright smile. "This is very interesting. A unique situation."

"You got the footprint?" Mac interrupted.

"Yes, it was tough to separate the trespasser's aura from Sophie's, though. The auras are somehow muddled together. It appears that the person attempted to camouflage themselves within Sophie's energy footprint. They just didn't realize that they'd be dealing with an expert." Larry pressed his hand to his chest to indicate who was the expert in case Sophie wasn't aware. "I'm dying to meet the person who managed this level of magic. Being able to blend your aura into someone else's would be quite the feat. I've never heard of someone who could pull this off. Oh, just imagine all the possibilities!"

Mac blew out an annoyed huff as Larry continued to exclaim his delight. "So, you got her, right?" Mac asked, pulling Larry back to the present.

Larry scoffed, somehow peering down his nose at Mac even though he was the shorter of the two. "I'm a professional. Of course, I got her. I just can't figure out how she was able to hide in someone else's aura."

Sophie nodded her head, thinking of how Snow White had been able to replace her face with Sophie's in all her visions. "That makes sense, actually."

Sophie looked at Mac and could tell they were thinking the same thing. Somehow, Snow White figured out who Sophie was and had started mimicking her right from the start.

"What do you mean? How does it make sense?" Larry asked eagerly like a dog who had caught a scent trail, looking back and forth between Sophie and Mac as if he could glean the answer from their unspoken communication.

"Sorry. It's classified," Mac replied with a shrug that clearly stated that he wasn't sorry at all.

"Seriously? I just helped you out here, and you can't tell me anything about this person of interest? Throw me a bone."

"What kind of Mythical could pull off this kind of magic?" Mac asked Larry, ignoring his petulant grousing. The question seemed to distract and calm him down.

Larry got a thoughtful look on his face. "Hmm. Good question. I'm not quite sure. Maybe Fae. Maybe witch."

"What about a warlock?" Sophie asked, teasing Larry.

"You said this is a woman. Women can't be warlocks."

"Oh, I see. You're sexist."

"I am *not—*"

"We're not interested in your excuses. We have more important things to deal with besides your sexism," Mac interrupted, giving Sophie a quick wink as Larry sputtered. "Can you do a location spell on the trespasser? She's a person of interest with the Conclave."

The mention of the Conclave seemed to settle Larry down and make him finally act in a professional manner.

Closing his eyes, Larry spread his arms out wide and then slowly swept his hands in close like he was scooping up water and trying to hold it in his curved palms. He pulled his cupped hands close in front of his sternum. While Larry muttered under his breath again, Sophie felt a hum fill the apartment. It made her want to stick her finger in her ear and wiggle it to get rid of the buzzing itch.

Larry's eyes popped open, and he gave Sophie another of his patented grins. Reaching into the air above his head, he appeared to pluck an invisible string.

"Wow! She's good. Like *really* good. I'm begging you to let me talk to her for just one minute once you catch her."

Stepping next to Sophie, Mac wrapped an arm around her waist, tugging her close. "You located her?"

"Nope! She laid down too many false trails. I can't grab onto them. They're too delicate, like gossamer threads." Larry strummed a few more invisible 'threads', his smile widening to disturbing proportions.

"What do you mean?" Mac growled. "You can't find her at all?"

"Nope! I'm pretty sure she's here in the city. Or… she could be on the east coast." Closing his eyes, Larry delicately plucked the invisible threads again. "Nah. She's here somewhere in the Bay Area. That's as close as I can trace her."

"What happens now?" Sophie asked.

"I want you to pack a bag – get enough for at least a few days. While he's –" Mac pointed at Larry "– pulling prints from the apartment, I'm going to find a safe place for you to stay. We have to assume that Snow White has been watching the apartment, and it's not safe for you here until she's caught."

"Where am I gonna go?"

"I'll make some calls and figure something out," Mac assured her.

Nodding her agreement, Sophie turned to enter her bedroom when a thought stopped her mid-step. "Wait. If Snow White's been watching me, then she's probably seen me with Birdie and Burg. Do you think they're in danger too?"

"Burg can handle himself, but I'll give him a warning. However, you might be right about Birdie. I'll have her pack a bag too."

After Mac promised to be back as quickly as possible with Birdie, Sophie rushed through her apartment, stuffing a duffel bag with clothes and toiletries until the seams of the pack started to creak.

Heading back out into her living room, Sophie tossed her bag by the front door. It landed with a *thwump*. Sitting on her futon, she watched as Larry twirled a soft-bristled brush through a compact of black powder. He was gently dabbing the brush over the entirety of the whiskey bottle's neck. Humming to himself, paying no attention to Sophie intently watching him work, Larry grabbed what looked like a piece of clear packing tape. Sophie leaned forward, resting her elbows on her knees, keen to see if this type of police work was accurately portrayed on TV. Larry pressed the tape onto the bottleneck, then slowly peeled it off. Holding the tape by its edges, Larry held it up to the light coming through the window. Sophie could just make out a gray smudge in the middle of the clear tape.

"Is that her fingerprint?" Sophie asked.

"Possibly. Statistically speaking, it's more likely that it's yours," Larry explained as he turned back to the table, fiddling with some items in a hard-sided briefcase that Sophie couldn't see into even when she strained sideways to peer into the briefcase's depths nosily.

"Mine?"

"Yeah. I'm going to need a set of your prints so I can compare. But let me finish up in here first," Larry said, heading into the kitchen. Curiosity forced Sophie to get off the sofa and follow him. She watched as he started pulling prints off her fridge and her cabinets.

"Any idea why you have a serial killer stalking you? What's so special about you?" Larry asked, a sly curiosity on his face.

"I'm not sure why," Sophie replied after taking a moment to gather her thoughts and school her face. "Maybe when I stumbled onto her crime scene, I saw something. Maybe I saw her or some other clue, and I didn't realize it. She must've followed me home. Maybe she just instantly became obsessed with me. Who knows how a crazy murderer thinks?"

"Bad luck, that. Sounds like the wrong place at the wrong time." Larry tutted his sympathy. Sophie attempted to put on an air of innocence, but thankfully the warlock was too busy pulling prints off her kitchen cabinets to notice her forced nonchalance.

He moved around Sophie's apartment, methodically pulling more prints from various surfaces. He explained that he was getting prints from areas that would have been the most likely touched by Snow White – the filing box, the bedroom windowsill, light switches, and doorknobs.

Birdie's voice calling out for her pulled Sophie away from Larry and back into her living room. When Birdie spotted her, something of Sophie's fear must have shown on her face because Birdie shoved her vintage suitcase into Mac's arms and rushed over. Pulling Sophie into a strong, bony hug, Birdie clucked about how worried Sophie had made her. Sophie aimed a smug grin at Mac over her shoulder.

She loves me more, Sophie mouthed at Mac, who just rolled his eyes.

"Turner, I'm going to get these two out of here. Can you manage the rest on your own?" Mac asked.

"Certainly," Larry responded with a negligent wave of his gloved hand. "I'm going to lay a spell on all the windows and doors so that if anyone, even our talented stalker, crosses the threshold of this apartment, I will know immediately."

"Aren't you smart?" Birdie cooed over Sophie's shoulder at the warlock, who, if Sophie didn't know better, was blushing.

"Where's Ginsberg?" Sophie asked, looking around.

"Burg agreed to watch him for me," Birdie explained.

"We should go," Mac said, glancing at the clock in the kitchen.

"I have some beignets in the fridge that I've been saving. Can I grab them, or do you need them for evidence?" Sophie asked, only half-joking.

Larry assured her that he'd already gotten the prints he needed from the kitchen, so she was free to grab her leftovers.

Opening her fridge, Sophie stared into its depths for a lost moment, unable to understand what she was seeing. The Styrofoam carton from Brenda's was where she left it on the top shelf of the refrigerator, laying open and empty. A lone smear of chocolate inside the white box was all that was left to indicate what was once inside.

"That *bitch*."

"What?" Mac asked, striding into Sophie's tiny kitchen, worry etched across his features.

"That bitch ate my beignets. I was saving those. What kind of monster—" Cutting off her rant with a growl, Sophie slammed the door closed on the fridge, which groaned its complaints at the rough treatment. Needing to get away from the empty take-out box before she completely lost her mind, Sophie stalked out of her kitchen, past her gawking friends, back stiff with tension and a headache starting to bloom behind her right eye.

Mac chased after Sophie, catching her by her elbow and pulling her to a stop as she reached her front door. Sophie turned to him, "I know. I know. I'm overreacting. They're just donuts. It's just... I was looking forward to them," she whined.

"You're not overreacting. You have every right to be angry."

"This whole thing is starting to get to me," Sophie softly confessed. Mac caught Sophie's hand within his, rubbing soothing circles over her knuckles with his thumb.

"We're gonna fix this. First though, we need to get you somewhere safe. I've found a place."

Blowing out her fear and annoyance on a slow breath, Sophie nodded her approval. Mac shouldered both her and Birdie's bags, leading them out of the apartment. The group was silent as they walked out of Brown Betty and got into Mac's spotless sedan.

Birdie barely got her door closed before starting her interrogation. "Okay, girlie, spill. What the hell is going on here?"

"I stumbled upon a murder scene the other day, and now we think that the murderer is stalking me," Sophie replied. This was technically the truth, but Sophie felt like the world's biggest jerk.

Birdie threw up a hand to forestall Sophie saying anything more. "You are a terrible liar. Do I look like I was born yesterday?"

"Not at all. You look like you were born a long time ago. Like a really, *really* long time ago."

Birdie scoffed and turned her attention from Sophie to Mac.

"You've pulled me into the middle of this. You're taking us into some 'safe house'. I deserve to know what is really going on. I'm neither deaf nor stupid, girl. Don't you try to feed me any more of your bullshit. What is really going on? Don't think I haven't noticed that you've both been acting strange lately."

Sophie exchanged a glance with Mac, who nodded his permission to spill the beans.

"Okay, I should start from the beginning..."

CHAPTER 15

a fter telling Birdie all about her ability to see death visions, how she accidentally uncovered a conspiracy, dug up a grave that culminated with her climbing up the Coit Tower clinging to an ogre's back, Sophie glanced over at her friend who appeared to have been rendered mute.

"And then there's Snow White," Sophie continued, apprehension slowing her words.

"Snow White?" Birdie repeated, her words faint.

By the time Sophie finished telling Birdie about her serial killer stalker and her problems with Alphonse and his wolf pack, Birdie had recovered her voice. What followed was a twenty-minute lecture from Birdie about not keeping secrets from her and how Sophie needed to work on keeping herself safer.

When Mac scoffed in agreement, Birdie turned her ire on him. Sophie was careful to hide her glee and be as quiet and unobtrusive as possible.

"Where are you taking us, by the way?" Sophie asked once Birdie had finished saying her piece. Mac was circling yet another block. Sophie assumed that he was attempting to lose any tails and hide their destination from anyone trying to follow them. Despite dozens of random turns and switchbacks, they had slowly meandered towards the west side of the city.

"I'm taking you to the Knights of the Red Branch. The clan leader owes me. He said that his clan would keep you both safe."

"Knights of the Red Branch," Sophie repeated slowly. "Like, medieval knights with swords and suits of armor?"

"Hardly," Mac scoffed. "You'll just have to see."

"The Knights of the Red Branch? Their hall burned down well over a decade ago. They never rebuilt. I thought they'd closed down," Birdie replied.

"After the incident with the basan shifter, they decided to rebuild in secret and not open their doors to the general public anymore," Mac explained.

"Basan shifter? What's that? I thought that fire was caused by faulty wiring. What really happened?" Birdie asked.

"A basan is an avian shifter – a huge fire-breathing rooster. They are originally from Japan but have a small community in Sausalito. The basan in question was drinking at one of the many bars inside the KRB hall. He got completely plastered, and the story I heard was that he was trying to impress the local ladies by blowing fire rings. Things got out of control, and he set the whole building on fire. Luckily, no one was injured, but they decided to close their doors to outsiders."

Flicking on his turn signal, Mac pulled his car out of the flow of traffic and into the driveway of a large apartment building squatting on the corner of Fulton and 6th Avenue in the Richmond District. It looked like an expensive place to live with the lines of bay windows on each floor and the fancy cornice molding along the roofline.

Birdie and Sophie followed Mac to the front ironwork gate and watched as he shifted both bags to one arm so he could ring the doorbell. He held the gate open for Birdie and Sophie to enter as they were buzzed in.

Sophie had expected to be standing in an apartment lobby

with the typical mailboxes next to elevators. Instead, she was standing in a grand entranceway. To her left was an archway leading to a pub filled with dark gleaming wood and low lights. Above a huge stone fireplace was a banner with a coat of arms – a red cross emblazoned on a yellow crest with two snarling wolves rearing on hind legs on either side.

Most of the tables in the pub were filled with people, despite the early hour, all quietly talking and laughing. They all fell silent and stared at the newcomers standing in the entryway, noiseless and wary. Quickly looking away from their gazes, Sophie stared down the empty hallway in front of her, then to the right. The hallway led towards the back of the building, with an ornate set of stairs rising along the right wall. There was one door on the right a few feet before the bottom of the stairs.

"Welcome to Clan Cú Faoil," boomed a voice from the top of the stairs. Looking up, Sophie spotted a diminutive man lounging against the handrail dressed in pressed slacks, a well-fitted vest, and a button-up shirt with the cuffs neatly rolled to his elbows. Despite his nonchalant posture, Sophie had the feeling that he was posing there for dramatic effect.

Suddenly, a hairy beast of a dog tried to leap past the man toward Sophie's group at the bottom of the stairs. The small man with the large voice snatched the dog mid-leap and casually tossed it back down the hall behind him without a backward glance. A muffled *woof* and the scrabble of claws on wood was the only sign left of the retreating dog. Sophie's mouth dropped open in shock at seeing a man who would barely reach her chin casually toss around a dog almost the size of a miniature horse.

Turning to Sophie, Mac chuckled at her slack-jawed surprise. "The Knights of the Red Branch are Irish wolfhounds."

"Like dogs? They're dog shifters?" Sophie whispered frantically. Mac didn't respond, just gave her a massive grin in response.

Stepping toward the foot of the stairs, Mac raised his hand in greeting, leaving behind a paralyzed Sophie. "Fergal, these are my friends I called you about."

"Mac, you sly fox." The man grinned, clearly pleased with his dad joke, and came down the stairs, pulling Mac into a brief, back-slapping hug. He had curly brown hair trimmed short with blunted bangs that reminded Sophie of an ancient Roman statue she had seen in a book once. "You didn't tell me you'd be dropping two incomparable beauties on my doorstep."

"Haha, sly fox," Mac deadpanned. "Never heard that one before."

"And who are these lovely ladies?" the man asked Mac, turning towards Birdie.

"Fergal O'Dwyer, I'd like you to meet Birdie Gafferty and Sophie Feegle. Thank you for offering them sanctuary on such short notice."

Sophie studied the clan leader as he leaned gallantly over Birdie's hand, placing a kiss on her knobby knuckles. Birdie twittered at the attention. Mossy green eyes flicked up towards Sophie, catching her in the act of observing him.

Holding her hand out in greeting, Sophie stated, "It's nice to meet you, Fergal. Thanks for taking us in."

"It's nice to meet you, too, Sophie. Mac here tells me that you've gotten yourself into a bit of a pickle. A murderous stalker, eh?" Fergal asked, turning back to Mac for confirmation.

"And she needs protection from the Sunset District pack, too. Alphonse has issued some threats against her," Mac reminded Fergal. "I'm hoping someone in your clan would also be willing to give her self-defense lessons."

"Oh my, Sophie, haven't you been a busy bee! I have just the guy to get Sophie into fighting form. Let's go to the bar on the second floor. That one has a kitchen attached. I'll get my wife to whip you up some food, and you tell old Fergal here what's going on."

"You have more than one bar here?" Sophie asked, glancing

over at the pub to her left. All the patrons were studiously looking everywhere but at her.

"Yes, we modeled this hall after the one on Mission Street that burnt down in 2007. It was a point of pride that the original hall had a bar on every floor," Fergal said as he looped both her and Birdie's hands over his biceps and led them up the wide staircase with Mac trailing behind them.

"This place is four stories. Do you really have four bars here?"

"Of course. It's tradition!"

The thunder of feet from above, combined with childish shrieks of delight, had Sophie snapping her head up from her admiration of the antique wooden newel post at the bottom of the stairs. Fergal tugged Birdie and Sophie flush against the railing as a gaggle of children interspersed with a couple of Irish wolfhound pups came thundering down the stairs.

"Oi! You lot! Watch out; we've got guests here. Do you want them to think we've got no manners?" Fergal bellowed after the herd of children.

The last child in the group, and the smallest, stopped and turned to Fergal. "Sorry, Unca Ferg!" the little girl chirped before racing after the other children as they piled out a door at the end of the hallway. Sunlight lit up the corridor for a moment as the door slammed shut behind the group. Sophie got a brief impression of a large outdoor playground and verdant greenery.

"Sorry, alpha! The little boogers got away from me," a woman called as she raced down the stairs past them and out the back door after her escapees.

"Kids, amirite?" Fergal chuckled while leading the group up the rest of the stairs.

The second floor had a similar layout to the first, with another bar on the left. This bar was slightly smaller than the one on the first floor but was more crowded. Almost every table was filled with people eating and laughing.

As they entered, everyone looked up from their plates, silent and wary, watching the newcomers.

"Make some room. We've got guests," Fergal called out. He pointed at a group of men gathered around a table near the long pub-style bar top. He flicked his hand in a shooing motion. The occupants quickly grabbed their plates and drinks and dispersed like dandelion fluff to the few empty stools lining the bar counter.

Fergal pulled out a chair for Birdie, then tried to do the same for Sophie, but Mac waved him off. Once everyone was seated, Fergal whistled a loud, sharp note.

Right away, a woman came stomping across the room; her mouth turned down in an irritated moue. Her shoulder-length black hair swept back and forth across her shoulders, bouncing with her strides. She wore a dark green apron over black pants and a black shirt. The woman made a beeline for Fergal, whose back was turned. She bopped him on the head with a small notepad.

"Don't you whistle at me, you mangy mutt," the woman lectured in a thick Irish accent while Fergal rubbed the top of his head, making a pitiful face at her.

"Riona, my love, I was just trying to—" Fergal started, but a sharp look from Riona had the words dying on Fergal's lips.

"This one thinks he's funny," Riona said to the rest of the table's occupants, nodding towards her husband.

"You said you fell in love with me because of my humor." Fergal paused, and Sophie watched as a bawdy gleam entered his eyes. "That, and the size—"

"If you finish that sentence, you'll be sleeping on the couch tonight," Riona interrupted, her voice stern. But a slight smile tugging at her lips. Fergal gave her an unrepentant grin.

"What would you guys like for breakfast? I recommend the full Irish," Fergal told the table.

"Uh… what's that?" Sophie asked.

"You've never had a full Irish breakfast?" Fergal asked, aghast. "Well, you've been missing out. Riona, would you be a dear and get everyone at the table a full Irish?"

"Of course, I'll have it out in just a few minutes. Coffee for everyone?" Riona asked.

Everyone nodded. Riona turned to leave, but Fergal grabbed her sleeve and pulled her back. When he pulled her down for a kiss, Sophie started to look away, but her eyes caught on their matching claddagh rings. Both were made from silver with an identical design of two hands holding a heart under a crown, but Fergal's band was a heavier, more masculine design compared to Riona's delicate ring.

With a final smacking kiss, Riona pulled herself from Fergal's lap. As she started to walk away, Fergal stopped her again. "You know what? Bring me a full Irish, too!"

"You've already had breakfast," Riona said with a frown.

"I'm half-starved. I swear we have a joint-eater in the building," Fergal replied, rubbing his flat stomach, making Riona shake her head and scoff, a fond look on her face.

"Fine, but don't come whining to me later when you've got a bellyache."

"What's a joint-eater?" Birdie asked after Riona headed to another table.

"It's an invisible fairy who sits next to their victim and eats half their food," Fergal explained.

As Riona disappeared through a swinging door just past the bar, Sophie felt a pang of jealousy. Or maybe it was hope. Riona and Fergal were so obviously and ridiculously in love with one another and yet settled and comfortable. They just seemed right together. Like they were meant to be.

Sophie glanced at Mac and found that he was watching her.

Riona arriving with mugs of steaming coffee broke the spell between Sophie and Mac. Sophie picked up the mug and brought it to her nose for a long sniff. The rich smell of coffee seemed to seep into her bones.

As she sipped, Sophie looked out some windows to her left that faced towards Golden Gate Park. Even with Fulton Street between the building and the park, the view was lovely. The sculpted yet rugged greenery of the park filled the window. Everything felt comfortable and relaxed here. Kids occasionally stampeded past the bar, giggling in human form or with wolfhound nails scrabbling on the floor and the occasional bark. With laughter and talk floating above her head, the smells of eggs and coffee in the air, Sophie finally felt some of the tension in her shoulders start to unravel.

"It's nice, innit? It's my favorite view in the clan house," Fergal said, noticing where Sophie's attention was.

"It's lovely. The location of your clan house is awesome," Sophie replied.

"Yeah, being this close to the park is perfect. We can let our hounds out to run in nature without having to travel far. We just have to keep to after dark so as not to scare the locals. It took us ages to buy up this block."

"You own the whole block?"

At Sophie's stunned face, Fergal explained, "We bought up all the houses and buildings on this entire street and the one behind it. That way, we could open the yards between the buildings. It gives everyone, especially the wee ones, a shared open space to shift and run without needing to worry about any humans seeing us."

All Sophie could think was, *In this real estate market?*

Just as Sophie was about to ask the impertinent question of how much it all cost, Riona and another woman showed up with the meal. Sophie's mouth dropped open when Riona deposited a platter of food before each person at the table. There was more food on the plate than Sophie typically ate in an entire day, especially during the bleak period when she'd previously been unemployed.

"A full Irish breakfast," Fergal announced with pride. With a fork, he pointed out each item on the platter. There was toast, fried tomatoes, beans, two fried eggs, mushrooms, bacon, sausages, and black pudding. It was an astounding amount of food.

Sophie had never heard of anyone eating beans for breakfast before, but everything smelled delicious. All the items on the platter were familiar, except the black puddings, which looked like black hockey pucks speckled with flecks of white.

"What's black pudding?" Sophie asked. Looking around the table, it appeared everyone else knew something she didn't. The smirks on Birdie and Mac's faces didn't bode well.

"It's blood sausage. It's my gran's recipe, made with pigs' blood, suet, oats, and barley. Give it a try. You're gonna love it."

Oh no, was all Sophie could think. Fergal speared one with his fork from his plate and tossed it in his mouth with relish. It reminded Sophie of an old neighbor's dog who would eat whole hotdogs without chewing, snatching them out of the air when tossed to him. Sophie missed that old German Shepherd.

Sophie cut off a small piece of the black pudding and took a timorous bite. As soon as it landed on her tongue, Sophie knew that blood sausage was not for her. Chewing as quickly as possible, Sophie swallowed down her bite and chased it with a large gulp of coffee. Sophie was surprised that it was crumbly. She'd expected it to be greasy, or perhaps gelatinous – like the texture of clotted blood. The mushy yet grainy texture was entirely revolting for Sophie, with a strange spicy aftertaste that had coppery undertones.

"Good, innit?"

"It's, um, great. That banner," Sophie said, pointing to the coat of arms over the fireplace, trying to distract Fergal away from her honest thoughts on black pudding. "Are those Irish wolfhounds next to the shield?"

When Fergal turned in his seat to look at the banner, Sophie took the opportunity to fork her blood sausages onto Mac's plate. Mac looked up from his devotion to his meal with a teasing grin at Sophie before returning his single-minded attention to demolishing his breakfast.

"Yes, that's the coat of arms for the Clan Cú Faoil. The Tuatha Dé Danann created the original Irish wolfhound as a war dog. They were famous for being able to pull a man right off his horse in the heat of battle. However, they were mostly used for hunting and protection against wolves."

"Ireland has wolves?"

"Not anymore," Fergal replied with a feral grin that was a little too sharp for Sophie's comfort, causing a shiver to run up her spine. "But those aren't just regular Irish Wolfhounds. Those are wolfhound shifters. The goddess Danu herself created my ancestors to protect Ireland. The shifter on the left is the Hound of Cúchulainn. He was a young warrior that killed King Conchobhar's favorite hound. He felt so bad that he offered to take its place until a new dog could be found. There are lots of legends and stories told in Ireland about Cúchulainn to this day. The one on the right is Failinis. I can trace my family roots right back to the great Failinis."

Sophie already knew she was going to regret asking but couldn't help herself. "Who's Failinis?"

"Failinis was the great war hound who served Lugh Lámhfhada of the Tuatha Dé Danann himself. He was instrumental in helping the Tuatha Dé Danann push the Fomorians out of Ireland. He was invincible in battle – caught every wild beast he encountered, and could magically change any running water he bathed in into wine. It was said that Failinis was so impressive that all the wild beasts in the world would bow down before him, and he was more splendid than the sun in his fiery wheels."

Sophie swallowed her snort of amusement as she watched Riona's mouth move along with her husband as she passed by carrying more platters of food.

At the look on Sophie's face, Fergal explained. "That's a quote from *Odiheadh Chloinne Tuireann*. I managed to acquire one of the manuscripts recently. It's almost 300 years old. It's so ancient that you have to store in a special facility."

"Hold on." Sophie stopped Fergal, who looked like he was gearing up for a monologue. "He turned his bathwater into wine. And people drank your great grandpa's dirty bathwater wine?"

"It would have been an honor to drink the wine created by the great Failinis," Fergal retorted indignantly.

Sophie nodded sagely, deciding not to challenge Fergal on the quality of wet dog wine.

While Fergal continued to regale them with stories of Failinis' grand adventures, Sophie turned her focus on the platter of food before her. Thankfully, the rest of the breakfast was delicious and she dug in heartily. Initially, the idea of beans for breakfast seemed strange, but they were quickly growing on her. As Sophie was dipping her toast into the beans and scooping them into her mouth, Fergal called out, "Conor. Liam. Patrick Junior. C'mere."

Three young men at a table across the room peeled themselves out of their seats and rushed to Fergal's side.

"Boys, this is Sophie Feegle. You're going to be guarding her whenever she leaves the clan house. Her safety is your top priority. Got it?"

"Yes, sir," the three boys chorused, practically saluting and vibrating at attention.

"I'll be giving your usual assignments to some of the others, so don't worry about that. You'll be at Sophie's beck and call. You'll do your clan proud," Fergal demanded, his tone brooking no argument. "Sophie, what time do you need to leave here tonight for work?"

Sophie told them when she needed to leave for work, and Fergal dismissed the threesome.

After the boys were out of earshot, Sophie swiveled to Fergal. "They're teenagers," she argued, trying to keep her voice low and calm.

"They're legal adults. Those boys are some of my best. Already battled-tested. You couldn't be in safer hands, I swear it. They'll drive you to and from work each day, and if you need to go anywhere, they'll be available to accompany you."

"Battle-tested? They're kids. I don't want any kids put into danger because of me. This is a terrible idea."

"They're all future alphas and are eager to prove themselves. You couldn't be in better hands." Fergal turned to Birdie, clasping her hand and giving her a warm smile. "I haven't gotten anyone selected to guard you yet, so let me know if you have somewhere you need to be."

"I don't have any plans, so don't worry about getting me a bodyguard. However, if I could use a phone, I need to call my boyfriend and tell him that I had to leave town for an emergency. He'll worry otherwise."

"Of course. Riona will show you both to your rooms when you've finished eating. She can also get you a phone. I've got duties to attend to, but please stay and enjoy your breakfast. It was lovely to meet you both." Fergal stood up, wiping his hands off on a napkin before calling out to his wife that the food was as excellent as always. He strode off before Sophie could form another counterargument.

She turned to Mac in disbelief. "You can't possibly think this is a good idea."

"They're wolfhound shifters," he replied with a shrug as if that was all that needed to be said. "They're tough, loyal to a fault, and deadly in a fight."

Sophie huffed in resignation. She'd just have to make sure no one got hurt because of her, especially over-enthusiastic teenagers. She'd stabbed a mushroom with her fork and started to bring it up to her lips but realized she was too full to take another bite. Looking down at her plate, she had barely finished a third of her food. Glancing over at Mac, her mouth dropped open as she watched him cleaning up the last scraps on his plate with a piece of toast. Wordlessly, she slid her unfinished food to Mac, who, with a grateful grin, pulled her plate on top of his empty one and dug in.

Riona stopped by, refilling their mugs from a large carafe. "Let me know when you've finished here, and I'll show you to your rooms."

Mac polished off his second plate of food almost as fast as the first.

"How are you not fat?" Sophie asked.

"Shifter metabolism," Mac replied with a shrug. "Shifting burns a ton of calories."

"Lucky," Birdie complained, making Sophie nod in agreement.

With a final slurp of his coffee, Mac said that he needed to get to the office and see if Larry had unearthed any additional clues. He promised to call if he found any new leads. Sophie stood up with Mac, not wanting him to leave. Although everyone at the clan house had been welcoming, she felt a bit like a stranger in a strange land. He must have recognized something on Sophie's face because he pulled her into a tight hug.

"It's going to be okay," he promised. Sophie took comfort in the gruffly whispered words. "We're going to catch Snow White, and we'll get you back into Brown Betty in no time. I promise. We're going to figure this out."

"I know. I just hate that she's out there running around free. I can't wait until she's rotting behind bars." Mac pulled back and gave Sophie a kiss that had Birdie cheering, which everyone in the room picked up. Sophie could feel a blush heat her cheeks.

"I don't want to leave you here, but I have to go. Call me if you need me, no matter the time."

"I will," Sophie promised.

Mac gave Sophie a final kiss and turned to leave. Birdie cleared her throat loudly. When Mac looked at her, she pointed at her cheek emphatically.

"Have a nice day, Birdie. Keep an eye on Sophie for me, would you?" Mac asked, bending down to place a chaste kiss on Birdie's cheek.

After Mac left, Riona stopped by to check if they were ready to see their rooms. She led them up another set of stairs to the third floor, explaining that someone had already dropped off their bags for them. They trailed after Riona as she took them to the end of the long hall, past several closed doors. The corridor ended at a large bay window looking out over the open space behind the clan house. This floor of the house was quiet, the noise and chatter of the house occupants muffled and far away.

"Here you go, your rooms are across from one another," Riona said, opening both doors. "Let me know if you need anything. I'll be in the kitchen for most of the day. You should be able to find me there, or if I'm not there, someone will know where I am."

Glancing inside, Sophie saw a bed with a bright quilt, a nightstand with a lamp, and the edge of a dresser. The room had a warmth and personalization to it, but it was still clearly a room reserved for guests.

Sophie and Birdie thanked Riona for her hospitality. With a final reminder to find her if they needed anything, Riona hustled back down the hallway, disappearing down the wide staircase.

"I need to call Milton. I'll see you in a bit?" Birdie said, ready to stay if Sophie needed her.

"Of course. Tell him I said hi. I think I'm going to try and get some rest," Sophie responded, watching as Birdie entered her room.

Stepping into her room, Sophie spotted her bag waiting for her on the dresser. Looking to her right, there was a painting of rolling green hills that dropped suddenly into gray cliffs. At the bottom of the cliffs, a dark sea roiled and churned. It was beautiful but filled Sophie with melancholy. There was a sense of loss to the painting. She assumed it was a painting of the Irish coast. Sophie ran a hand along the green and white patterned quilt on the way to look out the large window on the opposite side of the room, facing the backyard.

Stopping in front of the window, Sophie finally got to see the extent of open space out back that Fergal had bragged about. The clan house was one end of the long rectangle of space, giving Sophie a full view of the entire area. Below, there were tables and seats with umbrellas and an unlit fire pit. Beyond that was a playground, followed by gardens and morphing into a wooded area. People and wolfhounds swarmed over the area, some scurrying about and some lounging.

A soft knock at the door had Sophie drawing her attention away from the scene below. She called out for whoever was at the entrance to enter.

"It's me," Birdie called out as she opened the door and entered the room. She came over and joined Sophie, looking out at the bustling activity below.

"This place is interesting. The people seem nice. Lots of families," Birdie commented, pointing to two women pushing toddlers on swings.

"Yeah, it's nice. Did you get a chance to talk to Milton?" When Birdie nodded her head, Sophie asked, "Did the call go okay? Did he believe your story?"

"Oh yes, there's no problem there. I told him you were driving me down to Fresno to see a sick niece."

"I hate that you had to lie because of me. I'm sorry I dragged you into this."

"I'm not," Birdie retorted. "You didn't drag me into anything. I'm here of my own free will, and I'm happy to be here with you. This is fun."

"Fun? Are you crazy? This isn't fun. I've put you in danger."

"No, you haven't. Mac is just being cautious. I'm in no danger. It sounds like you're the one in real danger. And I'm glad that I'm here to watch your back. Besides, I'm considering this an adventure. And you know my middle name's Adventure."

"Your middle name is Roberta," Sophie scoffed.

Birdie airily waved away Sophie's statement. "Whatever. Either way, I'm glad to be here."

"I'm glad you're here too," Sophie admitted.

"I was going to find a TV and watch my shows. Do you want to come with me?" Birdie asked.

"Normally, I'd say yes. But it's been a long night, and I'm exhausted. I'm going to try and get some sleep."

"If you're sure," Birdie replied slowly.

"I'm sure, Birdie. Enjoy your shows."

Birdie gave Sophie a long, considering look before squeezing her arm with a bony hand and heading out. The door closed softly behind her as Sophie turned back to the window to watch the people marching to and fro below. They all seemed so happy and carefree. They didn't doubt themselves. They weren't scared.

Sophie stared down at the activity, feeling disconnected and out of sorts. She hated this feeling. She was sick of feeling frightened and insecure. The tide of recent events had been bashing against her and tossing her ashore only to drag her back again every time she felt like she'd got her feet back under her. Fear had taken root and was secretly brewing in her belly.

This wasn't like her. She wasn't timid. She wasn't a worrier. People didn't get to make decisions for her. She was never unsure and scared. She didn't let people intimidate her. Sophie kicked those kinds of people in the teeth. How had she let herself give in to doubt and fear?

The uncertainty needed to end. Now. She refused to live under the shadow of constant fear.

"Enough is enough," Sophie announced. She wasn't going to

wring her hands anymore. It wasn't who she was, and she wasn't going to let assholes like Alphonse and Snow White change her. She was allowing them to get to her and make her doubt herself. "No more," she vowed.

She decided that she couldn't ignore the danger in her life, but she would not let it rule her. She could acknowledge the fear and paranoia, then move past it. Sophie could feel herself shedding the invisible weight. Her shoulders straightened with her resolve.

Turning away from the window, she decided that taking a steaming hot shower and then getting some rest would probably help the most.

After vigorously scrubbing the night off, she slipped beneath the crisp cool sheets with a contented sigh. Despite the long shower, a full belly, and exhaustion weighing heavy on her, it took Sophie a long time to finally succumb to sleep.

CHAPTER 16

Sophie woke up feeling reinvigorated. Glancing out the window, she guessed that it was early evening. The rosy tint of the setting sun cast a blush on the buildings outside her window. Reaching over to the nightstand, Sophie snagged her phone. After checking and finding no messages, she quickly dialed Mac's number.

"Hey, Soph, everything okay?" Mac asked, his voice low and growly like he was about to turn furry and tear apart anything that threatened her. The idea made Sophie giddy. Sophie nestled back into her pillow; the phone pressed to her ear and a smile on her face.

"Everything's fine. I just woke up and wanted to check in with you. Any news?"

"Not really. Of the fingerprints Larry pulled from your apartment, almost all of them look like they belong to you. There are a few that weren't yours, but they're not matching anything in the database. We'll see if anything turns up, but I'm not that hopeful. Snow White seems like she's too careful to make a simple mistake like that."

"You're probably right," Sophie agreed.

"She's going to slip up and get caught soon though. I'm sure of it."

"How can you be so sure?"

"Because I'm damn good at my job," Mac growled, his voice deep and smoky.

Sophie swallowed a chuckle; Mac was in no danger of falling victim to false modesty.

Getting out of bed, Sophie walked over to the window. The shared space out back was still busy with people even as the evening rolled into dusk. She watched as a wolfhound puppy dashed under her window. The puppy was all long legs that vastly outsized its body. With a high-pitched yip, the hound morphed into a naked toddler who was then scooped up by a woman who Sophie assumed was the mother.

"If there are Irish wolfhound shifters, does that mean there are chihuahua shifters? Or Pomeranians?"

"Not as far as I know," Mac replied with a chuckle.

"What's the craziest kind of shifter you know of?"

"Hmmm. Well, let's see. I've met a few honey badgers. You'd like them. They were crazy, willing to fight anybody, and would eat just about anything. But the weirdest shifter I've ever heard of is the pangolin."

"A what?"

"A pangolin. They kinda look like what would happen if an armadillo and a pinecone had a baby. I've heard that there are very few pangolin shifters left in the world. I've personally never met one. But that is probably the craziest shifter type I know of."

"I would love to see that," Sophie said wistfully.

"Maybe we can someday. We just need to get through this first," Mac murmured.

"I was going to get dressed and wander down to get some food. Are you off work soon? Do you want to join me for dinner?"

"I wish I could, but I have a ton of work to finish here. I plan to take a photo of Alphonse and a few of his top pack members, including the late Zachary Dupree, and see if any of Derek Gibson's neighbors recognize them. But maybe we can coordinate your lunch hour at work tonight."

Sophie remembered Zachary Dupree vividly – she wasn't soon going to forget him begging to spare his human girlfriend's life. The other name was familiar, but Sophie was having trouble placing it.

"Derek Gibson – who's that?"

"That government guy killed by a pack of wolves, remember?"

"Oh jeez. How could I forget?"

Reggie had warned her that eventually Sophie would see so many dead bodies that she'd become numb to them. That the faces would start to blur and be easily forgotten. Sophie had shaken her head in silent denial. The death visions ensured that she would never become numb to the victim's death, especially the violent ones. Besides, she hadn't forgotten Derek Gibson. The image of his body crumpled on the forest floor at the feet of wolves while slowly bleeding out was still fresh in Sophie's mind. In a way, she felt like she had been there with him. His name was something Sophie had only seen written on a piece of paper, but his death was something she had experienced.

In the beginning, the deaths in her visions had been something Sophie had watched from the sidelines. Just a spectator. But more and more, she had been experiencing them as if she was the victim herself. It was impossible to forget or quickly move on from that. It had become harder and harder to separate herself from each death.

However, she realized she needed to find a way to let all their deaths go. It had all become too personal. If Sophie continued to carry the burden of each murder, she would burn herself out. She needed to stop putting all of herself into her job and her ability. It didn't mean she didn't care – she did, deeply – she just couldn't keep carrying the hurt and responsibility of each person's death in her heart. The strain was getting to be too much. She felt like a salmon continuously swimming upstream, with the unrelenting pressure trying to sweep her under and drag her down. How she would achieve that distance when she experienced all their fear and pain was a mystery.

"Well, there *has* been a lot going on lately," Mac teased, pulling Sophie out of her morose thoughts.

"There has? Hmm. I hadn't noticed," Sophie replied, tapping her chin in mock confusion. "You think some of Gibson's neighbors might have seen something?"

"I'm hopeful. If I can place some of Alphonse's people near the kidnapping, I can start asking uncomfortable questions."

They chatted for a few more minutes before Sophie promised to text him once she was safe inside the morgue later that night.

After a refreshing shower – did everyone in this city have decent water pressure besides her? – Sophie knocked on Birdie's door, wanting to check on her. When no answer came, Sophie decided to head down to the downstairs pub for dinner.

She wandered down the stairs and into the pub's dining area. Riona was bustling between tables, carrying plates and drinks, moving in a coordinated dance that spoke of years of practice. After depositing her last burden, Riona came over and waved Sophie towards an empty table.

"I was looking for Birdie. Have you seen her?"

"I think she's in the game room. It's right across the hall," Riona replied, pointing through the arched entry of the pub to a closed door on the other side of the hall.

Sophie thanked her and headed over to the game room. Cracking the door open, Sophie peeked in. There were several circular tables with people gathered around them, each holding playing cards in their hands. Sophie spotted Birdie at a game table across the room. Opening the door let light into the dim room, causing all the occupants to glance up from their games.

"Sophie!" Birdie called, waving Sophie over. She pointed to an empty chair on her right when Sophie approached the table. As she took the seat, Sophie gave the other three occupants around the table surreptitious looks. One was a woman with a soft cloud of white hair and a thick pearl necklace with a gentle smile. The other two were older men who could have passed for brothers. Both were wearing tweed Kerry caps, cable-knit sweaters in shades of brown and olive, and matching crooked grins.

Birdie introduced them as Colleen, Ethan, and William, each one greeting her with a "How are ya?" Sophie felt compelled to answer each with a "Not so bad. And you?"

Colleen started pointing out each person around the room, giving Sophie their name and relevant information, like if they were a cheat at cards or prone to bluffing. Sophie waved to each person, forgetting each name almost as soon as Colleen finished the introduction.

At first glance, Sophie thought they were playing poker, but they were holding too many cards for that. Birdie explained that they were playing bridge when Sophie inquired. She watched the action for a few minutes, trying to figure out how the game worked. Birdie explained the rules as the group at her table played.

"When you've finished with your game, would you like to join me for dinner?" Sophie asked.

"Oh, I already ate, Sophie. However, I would be happy to sit with you while you eat."

Sophie was shaking her head before Birdie completed her offer. "Absolutely not. Stay here with your friends. Enjoy your game."

After several minutes of assurances that she was fine to eat alone, Sophie headed back to the pub, waving goodbye to the room of geezers.

Grabbing a seat at an empty table, Sophie breathed deeply of the delicious aromas of food around her. A moment later, a teen girl approached Sophie asking if she'd like to eat.

"The cook made beef and barley stew or bangers with colcannon for dinner tonight."

Remembering the blood sausage, Sophie decided to stick to the familiar and picked the beef stew. The server was barely gone a minute before she returned, bearing a large steaming bowl with a hunk of bread. Sophie had the urge to rub her hands together like a villain. The first bite had Sophie groaning. By the third bite, she had left all civilization behind and was shoveling the food into her mouth like an animal.

A body landing in the chair to her left had her manners returning to her. Before she even glanced over, Sophie knew that it was Fergal. He had a presence that you could feel as well as see.

Turning in her seat, Sophie gave Fergal her full attention. "Good evening, Fergal. Thank you for taking me in."

"It's our pleasure. Happy to help Mac and any of his friends. I owe him my life, so giving someone a room is a small thing," Fergal replied. "I hope you are enjoying your stay. Is the room to your satisfaction?"

"Everything is great," Sophie replied fervently. "This place is amazing. I love what you've done here."

"I agree. I am very proud of the clan house and my clan. We've worked hard to make a place that is safe for my people. Not just where the wolfhounds are safe, but where they can thrive."

Fergal waved over the young woman as she walked past.

"Mom said you can't have any more stew," the girl lectured. The tone of voice sounded exactly like Riona's, making Sophie bite her lips to hold in a laugh.

"Well then, I'll take some apple cake. I am the clan leader, and I can have cake whenever I want."

"Fine, I'll get you a piece. But I'm telling mom," the girl warned.

"I'm not scared of her," Fergal retorted, but the girl's snort told a different tale.

Turning her attention back to her meal so Sophie could hide

her amusement, she could feel Fergal fix her with the sharp stare of an eagle, or perhaps more appropriately, a hound. Shoving a spoonful of stew into her mouth, Sophie returned his gimlet eye.

Normally, if someone were staring her down like this, she'd give them a hard time. Tell them to take a photo or give them the finger. However, something about Fergal made her pause. He seemed laidback and jovial at first glance, but there was something in his eyes that let Sophie know that Fergal was dangerous. He was joking and smiling at her, but Sophie knew that the moment she became any kind of threat to Fergal or his pack, he would cut her throat without a second's hesitation and not lose a single minute of sleep over it. He was not someone to be trifled with. Family and clan came first for Fergal, and the rest of the world came a very distant second. Sophie respected that and understood his unspoken stance, but she also knew that she was part of that distant second – even if she and Fergal eventually became friends.

Fergal's daughter dropping off the piece of cake interrupted their staring contest.

"So, tell me. How did you run afoul of Alphonse?" Fergal asked, forking a large bite of cake into his mouth. Turning, he waved his hand to get his daughter's attention, mouthing the word 'coffee' at her.

"I can't tell you that. It's part of an ongoing investigation. You'd need to ask Mac to get any information about that. However, I can tell you that he has a problem with a human working in the Mythical division of the ME's office."

Fergal harrumphed at her reply but seemed to accept the answer. "That sounds like the Alphonse I know. He's never met a human he didn't have a problem with. Patrick Senior has agreed to train you so we'll make you as prepared to deal with Alphonse as we can get a human. You'll start tomorrow morning. I promised Mac we'd take care of you, and we will. Hey, did Mac ever tell you how we met?" Fergal asked, a wide grin splitting his face. When Sophie shook her head, Fergal slouched back into his chair as if getting settled in.

"Back when my father was still the alpha of this clan, I was his second in command, training and preparing to take his place. My uncle, unbeknownst to my cousin Eoghan, decided that his son would be the superior choice to run the clan instead of me. Eoghan had zero desire to be the alpha, so I have no idea how my uncle John came to this conclusion. John knew that Eoghan couldn't beat me in a dominance fight – even if he could somehow have gotten Eoghan to challenge me. So this bleedin' idiot hired several bear shifters to murder me. They jumped me coming out of my favorite pub late one night. They dragged me behind the bar and did their darnedest to end my life. They surely would have killed me if Mac hadn't happened to have been driving past on patrol and saw them grab me.

"By the time he'd parked his car and made it around the back of the pub, I'd had to shift to my wolfhound form to defend myself. Despite that, I was being soundly thrashed. In my defense, there were four of them. He yelled and waved his gun and badge around, and the cowards ran off. He was checking me over when we heard the sirens of police approaching. We both needed to get away before any humans arrived. There's no good way to explain claw marks, if you know what I mean. I was too injured to make it out on my own, and my wolfhound form was too heavy for Mac to carry. I had to change back to human, and Mac had to carry me out of there. Naked as a newborn and bleeding like mad. Just picture my naked arse hanging out there for all the world to see as Mac carried me fireman-style and tossed me into the back of his patrol car. It's funny as hell now, and I like to tease him about it every chance I get, but he saved my life that night. I owe him a debt I don't think I'll ever be able to pay off."

The vivid picture Fergal painted made Sophie grin. She could just imagine the grumpy look on Mac's face while having a naked man slung across his shoulders.

"Wow. That's…" Sophie dropped her spoon back into her stew. "I'm just glad he was there to help you."

"I was fortunate he happened to be driving by. I've never forgotten the fact that Mac faced off against four bear shifters to save my life. I'm always going to watch out for him."

Sophie understood the unspoken message. If she ever hurt Mac, she might just end up with a pack of wolfhounds snapping at her heels.

"I'm just so glad he has a good friend like you to watch his back. I like that he has more than just me looking out for him." *Right back atcha*, Sophie thought, fluttering her eyes at Fergal.

Riona dropping off a mug of coffee was a welcome distraction.

"Are you giving this girl, who is under our sworn protection, a hard time?" Riona questioned, folding her arms in a manner befitting an angry schoolmarm.

"No, I was just telling Sophie the story of how Mac and I became friends," Fergal argued. He turned to Sophie while his wife shook her head at him. "By the way, I'll have you know that I'm such a good friend that I even paid to have his jacket from that night dry cleaned."

"He should have burned it," Sophie teased, making Riona laugh uproariously.

"I like her," Riona announced, giving Sophie a conspiratorial wink.

"Did I pass muster?" Sophie asked Fergal after Riona returned to the kitchen.

Fergal gave her a sharp, amused look. "You'll do."

Walked right into that one. Sophie rolled her eyes at herself.

CHAPTER 17

*S*everal hours later, Sophie found herself crammed into the backseat of a well-dented, souped-up sports car. It looked like the kind of vehicle that wanted to be a street racer but was primarily used for loudly revving its engine at red lights impotently. She was pressed elbow-to-elbow with one of her 'bodyguards' – Patrick. Patrick looked like he should be on a postcard for Ireland with his bright red hair and freckled face. In the front seats were Conor and Liam, who were brothers so similar in looks and age that Sophie couldn't tell them apart. Both had dark brown hair and eyes coupled with the slightly gangly look of teen boys in the middle of a growth spurt.

The boys weren't exactly Praetorian Guards. Sophie knew better than to expect Spartan warriors, but they still seemed like kids to Sophie. She couldn't take them seriously as soldiers. They smelled vaguely of Cheetos and Axe body spray. They barely had stubble gracing their chins. Looking at them made Sophie feel a thousand years old. She wasn't that much older than them, maybe six years or so, but it might as well have been thirty. She needed to find a good sturdy cane so she could shake it at the hooligans trespassing on her lawn. They talked about video games and social media personalities with dumb-sounding names and played music she'd never heard of so loud it made her ears throb.

Oh, to be young.

Finally, to Sophie's utter relief, they pulled into the parking lot of the Medical Examiner's building. Stepping out of the car to a chorus of goodbyes, Sophie patted her pocket, double-checking the reassuring lump of the taser hidden there.

"Sophie, wait!" Conor, or possibly Liam, called. Turning back to the vehicle, Sophie watched as he dangled a small cooler bag out the car window. "Miss Riona packed you a lunch."

Opening the bag, Sophie saw a transparent container filled with sausages and mashed potatoes with some sort of green vegetable mixed into it. "Please tell her I said thank you," Sophie requested, touched by the thoughtful gesture of the alpha's wife.

Stepping through the front doors of the building, Sophie looked back to see her bodyguards hanging out the car windows, watching to make sure she got inside safely. She waved them off as she entered the lobby.

Looking over toward the front desk, her feet stuttered to a stop when she saw the whole Odd Ones crew gathered in a circle and talking animatedly. Even Miss Zhao was involved.

"She's here!" Ace exclaimed, catching sight of Sophie frozen inside the lobby doors.

"Oh, thank god you're okay," Amira cried, skipping over to Sophie and pulling her into a hug.

In shock, Sophie awkwardly patted Amira on the back because she never would've pegged Amira as a hugger.

"Reggie told us everything. I can't believe Snow White broke into your apartment," Amira continued, pulling back to gaze into Sophie's face. "Are you okay?"

Sophie cleared her throat self-consciously. "I'm fine. Mac was able to find me a safe house, and he got me a couple of body-guards to escort me to and from work." Sophie specifically left out the fact that her bodyguards were not yet twenty years old and still had pimples.

"I'm just glad you're alright," Ace said gruffly, patting her shoulder before moving aside so Fitz could hug her.

Sophie gave Reggie a thankful look when he suggested to everyone that it was time to get to work.

"Miss Feegle," Miss Zhao called out, stopping Sophie as she followed the group towards their work area. Sophie shuffled back to Miss Zhao, feeling a bit like an unruly child being called to the front of the class.

Before Sophie could ask what Miss Zhao wanted, she stood up and clasped Sophie's hands in her manicured ones. "I'm glad that Detective Volpes has gotten you protection and a safe place to stay. However, you are welcome to stay with my dragon clutch if that would make you more comfortable. My family would be happy to watch over you."

"Oh wow. That's very generous. Thank you so much. I think I'm good where I am, but if I start to feel unsafe, I'll let you know."

"The offer is open. I'll make sure Detective Volpes knows too, in case of emergency."

When Sophie thanked her again, Miss Zhao inclined her head regally and turned back to her computer. Understanding that she had been dismissed, Sophie headed to the main autopsy room.

Sophie must have still looked confused or dazed when she joined Reggie in front of the schedule whiteboard. When Reggie asked what was wrong, Sophie told him about Miss Zhao's offer of protection.

"Why would she offer to help me? I was under the impression that she mostly tolerated me because she thought I was vaguely amusing. Like an unruly toddler."

"Miss Zhao wouldn't offer to take you in if she didn't care for you. Who knows how a dragon thinks? They're a bit of an enigma, even in the Mythical community. They guard their secrets even more fiercely than they do their treasure."

"Pssh, you're getting too deep for me, Reggie," Sophie teased. "You know what would take my mind off all my current troubles?"

"An autopsy?" Reggie suggested with a conspiratorial grin.

"Exactly! Let me go fetch our first customer of the night, and I'll be right back."

SOPHIE BECAME A CLOCK-WATCHER AS THE TIME WOUND CLOSER TO her lunch hour. Happy anticipation bubbled in her belly at the thought of seeing Mac. A knock on the door was their only warning before his grinning face popped through the opening.

Sophie peeled off her gloves and launched herself at Mac with a squeal, almost knocking him back into the hallway.

"Hey Reggie, I hope I'm not interrupting," Mac greeted, carrying Sophie back inside the autopsy room. His nose flared as he walked into the room, with Sophie still wrapped around his waist. "What is that smell?"

"A Jorōgumo," Sophie said, pointing to the body of a woman on the examination table, after releasing Mac but keeping an arm around his waist.

"A what?"

"A Jorōgumo is a spider shifter. They're found in Japanese mythology – always female. They only bear daughters, no sons. The legends say that the Jorōgumo was a beautiful young woman who lured unsuspecting men to their deaths," Reggie explained. "They're also known for their sweet vinegar smell."

The cloying scent of jasmine undercut with a sharp edge of vinegar filled the autopsy room, making Sophie more sympathetic to Amira's aversion to assisting Reggie. Still, Sophie decided that the strange scent of a Jorōgumo shifter wasn't even in the top ten of awful smells that Sophie had experienced during an autopsy.

"We're almost done here, so if you want to head to the breakroom, I'll be there in a few minutes," Sophie suggested to Mac.

"I can finish up here on my own, Sophie. Why don't you two go ahead and start your lunch break? I'll be there in a few minutes, and we can catch up," Reggie offered.

"You're the best boss ever," Sophie declared. Pink darkening his cheeks, Reggie waved off the compliment, turning back to the spider-woman on the autopsy table.

Dragging Mac behind her, Sophie poked her head into the breakroom, grinning when she found the room empty. Pulling Mac inside behind her, she crowded him against the door. Feeling like a tease, Sophie pressed close, hovering her mouth a breath away from Mac's. Mac's eyes gleamed with his predatory nature. Before he could make the first move, Sophie closed the gap between them, brushing her lips across his. She trailed her lips across his jaw to rub her cheek against Mac's, the rasp of stubble grabbing at her skin.

With a groan, Mac cupped Sophie's jaw, pulling her mouth back to his. Entwined together, they indulged in one another, sharing breath and kisses. Time passed in a flurry around them, colors and noise swirling past unnoticed. They made out against the door for an indeterminate while, lost in the play of tongues and the soft sound of kisses and pleasure trapped in the intimate space between them.

The sound of approaching voices broke into their awareness, making Sophie whine. With a final soft brushing of lips, they slowly unwound from each other. Sophie pushed Mac to a chair while she went to fetch her lunch.

Luckily, Riona packed enough food for Sophie that there was plenty to share with Mac. She suspected that Riona wasn't used to feeding humans. Despite having shared meals with her co-workers for months, Sophie still wasn't used to the sheer quantity of food shifters ate at each meal.

"Mac!" Ace called out happily as he entered the room, followed quickly by Amira, Fitz, and Reggie. Sophie thought that Ace and Mac barely tolerated each other's presence. Where was his usual grumpy attitude? It appeared that battling wolf shifters and Fae together at the top of a tower was some sort of male bonding experience. Amira, Fitz, and Reggie grabbed their lunches and joined Sophie and Mac at the table while Ace took his usual place at the sink to thoroughly scrub his food before he ate it.

Sophie watched as Amira pulled out a can opener from her bag and started opening yet another can of salmon. Sophie was just glad it wasn't sardines again. Watching Amira slurp down whole sardines like spaghetti noodles had put her off her lunch for a week.

"Any news?" Reggie asked Mac, taking a seat on the opposite side of Mac from Sophie.

Mac shook his head, his shoulders slumping. "No, we don't have any leads on Snow White. We still don't have any idea who she is or where she'll strike next. And we couldn't find Zachary Dupree's human girlfriend. I feel like we're just spinning our wheels while Snow White runs around free."

Sophie stared pensively at the worn Formica, tracing her finger along a groove in the tabletop, annoyed with the lack of progress. *What good is having these dreams and visions if I can't track down one person?*

"You'll get it figured out," Ace replied, unwavering confidence in his voice. Mac gave him a grateful look. Was Sophie getting to watch the birth of a bromance? She hid her snicker since it didn't seem like an appropriate time.

"We just need to make sure that we keep Sophie safe," Reggie said, drying up her amusement and making a lump form in her throat. Reggie was always looking out for her. Even after being friends for several months now, it never failed to move Sophie.

"We have someone watching Sophie's apartment, day and night. Plus, I have some bodyguards escorting Sophie to and from work. They're on the lookout for anything suspicious," Mac assured Reggie. "Thankfully, the chief is taking this seriously and allowing me to use department resources for Snow White. Not much more I can do until she reveals herself."

"Did you turn up anything at Derek Gibson's neighborhood? Did anyone see any of Alphonse's pack members grab him?" Sophie asked, deciding to change the subject.

"It was a total bust. I went door to door and showed photos of Alphonse's top pack members, but no one in the entire street recognized any of them. I was hoping that one of the neighbors had been the Good Samaritan that called it in. But nothing."

"Could it have been the human girlfriend?" Sophie asked, thinking of the now-missing woman.

"Neesa Jacobs? Possibly, but I doubt it. After talking to some of her known associates, I doubt that Dupree told her much. She wasn't exactly Good Samaritan material, but you never know. Her neighbor said that she was strung out so often that she was practically catatonic most times. That doesn't mean that she wasn't our caller. We need to find her to determine if she knew anything, but I suspect she won't be turning up alive."

If Alphonse's pack had got a hold of Neesa as they suspected, Sophie doubted that they'd ever see her alive again. Once they dealt with Snow White, Sophie was keen to turn her full attention to the Sunset District pack.

"Could it have been Snow White? You said the caller was a woman, right? In my dream, it felt like she'd been following Alphonse for a while now. Maybe she saw them grab Derek."

"Maybe. But why would she call the police about the kidnapping but not call-in warnings about the other killers she's offed? I don't know if it fits into her MO. She seems like she enjoys taking out the trash herself," Ace suggested as he finally joined everyone at the table. Sophie was surprised the apple he'd been washing still had any skin left.

Sophie tapped her nails on the Formica, trying to remember what it felt like to be in Snow White's head. Trying to remember her thought process felt like trying to hold sand. "In all my dreams and visions, Snow White only went for the kill if she could get her target alone. When the wolves grabbed Derek, there were a whole bunch of them."

"Can we get a copy of the call? At least then we'd possibly know what Snow White's voice sounds like. If it was her, that is," Fitz suggested.

Mac pulled out his notepad, quickly scribbling. "That's a good idea. I'll see what I can do."

Fitz gave Sophie a pleased grin like he was happy to be helping. Sophie watched as he speared an egg from his cobb salad and ate it.

"You're a snow goose shifter... It's alright for you to eat eggs?"

"This is a *chicken* egg," Fitz retorted, spearing another wedge of hard-boiled egg. "I'm a snow goose. It's an entirely different species of bird. It's not cannibalism."

Sophie briefly wondered if snow goose shifters laid eggs instead of giving live birth. She assumed that since shifters were primarily human with the ability to shift to other creatures, that made them mammals even if their other forms were not mammalian. She knew there were avian and even reptile shifters, but she assumed they were categorized as mammals. Maybe she'd ask Reggie later.

"Do cow shifters exist? And, if they do, would it be cannibalism if they ate a hamburger?"

Everyone groaned at the table, used to Sophie's questions about Mythicals by now.

"I've never heard of bovine shifters," Reggie stated. "Actually, I don't think I've heard of any shifters where the animal is used in farming agriculture. No chickens, pigs, cows, or even turkeys."

"Some people eat goose, right? I've never eaten goose," Sophie quickly assured Fitz. "But would a snow goose ever eat a regular goose? Would that be considered cannibalism?"

Fitz dropped his fork into his salad bowl with a shudder. "I don't know if that would be cannibalism, but I would never eat goose. Never. At the very least, it would be in poor taste."

For a moment, Mac looked at Sophie like he was dealing with a lunatic, but then a slow smirk spread across his face.

"I've heard that in the South, they eat raccoon. I've been told that it's pretty tasty, but the meat is tough and gamey," Mac said conversationally to Sophie, his eyes shining with repressed laughter.

Ace sputtered, almost choking on the sip of soda he'd just taken. "I'll show you tough, Mac. You two are disgusting." Ace growled, rolling his eyes at Amira as Sophie and Mac cracked up.

"If anyone makes a joke about cats and Chinese food, you're gonna get my bowl of salmon and rice dumped on your head," Amira warned, one manicured finger sharpened to a claw-like tip pointing at each person gathered around the table.

As laughter and jokes filled the room, Sophie was pleased to see the atmosphere had lightened up. Everyone was smiling and teasing. Snow White had been a dark cloud hovering over all their heads, not just Sophie's. What she wouldn't give to get rid of her permanently. And that couldn't happen until Snow White finally showed her face.

Sophie didn't like to sit on her hands, waiting for life to happen to her. She was sick and tired of waiting to see what Snow White would do next. She went out and made things happen. It chafed that she was stuck in the waiting game now.

Or was she?

"I have an idea, but you're not gonna like it," Sophie announced, turning in her seat to face Mac. "I hate sitting around waiting for Snow White to strike. We know she's interested in me, right? We should use me as bait. We can draw her out."

The uproar Sophie's suggestion created was impressive. Everyone was talking over one another, arguing the idea down. Sophie grimaced. She hadn't meant to obliterate everyone's good mood. However, it was just a little glorious that everyone was so outraged by the thought of Sophie putting herself in harm's way.

"Hell. No," Mac stated, his loud announcement cutting off the arguing. "We are not putting you into that kind of danger. Snow White killed a wolf shifter. One of Alphonse's top enforcers. It's too dangerous. It's not worth risking your life over."

"I think we can all agree that my life is already in danger," Sophie pointed out.

"You're staying in a safe house, and you have bodyguards. You're in a building guarded by a dragon. You're as safe as I can make you," Mac grabbed Sophie's hands. "I want to catch her just as badly as you, but we are not using you as bait. We'll find another way. There must be some other way to draw her out. Promise me you won't try to do anything stupid."

Sophie held Mac's gaze, not wanting to agree with his request but understanding his stance. She would feel the same way if Mac suggested putting himself in danger.

"Alright, I promise I won't do anything stupid. I just want to get this solved and get Snow White off the streets. People's lives are at stake, even if that person is Alphonse."

"What about using Alphonse as bait instead?" Amira suddenly announced. As one, everyone turned to look at her. The statement resonated through the abruptly silent room and hung, quivering in the air. The sudden silence held for a moment before Amira shrugged her shoulder, flipping a dark lock of hair back. "We know that Snow White has been following Alphonse too. I think that if we can find a way to dangle Alphonse in front of her, she won't be able to resist."

"I like it. But how do we do this without Alphonse knowing?

If he gets any idea that Snow White's after him or that we know about some of his recent actions, he'll circle the wagons, and we'll lose the opportunity," Mac argued.

"Is it ethical to use him as bait without his knowledge?" Reggie asked, biting his lip in worry.

"He's already bait. We just need more eyes on Alphonse. Or some way to track him. If we know where he is, then we can keep an eye out for Snow White. This will make him safer if you think about it," Mac said. "I'm going to talk to Larry in the morning and see if he has any ideas. Maybe he can put a tracking spell on Alphonse or something."

As everyone finished up their lunches, Sophie watched Mac stifle a yawn. It might be lunchtime for Sophie and her co-workers, but it was the middle of the night for the rest of the world. Sophie felt touched that Mac would get up in the middle of the night just to join her.

Bidding everyone a good night, Mac headed to the exit to get home and catch a few hours of sleep before he needed to be at the station in the morning.

Standing in the lobby, watching the taillights of Mac's sensible car turn the corner, Sophie felt a sense of impending doom – as if everyone she cared about was sprinting headlong towards disaster, and there was nothing she could do to stop it.

CHAPTER 18

*S*ophie's days had fallen into an easy rhythm. Most evenings, she had dinner with Mac at the clan house once his shift was over. Usually, Birdie joined them for the meal and to flirt with Mac. He caught them up on the progress – or, rather, the lack of progress – with Snow White's and Alphonse's cases. At night, Sophie assisted Reggie with autopsies, recording death visions on Reggie's phone. Her bodyguards drove her to and from the ME's office like clockwork each morning and night. The lads, as Fergal called them, had started to grow on Sophie. She still felt like a den mother in charge of a bunch of rowdy frat boys, but they were so good-natured it was impossible to hold their puppy-like exuberance against them. Once Sophie arrived back at the clan house in the morning, she had breakfast with Birdie and Fergal, then got her ass kicked by Patrick Senior. Once she went to bed, the cycle began all over again.

Where Patrick Junior was a lanky boy with hair the color of a new penny, his father was a mountain of a man with dark auburn hair. With his thick beard and wild mane of hair, he looked like he should've lived in a stone castle and worn a kilt. She suspected that some of his ancestors were probably called laird of the manor. Other than their red hair, father and son hardly looked related. Until you looked into their identical green eyes.

Patrick Senior, who preferred to be called Paddy, spent a great deal of time knocking Sophie to the ground and then making her get back up again, pointing out how she should've blocked his moves. He seemed to take great delight in pummeling his students. The first few days of lessons with Paddy had left Sophie's butt as one massive bruise.

However, slowly but surely, over the last week Sophie had started to improve. It was a relief to her poor ass. Paddy said she was a natural, but faced against a mountain in human form, it certainly didn't feel that way.

Sophie had started wishing that she'd have a dream about Snow White and her activities, even her murderous ones, before climbing into her bed each morning. Anything to move things along. However, her dreams had been annoyingly mundane for the last week. Sophie missed her apartment. She missed going to the pub and hanging out with Burg. She even missed arguing with her landlord. Sophie was more than ready for things to get back to normal. Well, her kind of normal, anyway.

On Thursday, Sophie – along with her escorts – had hit up a metaphysical supply shop and bookstore in the Haight-Ashbury district. Apparently, modern witches and warlocks no longer foraged for eye of newt and toe of frog in dank forests. They just hopped down to their local supply shop. Sophie had found a few books about lucid dreaming and astral projection.

She'd been reading them in the fervent hope that she could take better control of her dreams and visions. So far, she hadn't had any luck, but she still had two more books waiting for her on her nightstand.

A few days prior, Larry the Warlock had managed to put a tracking spell on Alphonse. When Sophie asked how, Mac explained that they'd used a strand of Alphonse's hair to make the spell work.

"How did you manage to get a hair off Alphonse?" Sophie had asked. Alphonse was such a pressure-cooker of rage and aggression that she couldn't imagine the danger involved in stealing anything from him.

"Carefully," Mac had replied with a breathless laugh. Sophie pulled a sulky face at that non-answer. Even after days of pestering him, Mac hadn't given up his secret hair-retrieval methods. Sophie suspected that he had just bribed one of his pack members, but Mac enjoyed getting on Sophie's nerves too much to give up his secret. Days later, Sophie was no closer to her answer. Maybe she'd ask Larry next time she saw him.

Despite the cheerful chatter of the other people filling the clan dining room tonight, a dark cloud hovered over Mac. He stabbed up a bite of shepherd's pie and stuffed it in his mouth like it had insulted his mother.

"Everything okay, sweetheart?" Birdie asked. Sophie was glad Birdie spoke up; she was worried that he'd damage the cutlery if he kept it up. He was so annoyed he wasn't even preening under Birdie's praise like usual.

"Alphonse is the worst bait in existence. He barely ever leaves his compound. Snow White can't reveal herself if Alphonse doesn't leave."

Mac pulled out a paper map of the city again with a grumble, checking if the red dot that represented Alphonse had moved from the pack headquarters on Noriega Street. Mac folded up the map with precise movements and a wordless snarl before tucking it back into his pocket, only to pull it out again five minutes later.

Alphonse had only left his house on a couple of occasions, and he never went far. Sophie asked if Alphonse had perhaps realized that he was being tracked. Mac explained that the alpha was known for being an isolationist, so his homebody tendencies weren't an indication that he was on to them.

Mac decided to drown his frustrations in the bottom of a pint glass. By the time Sophie needed to leave for work, he was in a much better mood, but in no shape to drive himself home. He happily accepted Sophie's offer for him to sleep in her room in the clan house. Perhaps if she hurried home in the morning, they could get in some alone time before Mac would have to head to the station and she had her training. If Mac wasn't too hungover, that was.

"Don't you need to work in the morning? How're you gonna function if you're hungover?" Sophie warned, watching Mac drain the last dregs of beer from his glass.

"Shifter metabolism." Mac shrugged. "It means that I'll be sober in just a few hours. I don't get hungover."

"Lucky," Birdie griped. Sophie nodded in agreement, thinking of her last hangover. Years later and the thought of gin and tonics still turned her stomach.

Sophie couldn't wait for the weekend so she could spend more time with Mac than just a shared meal. The bed at the clan house was soft and comfortable, but it was lonely. Sophie was sick of sliding into cold empty sheets each morning.

"We need a way to draw Alphonse out. It's taking too long for him to come out on his own."

"You're right," Mac exclaimed, straightening up from his slump. "If we set up when and how we get Alphonse out of his headquarters, we can draw him to a place of our choosing. That'll let us control the environment. We can set the perfect trap."

"How're we gonna do that?"

"I need to talk to the chief. If I tried to pull off an operation like this without his approval and input, he'd put my balls in a vice." The change in Mac's demeanor was almost instantaneous. He was now sitting up, tapping his thumbs on the table in thought, eyes gleaming.

Checking the time on her phone, Sophie let Mac know that she needed to leave. Tugging Mac from his chair, Sophie stopped so he could give Birdie her nightly kiss on the cheek. Then she led him down the stairs to where the lads would be waiting to take Sophie to work. As they got to the bottom of the stairs, Sophie spotted the boys loitering out front, waiting for her to show up. Conor turned and raised his hand in greeting when he spotted Sophie. She was finally able to tell the two brothers apart. Conor was the older brother. He was a little taller and more filled out. He also had a small scar through one of his eyebrows.

Mac twirled Sophie around, pressing her back against the wall. He gave Sophie a kiss that curled her toes, sparks of pleasure rolling down her back. With his lips a millimeter from her, his eyes shiny from drink, he whispered, "I wish you didn't have to go, hellraiser."

"Me too, dickhead," Sophie whispered back, watching as Mac gazed at her lips longingly. The look in his eyes made Sophie's stomach swoop like she was on a rollercoaster.

Shaking his head as if pulling himself out of a daze, Mac glanced over to the front door. Sophie followed his eyes to see her bodyguards all spin away, reminding her that they had an audience. She threaded her hand in Mac's hair, running her nails along his scalp before using the strands to tug his attention away from the boys and back to her.

"Do you have any plans this weekend?" Sophie asked once she'd caught his eyes.

"Take-out and you in my bed," Mac suggested with a devilish grin.

"That sounds perfect," Sophie replied with a groan of longing. Mac searched her face before dipping his head to fit their lips together in a lingering kiss.

Sophie made a whiny sound in her throat and pulled back, "I have to go."

"Just a minute more," Mac said between more kisses.

Several minutes later, Sophie stumbled out the door with the feeling of Mac's eyes on her warming her back. Sophie let herself look at Mac for a long moment, locking eyes with his bright blue ones.

"Come on, Sophie. We gotta go," one of the boys called, breaking through her reverie. Raising her hand in a final wave to Mac, Sophie headed out the door to the blushing boys who'd obviously witnessed her PDA with Mac. Sophie refused to be embarrassed by kissing her boyfriend, so she determinedly stepped past them and headed to the car parked on the street.

Standing next to the car, Sophie looked back to watch as the lads scurried after her.

Idiots, Sophie thought fondly as the boys elbowed and jostled each other. As usual, Patrick and Liam fought over who would get to sit in the front. The car belonged to Conor, the eldest of the three boys, so he always insisted on driving. He didn't trust anyone else to drive his 'baby'. After wrestling for a minute, Patrick locked Liam in a headlock, his red curls bouncing and arms straining as he struggled to keep Liam contained. Finally, red-faced and panting, Liam tapped out, signaling that Patrick could sit in the front tonight. With a triumphant fist pump, Patrick hopped into the front seat.

Another car merged into their lane as they pulled onto the 101, almost clipping Conor's front bumper. Braking and swerving out of the way, Conor laid down on his horn and cussed at the clueless driver that'd nearly run them off the road.

"Nice maneuvering. Just like Lewis Hamilton," Patrick said with a fist bump to Conor after the adrenaline wore off.

"Who's that?" Sophie asked.

"Lewis Hamilton... The racecar driver?" Liam repeated an incredulous look on his face. As if Sophie had just asked who the president was.

"Oh, yeah, I don't watch Nascar," Sophie explained.

Patrick gasped in outrage. "It's Formula 1, not Nascar!" If he'd been wearing pearls, he'd have clutched them.

Liam gave Sophie a sideways glance indicating he was dealing with a particularly dimwitted creature. Sophie felt whatever small amount of respect she'd built with the boys slipping away.

Figures.

As they drove to work, Sophie stared out the window wondering where Snow White was. Nearing her work building, Sophie tried to see if any car or pedestrian looked out of place. Paranoia had a stranglehold on her because everyone looked suspicious. She couldn't wait for Snow White to finally be caught so the sensation of always needing to look over her shoulder would go away.

~

SEVERAL HOURS LATER, SOPHIE WAS ZIPPING UP THE BODY BAG ON A staked vampire having just completed his autopsy.

Sophie was about to roll him back to the fridge when Reggie's demeanor pulled her up short. Peeling his gloves off and tossing them in the trash, Reggie started chewing on his thumbnail – a sure sign that he was worried about something.

"Everything okay, Reg?"

"The victim's Domus leader is going to be enraged when he finds out that one of his vampires has been going outside the Domus to feed on humans. What's worse is your vision makes me think this guy wasn't the only one doing so. Remember? He received that text from someone named Preston saying he wouldn't be able to join him for dinner just before this guy attempted to grab that woman. I'm almost certain they have been hunting humans together, and I'm sure the Domus leader Raphael will agree. As one of the bigger Domus houses in the city, they have dozens of Volos in-house to feed the vampires. No one in the Domus needs to feed outside their house. The fact that his vampire got caught by a group of hunters and staked only adds insult to injury. I know the Domus leader, and he is about to go apoplectic. Plus, when the Conclave finds out that Raphael's Domus has courted exposure to the human world... The sanctions are going to be steep. I almost feel bad for the Domus's members."

"If there are human hunters out there hunting vampires, doesn't that mean the secret is already out?"

Reggie shrugged. "Not widespread. Mythicals have been very efficient at hiding any evidence of our existence. Those hunters are far and few between. Plus, most people think they're just conspiracist nutjobs."

"I can't believe the whole world hasn't found out about the existence of Mythicals yet. With everyone having a camera in their phone, don't you think it's just a matter of time before you guys are discovered? Humans will freak out. Like aren't you worried that the government would kidnap your people and do experiments on them or something? Or that there would be mass panic if you guys were discovered?"

"I believe humans will react better than you think. Plus, I'm sure all the different Conclaves worldwide have plans in place for that contingency. We're also well-hidden. No one meeting most Mythicals would have any way to discover we aren't human. You didn't know I was a shifter until I told you," Reggie reminded Sophie.

Sophie wasn't so sure that humans couldn't figure out ways to unearth Mythicals if their existence became general knowledge, but she decided to keep that opinion to herself.

"And you just trust that these Conclaves have it all figured out? How can you trust them that much? Shouldn't you want to know what the plan is so you can be prepared? I'd want to know the plan."

"We take a lot of precautions to make sure humans don't find out about us. We have our people planted in the government, military, police, and media. Every Conclave has Fae on staff that can alter memories, that can remove incriminating videos from online. It's much more sophisticated than you realize."

"I hope for your sake that's enough to keep your people safe.

Now that I think about it, if you know that you need to keep the existence of Mythicals hidden from humans, why did you hire me, Reg? I'm human, and you didn't know me at all. I could have been a vampire hunter for all you knew. Plus, I'm honestly a bit unqualified for this job." She was more than a bit unqualified, but Sophie wasn't about to point that out to her boss. "How could you be sure I wouldn't spill the secret of Mythicals' existence? If I had been you, I wouldn't have hired me."

"Gut instinct. When I met you, I don't know, I just knew. My instincts have never steered me wrong yet. We're surrounded by magic every day. I've learned to trust in it," Reggie replied. Sophie suspected that Reggie just had a soft spot for people who were down on their luck, which was undoubtedly where Sophie had been when they'd found each other. Maybe she was just cynical, but Sophie would never blindly trust strangers as Reggie had. "However, speaking of being unqualified," Reggie continued, "I want you to look into getting your Medical Assistant Certification. City College has a program for it starting next month. It'll take less than six months to complete."

"Reg... I can't afford to pay for classes right now," Sophie replied, embarrassment making her cheeks darken. "I'll need to save up for a little bit before I can afford it."

"I'm certain that the ME's office will sponsor you as part of our Continuing Education program. I'm a member of the committee for that program so I know I can make it happen for you. So don't worry about the cost, just go get signed up. We'll figure it out."

Pressure pushed at Sophie's eyes from Reggie's care and thoughtfulness. Turning her head away, she had to blink away the wetness. Straightening her shoulders, she gave Reggie a wide smile.

"I don't wanna go back to school. I suck at school," Sophie play-whined, channeling her inner middle-schooler.

"Tough shit," Reggie snarked back, making Sophie bark out a

surprised laugh. Some of her potty mouth was starting to rub off on her sweet boss.

"I think I'm a bad influence on you," Sophie teased.

"Hardly," Reggie snorted. "There's something else I've been meaning to talk to you about. I have an acquaintance who is an expert in psychometry that I want you to meet with."

"Psychometry? What's that? Is it similar to psychiatry? Are you suggesting that I need a shrink?"

"Almost certainly," Reggie joked. "But, no, psychometry is what I think your gift is. I've been doing some research in this field. It's also called token-object reading. It's the ability to read the history of an object by touching it. My contact at UC Berkeley had never heard of psychometry that was tied specifically to death. However, after describing your abilities, she thinks it's possible. She's very interested in meeting you. I told her that'd be up to you."

Sophie *hmm*ed noncommittally, not sure she wanted anyone else to know about her ability. The more people that knew, the higher the odds that it wouldn't stay a secret.

"You're sure this person can be trusted?" Sophie confirmed, waiting for Reggie to nod before continuing. "I wish you had asked me first before you told a stranger about my abilities."

"I never told her your name or even how we know each other. You don't have to meet her, but she's an expert in her field, and I think she can help. Even if you don't meet her, she has some interesting ideas. She suggested that we should run some tests to see if you can get readings off murder weapons. And to touch things that people had been touching or holding when they died and see if you could pull any imprints. It'll help us determine if your gift only works on people or if we can expand your repertoire. Imagine if you could touch a knife and see what happened? We'd be able to solve even more crimes. Even ones without a body."

Sophie agreed that it would be worth exploring. Understanding the limits of her skills just made sense.

Excitement had grabbed ahold of Reggie, and he was throwing out ideas. "Have you ever got a reading on an animal's death? I wonder if we can find a way to get ahold of a dead animal..."

"I don't think so. I've never touched any recently deceased animals. But frankly, if I could see the final moments of every chicken nugget I tried to eat, I'd be a vegetarian already."

"I can imagine," Reggie grimaced. "I wonder if, during the process of butchering and handling the meat in the factories and stores, the visions get destroyed. I still think we should test it out. I know someone who owns a veterinarian clinic. We'll have to think of a good reason why we want you to touch one of the dead animals."

Sophie shrugged. She doubted she could get any visions from someone's dead cat or such, but she was willing to try.

"I'd like to run several tests. We haven't figured out the limits of your gift yet. Can you pull visions from a body that has been dead a long time, like years after they died? Or what about someone who's been dismembered? Could you get a reading from a small piece, like a finger? Could you imagine if you touched a mummy and could see their final moments? Imagine the possibilities!"

Sophie couldn't find it in herself to be annoyed in the face of Reggie's enthusiasm. "How would we get ahold of a mummy?" Sophie asked, only half-joking.

"I believe the San Francisco State University has a few. The mummies used to be in the collection owned by Adolph Sutro. I'll look into it. If I remember correctly, they put the artifacts on display periodically. I saw it on the news once," Reggie promised.

"Sutro? Like Sutro Tower?"

"He was the mayor in the 1800s. I assume the tower was named after him," Reggie replied with a shrug. Sophie briefly considered looking it up on her phone but decided she didn't care enough to bother.

"I would be shocked if I could pull a death vision off a mummy. However, if you get me one, I'll try it out," Sophie promised, pushing her vampire victim out of the room, Reggie's chuckle following her.

~

"Bye, Miss Zhao. Have a good day," Sophie called out. As she walked out, Sophie stuffed the brochure and application for the Medical Assistant Certification program that Reggie had given her into her messenger bag.

"You too, dear," Miss Zhao replied, unaware of Sophie's inner turmoil.

The weak morning sun broke through the clouds in patchy shades of gray. The light was feeble and watery, barely enough to warm Sophie's shoulders, but after enduring rain every day that week, it was a welcome relief. Squinting, Sophie looked to the spot where Conor usually parked. She couldn't stop her grin when she spotted Mac talking to her bodyguards. The hero worship plastered all over their faces was the cutest thing ever. Liam noticed Sophie and pointed over Mac's shoulder. Turning to face her, Mac gave Sophie a welcoming grin.

Several long strides later and Mac swept her up into his arms. His posture and expression vibrated with repressed excitement.

Laughing, Sophie pressed a kiss to Mac's chin. "You're certainly in a good mood. What's going on?"

"Would you guys give us a minute?" Mac asked the lads, pulling Sophie over to a bench out of the way when the boys started to walk away. "I talked to Dunham this morning, and he said that we can use Alphonse as bait to draw out Snow White."

"He did?" Sophie was surprised that the Chief of Police would risk the life of someone without their knowledge. That wasn't entirely true. Sophie didn't doubt that Dunham would willingly sacrifice someone to further his objectives. She was just surprised he was willing to do so with someone as dangerous as Alphonse. If things went south, Sophie did not doubt that Alphonse would exact revenge against anyone involved with this operation.

Thinking about the possible repercussions, Sophie was having doubts about the plan. She should try to put a halt to this entire endeavor. If Mac got hurt because of her hare-brained scheme, she'd never forgive herself.

"Yeah, the only drawback is that Alphonse has to agree to be bait. Dunham's going to be calling him later this morning to make the request. I tried to talk Dunham out of it, but he said that if we got caught trying to use the alpha as bait without his explicit consent, losing our jobs would be the least of our problems. Dunham is going to tell Alphonse that we believe he is being followed by the person who killed Roger and get him to go to a location where we can trap Snow White."

"I want to be there," Sophie said. Mac was already shaking his head before Sophie had finished the sentence. "I can be a help. For some reason, Snow White and I have a connection. I feel like I'll be able to sense her when she gets close. I will stay out of the way. Alphonse doesn't even need to know I'm there. I just have this feeling that you'll need me to help deal with Snow White."

Mac and Sophie argued until they found a compromise. Sophie would be far away from the action and out of sight, especially from Alphonse, and she had to have several bodyguards with her. That no matter what happened, she could not reveal herself.

"I want to see what she really looks like. In all my visions, she's wearing my face, and it's gotten to me. I just need to know that she doesn't look like me. That my face wasn't the last thing the people she murdered saw," Sophie explained.

"I know. We'll make sure you get a chance to see her," Mac promised.

Checking his phone, Mac declared that he needed to return to the station. He walked Sophie back to her minders.

"Once Dunham tells me what Alphonse says, I'll let you know," Mac swore in Sophie's ear as he hugged her goodbye.

"You better," Sophie jokingly threatened, nipping Mac's chin. Mac gave her a retaliatory nip with a happy grin before spinning away and getting into his car.

"Bye, Mac!" Patrick yelled out as Mac drove past. Mac raised a hand out the window in goodbye.

It was weird. Mac wasn't rude to the lads, but other than checking in with them occasionally to make sure that they were watching for tails or ensuring they were following 'protocol', he barely acknowledged them. However, they seemed to hang on Mac's every word and gesture. He certainly couldn't be called approachable. Even when he was friendly, there was a sharp edge to his charm. That sharp edge did strange things to Sophie's libido.

Sophie would think the hero worship was a respect for a police officer thing, but most teens weren't exactly pro-cop these days. The boys didn't treat anyone else except their alpha Fergal and Paddy with such deference. They treated Sophie like she was their little sister even though she was older than they were.

Sliding into the backseat, Sophie debated how to broach the subject.

"Mac's pretty great, huh?" Sophie asked without forethought. She wanted to slap herself. Sophie had the subtlety of a freight train and the tact of a bulldozer.

"Are you kidding?" Conor exclaimed from the front seat, not noticing Sophie's mortification. "He's awesome. He's the first non-apex shifter to join the Mythical police force. They tried to muscle him out when he first joined, but Mac wouldn't let them. He doesn't even have a big pack to back him up and sponsor him. He's only got his family pack, and most of them aren't even local."

"It's rumored that he defeated a gargoyle single-handedly," Patrick added, awe filling his voice.

"Gargoyle? Like the made-from-stone mythological creature?" Sophie clarified.

"Yeah. They're supposed to be some of the best fighters. And he took one down by himself."

"Everyone had to respect him after that," Liam piped up. "Stopped giving him shit for being a non-apex shifter."

Sophie had seen plenty of attitude from other shifters but decided not to disabuse them of the notion that Mac was the be-all-and-end-all. She bit her lip and leaned back in her seat, eagerly listening to stories about her boyfriend's greatness. She'd had no idea that she was dating someone so admired. It was strange to Sophie that Mac liked her, but she wasn't about to question her good fortune. Sophie liked who she was as a person, but no one would call her accomplished or claim that she was breaking any frontiers.

The lads dropped her off in front of the clan house and waited until she entered the front door before driving off to get to their morning classes. The thought of school made Sophie scowl as she knew she needed to sign up for the Medical Assistant classes by the end of this week.

Spotting Birdie at her usual table by the window, Sophie joined her, pulling up a chair and squeezing one of Birdie's hands in greeting. Riona's daughter Alexandra, who insisted everyone call her Lexa with a roll of her teenage eyes, placed a coffee in front of Sophie before she'd even settled. Sophie was starting to feel very guilty about the amount of food the clan had been feeding her, but when she offered to pay for her meals, Fergal acted as if she had mortally offended him.

Birdie caught Sophie up on clan gossip while they waited for their breakfast to be delivered. Fergal had created a tight-knit community of wolfhound shifters, but the price of that closeness was everyone in everyone else's business.

When her cell phone started chirping from her pocket, Sophie was just taking the first bite of her eggs and toast. She was annoyed until she saw who was calling.

"It's Mac," Sophie exclaimed when she saw 'Detective Dickhead' flash across her screen. "He must already have news."

"Hey, good morning," Sophie answered. As Sophie stood up to leave the table and find somewhere quiet to talk, Birdie frantically waved her hands to catch Sophie's attention. Grinning, Sophie informed Mac, "Birdie says hi."

Squeezing Birdie's shoulder on her way out, Sophie found a quiet corner in the hall outside the pub's doors. On the other end of the line, Sophie could hear the noise of a crowded room, then the sound of a door slamming shut and quiet.

"It's happening today," Mac growled.

"Huh?"

"Sorry, I'm flustered," Mac apologized. "Dunham asked Alphonse to be bait while I came to see you this morning. Alphonse agreed to be bait, but only if we set the dragnet up for later today. He said it has to occur today, or it won't be happening at all. It's a total shitshow here. The station is in complete chaos. We're scrambling to pull in all available officers. We haven't even had a chance to scout a location yet. We need to find a place where we can keep bystanders out and somehow hide half the Mythical police force division. I swear, Alphonse's doing this just to make things more difficult than they need to be."

"Could you close down a parking garage for a couple of hours? Or an abandoned warehouse?" Sophie suggested. "What about a place under construction, so you just have to clear out the workers and not the general public?"

"Hmm, I like the idea of a construction site. I'm gonna do some research. We need to find a place as soon as possible just to secure it. I need to figure something within the next hour. As soon as I have more details, I'll give you a call. The dragnet's not going to happen until dusk tonight, so you should try and get some rest," Mac suggested.

That would be easier said than done.

"I can still come?" Sophie asked. She'd understand if it was just too much to manage. She'd hate it, but she wouldn't kick up a fuss. Mac had enough on his plate without her throwing a bitch-fit.

"Of course. I promised, didn't I? I'm going to call Fergal next and see if he can escort you there and find a good place for you to watch the proceedings out of sight."

"You're the best boyfriend ever, you know that?" Sophie teased, then said in a more serious voice. "You're my favorite person."

"You're my favorite person too. Now tell me I'm pretty so I can go face this shitty day."

Sophie cackled like a hyena before sputteringly complying. "My God, Mac, you're *so* pretty. You're like a Disney princess."

"Damn straight," Mac replied. "Ergh, Turner's waving at me. I gotta go. I'll see you later, okay?"

"Okay. Good luck, Mac," Sophie replied, hanging up the call and returning to her now cold breakfast.

"Everything okay? You look worried," Birdie asked. Sophie recapped the call with Birdie while she tutted in sympathy.

Sophie was finishing the final bites of her meal, slumped in her chair, wondering how in the world she was going to get any sleep when the chair to her left screeched as it was pulled back from the table. Fergal sat down, pulling off his navy-striped suit jacket with precise movements. Every time Sophie had seen Fergal, he always looked like he was about to step into a boardroom. Riona dressed normally, so why didn't Fergal? She had never seen him leave the clan house, so why was he dressed so dapper?

"You're looking fancy," Sophie complimented.

"You gotta dress for the job you want. What kind of job are

you aiming for?" Fergal asked, giving Sophie a slow head-to-toe look.

"Harsh." Sophie tried to give Fergal a hurt look but ruined it by laughing. "Did you need something, or did you just stop by to make fun of my fashion sense?"

"We need to talk. Mac called and asked me to babysit you tonight. Making fun of you was just a bonus."

"Everyone in my life's a comedian," Sophie grumbled.

"I'll leave you two to your talk. Ethan and I are due to sweep the floor with Colleen in bridge. She thinks she's God's gift to cards. I need to take her down a peg or two," Birdie announced, getting up from the table. "I'll see you for dinner, Sophie?"

"I'll see you for dinner. If I'm going to be late, I'll text. No mercy for Colleen."

"No mercy," Birdie confirmed solemnly.

After Birdie left, Sophie turned and looked at Fergal expectantly. "What's the plan?"

"They're going to try and lure your stalker to Kezar Stadium. We'll need to get there before 5 so I can scout a good location where we can watch but not be seen."

"Kezar Stadium?"

It seemed like a weird place to set up an ambush. It was a wide-open space with Golden Gate Park to the west and north and Haight-Ashbury located to the east. The 49ers football team had used it in the 1960s, but now it was mainly used by minor local sports leagues. It was usually crawling with people playing pick-up games of soccer and joggers using the running track.

"Yeah. It's closed for some repairs, so they thought it would be a good place to set up an ambush. Mac thinks they'll be able to post plain-clothes officers all around the perimeter without drawing suspicion," Fergal explained with a shrug. "This isn't their first rodeo," Fergal added at Sophie's doubtful look.

"What time do you need me ready to go?"

"We're going to meet out front at 3 p.m. to head out."

"Is it going to take us two hours to get to the stadium?" Sophie asked, confused.

"Mac requested that I include an ogre as part of your bodyguard team. So, we need to head to the Tenderloin before we head to Kezar. I'm surprised that you have an ogre for a friend. They're not known for befriending humans, even cute ones like you. Who are you *really*, Sophie Feegle?" Fergal gave Sophie a penetrating stare like he was trying to see inside her brain and figure out all her secrets and mysteries. But there weren't any secrets – well, there was one – but Sophie was just Sophie. Her only secret was her strange ability, but that didn't change who she was as a person.

"The ogre is named Burg, and he owns the pub next to my apartment. It's not an exciting story. We became friends when I stopped at his pub for a drink. That's all."

"Okay," Fergal replied, his brows drawn in skepticism.

Sophie rolled her eyes in exasperation. "Anything else?"

"No, that's it. Get some rest, and I'll see you at 3," Fergal replied, standing up and leaving Sophie to her thoughts.

Get some rest? Fat chance.

CHAPTER 19

*a*fter tossing and turning for most of the day instead of sleeping, despite Paddy working her extra hard that morning, 3 o'clock found Sophie standing in her most inconspicuous black t-shirt and jeans in the foyer of the clan house, munching on a granola bar. Movement at the top of the stairs caught her attention. Fergal was coming down, clad in dark sweatpants and a gray t-shirt. Patrick and Conor were behind him in similar outfits, their faces stern and bodies rigid. Sophie had previously scoffed at the idea of the lads being 'battle-tested', but now she wasn't so sure seeing their game faces.

As Fergal joined Sophie in the entryway, she teased. "I hardly recognize you without a suit on. Why so casual?"

"If things go sideways and I need to shift, I don't want to get tangled in my clothing. Getting out of these will only take a moment. Besides, I wouldn't want to risk any of my suits. They're bespoke," Fergal scoffed.

"Where's Liam?" Sophie asked, looking for the third musketeer.

"Not enough room in the car since we're picking up your friend. Liam's the youngest, so he has to stay behind."

Liam wasn't quite eighteen yet, so it made sense to Sophie to leave him out of the fray. If anything went wrong, Sophie would feel awful about putting someone who wasn't an adult into harm's way. She would bet money that Liam wasn't in agreement; he probably hated being left behind.

Fergal led the team out of the clan house and over to a plain beige sedan parked on the street.

"Is this your car?" Sophie asked, thinking that Mac and Fergal had similar tastes in vehicles.

"One of them," Fergal replied nonchalantly.

"It's good to be the clan leader," Sophie snarked, earning a wink from Fergal.

Fergal held the door open while Sophie slid into the front passenger seat of the car. Patrick and Conor sat in the back, silent, and alert.

Traffic started to become congested as people headed home early from work. It seemed to Sophie like half the population of San Francisco was trying to sneak out of work before rush hour began in earnest. Fergal pulled over several blocks away from Brown Betty. At Sophie's confused look, he explained that he was cautioned against bringing her too close to home in case her stalker was watching for her there.

Sophie bounced in her seat when she saw Burg approaching; his long-legged stride was unmistakable. As he came even with the front bumper, Sophie flung herself out of the car to catch him in a hug.

"Sophie!" Burg hooted, swinging her up in a bone-crushing hug.

"Burg! I've missed you," Sophie exclaimed, squeezing her arms as best as she could around her barrel-chested friend.

As Fergal stepped out of the car and approached them, Burg set Sophie back on her feet and turned to the clan leader with a welcoming smile on his face.

Sophie introduced the men as they exchanged reserved handshakes. Despite probably weighing twice as much as Fergal, Burg treated him with quiet respect. Not that Burg was ever rude, but his usual gregariousness was noticeably absent.

Eyeing the car, Sophie suggested that Burg take the front seat, and she'd sit in the back with the lads. Patrick got out of the car and ushered Sophie into the middle seat.

When Burg slipped into the front seat of the vehicle, he turned to catch Sophie up on the local news. Sophie was about to introduce Conor and Patrick when she noticed the look on their faces. The greeting died on her lips as she watched both Conor and Patrick take deep sniffs and then simultaneously make wheezing sounds of shock. The look of astonishment and disbelief on their faces almost made her laugh out loud. They looked like a demon had just joined them, and they didn't know if they should be scared or excited.

"Burg, these are my bodyguards, Patrick and Conor. Patrick, Conor, this is Burg," Sophie introduced. The lads straightened up a bit when Sophie referred to them as bodyguards.

With wide eyes, they shook Burg's hand and murmured 'nice to meet you's. Sophie thought that Burg was quietly amused by their awe even if his face showed nothing but polite interest.

Burg turned his attention back to Sophie. "Sal and George have been asking after you. They've been missing you."

Sal and George were two regulars at The Little Thumb with whom Sophie had struck up a casual friendship over the mutual love of good whiskey.

"I'm hoping that after today I'll be able to come back and see them. I'll even buy them a round in celebration."

The lads' eyes ping-ponged between Burg and Sophie.

"I've just texted Mac to let him know that we're on our way to Kezar Stadium," Fergal announced, tucking his phone in his back pocket and pulling into traffic.

"Alpha O'Dwyer, it's nice to meet you finally. I've heard good things about your clan. The rumors are that your pubs are excellent. It's a shame you had to close them to the general public," Burg said to Fergal. It figured that to Burg, the most important thing about Fergal was his pub. "You'll have to come by The Little Thumb sometime. First round's on the house."

"You've got a deal. After we're done here today, would you like to join us at the clan house for dinner?"

"I would be honored to join you for a meal. You serve food out of your pub, right? My sister's been trying to talk me into serving food at the pub," Burg mentioned. "I'm considering it, but I'd need to hire a cook and a wait staff. Just not sure I want to take on that kind of headache."

A thirty-minute drive later found them parked on Frederick Street. They managed to find a spot within view of a side gate. From their vantage point, they'd be able to see the entirety of the stadium. It was perfect. Putting the car into park, Fergal grabbed his phone and quickly typed something into it.

"I just let Mac know that we're here," Fergal explained.

A minute later, the gate opened, and Mac jogged over. As everyone climbed out of the vehicle, Sophie nudged Conor out of the way. Fergal and Burg got to Mac before Sophie, so she waited while they shook hands. The lads were waiting behind her so she could hear them whispering to each other.

"Liam's gonna shit himself when he finds out we got to meet an ogre," Conor murmured to Patrick.

"He's gonna be even more pissed off that he had to stay home," Patrick commiserated.

Poor Liam. It can be tough being the youngest.

Sophie left the boys behind to join the conversation with Mac.

"They're setting up now. Our department warlock is setting a spell around the entire perimeter of the stadium that will trap her once she crosses the boundary of the spell."

Looking over Mac's shoulder, Sophie could see Larry carrying what looked like an industrial-sized sack of salt over his shoulder as he crossed the grass field in the center of the running track.

"Is there anything we can do to help?" Burg offered.

"No, the chief said you guys could observe but only if you promised not to interfere in any way," Mac replied. "We've got plain-clothes officers posted around the outside of the stadium, keeping an eye out for anyone approaching. Then we'll have a dozen of our best hidden behind an invisibility spell. So, when she shows up and triggers the trap, we can contain her."

"Once you trap her, will I get a chance to see what she looks like?" Sophie asked.

"Not here, but once I get her to the station and into an interrogation room, Dunham said you can watch through the mirror," Mac promised. "I got you a radio so you guys can listen in."

Mac handed the radio to Fergal and showed him which channel they were using. Everyone else headed back to the car while Mac pulled Sophie to the side.

"How's it going? Do you think this is going to work?" Sophie asked.

"If Snow White shows up, I think this could work. It all depends on if she's watching Alphonse like we think she is. We'll see in a bit," Mac said with a shrug. "How are you feeling?"

"I'm good. Just looking forward to this all being over."

"Me too," Mac agreed. "Do you have your taser?"

Sophie patted her pocket. "I don't leave home without it anymore."

Mac grimaced at the necessity but nodded in approval.

Sophie didn't like seeing Mac so stressed. It felt like it was her fault in a way. Sophie knew that was garbage – this was Snow White's fault – but the feeling persisted.

"The lads were telling me how you defeated a gargoyle and took on the entire police department to allow non-apex shifters on the force. They talk about you like you're a god or something.

I don't want to embarrass them, but it's the cutest thing I've ever seen," Sophie told Mac, wanting to see him grin.

"You have to understand: Irish wolfhound shifters were created to hunt wolves and wolf shifters in Ireland. They were bred to be world-class warriors, but most apex shifters treat them like they're no better than pets. They think of the wolfhounds as domesticated dogs, so the clan doesn't get the respect and standing it deserves in the Mythical community. If any of these idiots had ever seen an Irish wolfhound in their half-form, they'd be singing a much different tune. However, very few people that have ever seen one in their battle-form have lived to tell the tale."

"Huh, that makes sense," Sophie replied.

"I've got to get back. Alphonse should be here in about an hour, and I want to make sure everyone is in place well before that time."

"Good luck," Sophie wished him, giving him a quick hug and kiss. Nerves fluttered through her as she watched him head back through the gate and jog over to Larry, who was slowly walking along the top of the far bleachers, the bag cradled in his arms as a steady line of white poured from a hole in the corner of the sack.

Sophie examined the area, trying to imagine how this whole sting operation would work. The stadium was an open-air oval. Iron fencing and trees bordered the grounds, blocking most of it from the view from the surrounding areas. There was a grass field in the middle with a running track encircling it. The field and track area were below street level as if the area had been dug down. On the long sides of the oval were concrete bleachers rising along the natural slope of the hillside. To the west, on Sophie's left, was a huge, freestanding triumphal archway. Some parking and a large building with a red-tiled roof and cream stucco that matched the arch were on the right, to the east.

Sophie got back into the car, taking the middle seat again. Fergal turned up the volume on the radio and put it in a cupholder. They listened as Mac and other officers called out instructions and requests for help over the frequency.

As the waiting started to approach an hour, Sophie looked outside the vehicle with longing. Why did she choose to sit in the middle? Fergal and Burg had been discussing things like inventory and overhead for the entire hour. Sophie had learned more about licensing requirements and restaurant equipment than she ever thought she would. It was an interesting discussion for the first twenty minutes, but now she just longed for freedom. Even Conor and Patrick looked bored. Their excitement at the adventure waned as the hour drew to a close.

"Alphonse just messaged and said he's about ten minutes away," Mac's voice crackled over the radio, making Sophie straighten from her slump between Conor and Patrick as if someone had poked her with a cattle prod. "He will be approaching from the west. Larry, go ahead and activate the invisibility spell for Team A."

Several voices called out an affirmative. Larry approached a group of eight men and women waiting near the entrance archway. He herded the group to the side and started another circle with Larry and the officers inside. Instead of salt, this time Larry used some kind of black powder to create the ring. Sophie watched as Larry spoke his spell, his arms and hands moving in complicated patterns. Between one moment and the next, the entire group, including Larry, disappeared. In their place was unblemished grass, not even a footprint left to give away their location.

"Cool," Conor whispered, echoing Sophie's thoughts.

"Everyone in place?" Mac asked. After several murmured acknowledgments, Mac said, "If anyone sees anything suspicious, let us know immediately. Otherwise, I want radio silence from here on out."

Sophie strained her eyes, trying to locate Mac's other team members, but they had melted into the trees and surrounding buildings. Everything was still and quiet as if the stadium was holding its breath in anticipation.

An eternity of waiting later, Mac's voice whispered, "Alphonse approaching now. Everyone, stay in your post and keep your eyes open."

Alphonse marched through the archway and onto the middle of the field as if he didn't have a care in the world. He knelt, fiddling with his shoes as if he needed to tie his laces. He stayed in that position rather than get back up. Maybe he was trying to look less intimidating? *Or maybe he's praying*, Sophie thought.

There was a quiet buzz, then a voice whispered over the radio, "Movement by the north bleachers. By the restrooms."

Fergal pulled binoculars from the center console, scanning the area with them. Sophie wished she'd thought to bring binoculars for herself.

"Do you see anything?" Sophie whispered, straining her eyes.

Scanning back and forth, Fergal grunted, "Not yet." A moment later, his hands tensed on the binoculars.

Mac's voice crackled over the radio. "Hold your places. Wait for my sig—"

"GET HER!" Alphonse's voice suddenly roared out over the stadium.

People came surging out of the trees, buildings and car parks dotted around the stadium like ants from a kicked anthill. Sophie whipped her eyes away from the restrooms to see Alphonse loping across the field, bellowing and pointing at the small restroom building at the top of the bleachers.

"What the—" Sophie started to exclaim.

"No! No, no, no. She hasn't crossed over the salt line yet!" Larry's voice cut across over the chatter on the radio.

"Shit. She's getting away," Fergal growled, pointing towards the top of the bleachers, the binoculars still in place. "They pulled the trigger too soon. I don't know if they're gonna be able to catch her."

A flash of movement near the corner of the building was all Sophie saw before a dark figure turned away, quickly cresting over the hill behind the bathrooms and disappearing from view. Dozens of people were leaping up the bleachers, taking several steps at a time, scrambling to catch up to Snow White. Sophie looked back at the center of the field to see Mac racing across the grass while simultaneously yelling into his radio. Even from a distance, Sophie could see the rage etched across his face.

"Should we help?" Sophie asked quietly, already knowing what Fergal would say but still needing to make the suggestion. Sitting on her ass while the whole plan fell apart sucked.

"It's out of our hands. We promised to stay in the car, and that's what we're gonna do," Fergal replied flatly. "Hopefully, the officers stationed on the far side of the stadium can intercept her."

An excited voice crackled over the radio, "I see her! She's crossing Kezar Drive, heading north. Black hoodie, dark pants," dashing the brief hope Fergal had inspired in Sophie.

"Keep on her," Mac's voice replied, his breath panting. He dashed up the concrete bleachers in a few long leaps, only a few steps behind the rush of people. And he was closing that distance quickly.

"Who were all those people? Were they cops?" Sophie asked.

"No. It looks like Alphonse planted some of his people in the area. I recognized a couple of them," Fergal explained.

Only a few scant moments had passed from Alphonse's first bellow to Mac disappearing over the hill. Sophie sat in the car in shock, looking from Fergal to the empty stadium and back again.

In the distance, Sophie could hear several honking car horns and screeching tires. Leaning between the two front seats to better hear the radio, her fingers cramped from her tight grip on Burg's armrest.

"She's made it across Kezar, still heading north. Right for the park," a disembodied voice said over the radio.

Sophie dropped her head into her hands, gripping her forehead in frustration. A headache was forming right between her eyes.

"Larry, keep your team onsite. We can't be sure that it's her or not. Everyone else, catch and detain until we can confirm it's our target," Mac barked across the radio.

"Shit. She's heading right for Koret playground," a panting voice called out.

Fergal groaned, shaking his head. "Damn it. Koret's going to be brimming with kids and families right now." Fergal was right. The area was typically packed with families once the business day ended.

Chewing her thumbnail down to the quick, Sophie listened to the officers coordinate their search for Snow White. What little hope Sophie had left slowly drained away as the voices over the radio sounded more and more frustrated.

"We lost her in the crowd. I think she might have headed over to the soccer fields. There's a bunch of little league teams playing," a voice announced.

Mac directed officers in pairs to spread out throughout the area. He sent a few to the carousel; the rest were sent to Hippie Hill, the tennis center, and the soccer fields. Golden Gate Park was crisscrossed with dozens of trails and paths. Snow White could be anywhere.

"Larry, any movement by you?" Mac asked.

"No. All clear here."

"Okay, I'm heading back your way," Mac replied. "Go ahead and drop the invisibility glamor. I don't think there's any point now. Send Pérez, Spencer, and Federov to canvas Stanyan Street in case the suspect turned east. Have the rest of your team join Alinksy – he's at the carousel – and he'll coordinate the rest of the search. If anyone comes across any of Alpha Alphonse's people, inform them that they are hindering an active police operation. They are not sanctioned to participate in this activity."

Larry's team popped into existence on the field a moment later. Three members of the group peeled off and headed to the right. The rest clambered over the bleachers, passing by Mac as he returned to the stadium. He gave them a clipped nod, phone glued to his ear, talking rapidly.

Mac headed directly to Larry. After a quick conversation, Larry turned and headed towards the restrooms. He stopped in the same spot Sophie last saw Snow White, lifting his hands in the air.

"Turner's going to try a tracking spell on the suspect. Stand by," Mac announced over the radio.

Larry spent several minutes waving his hands around in complicated designs, turning several times to face different directions. His shoulders slumped, and he shook his head at Mac.

Mac raised the radio to his lips. "The spell was a bust, folks. Go ahead and keep looking for the suspect. Female, black hoodie, dark pants, around 5'6", medium build. Did anyone get a look at her face?"

Several voices returned a negative, further dampening Sophie's hopes.

Mac paced back and forth around the grass field, issuing commands and receiving occasional feedback from the officers roaming the area. Sophie stopped listening to the radio chatter after a while, just worriedly watching Mac. Even from a distance, he radiated tension and frustration. A sympathy headache throbbed at Sophie's temples. It was evident that Snow White had escaped. The likelihood of her being caught at this point was about the same as Sophie winning a Miss Congeniality contest.

"Oh no," Fergal announced suddenly. Following his gaze, Sophie spotted Alphonse cresting the hills, looking like a thunderstorm, stomping down the slope with a couple of his people following closely on his heels. Alphonse headed directly for Mac and got right in his personal space. He loomed over Mac, muscles bulging, screaming in his face. Mac held stone still, tensed but outwardly unfazed by Alphonse's threatening behavior, only the tension in his frame betraying his anger. The alpha was screaming so loudly that Sophie could hear him. She couldn't make out the words at this distance, but she could hazard a guess. Mac slashed a hand, negating whatever Alphonse was saying. Stepping back from Alphonse, who was practically on his toes, Mac pointed his finger at Alphonse's chest, then indicated the salt line encircling the stadium. The two men looked moments from coming to blows.

The whole day had become a complete disaster, and it was clear that it was Alphonse's fault. However, he was the type of guy who would never admit when he was wrong. Sophie hoped that Mac was verbally tearing Alphonse a new asshole for ruining their chance at catching Snow White. She was probably on her way to Oregon by now. Whatever Mac had to say seemed to set Alphonse off even more. The alpha's back hunched, and he looked like he was ready to start swinging. As Alphonse took another threatening step towards Mac, Sophie found herself trying to climb over Patrick and get out of the car.

She hadn't even realized she'd moved when a firm hand grabbed the back of her shirt and yanked her back to her seat.

"Sophie, if you interfere, it'll only make the situation worse," Burg warned. Sophie puffed up, ready to argue, but Burg's implacable logic quickly deflated her.

"I know. I just..." Sophie sighed. "I really don't like that guy. How dare he yell at Mac when this was obviously his fault?"

Saying that she didn't 'like' Alphonse was a bit of an understatement. Sophie would love to see him taken down a peg or two. If she never saw the alpha again for the rest of her life, it would still be a day too soon.

"If she tries to get out of this car again, lads, you have my permission to sit on her," Fergal instructed Patrick and Conor. Patrick gave Sophie a look of sympathy but gave his assent along with Conor.

Larry slid into the space between Mac and Alphonse, facing the enraged alpha. He made a pushing motion with his hands as if shoving against an invisible weight. Despite Larry not even physically touching Alphonse, the alpha slid a few feet back, his shoes leaving dug up tracks in the grass.

"Wow." Burg whistled. "He's good."

"Larry told me that he's a warlock. What is that exactly? He said it wasn't like a witch," Sophie asked.

"A warlock is almost any male that can manipulate magic. They're born with the ability to absorb magic, like a battery, then manipulate and use it. They use words, gestures, and sometimes objects to direct and control their magic. They're often human but can be born to any species."

Based on only gut instinct, Sophie thought that Larry might be a human wizard. She was getting better at spotting the idiosyncrasies that indicated when someone wasn't human. They all had little tells if one knew what to look for.

"Why can't women be warlocks?" Sophie asked, feeling a swell of feminist annoyance rising inside her.

"I suppose they could. It's just a name for a male magic user who doesn't have a specialty," Burg replied.

"A specialty?"

"From what I understand, warlocks generally don't subscribe to one single discipline. They use Fae magic, witch, shaman, sorcerer, anything. They'll borrow and steal spells and magic from wherever and whoever they can. If they've got the power to harness it, they can perform it."

"What's the female equivalent then?"

Burg shrugged. "I'd say a witch or a sorceress, perhaps."

"Most witches use earth magic. Although more and more have been using blood and sex magic. They can absorb ambient magic from the very ground if they're strong enough. Most use things like herbs and ritual knives and crystals to focus their energy.

Witches, like warlocks, are a catchall for a large group of magic users with lots of different specialties and focuses."

At the mention of sex magic, both Patrick and Conor became more alert. If they'd been in their Irish wolfhound form, Sophie could imagine their ears pricked up in attention, heads tilted to the side.

Burg nodded, turning to face Sophie in the backseat. "It's interesting that he's on the police force. Most of those guys freelance because they can get paid a ton. Since they don't have a single focus, they're in high demand. They've got flexibility where other magic users are more restricted. They're infamous for mashing styles up and creating entirely new spells on the fly."

Whatever Larry was saying to Alphonse seemed to finally calm him down. After a few minutes of intense conversation, Alphonse turned on his heel heading back towards the arched entrance. Waving his arm in a 'come on' gesture, his people trotted after him. Mac and Larry stood rigid, in the middle of the field, watching his retreating back. Mac waited a few extra minutes after Alphonse was gone before turning and heading in Sophie's direction. His stride was purposeful but unrushed.

Sophie nudged Patrick to get out of the way so she could get out of the car, but Patrick gave her a stubborn tilt of his chin and shook his head, eyes cutting to Fergal seated in front of him.

"Move," Sophie growled, trying to shove Patrick out of the way. Patrick gave Sophie an apologetic look but refused to budge.

"It's fine. The danger's over," Fergal told Patrick. Sophie huffed when Patrick climbed out of the car and held the door open for her. She was sick of being babysat by teenagers. Getting out of the car, she forgot her irritation as Mac stepped out of the gate with stiff movements and onto the sidewalk.

Before Sophie could say a word, Mac dragged her into a tight hug. She could feel the tension vibrating through his frame. Understanding the need for comfort after that debacle, Sophie zipped her lips and snuggled into the hug, running a soothing hand up and down Mac's back.

Sophie pulled back from the hug, holding Mac at arm's length, examining his face. He looked positively murderous. "Are you okay?" she asked.

At first glance, Mac appeared composed, but his blue eyes blazed with rage. The clench of his jaw and trembling fists at his sides reflected Sophie's own desire to hunt down Alphonse and do Snow White's job for her.

"I'm fine. Just pissed." He was more than just 'pissed', but Sophie wasn't about to point that out. "We've lost our opportunity to grab Snow White. She knows we're on to her now. We'll never see her again. What a clusterfuck. She's gonna go to ground at the very least but will probably move on and leave the city. Then I don't know how we'll ever find her. She's probably halfway to Alaska by now," Mac complained. "Alphonse is the biggest idiot I've ever had the displeasure to know. If I didn't know better, I'd think he let her get away on purpose."

"Why did he do that? Yell for his men?"

"He claimed that it was his right to deal with his stalker as he saw fit. His master plan was to have his people grab her before we could get her ourselves and then claim alpha rights. I'm sure he was planning to make a whole production out of her execution for killing Roger Lammar."

"He can do that?" Horror filled Sophie at the thought of Alphonse having that kind of power. To decide who lived and who died without due process.

"He claimed that she is an 'imminent threat' and he was within his rights as the alpha of his pack to protect his people. The Conclave wouldn't have sanctioned such an action, but it would have been too late for Snow White if he'd got his hands on her. I'm almost glad she got away."

"What a prick. I thought you guys were about to get into a fistfight."

GWEN DEMARCO

"A part of me was hoping he'd take a swing at me. But Alphonse knew that if he attacked me first, I'd be able to wipe the floor with him and face no repercussions. I don't know if I could win a fight against him, but, man, would I love to find out. He'd never willingly fight someone he wasn't sure he could beat. It would ruin his standing as pack alpha if he lost a fight, especially to someone who isn't considered an apex shifter. So instead of fighting me, Alphonse announced that he was going to make a formal complaint against me to the Conclave. He's claiming incompetence. He even tried to suggest that I let Snow White escape on purpose. I don't know how his pea brain came to that conclusion."

"What will happen then? Is your job in trouble?"

"Nah, there's no way his complaint will stand once some of my officers submit their bodycam footage. Alphonse blew this whole operation. I hope he does make a complaint. I will take *great pleasure* in making him look like the damn fool he is," Mac said.

Fergal, Burg, and the lads must have decided that Sophie and Mac had enough alone time because they all got out of the car and strolled over. When Mac explained the situation, both Fergal and Burg offered to stand as witnesses on Mac's behalf.

"I appreciate the offer. Hopefully, it won't come to that. But with both your reputations in the Mythical community, it would certainly lend extra weight to my testimony," Mac said, shaking both men's hands.

Mac pushed a button on the radio strapped to his shoulder and requested all the teams check in. One by one, each team responded, letting him know that Snow White was nowhere to be seen.

Mac didn't look surprised, but he did look disheartened. Fergal clapped Mac on the shoulder in sympathy, then headed back to the sedan. The rest of the group followed, giving Sophie and Mac space.

"I've got to get back to the team. I just wanted to check on you and make sure you're okay," Mac said.

"I'm fine. Disappointed, but fine. What happens now?"

"My day is just starting. I've got to call Dunham and apprise him of the situation, so I'm not looking forward to that. We'll keep searching the area for at least another hour unless Dunham recalls the team. Then I've got to head back to the station and deal with the chief and all the paperwork. This couldn't have gone worse," Mac lamented. "You should probably head back to the clan house. There's nothing you can do to help here."

Sophie pulled Mac into a tight hug, hoping to make him feel better. A buzzing from Mac's pocket had him pulling back and checking the screen.

"Shit. It's Dunham. I bet Alphonse already called him. Do you want to take this call for me?" Mac joked.

"Absolutely not."

Mac grinned at Sophie, putting the phone to his ear.

"Chief," Mac greeted, then gave Sophie a quick distracted kiss before turning his full attention to the call.

Sophie mouthed 'good luck' and waved at Mac, who returned it – a grimace on his face as he listened to whatever Dunham was saying – before heading back to her entourage.

The drive back to the clan house was quiet. Sophie chewed away her remaining thumbnail, worrying about what Mac was having to endure. Dunham better not have given him a hard time. Hoping that maybe she could help Mac, Sophie closed her eyes and tried to find her connection to Snow White despite being wide awake. It was a long shot, but Sophie was willing to try anything at this point.

No matter how hard she concentrated, she felt nothing. She tried to project her soul towards Snow White, but she stayed firmly in her body. No connection, no visions. Nothing. Sophie decided to try and fall asleep in the hopes of getting a vision, but they were pulling up to the clan house before she had a chance to settle down.

"Anyone hungry?" Fergal asked.

"No, thank you. I'm going to try and take a nap," Sophie responded, earning a strange look from Fergal, who checked his watch with a frown.

"Now? It's been a long day. Let's get a bite to eat, and then you can take a nap," Fergal suggested. When Sophie's stomach growled in response, Fergal grabbed her by an elbow and steered her to the dining hall. Sophie followed, docile as a lamb, too emotionally drained to put up a fight.

Taking the seat next to Sophie, Burg looked around the pub with an eager eye, absorbing every detail.

Being the consummate professional and officially Sophie's favorite person in the world, Riona dropped off pints of ale before they'd barely settled into their seats. Sophie swiftly grabbed hers and clutched it to her chest like it was her precious. Maybe it was years of practice, or she just recognized the look on her husband's face, but somehow Riona knew they needed a drink without having to ask.

"Didn't go well?" Riona tutted.

"I'm not sure it could have gone worse," Sophie muttered, gulping giant slurps of her beer, uncaring of the foam mustache she was sporting.

"Alphonse jumped the gun and startled the target away. It completely blew the entire operation and wasted everyone's time. Then he kicked up a big fuss trying to blame Mac for his screw-up. Typical Alphonse behavior," Fergal grumbled.

"Do you know him well?" Sophie asked.

"I've had to deal with his bullshit for almost ten years now. I can't tell you how sick of Alphonse we all are. The Golden Gate Park sits directly in between our territories. As you can imagine, all shifters love to run in the park after dark – let their animal side run free. For a few years, we had run-ins with his pack almost monthly. Finally, the Conclave had to step in and divide up the park into sections. His people love to test our mettle, trying to sneak across the borders and start skirmishes. So now, no one can run the entire thing; you must stick to your designated section. But the Sunset pack is always infringing on our borders, pushing us. I believe that Alphonse encourages that behavior in his pack mates, hoping to get us to engage. He's hoping that he can cry foul and push for reparations from the Conclave if we react. He's been trying to expand his territory ever since he defeated the last alpha and took leadership. He's a thorn in my side. A loud, obnoxious thorn."

"He stepped in it today, though. He's going to lose face with the Conclave when the details of how badly he screwed up the operation comes out," Burg consoled Fergal.

Riona clucked her tongue before promising to bring everyone dinner.

"After we finish here, I'll take you on a tour of the kitchen," Fergal promised Burg.

"I'd really like that. Thank you for your hospitality. This place is fantastic. And the smells coming from your kitchen are making my mouth water."

Pride beamed from Fergal at Burg's fervent praise. Despite Sophie's sour mood, watching another budding bromance bloom right in front of her eyes was amusing.

Just as Riona and her daughter deposited plates of food at the table, Liam came clattering down the stairs. Rushing towards the group, he stopped short, frozen in place. Ramrod straight, nose quivering, Liam's head swiveled towards Burg. His mouth dropped open, but no words came out.

"Liam," Fergal said, snapping him out of his trance. "Join us." Fergal snagged a chair and pulled it up to the table. With slow, careful movements, as if he was trying not to startle a wild animal, Liam slid into the chair.

While Sophie pushed food around her plate, pretending to

eat, Conor and Patrick retold Liam about the day's adventures. Liam kept occasionally cutting glances toward Burg, his eyes owl-wide at sharing a table with an ogre.

Fergal watched Sophie with fatherly concern, nudging her plate closer to her. With an internal sigh, she ripped off a piece of her soda bread and stuffed it into her mouth.

Finally having eaten enough to satisfy her host, Sophie excused herself and headed up to her room. If she could fall asleep quickly, Sophie could get an hour of sleep. Setting the alarm and shucking off her boots and socks, Sophie got under her blanket. Fluffing her pillow, she closed her eyes and willed herself to sleep.

Find Snow White. Find Snow White, she silently chanted. The books said that you had to picture the person or item you were targeting with as much detail as possible. Sophie focused on how it felt to be inside Snow White's mind. Sophie thought about her determination, her glee, her enjoyment of the hunt.

When her alarm blared an hour later and Sophie's eyes snapped open, she had to bite off a strangled yell behind clenched teeth. She hadn't gotten a single second of sleep. Her mind wouldn't shut up, her thoughts running like a hamster on a wheel, obsessing over needing to sleep. She had tried turning her mind blank, then tried to find her happy place – a beach with swaying palm trees. She'd tried calming, meditative thoughts. At one point, she'd even downloaded a sleep app that used calming music to lull people to sleep. That was a waste of a dollar.

She would have counted sheep if she'd thought it would've worked.

With a groan, she sat up, snatching up her phone and turning off the alarm. Checking the time, she decided she had time for a shower before she needed to leave for work. She sent a quick text to Mac to check in with him. When she got out of the shower, she found a text waiting for her stating that he was back at the station, followed by an angry-faced emoji with steam coming out of its nose.

Yikes. Try not to shoot anyone. Unless it's a particular alpha asshole, then feel free.

Mac texted back that he couldn't make that promise. He explained that most of the Conclave had shown up at the station, along with several members of Alphonse's pack, including the alpha himself. Most of the members of Mac's team were there to give their recounting of the event too. There was a lot of grand-standing going on by the Conclave, along with a side of finger-pointing. Mac promised to call her when he could and catch her up.

Sending off a kissy-face emoji, Sophie slid her phone into her pocket, stuffed her feet into her boots, and grabbed her bag. A long night loomed ahead of her, but Sophie determinedly left her room to find the lads and head to work.

Marching down the stairs, Sophie could hear offkey singing coming from the dining room. It sounded like one of the soccer chants the regulars at The Little Thumb occasionally sang while watching the game on one of Burg's televisions. Once they started yelling 'Olé, olé, olé', it was Sophie's signal to get out of the pub and back to Brown Betty.

Coming into the dining room, Sophie immediately spotted Burg and Fergal, arms slung around one another, listing in their seats like unbalanced warships on stormy seas, drunk as skunks.

"Sophie," both men cheered as she entered the dining room. Riona caught Sophie's eye, shaking her head at Fergal and Burg's antics.

"Come join us, Sophie. You gotta try this whiskey! Fergal's family makes it special themselves. Just for shifters. It's extra potent," Burg bellowed, almost falling out of his chair, trying to wave Sophie over.

Fergal closed one eye, squinting in Sophie's general direction. She wondered how many Sophies he was seeing. "Yes, you should have a quick dram. Although you *are* human, so you can only have a wee bit," Fergal announced, holding up the bottle in his hands toward Sophie. He looked surprised to see that it was empty.

"Riona, my beautiful bride! This bottle is empty. We need another." Fergal shook the bottle at his wife to show her its unfilled state.

While they were distracted, Sophie slipped out to find the lads. Heading down the stairs, she spotted Birdie heading up.

"Hey, girlie," Birdie greeted. "I heard today went poorly."

There were no secrets in the clan house. Sophie had lain down for just over an hour.

"That's putting it lightly. It was an unmitigated disaster." Sophie shrugged. "I'd tell you all about it, but I have to get to work. Burg's up in the pub. He was there and can fill you in."

They gave each other a quick hug before Birdie headed up the stairs. As Sophie landed in the foyer, she heard Fergal and Burg cheer "Birdie" from up above. Oh boy. Maybe she shouldn't have sent Birdie to the pub. Sophie had a feeling that Birdie would be nursing a hangover by the time she returned from work in the morning.

Oh, well. Not her circus, not her monkeys.

CHAPTER 20

*H*er bodyguards were in their usual spot – lounging around the front stoop – waiting for Sophie.

Patrick let Liam sit in the front seat without argument. Sophie assumed that it was because they felt terrible that Liam had to miss all the action earlier.

"I can't believe you're friends with a real-life ogre!" Conor exclaimed. "I've never met one before. They're supposed to be super mean and aggressive. They hate everyone but other ogres."

Sophie scoffed. "You've met Burg. Did he seem mean to you? He owns a pub that is considered neutral territory for all Mythicals. If he hated everyone, why would he allow any Mythical to come inside? Maybe other ogres are jerks, but not Burg. He's a sweetheart. The pub's next to my apartment, so we became friends when I stopped in to get a drink. He's one of the friendlier people I've ever known."

"You went into an ogre pub? Alone?" Liam questioned.

"Yeah. It's just a pub. I mean, it's in the Tenderloin, so there's plenty of dangerous characters around, but The Little Thumb is safe."

"You live in the Tenderloin? Huh, you're cooler than you

seem," Liam said as if that was a compliment. Sophie opened her mouth to respond with something scathing, but nothing came to mind.

"I'm cool," she protested weakly.

"Oh, you totally are, Sophie," Patrick replied, his voice sugar-sweet.

"Did your mom tell you that?" Conor snarked at the same time.

Patronizing little shits, Sophie thought, glaring at the brats. Sophie's scowl only made Patrick laugh louder.

The lads dropped her off, making sure that Sophie arrived through the lobby doors. Despite being goofballs, they certainly took their job seriously.

Sophie found Reggie reviewing charts in his office. She pulled him into the main office. Amira, Ace, and Fitz were all at their desks when they entered the room.

"What did you need to tell us, Sophie?" Reggie asked.

Settling her hip against an empty desk, Sophie proceeded to give the team a recap of the day. Ace threw his hands up in the air in aggravation when Sophie told them how Alphonse tried to grab Snow White before she crossed the threshold of the spell, ruining the entire operation.

"No way! Tell me he didn't," Reggie exclaimed, eyebrows raised.

"Oh, yes, he did. And now he's trying to put the blame on Mac that she escaped," Sophie retorted, hands clenching with the desire to wring Alphonse's thick neck.

"What happened then?" Fitz asked.

"Mac and his team were still searching for Snow White when I left. But he thinks she is long gone. Last I talked to him, he was at the police headquarters. Most of the Conclave had arrived, and everyone was pointing fingers."

"Do you want me to—" Reggie started to say, but the ringing of Sophie's phone interrupted him.

"It's Mac," Sophie said, answering the call. "Hey, Mac. What's happening? Are you okay?"

"Yeah, I'm good. I just wanted to call to hear your voice and to give you an update."

"Hey, I'm here with the Odd Ones. Can I put you on speaker?"

When Mac gave his permission, Sophie placed her phone on a table between her friends.

"We're all here. What happened after I left today?" Sophie asked.

"It went exactly as you can imagine. My team searched the entire area for hours before the chief called us all back to the station. When I walked in the door, Alphonse, Dunham, Marcella, and most of the Conclave were making a fuss in the middle of the bullpen. When I walked in, Alphonse tried to attack me. He ended up under a pile of most of the Mythical division of the police force," Mac explained with a chuckle. "All of my team ended up giving their statements which, along with the bodycam footage, proved a bunch of Alphonse's accusations as false. I don't know what he was thinking. He made himself look like a fool and a liar in front of the Conclave. He just stormed out of here a few minutes ago. A couple of members of the Conclave left to find him and try to bring him back. I hope he doesn't come back, to be honest. Marcella looks ready to start removing heads from shoulders, but that's directed mostly at Alphonse. I think he lost standing in the community today, especially because he aired this all out in the middle of the bullpen in front of a crowd. Everyone is going to be talking about this. If he'd just shut up, it could have been swept under the rug. I've got one hell of a headache, but it was worth it to watch Alphonse shoot himself in the foot."

"Wow. I wouldn't be surprised if Alphonse gets deposed from his throne by an ambitious pack member soon," Reggie said. "I've heard his brother is just as ruthless as he is. I'd be willing to bet that he might try to stage a coup. Alphonse might end up having to deal with a lot of challenges. He's a tough son of a bitch, but if he has to deal with a gauntlet of dominance battles, he might lose. If enough people step up to fight him, he'll eventually get worn down. It'll be interesting to see how this plays out." Reggie looked worried by that prospect. Sophie thought getting rid of Alphonse couldn't be anything but a good thing. Maybe it was a the-devil-you-know kind of situation.

"I feel bad for his pack. They've had to deal with his tyranny for years. But if he gets challenged and is defeated, it's going to throw the pack into turmoil unless the new alpha is strong enough to hold them together and exert control. An unstable pack is a dangerous pack. Especially for its weaker members," Amira said. She shuddered at the thought.

"Bramwell and his entourage are back," Mac announced over the line. "I don't see Alphonse. They must not have caught up to him. Either that or he refused to come back. I'm not sad either way. Ugh, Dunham and Marcella are waving me over. I've got to go."

Everyone wished Mac luck, then Sophie took it off speaker and left the room to say goodbye.

"Hey, if you think Snow White's left town, when do you think I could go home?" Sophie asked. "I miss my bed."

Mac blew a breath out over the phone. "I'd rather err on the side of caution. Until she's caught or we have proof that she's gone, you should stay hidden."

Sophie knew that was what Mac was going to say, but it never hurt to check. In many ways, she liked staying at the clan house. Who wouldn't enjoy hot meals delivered on-demand with no need to do dishes? But she missed her apartment. It was a place that was all hers. She even missed the crappy little shower with its meager water pressure. It was her sanctuary.

"No, it makes sense. I think I'm just a little homesick."

"Dunham's looking annoyed. I've gotta go," Mac growled.

"Call me when you're done there. It doesn't matter what time; I'll answer even if I'm in the middle of an autopsy. I know Reggie won't mind. I just want to make sure you're okay," Sophie quietly told Mac.

"I will. I miss you. Wish you were here," Mac replied.

"Me too."

Sophie popped her head back into the office to let Reggie know that she just needed to get into her scrubs, and she'd be ready to start her shift.

The rest of the night, Sophie did her job distractedly. Mac called about an hour into her shift. He sounded exhausted but satisfied with the turn of events. It looked like, at a minimum, the Conclave was going to put sanctions against the Sunset District pack for interfering in a police matter. The Conclave was also discussing the option of forcing Alphonse to make a public apology to the Mythical division and specifically Mac himself. However, Mac thought that hell would freeze over before Alphonse agreed to those terms. They couldn't do much about Alphonse unless they were willing to remove him as alpha entirely. The Conclave didn't take drastic measures like that unless the Mythical in question was in danger of revealing Mythicals' existence to humans with their behavior.

Rolling a cart out of the autopsy room to head back to the fridge, Sophie almost ran over Ace. She called out an apology, but he just growled at her to watch where she was going.

Talking to Mac should have settled her nerves, but she couldn't stop replaying the day in her head. She was distracted and unable to pay attention to her surroundings like usual. Thankfully, she was proficient enough at her job by now that she could do most of it by rote. The visions also didn't take any real effort. She just had to touch a dead body and see what vision came. For such a valued ability, it didn't take any real skill – not that Sophie was complaining.

At lunch, Sophie let the conversation wash over her. It was all about Alphonse, Snow White, and what everyone thought would happen next. Thankfully, her appetite had come back, so she was able to eat her meal. She hardly registered what she ate, just glad to have warm food provided for her. That would be what she missed most about leaving the clan house – Riona's cooking. Well, that and having someone else do the dishes.

When her shift was finally over, the last twenty-four hours had started to catch up with Sophie. She felt like a zombie shuffling out of the building. She almost forgot to say goodbye to Miss Zhao, only remembering when she was almost out the door. Good thing, too – the best policy was to stay on the good side of a dragon.

"Get some sleep, dear," Miss Zhao advised.

"Yes, ma'am," Sophie replied, walking out into the morning sun.

Heading for the lads' car, a man's yell of 'give it back' caught her attention. Two bedraggled, homeless men were wrestling over something on the far side of the parking lot. It looked like a cloth bag. The bigger of the two men yanked on the bag, dragging the smaller man off his feet. Once on the ground, the smaller man started kicking up at the other man's arms, trying to get him to release the sack. Profanities were pouring out of both men's mouths.

She was *so* not in the mood to break up a fight, but nonetheless turned toward the battling men with a determined step. The lads had also climbed out of their car and were turned in the same direction. Excellent. She'd get them to break up the fight. Who said Sophie wasn't management material?

Before getting more than one step towards the battling men, a hand clamped over Sophie's mouth, an arm wrapped around her neck, yanking her off her feet. Flailing, Sophie tried to get her feet under her as she was quickly dragged around the corner of the Medical Examiner's building and out of sight from the parking lot. She tried to yell out to the lads but couldn't be heard over the homeless men's fight. As she was hauled around the corner, the last thing she saw was a van pulling into the parking lot. Screeching to a halt, the side door slid open, and men poured out of the vehicle, heading for the lads.

The arm around her neck tightened, cutting off her oxygen, as she was dragged further away. They were headed toward the waterfront with its jumble of shipping docks, warehouses, and unfinished construction – a perfect place for an assault or murder. Sophie opened her mouth as wide as she could, clamping her teeth around the meaty part of the hand over her mouth. She bit the flesh as hard as she could, feeling the bones shift beneath the muscle. Because of Reggie's habit of telling her facts about human bodies, Sophie knew that she had enough power in her jaw to bite off his fingers. The man holding her roared, trying to shake her off, but Sophie held on even when she tasted blood. The arm around her neck loosened but didn't let her go. She wasn't going to release his hand until she got free, so even when he shook her like a dog with a rat in its mouth, Sophie clamped down and held on.

With the man distracted, Sophie slid her hand into her pocket and palmed her taser. She shoved it into the torso behind her and triggered the current. Pressing the button on her taser got an immediate reaction. With a strangled gurgle, the man shoved her away. Landing on her hands and knees, Sophie flipped over and scuttled back like a terrified crab.

Alphonse was bent over with his hands on his knees, wheezing and shaking, but still on his feet. That should have put him on the ground. That was a bad sign. With a growl, he shook off the effects of the taser and straightened up. The look on his face spelled Sophie's imminent death.

Never let them get you on the ground, the voice of Paddy yelled in her mind. Scrambling to her feet, Sophie faced Alphonse, holding out the taser and keeping it trained on him.

Quickly glancing left and right, Sophie realized that they hadn't made it as far as she first thought. They were just behind the ME's building, just out of sight from the main road, with hedges hiding them from view.

The sounds of yelling and fighting floated in the air from the front of the building.

"What do you want?" Sophie yelled at Alphonse, hoping for a villain monologue to buy time for the cavalry to arrive.

Alphonse took a menacing step toward Sophie, so she stepped back, keeping the same distance between them. She could see Alphonse visually measuring the distance, deciding if he could leap across it and get her.

"What is your problem? I tried to save your packmate!"

"Like you don't know," he sneered. "You need to come with me. I have questions for you. Make this easy on yourself and come willingly. If you fight me, I'm going to make you suffer in ways you can't imagine."

Sophie was entirely certain that if she went anywhere with Alphonse, willingly or not, suffering would be in her future.

Alphonse took another step towards her, his hands up as if to show he had no ill intentions. Yeah, right. Alphonse growled in annoyance as Sophie took another matching step back. As he dropped the pseudo-friendly façade, claws slowly grew from his fingertips: curved, black, and almost as long as Sophie's pinky.

"We don't need to do this," Sophie said. "Ask your questions. I'll answer whatever you want. But I'm not going anywhere with you."

After another step that Sophie countered, she realized he was maneuvering her further away from the safety of the building and towards the waterfront. He was herding her.

"Who else knows about your visions? Who've you told about what I've done?" Alphonse demanded.

Sophie's poker face failed her for a moment as her mouth dropped open in shock. How could Alphonse possibly know about her visions?

A moment too late to be believable, Sophie sputtered out, "Visions? I don't know what you're talking about."

"Bullshit. I know that's why you've been stalking me and attacking my people. Frank saw you yesterday when you ran away like a gutless coward."

"Saw me? That's not possible. I wasn't there, and I haven't been stalking you. I don't know who your people saw, but it wasn't me. I swear!"

With Alphonse's back to the ME's building, he didn't see a person quickly peek around the corner, a few feet behind him. It was just a flash of movement, but Sophie saw them. Finally. The cavalry had arrived.

A moment later, the person dashed from around the corner. Sophie tried to keep Alphonse's attention on her, but when she saw her own face looking back at her, something must have registered in her eyes. It had to be Snow White, and she was wearing Sophie's face.

As Alphonse started to turn, Snow White sank a syringe into his shoulder. Before she could depress the plunger, Alphonse backhanded her, then grabbed her by her arm, tossing Snow White in Sophie's direction. She skidded across the concrete, coming to a crumpled heap several yards behind Sophie.

A bloody knife came skittering across the asphalt, coming to rest near Sophie's foot. Panting, Alphonse ripped the syringe out of his shoulder, tossing it away. Blood bloomed on Alphonse's bicep. Snow White must have managed to cut him as he threw her.

As blood started to drip from Alphonse's arm, he roared, "There's two of you!" It was so loud that it washed over Sophie like a wave. The seams on his shirt started to split as he grew taller, his muscles bulging and hair sprouting over his arms. The roar coming from his mouth morphed into a haunting howl.

"Oh, fu—" a voice that sounded precisely like Sophie's cried out from behind her, scared and shocked, but Sophie couldn't focus on that. Snatching up the knife, Sophie leaped at Alphonse. She tried to stab him in the chest, but he sprang back, and Sophie ended up stabbing the knife into his thigh. With a bellow, Alphonse seized the wrist holding the knife, twisting until Sophie felt something give. Letting go of the blade still sticking out of Alphonse's thigh, Sophie yanked on her arm, trying to pry it from Alphonse's grip. Screaming in pain, she kicked and scratched at Alphonse like a wild animal in a snare, only intent on escape at any cost. Her cry of pain was quickly cut off as Alphonse grabbed her by the throat, lifting her off her feet with one hand. Her feet kicked uselessly, trying to find purchase on the ground.

Sophie scrabbled one hand over his fingers, trying to pry his hand off her throat. The other hand was still grasped in Alphonse's tight grip. He twisted that arm, putting strain on her shoulder until it was screaming in protest. Vision darkening, Sophie kicked her feet, trying to peg him in the balls.

A boom rang out, so deafening that Sophie felt it as much as she heard it. At that exact moment, a hunk of Alphonse's temple disappeared in a splash of red and pink. Just as suddenly, Sophie was dropped, her knees crumpling under her. Alphonse still had a hold of Sophie's arm, so he pulled her over on top of him when he toppled over. Laying on Alphonse, gasping great heaving breaths, Sophie felt the air leave Alphonse's body.

Coughing raggedly, Sophie scrambled off Alphonse's chest, falling on her ass. She scrambled, scooching on her ass until she was several feet away. Sitting on the cold asphalt, Sophie held her injured arm and stared at Alphonse's bloodied body. She knew he was dead, but there was a part of her that couldn't accept that reality.

"Sister! Are you okay, Sophie?"

Sophie twisted around in horror. *Sister? What the—*

Snow White was walking towards her, a gun in her hand.

Sophie blinked as the sky went dark. Looking up, all Sophie saw was golden-brown scales the size of salad plates above her head. Snow White started screaming. Sophie looked back at her doppelganger in time to see a giant claw pin her to the ground. The gun was flicked out of Snow White's hand by one rolling pin-sized black claw. It clattered away across the asphalt.

A giant sinuous dragon, the size of a bus, loomed over Snow White. She screamed with mindless terror.

The dragon had a long, twisting body, almost snake-like, shimmering with coppery-brown scales, its snout was blunt with large round nostrils. Frills swept back from its head and down its back like a fringed mane. Surprise slapped Sophie that the dragon didn't have wings. All the stories and art had always showed them with wings.

The dragon coiled around Snow White, twining around her like a boa constrictor about to squeeze out the breath from its victim. The dragon dropped its giant head close to Snow White, snarling, displaying rows of fangs the size of baseball bats.

"You need to hush up now," the dragon advised Snow White in Miss Zhao's prim voice. The volume was commanding. A rumble rolled across the lot, raising the hairs on the back of Sophie's neck. Snow White's screaming cut off like a switch had been thrown, her teeth clicking as she clamped her mouth shut.

"Miss Zhao?" Sophie gasped. The dragon blinked its giant golden eyes at Sophie, tilting its head like a dog.

"Yes, it's me, dear. Are you okay?"

"I... uh... I think so," Sophie replied, not sure if she was telling the truth.

Sophie could hear breathless whispering that sounded like prayers.

Miss Zhao's head swiveled back to Snow White in a cobra-like move on an agile neck.

"Don't kill her yet. I have questions for her," Sophie called out.

Miss Zhao huffed a steaming breath from her nostrils, as if disappointed. A long-forked tongue flicked at Snow White, making her squeal. It was harder to tell with Miss Zhao's dragon eyes, but Sophie thought she could detect amusement.

The dragon leaned its face closer to Snow White, a slow grin spreading across its fringed viper face, dozens of rows of razor-sharp teeth on display. Brown scales with a copper iridescence glinted in the sun as Miss Zhao huffed a breath over Snow White's prone form.

"Hmm. She's human. Strange."

Sophie looked at the woman pinned under Miss Zhao's eagle-like claw. Except for a different haircut and a lack of visible tattoos, Snow White was a dead ringer for Sophie.

An angry voice screamed out, "Alphonse! You killed my brother, you bitch!"

Both Sophie and Miss Zhao whipped their head to the empty access road behind the building. A large man with shaggy brown hair was sprinting towards them. His focus seemed to be on Sophie and Snow White, blatantly ignoring the enormous dragon in front of him.

"Alphonse!" he screamed brokenly, looking at the still form of the alpha on the ground, a pool of blood forming under what was left of his head. Looking back at Snow White, he bellowed, "I'll kill you!"

Miss Zhao used her other paw to pin this new guy on the ground next to Snow White with a resigned huff. He wiggled and heaved, screaming obscenities but could not budge the scaled claw the size of a manhole cover from his chest.

"Sophie! Oh my god, there you are!" Mac's voice called out, followed by the thunder of several running feet.

Mac sprinted toward Sophie, flanked by three shaggy gray monsters. Reggie, Ace, Amira, Fitz, Larry, and several police officers were right on their heels, seemingly unconcerned about the hairy beasts in their midst, towering over them. The monsters were similar to the wolf shifters that Sophie had seen at Coit Tower – if those shifters had grown a foot in height and got 'roided up. They were the stuff of nightmares with shreds of clothing hanging off their forms and blood dripping from their claws and smeared on their muzzles. The monsters' steps faltered only for a moment when they spotted the dragon behind Sophie.

"Whoa, a dragon," Liam's voice came out of one of the monster's mouths.

Halfway to her feet, Sophie froze, mouth agape. Mac said that Irish wolfhound shifters were created for war, but nothing had prepared her to see the lads in their battle-form.

Mac crossed the distance between them in a few quick strides and hauled Sophie into his arms, burying his face in her hair. Her face was pressed into his chest. Every ragged breath, every beat of his heart, echoed in Sophie's cheek and sent minor tremors through her.

"Soph! Oh my god, Sophie! Are you okay?" Mac kept repeating, his body shuddering against hers, distracting her from her bodyguards' scary half-forms.

"I'm okay. I'm okay," Sophie reassured Mac.

"Thank god, you're alright. I thought I was too late." Mac pulled out of the hug and started frantically checking her over. Sophie hissed when he palpated her wrist.

"What happened?" Mac asked.

As Sophie explained what occurred with Alphonse, Mac's face became a rigid mask, eyes like a glacier. If Alphonse wasn't already dead, Sophie did not doubt that Mac would have tried to kill him. Mac ran a gentle finger down Sophie's throat. It was sore as hell and probably already turning purple.

Leaning closer, Sophie whispered in Mac's ear, "Snow White saved my life. Why would she do that? I thought she was after me."

"I have no idea. Nothing about this makes sense."

Several police cars arrived with lights flashing, followed by an ambulance, blocking the small access road behind the office. Everyone was babbling around them; police and friends speculating, Alphonse's brother was screaming about Alphonse and promised retribution for his death, Snow White was trying to explain that she was just helping save her 'sister'.

"Sister?!" Mac exclaimed, looking at Snow White then back to Sophie incredulously.

"That is *not* my sister! I don't know what magic she's using to look like me, but I do not have a sister. She's insane."

"She smells entirely human," Miss Zhao announced, giving Snow White another long sniff.

"You sure?" Mac asked. When Miss Zhao nodded her giant head regally, Mac shook his head.

"Are those antlers?" Sophie whispered, still staring at Miss Zhao. Calling them antlers was a bit of an understatement. Sharp, branching horns arched from Miss Zhao's brow, sloping back away from her face.

"Yes, she's a dragon," Mac responded as if it was self-explanatory. He turned to Larry. "Can you set up a repel spell around the perimeter? Shut down all access to the building and send all human employees home for the day. I don't want any humans wandering into the crime scene. Let's set this up as a thwarted mugging for the records."

Larry rubbed his hands together with glee. "Gladly." Heading back to the front of the building, he stopped and turned to Sophie. "Hey, I'm glad you're okay."

"Me too," Sophie agreed wholeheartedly.

Mac ordered officers to handcuff Snow White and Alphonse's brother, whose name was Antonio, and put them into police cars. It took four police officers to subdue Antonio and carry him into a police cruiser. Snow White allowed the officers to handcuff her, unresisting and obedient. She cheerfully thanked the officer who helped her to her feet. As they escorted her to a waiting vehicle, she tried to wave and get Sophie's attention, an excited smile on her face. Sophie watched her in consternation but didn't acknowledge Snow White's attempts.

"Okay, that's weird, right?" Sophie said.

Everyone concurred that Snow White's behavior was strange. She didn't even seem fazed that she was being arrested.

Once Miss Zhao gave up her captives, she said an unfamiliar word, raising her paws to the sky. A cloud of glittering brown smoke swirled around Miss Zhao's dragon form, swallowing her whole. The cyclone slowly shrunk as if it was being sucked down a drain, leaving in its stead Miss Zhao. Miss Zhao carefully dusted off the arms of her tan suit jacket and patted her hair to make sure her bun was still in place.

"Thank you for saving my life, Miss Zhao. I owe you," Sophie called out.

Miss Zhao waved away Sophie's words. "That's what you do for friends."

"Still. Thank you."

Miss Zhao gave Sophie a slight nod then headed back to the front of the building. Sophie silently vowed to get her a nice gift of appreciation. The Mid-Autumn Festival was coming up soon; perhaps Sophie would pick up some mooncakes.

According to Mac, Alphonse had over half a dozen of his pack members create a diversion out front so he could grab Sophie undetected. A police van arrived to pick them all up. Right on the tail of the police van, two sleek black SUVs arrived. The doors opened and out spilled Chief Dunham, Marcella, Bramwell, and – according to Reggie – several members of the Conclave.

Imperious as a queen, Marcella approached Sophie. "This is her? The one with the visions?" Marcella asked Dunham. Sophie's spine snapped straight while Mac growled low in his throat next to her.

"Excuse me?" Sophie exclaimed. "How does she know that? I was promised that if I worked with you that you would keep my ability secret." Sophie stared at Dunham, who stared back at her unfazed.

"I only told Marcella. As the Conclave Magistrate, I must

271

inform her when I acquire a new asset. Your secret is perfectly safe with her," Dunham replied.

Asset?! The nerve of this guy.

"Oh, yeah? She just announced it to everyone here, didn't she?" Sophie pointed around the backlot, where dozens of people were watching them. "Plus, Alphonse knew about my visions. That's why he tried to murder me just now. You should *never* have told anyone without clearing it with me first. I don't trust you," Sophie yelled, pointing at Dunham. "And I sure as hell don't trust her."

"You work for us now. We'll keep you safe," Marcella replied, obviously going into soothing mode. "Your talent is incredibly valuable to the Mythical community. We will make sure you are protected so you can continue your work and help keep murderers off the street. Chief Dunham told me how passionate you are about saving people."

"You're gonna keep me safe, huh? You've done a bang-up job so far," Sophie replied, sarcasm laid on thick, pointing to her purple and blue throat.

After realizing that Sophie was only getting angrier, Dunham led Marcella and the Conclave members away, promising to talk with her more later. Bramwell lingered for a moment, giving Sophie a long, considering look. It took every shred of Sophie's willpower not to give the wizard-lookalike the bird.

When another ambulance pulled up, Mac tried to talk Sophie into going to the hospital to get her wrist and neck looked at. Sophie refused to go. No amount of blustering, cursing, or cajoling was going to get Sophie to budge.

"Get Reggie to take a look at me. He's a doctor. I want to stay here and see what happens. I need to find out who Snow White really is."

Reggie examined Sophie and determined that her wrist was sprained but thankfully not broken. Her neck was severely bruised. Luckily, there didn't appear to be any permanent damage. He cleaned the scrapes on her hands and knees and declared that she would survive.

"However, at some point today, you should go get a second opinion at the hospital. Plus, they can give you pain medication which, I promise, you are going to want once the adrenaline wears off," Reggie predicted.

Mac led Sophie to an ambulance with its back doors wide open and waiting. He had her sit on the bumper so she would be out of the way but could watch everything. There was a paramedic inside fiddling with her equipment. She gave Mac an emergency blanket when he requested it. Snapping open the mylar blanket, he wrapped it around Sophie's shoulders with a stern command to stay put. Mac gave the paramedic a significant look. The woman quickly assured Mac that she would make sure Sophie stayed in the vehicle.

"Hey," Sophie called out as Mac started to walk away. "How'd you get here so fast?"

"The tracking spell showed that Alphonse was here at the ME's building. Larry and I were on our way to check out the situation when we got a call from Reggie saying that a group of wolf shifters were attacking some teenagers in the parking lot. I would have gotten to you sooner, but it took us a while to get through Alphonse's people, even with the help of the wolfhounds."

"You weren't kidding about Irish wolfhounds," Sophie exclaimed, glancing over at the lads who were back in their human forms and dressed in some scrubs borrowed from the Medical Examiner's department stash.

"I told you," Mac replied, flashing Sophie a grin. Sophie was glad to see Mac acting more like his usual self rather than a robot with murderous intentions. Although, given the circumstances, Sophie could understand needing to lock down his anger before he exploded. If someone had attacked Mac, Sophie didn't think she'd be able to control herself half as well.

Mac headed over to a circle of police officers clustered around Dunham. As he started talking to the chief, looking pissed off, Fitz and Ace rolled a gurney out the back door and parked it next to Alphonse's body. They stood waiting while Reggie and an unfamiliar woman in a white lab coat took pictures and samples from the scene, heads together over a clipboard. Sophie assumed that the woman was the crime scene technician that the Mythical division used. Reggie mentioned once that she was really nice. And unless Sophie was entirely mistaken, there was an interesting vibe between Reggie and the woman. Was that a blush on Reggie's cheeks?

Reggie and the technician wrapped up their work, waving over Fitz and Ace. With their help, they rolled Alphonse's body into a body bag and lifted him onto the gurney. Fitz moved the gurney back into the morgue while Reggie and the woman walked over to join Dunham.

The more people that stopped by and talked to Dunham, the angrier he started to look. He was looking almost as mad as Mac, which was quite a feat. He looked like a bulldozer in human form. His bulldog jowls were quivering with anger, and junkyard dog eyes stared down everyone who came over to interrupt him.

Without anything else to distract her, Sophie's teeth started chattering, and she shivered despite being wrapped in an aluminum blanket. Mentally, Sophie began to list off complaints. Her left ear was still ringing from the blast of the gun, her wrist ached under the wrap on her arm, she had a black eye, she had scrapes and bruises all over her body, especially on her knees, and her throat ached like a bitch. She was hungry and tired. And there was a crazy, murderous woman claiming to be her sister.

Amira sauntered over, looking annoyingly put together. Hopping onto the bumper next to Sophie, Amira bumped shoulders with her.

"How are you holding up?" she asked.

"I want pie," Sophie complained. "I deserve pie."

Amira's eyebrows rose, but she rolled with it. "Okay. That's weird. Any specific kind?"

"Blueberry. No, wait. Chocolate silk."

"Good choice. I'll see what I can do," Amira replied, giving the paramedic in the truck a long look.

The lovely lady in a navy-blue paramedic's outfit informed Amira that Sophie was probably in shock. How rude to talk about Sophie as if she wasn't sitting right there. She also told Sophie she was lucky that her wrist wasn't broken, only sprained. The way it ached, her pulse throbbing rhythmically as if set to a metronome, Sophie didn't feel lucky. The aches and pains were starting to make themselves known, and Sophie felt like garbage.

Amira kept Sophie company as the police started to wrap up the crime scene. The paramedic lady, whose name turned out to be Beth, gave Amira wet wipes so she could try to clean the blood and gore off Sophie's face.

"Could Snow White really be your sister? Were you adopted?" Amira asked suddenly.

Sophie rubbed her throbbing temple with her uninjured hand. "My parents never said anything about me being adopted. And they *never* said anything about a sister. I'm hoping there's another reason why she looks exactly like me."

Sophie glanced over at the car where Snow White was located. When Snow White saw Sophie looking, she waved enthusiastically, gesturing for Sophie to come over. Sophie determinedly looked away, ignoring the psycho trying to get her attention.

"Good god, what the hell?" Amira exclaimed. "She looks exactly like you."

"I know. It's creepy." Sophie shrugged, unable to explain what was happening.

"Sophie, you look like something the cat dragged in," a voice called out, making Sophie snort.

Looking to her right, Sophie spotted Fergal heading her way.

She introduced Amira and Fergal but noticed a strange tension radiating between them. Her typically gregarious friends were almost standoffish with one another. In particular, Amira seemed uncomfortable. Usually, when Amira didn't like someone, they were the first to know. Weird.

Fergal clucked over Sophie's bedraggled state. "I'll make sure Riona whips up some soup for you. It'll help soothe your throat," he promised. Never one to turn down free food, Sophie thanked him.

"Are the lads alright? I'm really sorry they got dragged into a fight because of me," Sophie apologized.

"Are you kidding? They're gonna be bragging about this day for years to come. They held their own against a dozen wolf shifters."

Fergal left, announcing that he needed to get the lads home now that the action was over. Fergal walked over to the lads who were still watching the cops work with interest. He clapped them each on their shoulders, beaming with pride. Mac walked over and shook Fergal's and the lads' hands before they turned to leave.

"What was that all about?" Sophie asked Amira.

Amira pointed at herself. "Cat." Then she pointed at Fergal. "Dog."

"Huh. I guess that makes sense. Well, sorta." Sophie shrugged, deciding that some things you just had to accept, even if she thought it was weird.

"Bye, Sophie!" Conor yelled as they walked past. Sophie waved goodbye as Patrick and Liam echoed Conor's farewell.

Not long after, Mac stopped by letting Sophie know that they were taking Snow White, Antonio, and the rest of the wolf shifters to the station to be interrogated.

"I assume you want to come and watch?" Mac offered. When Sophie nodded enthusiastically, Mac informed her that Reggie had offered to drive her to the police headquarters.

Within thirty minutes, Sophie was in Reggie's car, along with Fitz and Ace, who also didn't want to be left out. Amira said she'd meet them there, that she wanted to take her own car.

There was a mass exodus of vehicles as everyone left, heading to the police station or back on patrol. They left a few police officers to finish the clean-up and keep out trespassers.

CHAPTER 21

$\mathcal{M}$ac and Larry showed everyone into a small room with a large window looking into an interrogation room. Sophie was joined by Reggie, Fitz, and Ace. Amira hadn't arrived yet. Snow White was sitting at a table inside the interrogation room with her cuffed hands resting on the table in front of her. She looked around the bare room with interest. Several times, her eyes flitted to the two-way mirror that hid Sophie and her friends. Sophie wondered if Snow White was aware of her presence.

Mac and Larry entered the interrogation room.

Snow White straightened in her seat. "I want to talk to my sister."

"No talking yet," Mac commanded her. Turning to Larry, he asked, "You ready?"

"Yeah, give me a moment," Larry responded.

Larry opened an old-fashioned medicine bag on the table. Snow White watched with interest as he pulled out a mortar and pestle. For the next several minutes, Larry pulled out various vials and pouches, sprinkling items into the bowl.

Mac sat cattycorner to Snow White, his profile facing Sophie,

278

staring her down. Larry ground the mortar contents with a pestle, chanting words in an unfamiliar lyrical language. Mac sat a purse down on the table and started taking out items and lining them up on the table: wallet, knife, vial half-filled with clear liquid, another knife, a packet of gum, and a couple of hair ties.

After a few minutes, Larry dipped a thumb into the concoction. He approached Snow White, commanding her to hold still. Pressing his thumb to her forehead, Larry intoned a single word, then stepped back, leaving behind a brownish-gray smudge. Pressing the same thumb to his own brow, Larry repeated the word.

The door behind Sophie opened, and Marcella slunk into the room, reminding Sophie of a starved alley cat. Bramwell and the rest of the Conclave members were notably absent. Taking a spot next to Sophie at the window, Marcella looked at her, but Sophie ignored her presence.

"Do these items all belong to you?" Mac asked Snow White.

Snow White briefly looked over the items on the table. "Yes, those are all mine."

"Truth," Larry intoned. Snow White looked at Larry, startled.

"Please state your name," Mac requested, looking down at Snow White's license.

"Ruby Rivers," Snow White replied slowly.

Ruby Rivers? Sophie exchanged a look with Reggie. "Sounds like a stripper name," she stage-whispered. Reggie nodded in agreement.

"Truth," Larry announced.

"City of residence?" Mac asked.

"Well, it was Los Angeles, but I'm thinking of staying here in San Francisco. I like it here. Plus, I'm hoping to get to know my sister," Ruby Rivers replied enthusiastically. She was awfully cheerful for someone who'd just been arrested for murder.

On her side of the glass, Sophie made a strangled noise.

"Truth," Larry announced again.

"Alright. I need you to say, 'Today is the 6th', okay?" Mac requested.

"But it's the 15th," Ruby protested.

"Just repeat the words."

"Fine. Today is the 6th."

"Lie," Larry said, a pleased smile spreading across his face.

Sophie felt her face go slack in surprise. Larry was a walking, talking lie detector test.

"Oh wow! Is this magic?" Snow White exclaimed, pointing at the mark on her forehead. "That's so cool. My favorite color is purple. Is that the truth? I hate carrots. Can you tell that's a lie? I love carrots. Are you a witch?"

Sophie had to smother a giggle at the pained look on Larry's face.

"Why aren't you more scared right now?" Mac asked Ruby, his brows drawn in confusion.

"Well, I never expected to make it this long, ya know? I figured eventually I would either get caught, or one of my marks would kill me. It was a good run," Ruby replied. "I know I did the right thing. I killed evil people who needed to be stopped. And I stopped them. No one else was doing anything about it. Who knows how many people I saved?"

"That's not how you save people. The men you killed deserved to have their day in court, not be murdered in cold blood. You should have left it to the people trained to stop murderers. The actual police."

"You think I didn't try that?" Ruby scoffed, rolling her eyes. "With every single one I found, I called in tips to the police first. A couple of times, those tips were followed up on, and those people got caught. But usually, I got ignored or I was treated like a crazy person, or they were too late. Each time I found a new killer, I gave the police a chance to catch them first. If you guys would've done your job, I wouldn't have needed to do it for you."

"Truth."

"I bet she was the Good Samaritan," Sophie said to Reggie, who nodded in agreement. Marcella looked intrigued by Sophie's statement but didn't say anything.

"How many people have you killed?" Mac asked.

"Twelve. No, thirteen – if you count today," Ruby replied.

"Tell me about them," Mac asked, pulling out his notepad and pen.

As Ruby went into details about the men she killed, Amira arrived, carrying in a long baguette and two pies: one mixed berry, the other chocolate. The baguette she handed to Fitz, who snatched it out of her hand and clutched it to his chest.

"I couldn't find blueberry," Amira apologized.

"No, this is perfect. I think I love you," Sophie proclaimed.

"I get that a lot," Amira teased.

"Are you going to share the bread?" Ace grumbled.

"Let him have his emotional support bread. It's been a long morning," Reggie suggested.

While watching Mac interrogate Ruby, Amira passed out slices to everyone present except Marcella, and Marcella didn't ask. She didn't even acknowledge anyone else's presence in the crowded room.

"What makes you certain that Sophie is your sister?" Mac asked, switching gears. Ruby looked at him like he was stupid, then waved her hand over her face. "Sophie said she doesn't have a sister. What magic did you use to make yourself look like her?"

"There's no magic. This is what I look like. I didn't even know magic existed until I saw Alphonse and his people turn into wolves at Muir Woods. Is Sophie watching right now?" Ruby waved to the mirror.

Mac looked at Larry expectantly. "Truth," Larry said.

"Are you adopted?" Mac asked. Ruby shook her head no. "Did your parents ever mention a sister?"

"No, they never said a thing. I had no idea. As far as I know, I wasn't adopted."

"Where are your parents now? I'm going to need to talk to them."

"They died in a car crash several years ago." Ruby pinched her nose like the thought of her parents hurt her. It was strange feeling sympathy for Ruby, but Sophie did. It was difficult for Sophie to think about her parents too. It's hard to lose your parents young.

Mac hummed noncommittally. Flipping a page on his notepad, he looked back at Ruby, staring at her silently until she started to squirm in her seat.

"When did you first see Sophie?" Mac asked.

"I was following Alphonse and his lackey. After I killed Roger – defending myself, I might add – I was walking away when I saw her run around the corner. I thought I was hallucinating at first. I hung around, watched for a while. Saw you two kissing." Ruby waggled her eyebrows. "When you walked her home, I followed."

"Why did you never approach her? Why break into her apartment and follow her around instead?"

"I couldn't just approach her! What if she was the evil twin sister? Haven't you watched any of the movies? I needed to gather more information first."

"Wait. You thought *Sophie* was the evil twin?" Mac asked. Ruby nodded enthusiastically, Mac's sarcasm flying right over her head. "You're a serial killer!" he exclaimed.

"I prefer the term 'vigilante'. I was forced to take justice into my own hands."

Mac looked at Larry, flabbergasted. "Truth," Larry said with a shrug.

Mac shook his head and turned his attention back to his notebook. "How did you find these men? And how can you be sure they were killers?"

"If a person has killed someone and I touch them. I get a vision of what they did," Ruby explained. "I never went looking for these men. I would brush against someone walking down the street. Or bump against them on the bus, and boom! Vision. I actually found quite a few of them when I worked as Snow White at Disneyland. Weirdos flocked to that character."

"Truth," Larry said.

The pie suddenly sat in Sophie's stomach like a brick. Snow White got death visions, just like her. Well, not exactly like hers, but similar enough to not matter.

"What do you mean? Explain exactly what happens when you touch a murderer," Mac commanded.

Marcella leaned closer to the glass, a calculating look on her face that Sophie didn't like one bit.

"Okay, so the first time it ever happened, I was in a restaurant. I bumped into this guy – Daniel Friedman – coming out of the bathroom. I had a vision of him killing his wife and sealing her body in a plastic barrel in his shed. You can imagine how confused I was. I thought I was going crazy." Sophie scoffed at that. It was clear to Sophie that Ruby was crazy. "Just to make sure I wasn't losing my mind, I followed him home. I waited outside the house until dark and snuck into his backyard. Guess what I found? A barrel, just like the one I saw in my vision, sitting right there in his shed. And it smelled awful, too."

Mac looked over at Larry, who nodded to confirm that Ruby was telling the truth. "What'd you do then?" he asked.

"I left the barrel as it was. I didn't want to tamper with it in case she really was in there. I called the police and told them that I was a neighbor and saw him stuffing his wife's body into the barrel. Apparently, I wasn't the only one who called about the smell because they sent out an officer to check it out. I watched from down the street as they arrested him, and the ambulance showed up."

"When did this happen? And what city?"

"About two years ago, maybe? This was in Anaheim."

"What were the names of the other people whom you didn't

kill but got arrested?" Mac asked. He studiously wrote down names, dates, and details for each person.

"You say that you can see if someone has killed," Mac said, a strange look on his face. Holding out his hand to Ruby, he challenged her. "Tell me what you see."

Placing her hand in Mac's, Ruby sucked in a breath. "You're approaching a hovel. The place is a dump. The front door is hanging off the hinges, so you're able to slip inside. You're trying not to make a sound. Peeking your head around the corner, there's some kind of… creature in the living room. Oh gross! He's eating somebody. You yell for him to freeze and raise his hands, but instead, he jumps up and throws an ax at you. It hits you in your left shoulder and sticks there. Ouch! You shoot him a bunch in the face and kill him," Ruby finished, letting go of Mac's hand and looking at him expectantly. "Did I get it right?"

Sophie sat down in a chair next to the window, her breath whooshing out. Just the other morning, she had trailed kisses along a long, narrow scar on Mac's left shoulder when they had showered together. She had asked about it, and he'd told her that a cannibalistic troll had hit him with an ax. She'd thought he'd been pulling her leg.

"Interesting," Marcella murmured.

The door behind Sophie opened, and a man that Sophie recognized from earlier in the day stuck his head in the room. Sophie knew he was a member of the Conclave. He cleared his throat nervously.

"Magistrate Venturi? There's an issue," he said.

"Not now, Frederick. This is important," Marcella replied, waving the man away.

"Actually, ma'am, it's serious. We need to talk."

Huffing in annoyance, Marcella left the room without saying goodbye or acknowledging anyone. When the door closed behind her, Sophie blew out a relieved breath, glad that Marcella was gone.

A minute later, the door to the interrogation room opened, and a uniformed police officer approached Mac. Leaning down, the man quickly whispered in Mac's ear.

Mac reared back, looking at the officer in shock. "Are you serious?"

"Yes, sir, Dunham sent me to tell you as soon as he found out."

A barrage of expletives fell from Mac's mouth. Standing up, he pointed at the officer. "Return her to her cell. Take Turner with you. I want at least two officers guarding this woman at all times. She doesn't leave your sight. You got it?"

The man saluted. "Yes, sir."

"What's going on?" Larry asked.

"They were interrogating Alphonse's pack members, and it turns out that Bramwell was working with Alphonse. That's how Alphonse knew about Sophie's abilities."

"What?!" exclaimed Larry.

"Yep. And now, no one can find Bramwell. He's gone."

Mac turned and addressed the mirror. "Reggie, can you stay with Sophie? I'm going to get some people to guard your door until we know it's safe."

"Come with me, ma'am," the officer said to Ruby, helping her up from her chair.

"I want to talk to my sister," Ruby protested.

"That can't happen right now. You need to come with me," he replied.

Mac strode out of the room with steam almost rolling out of his ears; the rest of the group followed quickly on his heels.

"Holy shit. That was crazy," Fitz blurted.

Sophie sat in a daze as her friends' excited voices washed over her. Could Ruby Rivers really be Sophie's long-lost twin sister? What the hell? It didn't make any sense. How could she have never been told?

"We'll test both of their DNA to confirm," Ace stated. "Then we can be completely sure whether they're identical twins or not."

The door opened again, and a new, unfamiliar police officer popped his head in the room. "I'm Officer Benson. Detective Volpes asked us to guard your door." Sophie could see another police officer hovering behind him, his face curious as he looked over Benson's shoulder. "This is Officer Nguyen. If you need anything, let us know."

Sophie briefly considered asking them for a bottle of vodka but figured they wouldn't comply. Reggie thanked the men and started to close the door on their curious faces.

"She's tiny. I can't believe she killed Alphonse," Sophie heard one of the men say right before the door swung shut.

"Wait. What?" Sophie croaked. "People think I killed Alphonse?"

"We'll make sure to set the record straight," Reggie tried to assure her, patting her hand. Sophie appreciated Reggie's unwavering support, but she figured that this was a disaster in the making.

When the door opened again, at least two hours had passed and the pies were long gone. And so were all of Sophie's nails, chewed away. She had been unable to take another bite of the pies, nausea swirling through her stomach as her friends speculated about what was happening.

Sophie bounced up from her seat when Mac came in. He swept her up in a tight hug, making her bones groan, but she didn't utter a sound of complaint. She needed as much comfort as she could get after such a weird, crappy day.

"What happened?" Ace asked.

With a sigh, Mac set Sophie back on her feet. He had everyone sit down.

"When they were interrogating Alphonse's people, we found out that Alphonse and Bramwell had been working with Edwyn. Alphonse had been using lone shifters from other regions of the country as hired muscle to kill the people who wouldn't sell their properties.

"They had planned to close the Fae portal then buy up as much of the land in the city as possible, starting with real estate located on the ley lines. There are two in the city. With control of the lines, Edwyn and Bramwell planned to use their magic to slowly replace all humans in power positions with their people. It would have been a targeted repel spell to make specific individuals want to leave. We think they were planning to move more Mythicals from around the country into the city. We believe Bramwell has some questionable connections to a few other Conclaves. If they had succeeded, all that would've been left in San Francisco when they were done would've been human workers. They'd have their kingdom to rule, and no one would have known it was happening until it was too late."

"Is that why they killed Derek Gibson?" Sophie asked.

"Yes, he was a key member of the city Planning Commission. He had a lot of control over building permits and zoning. They were going to replace him with one of their people. There were others. We're trying to find them all. It's going to take months to unravel."

"How pissed is Marcella?" Reggie asked.

"I think she's putting on a good show, but in a way, this is good for her. She'll be able to consolidate more power with Edwyn, and now Bramwell, being gone. I initially thought she was close to Bramwell, but I suspect it was more of a keep-your-enemies-closer situation.

"In good news, she brought in one of her Fae to start putting a geas on everyone, so they won't remember that you have visions. I think Marcella is eager to keep you on her good side."

"A geas?" Sophie repeated.

"It's a spell that makes a person forget something, or sometimes it just prohibits a person from talking about something," Fitz explained.

"Can they do the same thing with Alphonse's death? I over-heard some cops saying they thought it was me that killed him."

"They will try, but that's going to be almost impossible. Very few people overheard what Marcella said about your visions. She told a few people on the Conclave, but other than that, no one knows. Even Antonio didn't know about the visions. He just thought that you were a stalker who killed Roger. I don't think Alphonse trusted his brother much. The trouble we're facing is that Alphonse's death is already news all over the city. People are already talking about the human woman who killed him. We're putting out conflicting stories to create confusion – that Antonio killed him in a challenge, that Bramwell killed him, that a rival pack took him out and such. Most Mythicals might have a hard time believing that two human women killed one of the strongest alphas in a generation. It would be easier to believe that Antonio killed him than a human woman. Their egos would never recover."

"What about Antonio? Won't he just tell everyone what he saw?"

"We've convinced him that it's in his best interest for everyone to believe that he killed his brother in challenge. Alphonse was not well-liked, so it won't be hard for Antonio to convince people that he was sick of his brother's brutal leadership."

"What happened with Bramwell?" Amira asked.

"Disappeared. He must have seen the writing on the wall when we started interrogating Alphonse's people. Larry tried to track him, but it's as if he never existed. Bramwell has strong magic, so I'm not surprised he could block Larry's spell. Dunham put out an APB on him, but I don't have much hope for that working. However, Marcella's going to throw her considerable resources at finding him. She's furious. If she gets ahold of him, I imagine he won't be long for this world."

Sophie shuddered a little. The idea of being the focus of

Marcella's ire was a horrible thought. "Do you think Bramwell will come after me?"

"I think you're the least of his worries. However, I'd like for you to stay at the safe house for a little bit longer."

"Can Birdie go home at least? Her boyfriend is starting to become concerned."

"I think we can get her back home before dinnertime," Mac promised. "If you guys want to head home, there's not much more you can do here. I'll take Sophie back to the safe house."

"Do you want to take tonight off, Sophie?" Reggie offered. "It's been a trying day, and you deserve some downtime."

"I think I'd rather be at work. It'll help keep my mind off the craziness of the day. I need a distraction."

Everyone started shuffling out, giving Sophie a hug – even Ace. "Things never are boring with you around," he teased. Sophie stuck her tongue at him making him chuckle.

Amira hugged her, then grabbed her hand and examined her nails. She announced that they needed to get their nails taken care of later in the week with a *tsk*. "Oh, we should bring Birdie too."

"Birdie would love that. Let's pick a day, and I'll let her know," Sophie promised.

Reggie lingered the longest, his round face concerned. "Soph, if I'd lost you today... I don't know what I would've done. Don't ever scare me like that again."

"Scared me too," Sophie whispered, hugging Reggie just a little tighter.

After all her friends left, and only she and Mac were left in the viewing room, Mac picked her up and sat down with her in his lap. Turning sideways, Sophie rested her head on his shoulder, arms loosely wrapped around his neck.

Pressing a kiss to her temple, Mac whispered, "You scared about ten years off my life today. Don't ever do that to me again, hellraiser."

"Yeah, I have no plans ever to try to get into a fight with an alpha ever again. That sucked."

Sophie snuggled into Mac's arms, happy to finally be alone with her boyfriend. She snuck her hands under Mac's jacket, resting her palms on his ribs. His steady breaths and his hand rubbing her back had almost lulled Sophie to sleep when a thought popped into her head.

"Hey, I have a question. Alphonse said that someone named Frank saw me at Kezar Stadium. Obviously, that was Ruby, but who is Frank, and how does he know who I am and what I look like?"

"That has to be Frank Russo. He's a part of Alphonse's inner circle. A real prick. Drives a white mustang. He's a baseball nut."

"Ah. I know who that guy is... Number 1 Sports Fan. He was the guy who threatened me in front of the ME's office."

They snuggled in silence for several minutes, just basking in the quiet and relief of having survived the day. Mac's phone beeping broke into their reverie. Checking it, Mac let Sophie know that Burg and Fergal had a car out front to return her to the clan house.

"Before we go, would it be possible for me to talk to Snow White – I mean Ruby – for a minute?"

"You sure? You don't ever need to see her again," Mac reassured her.

"Yeah, I'm sure. If she's really my sister, I just want to see her face to face for a minute, you know? Just to reassure myself that this is all real. Hear her voice and look into her eyes."

"Larry can accompany us," Mac suggested. He shot off a quick text and received an immediate reply. "He's on his way."

A knock on the door came a minute later. On the other side of the door stood Larry, looking a little frazzled, his usual fedora noticeably absent from his head. His hair stood up on ends as if he'd run his fingers through the strands repeatedly.

"I can't believe you can detect lies like that. Larry, you're kind of a badass," Sophie exclaimed.

"Truth," he teased, a pleased smile on his face.

Larry and Mac escorted Sophie through a convoluted series of hallways. They passed a staffed desk where the officer behind it gave both men a nod and Sophie a curious glance. With a buzz, the officer let them into a door off to the side. Once through the door, a series of cells stretched down a long hall. Midway down the aisle, two officers, one on either side of a cell, faced forward. Sophie wondered briefly where Alphonse's people were being kept but quickly decided it was irrelevant as they approached the cell.

As they came into view, Ruby bounced up from the cot where she was lounging.

"You're here!" she squealed, scurrying to the bars and pressing her face into the gap between the metal poles with a happy smile.

Now that she was there, Sophie wasn't sure what she wanted to say to this woman. She just looked at her, from her sleek ankle boots to her skinny jeans up to her expensive-looking blouse. Sophie's quiet perusal didn't seem to dim Ruby's enthusiasm. She might look like Sophie, but she didn't act anything like her. The opposite, in fact.

"I'm so glad you're here! These guys are boring and won't talk to me," Ruby claimed, nodding at the two police officers.

"Could you guys give us a minute?" Mac asked the attending officers. With a nod, both men walked away, heading out the door.

"I've always wanted a sister!" Ruby exclaimed once they were alone.

"I don't think we're sisters. I think you're an imposter."

Ruby thrust her hand through the bars, reaching toward Sophie. Out of curiosity, Sophie started to reach for her as well. For some reason, she felt like Ruby wouldn't be real until she'd touched her.

"What the hell! Don't touch her. You're going to disrupt the space-time continuum or something!" Larry barked.

"She's not from the future," Sophie said. "I mean, you're not... Are you?"

Ruby giggled. "No, silly. I'm from now." Turning from Larry, she stared at Sophie. "We're linked together. Don't you feel it? I've had dreams about you. I was super confused for a while. I couldn't figure out why I kept having dreams about dead bodies and autopsies. I thought I was going crazy. But when I looked around your apartment, I found a pay stub, and it all made sense. I was dreaming about you."

"You drank some of my whiskey."

"I know I shouldn't have. It's my one vice."

"Your one vice? You don't think killing people is a vice?"

"Oh no, that's a calling," Ruby explained, entirely serious. "Do you have dreams about me?"

Sophie didn't answer, but even a non-answer was telling.

"You have! I knew it! Is that how you found me? Because you found me first. This is going to be awesome. We're going to be the bestest of friends!"

Sweet mother of god. This woman wanted to be best friends. Mac made a choked sound next to Sophie. She couldn't tell if he was horrified or trying not to laugh.

"Why did you come to my work today?" Sophie asked, ignoring the happy, hopeful look on Ruby's face.

"After Alphonse set a trap for me yesterday. I knew I needed to leave town. But I didn't want to go without meeting you first. I just didn't expect Alphonse to show up and try to kill you. It's a good thing I was there!"

Sophie was chagrined to admit that Ruby wasn't wrong.

"We must have been separated at birth. Like one of those fairy tales. Oh! Or like that long-lost Russian princess. What was her name?"

"Are you talking about Anastasia?" Mac clarified.

"Yes! That's the one!"

"I hate to be the bearer of bad news, but they found her bones like a decade ago. She was killed with the rest of her family," Mac replied in a deadpan voice.

"Huh. Well, then not like her, but we could still be long-lost princesses!"

"It's probably better for our long-term health if we're not long-lost royalty," Sophie argued.

"Jeez, negative much? It looks like I'm going to be the fun sister!" Ruby said with a giggle.

Sophie exchanged an exasperated look with Mac.

"I think we can go now," Sophie said to Mac and Larry.

"Wait! Don't go yet. We've barely gotten a chance to get to know one another."

"I think I've seen enough. I'm ready to go," Sophie replied.

"Will you come back and see me? I want us to be friends," Ruby begged.

"I'm not sure yet. I don't know what's going to happen. And frankly, I don't know how I feel about all this. I need answers about my past before I can think about any kind of future with you in it."

"Well, I guess I can understand that."

"Let's go, guys."

Sophie and the guys turned and headed away.

"I'm fun," Sophie complained as they walked away.

"Of course you are," Mac placated.

"Call me!" Ruby called from her cell just as they exited the hallway.

"Does she think I somehow have her number? She's crazy," Sophie said to Mac.

"Oh, she's definitely insane, but weirdly, I'm starting to think that she's not evil," Mac replied.

"I agree. She seems to have a moral code that she adheres to. It's a skewed moral code, but she has one. I haven't had much time to follow up on the people she had arrested or that she killed, but what I've found so far confirms what she said. They were all evil – every single one of them," Larry said.

They dropped Larry off back at his desk and got on the elevator. Right as the doors closed, Mac said, "Here," dropping his jacket over her shoulders and zipping it up, flipping the collar up.

"Wha?" Sophie asked.

"Your clothes are covered in blood. Your neck is a lovely shade of blue-black. We're about to head into the regular world where that kind of thing draws attention," Mac teased. "Can't do much about that shiner you're sporting."

"Gross. Your poor jacket. I'm going to get blood and stuff on it," Sophie whined, but Mac shrugged as if he could care less.

"Can I take you to the hospital now to get you checked over?" Mac asked.

"Reggie already checked me over. And to be honest, I don't feel that bad. My wrist already feels better, and although my neck is sore, it's not that bad."

"Well, let the record show that I recommended seeing a doctor."

"Duly noted."

As the elevator announced its arrival at the lobby, Mac gave Sophie a serious look. "How much do you want Burg and Fergal to know? I can have the geas put on them as well," Mac offered.

"No. They've both gone out of their way to protect me. I trust them," Sophie replied, tugging Mac towards her waiting friends.

"You okay?" Fergal asked when they got in the backseat.

"I'm good. Just tired and a little overwhelmed," Sophie replied.

"What happened? Fergal said he couldn't tell me until he got approval from you both," Burg asked.

"You tell him," Sophie requested, poking Mac in the side. "I'm too tired."

Mac snuggled in the back seat with Sophie, catching them up

on what they'd learned about Ruby, Alphonse, Bramwell, and the whole debacle from that morning.

"I've told the lads that they can't breathe a word of what they saw today. They gave me their vow," Fergal assured Sophie and Mac.

Parking in front of the clan house, the group trudged up the front steps. The first thing Sophie saw was Birdie and a couple of her bridge friends halfway down the stairs.

"Sophie," Birdie cheered. "Do you want to join us for a game?"

Sophie was opening her mouth to decline when Birdie took a better look at Sophie's face.

"What happened?" Birdie demanded. "Are you okay?"

"Yes, I'm fine. I've just had a long, weird morning. I'll tell you all about it after I get some sleep."

Birdie left her friends behind and finished coming down the stairs to stop in front of Sophie with a worried look on her face.

"Is that blood?" Birdie cried, reaching a finger towards Sophie's hairline where Amira couldn't scrub out Alphonse's blood.

"Yes, but it's not mine," Sophie replied, hoping to reassure her friend.

Birdie, interestingly enough, did not look reassured.

"Let's talk in my office," Fergal offered. He led them through the 2nd-floor pub, then through the kitchen to a door next to the walk-in fridge.

"Riona, sweetheart, can you make sure no one interrupts us?" Fergal called out to his wife, who was elbow deep in a bowl of dough. Riona waved a dough-covered hand in assent.

Fergal ushered everyone through the door. Sophie looked around in confusion.

"This is your office?"

Half the office appeared to be a pantry of dry goods. Shelving ran floor to ceiling along an entire wall. The other half of the room was a sophisticated office with tufted leather seating, a mahogany desk, and bookcases with leather-bound books. It was the kind of place where men in Regency romance novels shared cigars and brandy.

"Yes, I converted half of the pantry. I used to have an office on the top floor, but I didn't get enough time with my wife with my long work hours. I had to knock out a wall to make the room, but it was worth it. Every time Riona needs a spice or more flour, I get to see her."

"That's disgustingly sweet. Also, a bit crazy, but mostly sweet," Sophie said, only partially joking.

"Alright, tell me, what is going on? Why do you have a black eye and blood in your hair?" Birdie demanded.

"You haven't even seen her neck yet," Mac crowed.

"Thanks," Sophie growled, giving Mac the stink eye.

"Your neck?" Birdie cried, grabbing the zipper on Sophie's jacket and tugging it down. "Oh my god! Sophie. What the hell happened to you?"

"An alpha wolf shifter tried to kill me this morning because he mistook me for my long-lost identical twin who has been going around town and murdering serial killers like some kind of psycho vigilante."

"You have a sister?"

"That's what I said too!" Sophie cried.

"Why don't you start at the beginning?" Mac suggested.

So that's what Sophie did.

Despite her initial shock, Birdie recovered from the story faster than Sophie expected. She should have known better, though; Birdie was used to rolling with the punches life sometimes threw her way. "You must've been separated at birth! I saw a very similar story on Dateline. It happens more often than you think. So, what is she like?"

"Crazy. Also, kinda weirdly sweet? And *way* too cheerful," Sophie said with a wince.

"Cheerful?" Birdie repeated, baffled. "You sure she's your

sister?"

"No, I'm not at all sure. I'm currently hoping that it's magic that makes her look exactly like me."

"How much does she look like you? Could she be a younger sister, not a twin?" Birdie asked.

"No, they're almost perfectly identical – different hair. No tattoos. Ruby doesn't have this scar." Mac rubbed his thumb across a small scar on Sophie's chin. "But other than that, they're mirror images of one another."

"It's disturbing," Sophie complained.

"What happens next?" Birdie asked.

"You'll get to go back to Brown Betty now that Alphonse is dead and Ruby is behind bars," Mac said. "Sophie is going to stay here for a bit longer. Other than that, we don't know. It's going to depend on what the police chief wants to do with all the culprits. We'll just have to wait and see."

"Girlie, you look dead on your feet," Birdie clucked.

"Are you hungry?" Fergal asked. Did that man think about anything other than food?

"No. I just want a shower and to sleep for twenty-four hours straight."

"Come on, hellraiser, let's make that happen," Mac offered, rezipping up the jacket, hiding the blood and bruises.

As a group, they headed out of Fergal's office-slash-pantry, through the kitchen, and into the pub. Sophie and Mac left the rest of the group behind to head up the stairs and to Sophie's room. Mac steered her towards her bathroom. Helping her peel out of her disgusting clothes that Sophie had every intention of burning, Mac turned on the water in the shower and guided Sophie under the stream. A moment later, he joined her. Pouring some shampoo in his hand, he tilted her head under the water and then started to scrub. Looking down for a second, Sophie watched red water swirl down the drain.

"Do I have brain matter in my hair?" Sophie asked as Mac scrubbed at a spot on her temple.

"Only a little," Mac replied as if that should be reassuring.

Sophie allowed herself to be maneuvered around the shower as Mac scrubbed off all the blood and grime. She was too worn out to care and all too happy to allow someone else to be in charge for a bit.

After her shower, Mac tucked Sophie into her bed.

"Can you stay? I don't want to be alone," Sophie asked.

"I can't stay all day, but I will stay until you fall asleep. Is that okay?"

"Yes, please. But you have to be the big spoon."

"Deal," Mac replied, getting into the bed and pulling Sophie into his arms.

Sophie tried to relax her muscles and clear her head, but the morning kept replaying in her mind.

"Sophie, let it all go. Sleep now," Mac rumbled in her ear. It shouldn't have worked, but somehow Sophie felt herself slip into sleep.

BORED. I'M SO BORED. BORED BORED BORED. THIS PLACE SUCKS. There isn't even a TV in here.

"Hey, do you know when they serve lunch here? I'm hungry. Could someone get me a box of Good & Plenties?" she asks. "Come on, talk to me!"

The two police officers guarding her prison cell ignore her again, just like they've been doing for the last several hours.

"Can you at least get me a book or something?"

The click of the door opening at the end of the hallway has her sitting up in bed. Maybe her sister's come back. Instead of her sister, a tall, thin woman with steel gray hair approaches her cell. She watches the woman approach warily. She is bone thin as if life has whittled her down, turning her sharp. Ruby has the sensation of being a bug caught in a web where the spider is fast approaching.

The woman stops in front of the cell and stares at Ruby for a minute.

"You two are dismissed," the woman says to the guards, who quickly march out the door. Ruby watches them leave, almost missing their stoic presence.

"I'm Marcella Venturi. You're Ruby Rivers, yes?"

Ruby slowly nods, having lost her voice.

"I'd like to offer you a job," Marcella says.

"A job?" She couldn't have been more shocked if Marcella slapped her instead.

"Yes. You see, I'm in charge of the Mythical creatures in the city. It's my job to protect them, to keep the peace, to provide safety for them. But it's also my job to make sure my people follow the rules of society. I need you to help keep killers off the street."

"I don't know. I mean, I don't even really know you."

"That's understandable. But I want to give you a chance to use your powers for good. To help people. You won't ever have to kill anyone ever again. I'll make sure that your visions are believed and that evil-doers will pay for their crimes."

That's a pretty good sales pitch, *she thinks.*

"That's all I ever wanted to do," Ruby replies. She looks at this woman for a long time, trying to determine if she is the real deal. "Can you get me out of this cell?"

"Yes, I can. I can get you out right now," Marcella offers.

"Okay, you have a deal. But. Only if you can get me a chance to spend time with my sister."

Marcella says, "Deal. I'd shake on it, but well... it'd be better if we refrained."

"You're scary," Ruby responds cheerfully.

"I prefer efficient," Marcella says with a smile, pulling a key out of her pocket and heading toward the cell door.

~

SOPHIE CAME AWAKE WITH A GASP. LOOKING AROUND, SHE realized she was alone in her room. Mac was gone.

"That conniving b—" Sophie bit off the words with a strangled growl. Grabbing her phone, she dialed Mac.

"Hey, Soph, you should be sleeping," Mac said, picking up after the second ring.

"Marcella took Ruby. I just dreamed it," Sophie gasped out, still trying to shake off the feeling of being in Ruby's head.

"That's not possible," Mac growled.

"She asked Ruby to work for her."

"Son of a—" Mac yelled. "Of course she did. Larry! Come here. We need to check Ruby's cell."

Sophie listened over the phone as Mac and Larry headed to Ruby's cell, Mac explaining the situation to Larry on the way.

Sophie could hear rustling, the sound of footsteps, followed by a door opening. There was a beat of silence before Mac yelled, "Damn it!"

"She's gone?" Sophie asked.

"Yep," Mac confirmed. "This is bullshit. I'm going to talk to Dunham."

But Sophie knew it was useless. Dunham didn't have any power to say no to Marcella or the Conclave.

"Alright, I'm gonna go now. I need more sleep. There's nothing I can do about any of this anyways," Sophie said around a yawn.

"I'm sorry, Soph," Mac said, his voice filled with regret.

"You have no reason to be sorry. This isn't your fault," Sophie assured him.

Hanging up, Sophie snuggled back under her comforter and went back to sleep.

EPILOGUE

*A*djusting her headphones to fit more firmly over her ears, Sophie followed Mac down the corridor lined with two stories of prison cells. The green walls in dim lighting made the whole place feel extra spooky. Mac stopped before a closed cell door on the first floor. He glanced back at Sophie, grinning, his eyes alight. In the headphones, a soothing voice explained that this particular cell was occupied by Frank Morris, one of three men who managed to escape Alcatraz by digging through the walls with sharpened spoons and making a raft from stolen raincoats.

Sophie was happy to see Mac having a good time and finally relaxing. The last few weeks had almost driven him mad. Antonio – the Sunset District pack's new alpha – and his pack members had been causing problems for the Conclave and the entire Mythical police department. They claimed that the Conclave set Alphonse up as a scapegoat for Edwyn and Bramwell's nefarious plans, that he was killed to cover up the scandal. Mac suspected that he was making a bunch of noise, hoping that the Conclave would give him more territory just to get him to shut up.

It always seemed to come back to real estate with these guys.

It hadn't helped Mac's mental state when Marcella somehow got a hold of Sophie's phone number and gave it to Ruby. At Marcella's request, Sophie agreed to talk to Ruby, but she informed them that she would only communicate with Ruby via text. She wasn't ready to speak to Ruby on the phone yet.

It turned out that texting with Ruby typically involved a lot of emojis and exclamation points. Sophie was dreading the day she figured out gifs. Slowly, Sophie was starting to thaw to her sister. It was hard to keep someone that cheerful at arm's length.

Yes, sister.

They had tested both their DNAs, and they were an exact match. Ruby Rivers was Sophie's identical twin sister. Sophie had been hanging her hope on Ruby being a changeling.

Dunham had people digging into their pasts, trying to figure out where they came from. The current theory going around was that one of their parents was a high-ranking Fae. Because both of them had an affinity to death, it was assumed that they inherited their gifts from someone with death magic or someone associated with death. It turned out there were a lot of Mythical beings related to death: banshees, the Dullahan, the lady in white, and even the Fae Queen's consort's line. Heck, the Irish fairy monarch Finvara was the King of the Dead.

As the narrator continued to recount the harrowing tale of the prisoners' escape, Sophie linked her hand with Mac's. He gave her another grin and pressed a quick kiss to her lips.

"Best date ever," Mac praised.

Leaning down to get a closer look at the paper mâché dummy that Frank Morris had left in his bed, the muscles in Sophie's legs protested. They were still so sore from that morning's training session. She was hobbling around Alcatraz like an old lady. Sophie was happy that Paddy never took it easy on her even though she was human, but she was sore in places she didn't even know had muscles. The man made drill sergeants look like sweethearts.

At the first lesson after Alphonse's death, Paddy had looked at Sophie's neck, which had turned a lovely shade of sickly yellow and green, and promised that he'd make it so that would never happen to Sophie again. Sophie tried to make him pinkie promise, but Paddy just rolled his eyes at Sophie, and then swept her feet out from under her.

Mac tugged Sophie up some stairs, opening a door that led to the roof. At the top of Alcatraz, the panorama of San Francisco lay out before them – the Bay Bridge lit up the sky to the left, and Oakland was behind them. They turned towards San Francisco, leaning against the railing and watching the sun set over the city. As dark descended over the cityscape, lights blazed from all the skyscrapers and streetlights, giving it a magical golden glow.

The temperature dropped as the sky turned dark, but Sophie was warm in Mac's arms.

ACKNOWLEDGMENTS

Thank you for reading Portents and Oddities – the second book in the Sophie Feegle series. I'd like to thank my killer husband and kids. I'd also like to thank my editor Arundhati Subhedar and book cover designer Rebecacovers. Lastly I'd like to thank my beta readers: David, Jessica, Joanne, Karen, Paige, Pam, and Tina!

If you've read the first Sophie Feegle book (and I hope you have or this book might not have made any sense at all!), you'll know that I like to include facts and history about San Francisco within the story.

The Mission Bean was based off my neighborhood coffee joint The Beanery. They do roast their beans in house and you can smell it for blocks. Both Cal Surplus and Out of the Closet are thrift stores in the city and a fun place to shop. Who doesn't like a bargain? The Hunky Jesus contest is real and it's as funny as you imagine it to be. Brenda's French Soul Food is amaaaazing. The beignets are the real deal and so is the wait. Go early. It's worth it.

The Three Pigs Bakery is fake. I was making a wolf joke. However, there are tons of great bakeries in San Francisco. I was always partial to La Boulange.

Lastly, if In & Out Burger isn't the state restaurant of California, it should be. The locals are very, *very* proprietary of it. My recommendation is to get your French fries 'animal style'. It's not on the menu, but it's so yummy.

If you liked the book, please leave a review on Amazon. It really helps us independent writers get more exposure. Plus, I read and obsess over every review.

Please visit my website at www.gwendemarco.com or send me an email at gwen@gwendemarco.com.

ABOUT THE AUTHOR

Gwen DeMarco is an avid reader, wine & coffee drinker, gardener and a lover of all things nerdy. Gwen loves to write paranormal romance novels with a focus on the weird and wonderful. She loves to write a good snarky heroine and a grumpy male lead. Sophie Feegle is her first foray into the world of shifters, fae, ogres and vampires.

Gwen is happily married to her high school sweetheart and has two teenage children. She can often be found with her nose in a book and a glass of wine or mug of coffee in her hand.

To learn more, please visit my website and sign up for my mailing list to receive updates at www.GwenDeMarco.com

Made in the USA
Monee, IL
30 March 2024

55919175R00184